# Burlesques by William Makepeace Thackeray

The great author of Vanity Fair and The Luck Of Barry Lyndon was born in India in 1811.

At age 5 his father died and his mother sent him back to England. His education was of the best but he himself seemed unable to apply his talents to a rigorous work ethic.

However, once he harnessed his talents the works flowed in novels, articles, short stories, sketches and lectures.

Sadly, his personal life was rather more difficult. After a few years of marriage his wife began to suffer from depression and over the years became detached from reality. Thackeray himself suffered from ill health later in his life and the one pursuit that kept him moving forward was that of writing. In his life time, he was placed second only to Dickens. High praise indeed.

## Index of Contents

GEORGE DE BARNWELL

BY SIR E. L. B. L., BART

VOLUME I

In the Morning of Life the Truthful wooed the Beautiful, and their offspring was Love. Like his Divine parents, He is eternal. He has his Mother's ravishing smile; his Father's steadfast eyes. He rises every day, fresh and glorious as the untired Sun-God. He is Eros, the ever young. Dark, dark were this world of ours had either Divinity left it—dark without the day-beams of the Latonian Charioteer, darker yet without the daedal Smile of the God of the Other Bow! Dost know him, reader?

Old is he, Eros, the ever young. He and Time were children together. Chronos shall die, too; but Love is imperishable. Brightest of the Divinities, where hast thou not been sung? Other worships pass away; the idols for whom pyramids were raised lie in the desert crumbling and almost nameless; the Olympians are fled, their fanes no longer rise among the quivering olive-groves of Ilissus, or crown the emerald-islets of the amethyst Aegean! These are gone, but thou remainest. There is still a garland for thy temple, a heifer for thy stone. A heifer? Ah, many a darker sacrifice. Other blood is shed at thy altars, Remorseless One, and the Poet Priest who ministers at thy Shrine draws his auguries from the bleeding hearts of men!

While Love hath no end, Can the Bard ever cease singing? In Kingly and Heroic ages, 'twas of Kings and Heroes that the Poet spake. But in these, our times, the Artisan hath his voice as well as the Monarch. The people To-Day is King, and we chronicle his woes, as They of old did the sacrifice of the princely Iphigenia, or the fate of the crowned Agamemnon.

Is Odysseus less august in his rags than in his purple? Fate, Passion, Mystery, the Victim, the Avenger, the Hate that harms, the Furies that tear, the Love that bleeds, are not these with us Still? are not these still the weapons of the Artist? the colors of his palette? the chords of his lyre? Listen! I tell thee a tale—not of Kings—but of Men—not of Thrones, but of Love, and Grief, and Crime. Listen, and but once more. 'Tis for the last time (probably) these fingers shall sweep the strings.

E. L. B. L.

NOONDAY IN CHEPE.

'Twas noonday in Chepe. High Tide in the mighty River City!—its banks wellnigh overflowing with the myriad-waved Stream of Man! The toppling wains, bearing the produce of a thousand marts; the gilded equipage of the Millionary; the humbler, but yet larger vehicle from the green metropolitan suburbs (the Hanging Gardens of our Babylon), in which every traveller might, for a modest remuneration, take a republican seat; the mercenary caroche, with its private freight; the brisk curricle of the letter-carrier, robed in royal scarlet: these and a thousand others were laboring and pressing onward, and locked and bound and hustling together in the narrow channel of Chepe. The imprecations of the charioteers were terrible. From the noble's broidered hammer-cloth, or the driving-seat of the common coach, each driver assailed the other with floods of ribald satire. The pavid matron within the one vehicle (speeding to the Bank for her semestrial pittance) shrieked and trembled; the angry Dives hastening to his office (to add another thousand to his heap,) thrust his head over the blazoned panels, and displayed an eloquence of objurgation which his very Menials could not equal; the dauntless street urchins, as they gayly threaded the Labyrinth of Life, enjoyed the perplexities and quarrels of the scene, and exacerbated the already furious combatants by their poignant infantile satire. And the Philosopher, as he regarded the hot strife and struggle of these Candidates in the race for Gold, thought with a sigh of the Truthful and the Beautiful, and walked on, melancholy and serene.

'Twas noon in Chepe. The ware-rooms were thronged. The flaunting windows of the mercers attracted many a purchaser: the glittering panes behind which Birmingham had glazed its simulated silver, induced rustics to pause: although only noon, the savory odors of the Cook Shops tempted the over hungry citizen to the bun of Bath, or to the fragrant potage that mocks the turtle's flavor—the turtle! O dapibus suprimi grata testudo Jovis! I am an Alderman when I think of thee! Well: it was noon in Chepe.

But were all battling for gain there? Among the many brilliant shops whose casements shone upon Chepe, there stood one a century back (about which period our tale opens) devoted to the sale of Colonial produce. A rudely carved image of a negro, with a fantastic plume and apron of variegated feathers, decorated the lintel. The East and West had sent their contributions to replenish the window.

The poor slave had toiled, died perhaps, to produce yon pyramid of swarthy sugar marked "ONLY 6 1/2d."—That catty box, on which was the epigraph "STRONG FAMILY CONGO ONLY 3s. 9d," was from the country of Confutzee—that heap of dark produce bore the legend "TRY OUR REAL NUT"—'Twas Cocoa—and that nut the Cocoa-nut, whose milk has refreshed the traveller and perplexed the natural philosopher. The shop in question was, in a word, a Grocer's.

In the midst of the shop and its gorgeous contents sat one who, to judge from his appearance (though 'twas a difficult task, as, in sooth, his back was turned), had just reached that happy period of life when the Boy is expanding into the Man. O Youth, Youth! Happy and Beautiful! O fresh and roseate dawn of life; when the dew yet lies on the flowers, ere they have been scorched and withered by Passion's fiery Sun! Immersed in thought or study, and indifferent to the din around him, sat the boy. A careless guardian was he of the treasures confided to him. The crowd passed in Chepe; he never marked it. The sun shone on Chepe; he only asked that it should illumine the page he read. The knave might filch his treasures; he was heedless of the knave. The customer might enter; but his book was all in all to him.

And indeed a customer WAS there; a little hand was tapping on the counter with a pretty impatience; a pair of arch eyes were gazing at the boy, admiring, perhaps, his manly proportions through the homely and tightened garments he wore.

"Ahem! sir! I say, young man!" the customer exclaimed.

"Ton d'apameibomenos prosephe," read on the student, his voice choked with emotion. "What language!" he said; "how rich, how noble, how sonorous! prosephe podas—"

The customer burst out into a fit of laughter so shrill and cheery, that the young Student could not but turn round, and blushing, for the first time remarked her. "A pretty grocer's boy you are," she cried, "with your applepiebomenos and your French and lingo. Am I to be kept waiting for hever?"

"Pardon, fair Maiden," said he, with high-bred courtesy: "'twas not French I read, 'twas the Godlike language of the blind old bard. In what can I be serviceable to ye, lady?" and to spring from his desk, to smooth his apron, to stand before her the obedient Shop Boy, the Poet no more, was the work of a moment.

"I might have prigged this box of figs," the damsel said good-naturedly, "and you'd never have turned round."

"They came from the country of Hector," the boy said. "Would you have currants, lady? These once bloomed in the island gardens of the blue Aegean. They are uncommon fine ones, and the figure is low; they're fourpence-halfpenny a pound. Would ye mayhap make trial of our teas? We do not advertise, as some folks do: but sell as low as any other house."

"You're precious young to have all these good things," the girl exclaimed, not unwilling, seemingly, to prolong the conversation. "If I was you, and stood behind the counter, I should be eating figs the whole day long."

"Time was," answered the lad, "and not long since I thought so too. I thought I never should be tired of figs. But my old uncle bade me take my fill, and now in sooth I am aweary of them."

"I think you gentlemen are always so," the coquette said.

"Nay, say not so, fair stranger!" the youth replied, his face kindling as he spoke, and his eagle eyes flashing fire. "Figs pall; but oh! the Beautiful never does. Figs rot; but oh! the Truthful is eternal. I was born, lady, to grapple with the Lofty and the Ideal. My soul yearns for the Visionary. I stand behind the counter, it is true; but I ponder here upon the deeds of heroes, and muse over the thoughts of sages. What is grocery for one who has ambition? What sweetness hath Muscovada to him who hath tasted of Poesy? The Ideal, lady, I often think, is the true Real, and the Actual, but a visionary hallucination. But pardon me; with what may I serve thee?"

"I came only for sixpenn'orth of tea-dust," the girl said, with a faltering voice; "but oh, I should like to hear you speak on for ever!"

Only for sixpenn'orth of tea-dust? Girl, thou camest for other things! Thou lovedst his voice? Siren! what was the witchery of thine own? He deftly made up the packet, and placed it in the little hand. She paid for her small purchase, and with a farewell glance of her lustrous eyes, she left him. She passed slowly through the portal, and in a moment was lost in the crowd. It was noon in Chepe. And George de Barnwell was alone.


VOLUME II

We have selected the following episodical chapter in preference to anything relating to the mere story of George Barnwell, with which most readers are familiar.

Up to this passage (extracted from the beginning of Vol. II.) the tale is briefly thus:

The rogue of a Millwood has come back every day to the grocer's shop in Chepe, wanting some sugar, or some nutmeg, or some figs, half a dozen times in the week.

She and George de Barnwell have vowed to each other an eternal attachment.

This flame acts violently upon George. His bosom swells with ambition. His genius breaks out prodigiously. He talks about the Good, the Beautiful, the Ideal, &c., in and out of all season, and is virtuous and eloquent almost beyond belief—in fact like Devereux, or P. Clifford, or E. Aram, Esquires.

Inspired by Millwood and love, George robs the till, and mingles in the world which he is destined to ornament. He outdoes all the dandies, all the wits, all the scholars, and all the voluptuaries of the age—an indefinite period of time between Queen Anne and George II.—dines with Curll at St. John's Gate, pinks Colonel Charteris in a duel behind Montague House, is initiated into the intrigues of the Chevalier St. George, whom he entertains at his sumptuous pavilion at Hampstead, and likewise in disguise at the shop in Cheapside.

His uncle, the owner of the shop, a surly curmudgeon with very little taste for the True and Beautiful, has retired from business to the pastoral village in Cambridgeshire from which the noble Barnwells came. George's cousin Annabel is, of course, consumed with a secret passion for him.

Some trifling inaccuracies may be remarked in the ensuing brilliant little chapter; but it must be remembered that the author wished to present an age at a glance: and the dialogue is quite as fine and correct as that in the "Last of the Barons," or in "Eugene Aram," or other works of our author, in which Sentiment and History, or the True and Beautiful, are united.


CHAPTER XXIV

BUTTON'S IN PALL MALL

Those who frequent the dismal and enormous Mansions of Silence which society has raised to Ennui in that Omphalos of town, Pall Mall, and which, because they knock you down with their dulness, are called Clubs no doubt; those who yawn from a bay-window in St. James's Street, at a half-score of other dandies gaping from another bay-window over the way; those who consult a dreary evening paper for news, or satisfy themselves with the jokes of the miserable Punch by way of wit; the men about town of the present day, in a word, can have but little idea of London some six or eight score years back. Thou pudding-sided old dandy of St. James's Street, with thy lacquered boots, thy dyed whiskers, and thy suffocating waistband, what art thou to thy brilliant predecessor in the same quarter? The Brougham from which thou descendest at the portal of the "Carlton" or the "Travellers'," is like everybody else's; thy black coat has no more plaits, nor buttons, nor fancy in it than thy neighbor's; thy hat was made on the very block on which Lord Addlepate's was cast, who has just entered the Club before thee. You and he yawn together out of the same omnibus-box every night; you fancy yourselves men of pleasure; you fancy yourselves men of fashion; you fancy yourselves men of taste; in fancy, in taste, in opinion, in philosophy, the newspaper legislates for you; it is there you get your jokes and your thoughts, and your facts and your wisdom—poor Pall Mall dullards. Stupid slaves of the press, on that ground which you at present occupy, there were men of wit and pleasure and fashion, some five-and-twenty lustres ago.

We are at Button's—the well-known sign of the "Turk's Head." The crowd of periwigged heads at the windows—the swearing chairmen round the steps (the blazoned and coronalled panels of whose vehicles denote the lofty rank of their owners),—the throng of embroidered beaux entering or departing, and rendering the air fragrant with the odors of pulvillio and pomander, proclaim the celebrated resort of London's Wit and Fashion. It is the corner of Regent Street. Carlton House has not yet been taken down.

A stately gentleman in crimson velvet and gold is sipping chocolate at one of the tables, in earnest converse with a friend whose suit is likewise embroidered, but stained by time, or wine mayhap, or wear. A little deformed gentleman in iron-gray is reading the Morning Chronicle newspaper by the fire, while a divine, with a broad brogue and a shovel hat and cassock, is talking freely with a gentleman, whose star and ribbon, as well as the unmistakable beauty of his Phidian countenance, proclaims him to be a member of Britain's aristocracy.

Two ragged youths, the one tall, gaunt, clumsy and scrofulous, the other with a wild, careless, beautiful look, evidently indicating Race, are gazing in at the window, not merely at the crowd in the celebrated Club, but at Timothy the waiter, who is removing a plate of that exquisite dish, the muffin (then newly invented), at the desire of some of the revellers within.

"I would, Sam," said the wild youth to his companion, "that I had some of my mother Macclesfield's gold, to enable us to eat of those cates and mingle with yon springalds and beaux."

"To vaunt a knowledge of the stoical philosophy," said the youth addressed as Sam, "might elicit a smile of incredulity upon the cheek of the parasite of pleasure; but there are moments in life when History fortifies endurance: and past study renders present deprivation more bearable. If our pecuniary resources be exiguous, let our resolution, Dick, supply the deficiencies of Fortune. The muffin we desire to-day would little benefit us to-morrow. Poor and hungry as we are, are we less happy, Dick, than yon listless voluptuary who banquets on the food which you covet?"

And the two lads turned away up Waterloo Place, and past the "Parthenon" Club-house, and disappeared to take a meal of cow-heel at a neighboring cook's shop. Their names were Samuel Johnson and Richard Savage.

Meanwhile the conversation at Button's was fast and brilliant. "By Wood's thirteens, and the divvle go wid 'em," cried the Church dignitary in the cassock, "is it in blue and goold ye are this morning, Sir Richard, when you ought to be in seebles?"

"Who's dead, Dean?" said the nobleman, the dean's companion.

"Faix, mee Lard Bolingbroke, as sure as mee name's Jonathan Swift—and I'm not so sure of that neither, for who knows his father's name?—there's been a mighty cruel murther committed entirely. A child of Dick Steele's has been barbarously slain, dthrawn, and quarthered, and it's Joe Addison yondther has done it. Ye should have killed one of your own, Joe, ye thief of the world."

"I!" said the amazed and Right Honorable Joseph Addison; "I kill Dick's child! I was godfather to the last."

"And promised a cup and never sent it," Dick ejaculated. Joseph looked grave.

"The child I mean is Sir Roger de Coverley, Knight and Baronet. What made ye kill him, ye savage Mohock? The whole town is in tears about the good knight; all the ladies at Church this afternoon were in mourning; all the booksellers are wild; and Lintot says not a third of the copies of the Spectator are sold since the death of the brave old gentleman." And the Dean of St. Patrick's pulled out the Spectator newspaper, containing the well-known passage regarding Sir Roger's death. "I bought it but now in 'Wellington Street,'" he said; "the newsboys were howling all down the Strand."

"What a miracle is Genius—Genius, the Divine and Beautiful," said a gentleman leaning against the same fireplace with the deformed cavalier in iron-gray, and addressing that individual, who was in fact Mr. Alexander Pope. "What a marvellous gift is this, and royal privilege of Art! To make the Ideal more credible than the Actual: to enchain our hearts, to command our hopes, our regrets, our tears, for a mere brain-born Emanation: to invest with life the Incorporeal, and to glamour the cloudy into substance,—these are the lofty privileges of the Poet, if I have read poesy aright; and I am as familiar with the sounds that rang from Homer's lyre, as with the strains which celebrate the loss of Belinda's lovely locks"—(Mr. Pope blushed and bowed, highly delighted)—"these, I say, sir, are the privileges of the Poet—the Poietes—the Maker—he moves the world, and asks no lever; if he cannot charm death into life, as Orpheus feigned to do, he can create Beauty out of Nought, and defy Death by rendering Thought Eternal. Ho! Jemmy, another flask of Nantz."

And the boy—for he who addressed the most brilliant company of wits in Europe was little more—emptied the contents of the brandy-flask into a silver flagon, and quaffed it gayly to the health of the company assembled. 'Twas the third he had taken during the sitting. Presently, and with a graceful salute to the Society, he quitted the coffee-house, and was seen cantering on a magnificent Arab past the National Gallery.

"Who is yon spark in blue and silver? He beats Joe Addison himself, in drinking, and pious Joe is the greatest toper in the three kingdoms," Dick Steele said, good-naturedly.

"His paper in the Spectator beats thy best, Dick, thou sluggard," the Right Honorable Mr. Addison exclaimed. "He is the author of that famous No. 996, for which you have all been giving me the credit."

"The rascal foiled me at capping verses," Dean Swift said, "and won a tenpenny piece of me, plague take him!"

"He has suggested an emendation in my 'Homer,' which proves him a delicate scholar," Mr. Pope exclaimed.

"He knows more of the French king than any man I have met with; and we must have an eye upon him," said Lord Bolingbroke, then Secretary of State for Foreign Affairs, and beckoning a suspicious-looking person who was drinking at a side-table, whispered to him something.

Meantime who was he? where was he, this youth who had struck all the wits of London with admiration? His galloping charger had returned to the City; his splendid court-suit was doffed for the citizen's gabardine and grocer's humble apron.

George de Barnwell was in Chepe—in Chepe, at the feet of Martha Millwood.


VOLUME III

THE CONDEMNED CELL

"Quid me mollibus implicas lacertis, my Elinor? Nay," George added, a faint smile illumining his wan but noble features, "why speak to thee in the accents of the Roman poet, which thou comprehendest not?

Bright One, there be other things in Life, in Nature, in this Inscrutable Labyrinth, this Heart on which thou leanest, which are equally unintelligible to thee! Yes, my pretty one, what is the Unintelligible but the Ideal? what is the Ideal but the Beautiful? what the Beautiful but the Eternal? And the Spirit of Man that would commune with these is like Him who wanders by the thina poluphloisboio thalasses, and shrinks awe-struck before that Azure Mystery."

Emily's eyes filled with fresh-gushing dew. "Speak on, speak ever thus, my George," she exclaimed. Barnwell's chains rattled as the confiding girl clung to him. Even Snoggin, the turnkey appointed to sit with the Prisoner, was affected by his noble and appropriate language, and also burst into tears.

"You weep, my Snoggin," the Boy said; "and why? Hath Life been so charming to me that I should wish to retain it? hath Pleasure no after-Weariness? Ambition no Deception; Wealth no Care; and Glory no Mockery? Psha! I am sick of Success, palled of Pleasure, weary of Wine and Wit, and—nay, start not, my Adelaide—and Woman. I fling away all these things as the Toys of Boyhood. Life is the Soul's Nursery. I am a Man, and pine for the Illimitable! Mark you me! Has the Morrow any terrors for me, think ye? Did Socrates falter at his poison? Did Seneca blench in his bath? Did Brutus shirk the sword when his great stake was lost? Did even weak Cleopatra shrink from the Serpent's fatal nip? And why should I? My great Hazard hath been played, and I pay my forfeit. Lie sheathed in my heart, thou flashing Blade! Welcome to my Bosom, thou faithful Serpent; I hug thee, peace-bearing Image of the Eternal! Ha, the hemlock cup! Fill high, boy, for my soul is thirsty for the Infinite! Get ready the bath, friends; prepare me for the feast To-morrow—bathe my limbs in odors, and put ointment in my hair."

"Has for a bath," Snoggin interposed, "they're not to be 'ad in this ward of the prison; but I dussay Hemmy will git you a little hoil for your 'air."

The Prisoned One laughed loud and merrily. "My guardian understands me not, pretty one—and thou? what sayest thou? From those dear lips methinks—plura sunt oscula quam sententiae—I kiss away thy tears, dove!—they will flow apace when I am gone, then they will dry, and presently these fair eyes will shine on another, as they have beamed on poor George Barnwell. Yet wilt thou not all forget him, sweet one. He was an honest fellow, and had a kindly heart for all the world said—"

"That, that he had," cried the gaoler and the girl in voices gurgling with emotion. And you who read! you unconvicted Convict—you murderer, though haply you have slain no one—you Felon in posse if not in esse—deal gently with one who has used the Opportunity that has failed thee—and believe that the Truthful and the Beautiful bloom sometimes in the dock and the convict's tawny Gabardine!

In the matter for which he suffered, George could never be brought to acknowledge that he was at all in the wrong. "It may be an error of judgment," he said to the Venerable Chaplain of the gaol, "but it is no crime. Were it Crime, I should feel Remorse. Where there is no remorse, Crime cannot exist. I am not sorry: therefore, I am innocent. Is the proposition a fair one?"

The excellent Doctor admitted that it was not to be contested.

"And wherefore, sir, should I have sorrow," the Boy resumed, "for ridding the world of a sordid worm;* of a man whose very soul was dross, and who never had a feeling for the Truthful and the Beautiful? When I stood before my uncle in the moonlight, in the gardens of the ancestral halls of the De Barnwells, I felt that it was the Nemesis come to overthrow him. 'Dog,' I said to the trembling slave, 'tell me where thy Gold is. THOU hast no use for it. I can spend it in relieving the Poverty on which thou tramplest; in aiding Science, which thou knowest not; in uplifting Art, to which thou art blind. Give Gold, and thou art free.' But he spake not, and I slew him."

"I would not have this doctrine vulgarly promulgated," said the admirable chaplain, "for its general practice might chance to do harm. Thou, my son, the Refined, the Gentle, the Loving and Beloved, the Poet and Sage, urged by what I cannot but think a grievous error, hast appeared as Avenger. Think what would be the world's condition, were men without any Yearning after the Ideal to attempt to reorganize Society, to redistribute Property, to avenge Wrong."

"A rabble of pigmies scaling Heaven," said the noble though misguided young Prisoner. "Prometheus was a Giant, and he fell."

"Yes, indeed, my brave youth!" the benevolent Dr. Fuzwig exclaimed, clasping the Prisoner's marble and manacled hand; "and the Tragedy of To-morrow will teach the World that Homicide is not to be permitted even to the most amiable Genius, and that the lover of the Ideal and the Beautiful, as thou art, my son, must respect the Real likewise."

"Look! here is supper!" cried Barnwell gayly. "This is the Real, Doctor; let us respect it and fall to." He partook of the meal as joyously as if it had been one of his early festals; but the worthy chaplain could scarcely eat it for tears.

* This is a gross plagiarism: the above sentiment is expressed much more eloquently in the ingenious romance of Eugene Aram:—"The burning desires I have known—the resplendent visions I have nursed—the sublime aspirings that have lifted me so often from sense and clay: these tell me, that whether for good or ill, I am the thing of an immortality and the creature of a God. . . . I have destroyed a man noxious to the world! with the wealth by which he afflicted society, I have been the means of blessing many."


CODLINGSBY

BY D. SHREWSBERRY, ESQ.

I

"The whole world is bound by one chain. In every city in the globe there is one quarter that certain travellers know and recognize from its likeness to its brother district in all other places where are congregated the habitations of men. In Tehran, or Pekin, or Stamboul, or New York, or Timbuctoo, or London, there is a certain district where a certain man is not a stranger. Where the idols are fed with incense by the streams of Ching-wang-foo; where the minarets soar sparkling above the cypresses, their reflections quivering in the lucid waters of the Golden Horn; where the yellow Tiber flows under broken bridges and over imperial glories; where the huts are squatted by the Niger, under the palm-trees; where the Northern Babel lies, with its warehouses, and its bridges, its graceful factory-chimneys, and its clumsy fanes—hidden in fog and smoke by the dirtiest river in the world—in all the cities of mankind there is One Home whither men of one family may resort. Over the entire world spreads a vast brotherhood, suffering, silent, scattered, sympathizing, WAITING—an immense Free-Masonry. Once this world-spread band was an Arabian clan—a little nation alone and outlying amongst the mighty monarchies of ancient time, the Megatheria of history. The sails of their rare ships might be seen in the Egyptian waters; the camels of their caravans might thread the sands of Baalbec, or wind through the date-groves of Damascus; their flag was raised, not ingloriously, in many wars, against mighty odds; but 'twas a small people, and on one dark night the Lion of Judah went down before Vespasian's Eagles, and in flame, and death, and struggle, Jerusalem agonized and died. . . . Yes, the Jewish city is lost to Jewish men; but have they not taken the world in exchange?"

Mused thus Godfrey de Bouillon, Marquis of Codlingsby, as he debouched from Wych Street into the Strand. He had been to take a box for Armida at Madame Vestris's theatre. That little Armida was folle of Madame Vestris's theatre; and her little brougham, and her little self, and her enormous eyes, and her prodigious opera-glass, and her miraculous bouquet, which cost Lord Codlingsby twenty guineas every evening at Nathan's in Covent Garden (the children of the gardeners of Sharon have still no rival for flowers), might be seen, three nights in the week at least, in the narrow, charming, comfortable little theatre. Godfrey had the box. He was strolling, listlessly, eastward; and the above thoughts passed through the young noble's mind as he came in sight of Holywell Street.

The occupants of the London Ghetto sat at their porches basking in the evening sunshine. Children were playing on the steps. Fathers were smoking at the lintel. Smiling faces looked out from the various and darkling draperies with which the warehouses were hung. Ringlets glossy, and curly, and jetty—eyes black as night—midsummer night—when it lightens; haughty noses bending like beaks of eagles—eager quivering nostrils—lips curved like the bow of Love—every man or maiden, every babe or matron in that English Jewry bore in his countenance one or more of these characteristics of his peerless Arab race.

"How beautiful they are!" mused Codlingsby, as he surveyed these placid groups calmly taking their pleasure in the sunset.

"D'you vant to look at a nishe coat?" a voice said, which made him start; and then some one behind him began handling a masterpiece of Stultz's with a familiarity which would have made the baron tremble.

"Rafael Mendoza!" exclaimed Godfrey.

"The same, Lord Codlingsby," the individual so apostrophized replied. "I told you we should meet again where you would little expect me. Will it please you to enter? this is Friday, and we close at sunset. It rejoices my heart to welcome you home." So saying Rafael laid his hand on his breast, and bowed, an oriental reverence. All traces of the accent with which he first addressed Lord Codlingsby had vanished: it was disguise; half the Hebrew's life is a disguise. He shields himself in craft, since the Norman boors persecuted him.

They passed under an awning of old clothes, tawdry fripperies, greasy spangles, and battered masks, into a shop as black and hideous as the entrance was foul. "THIS your home, Rafael?" said Lord Codlingsby.

"Why not?" Rafael answered. "I am tired of Schloss Schinkenstein; the Rhine bores me after a while. It is too hot for Florence; besides they have not completed the picture-gallery, and my place smells of putty. You wouldn't have a man, mon cher, bury himself in his chateau in Normandy, out of the hunting season? The Rugantino Palace stupefies me. Those Titians are so gloomy, I shall have my Hobbimas and Tenierses, I think, from my house at the Hague hung over them."

"How many castles, palaces, houses, warehouses, shops, have you, Rafael?" Lord Codlingsby asked, laughing.

"This is one," Rafael answered. "Come in."

II.

The noise in the old town was terrific; Great Tom was booming sullenly over the uproar; the bell of Saint Mary's was clanging with alarm; St. Giles's tocsin chimed furiously; howls, curses, flights of brickbats, stones shivering windows, groans of wounded men, cries of frightened females, cheers of either contending party as it charged the enemy from Carfax to Trumpington Street, proclaimed that the battle was at its height.

In Berlin they would have said it was a revolution, and the cuirassiers would have been charging, sabre in hand, amidst that infuriate mob. In France they would have brought down artillery, and played on it with twenty-four pounders. In Cambridge nobody heeded the disturbance—it was a Town and Gown row.

The row arose at a boat-race. The Town boat (manned by eight stout Bargees, with the redoubted Rullock for stroke) had bumped the Brazenose light oar, usually at the head of the river. High words arose regarding the dispute. After returning from Granchester, when the boats pulled back to Christchurch meadows, the disturbance between the Townsmen and the University youths—their invariable opponents—grew louder and more violent, until it broke out in open battle. Sparring and skirmishing took place along the pleasant fields that lead from the University gate down to the broad and shining waters of the Cam, and under the walls of Balliol and Sidney Sussex. The Duke of Bellamont (then a dashing young sizar at Exeter) had a couple of rounds with Billy Butt, the bow-oar of the Bargee boat. Vavasour of Brazenose was engaged with a powerful butcher, a well-known champion of the Town party, when, the great University bells ringing to dinner, truce was called between the combatants, and they retired to their several colleges for refection.

During the boat-race, a gentleman pulling in a canoe, and smoking a narghilly, had attracted no ordinary attention. He rowed about a hundred yards ahead of the boats in the race, so that he could have a good view of that curious pastime. If the eight-oars neared him, with a few rapid strokes of his flashing paddles his boat shot a furlong ahead; then he would wait, surveying the race, and sending up volumes of odor from his cool narghilly.

"Who is he?" asked the crowds who panted along the shore, encouraging, according to Cambridge wont, the efforts of the oarsmen in the race. Town and Gown alike asked who it was, who, with an ease so provoking, in a barque so singular, with a form seemingly so slight, but a skill so prodigious, beat their best men. No answer could be given to the query, save that a gentleman in a dark travelling-chariot, preceded by six fourgons and a courier, had arrived the day before at the "Hoop Inn," opposite Brazenose, and that the stranger of the canoe seemed to be the individual in question.

No wonder the boat, that all admired so, could compete with any that ever was wrought by Cambridge artificer or Putney workman. That boat—slim, shining, and shooting through the water like a pike after a small fish—was a caique from Tophana; it had distanced the Sultan's oarsmen and the best crews of the Capitan Pasha in the Bosphorus; it was the workmanship of Togrul-Beg, Caikjee Bashee of his Highness.

The Bashee had refused fifty thousand tomauns from Count Boutenieff, the Russian Ambassador, for that little marvel. When his head was taken off, the Father of Believers presented the boat to Rafael Mendoza.

It was Rafael Mendoza that saved the Turkish monarchy after the battle of Nezeeb. By sending three millions of piastres to the Seraskier; by bribing Colonel de St. Cornichon, the French envoy in the camp of the victorious Ibrahim, the march of the Egyptian army was stopped—the menaced empire of the Ottomans was saved from ruin; the Marchioness of Stokepogis, our ambassador's lady, appeared in a suite of diamonds which outblazed even the Romanoff jewels, and Rafael Mendoza obtained the little caique. He never travelled without it. It was scarcely heavier than an arm-chair. Baroni, the courier, had carried it down to the Cam that morning, and Rafael had seen the singular sport which we have mentioned.

The dinner over, the young men rushed from their colleges, flushed, full-fed, and eager for battle. If the Gown was angry, the Town, too, was on the alert. From Iffly and Barnwell, from factory and mill, from wharf and warehouse, the Town poured out to meet the enemy, and their battle was soon general. From the Addenbrook's hospital to the Blenheim turnpike, all Cambridge was in an uproar—the college gates closed—the shops barricaded—the shop-boys away in support of their brother townsmen—the battle raged, and the Gown had the worst of the fight.

A luncheon of many courses had been provided for Rafael Mendoza at his inn; but he smiled at the clumsy efforts of the university cooks to entertain him, and a couple of dates and a glass of water formed his meal. In vain the discomfited landlord pressed him to partake of the slighted banquet. "A breakfast! psha!" said he. "My good man, I have nineteen cooks, at salaries rising from four hundred a year. I can have a dinner at any hour; but a Town and Gown row" (a brickbat here flying through the window crashed the caraffe of water in Mendoza's hand)—"a Town and Gown row is a novelty to me. The Town has the best of it, clearly, though: the men outnumber the lads. Ha, a good blow! How that tall townsman went down before yonder slim young fellow in the scarlet trencher cap."

"That is the Lord Codlingsby," the landlord said.

"A light weight, but a pretty fighter," Mendoza remarked. "Well hit with your left, Lord Codlingsby; well parried, Lord Codlingsby; claret drawn, by Jupiter!"

"Ours is werry fine," the landlord said. "Will your Highness have Chateau Margaux or Lafitte?"

"He never can be going to match himself against that bargeman!" Rafael exclaimed, as an enormous boatman—no other than Rullock—indeed, the most famous bruiser of Cambridge, and before whose fists the Gownsmen went down like ninepins—fought his way up to the spot where, with admirable spirit and resolution, Lord Codlingsby and one or two of his friends were making head against a number of the town.

The young noble faced the huge champion with the gallantry of his race, but was no match for the enemy's strength and weight and sinew, and went down at every round. The brutal fellow had no mercy on the lad. His savage treatment chafed Mendoza as he viewed the unequal combat from the inn-window. "Hold your hand!" he cried to this Goliath; "don't you see he's but a boy?"

"Down he goes again!" the bargeman cried, not heeding the interruption. "Down he goes again: I likes wapping a lord!"

"Coward!" shouted Mendoza; and to fling open the window amidst a shower of brickbats, to vault over the balcony, to slide down one of the pillars to the ground, was an instant's work.

At the next he stood before the enormous bargeman.

After the coroner's inquest, Mendoza gave ten thousand pounds to each of the bargeman's ten children, and it was thus his first acquaintance was formed with Lord Codlingsby.

But we are lingering on the threshold of the house in Holywell Street. Let us go in.

III.

Godfrey and Rafael passed from the street into the outer shop of the old mansion in Holywell Street. It was a masquerade warehouse to all appearance. A dark-eyed damsel of the nation was standing at the dark and grimy counter, strewed with old feathers, old yellow hoots, old stage mantles, painted masks, blind and yet gazing at you with a look of sad death-like intelligence from the vacancy behind their sockets.

A medical student was trying one of the doublets of orange-tawny and silver, slashed with dirty light blue. He was going to a masquerade that night. He thought Polly Pattens would admire him in the dress—Polly Pattens, the fairest of maids-of-all-work—the Borough Venus, adored by half the youth of Guy's.

"You look like a prince in it, Mr. Lint," pretty Rachel said, coaxing him with her beady black eyes.

"It IS the cheese," replied Mr. Lint; "it ain't the dress that don't suit, my rose of Sharon; it's the FIGURE. Hullo, Rafael, is that you, my lad of sealing-wax? Come and intercede for me with this wild gazelle; she says I can't have it under fifteen bob for the night. And it's too much: cuss me if it's not too much, unless you'll take my little bill at two months, Rafael."

"There's a sweet pretty brigand's dress you may have for half de monish," Rafael replied; "there's a splendid clown for eight bob; but for dat Spanish dress, selp ma Moshesh, Mistraer Lint, ve'd ask a guinea of any but you. Here's a gentlemansh just come to look at it. Look 'ear, Mr. Brownsh, did you ever shee a nisher ting dan dat?" So saying, Rafael turned to Lord Codlingsby with the utmost gravity, and displayed to him the garment about which the young medicus was haggling.

"Cheap at the money," Codlingsby replied; "if you won't make up your mind, sir, I should like to engage it myself." But the thought that another should appear before Polly Pattens in that costume was too much for Mr. Lint; he agreed to pay the fifteen shillings for the garment. And Rafael, pocketing the money with perfect simplicity, said, "Dis vay, Mr. Brownsh: dere's someting vill shoot you in the next shop."

Lord Codlingsby followed him, wondering.

"You are surprised at our system," said Rafael, marking the evident bewilderment of his friend. "Confess you would call it meanness—my huckstering with yonder young fool. I call it simplicity. Why throw away a shilling without need? Our race never did. A shilling is four men's bread: shall I disdain to defile my fingers by holding them out relief in their necessity? It is you who are mean—you Normans—not we of the ancient race. You have your vulgar measurement for great things and small. You call a thousand pounds respectable, and a shekel despicable. Psha, my Codlingsby! One is as the other. I trade in pennies and in millions. I am above or below neither."

They were passing through a second shop, smelling strongly of cedar, and, in fact, piled up with bales of those pencils which the young Hebrews are in the habit of vending through the streets. "I have sold bundles and bundles of these," said Rafael. "My little brother is now out with oranges in Piccadilly. I am bringing him up to be head of our house at Amsterdam. We all do it. I had myself to see Rothschild in Eaton Place this morning, about the Irish loan, of which I have taken three millions: and as I wanted to walk, I carried the bag.

"You should have seen the astonishment of Lauda Latymer, the Archbishop of Croydon's daughter, as she was passing St. Bennet's, Knightsbridge, and as she fancied she recognized in the man who was crying old clothes the gentleman with whom she had talked at the Count de St. Aulair's the night before." Something like a blush flushed over the pale features of Mendoza as he mentioned the Lady Lauda's name. "Come on," said he. They passed through various warehouses—the orange room, the sealing-wax room, the six-bladed knife department, and finally came to an old baize door. Rafael opened the baize door by some secret contrivance, and they were in a black passage, with a curtain at the end.

He clapped his hands; the curtain at the end of the passage drew back, and a flood of golden light streamed on the Hebrew and his visitor.

## CHAPTER XXIV

They entered a moderate-sized apartment—indeed, Holywell Street is not above a hundred yards long, and this chamber was not more than half that length—it was fitted up with the simple taste of its owner.

The carpet was of white velvet—(laid over several webs of Aubusson, Ispahan, and Axminster, so that your foot gave no more sound as it trod upon the yielding plain than the shadow did which followed you)—of white velvet, painted with flowers, arabesques, and classic figures, by Sir William Ross, J. M. W. Turner, R. A., Mrs. Mee, and Paul Delaroche. The edges were wrought with seed-pearls, and fringed with Valenciennes lace and bullion. The walls were hung with cloth of silver, embroidered with gold figures, over which were worked pomegranates, polyanthuses, and passion-flowers, in ruby, amethyst, and smaragd. The drops of dew which the artificer had sprinkled on the flowers were diamonds. The hangings were overhung by pictures yet more costly. Giorgione the gorgeous, Titian the golden, Rubens the ruddy and pulpy (the Pan of Painting), some of Murillo's beatified shepherdesses, who smile on you out of darkness like a star, a few score first-class Leonardos, and fifty of the master-pieces of the patron of Julius and Leo, the Imperial genius of Urbino, covered the walls of the little chamber. Divans of carved amber covered with ermine went round the room, and in the midst was a fountain, pattering and babbling with jets of double-distilled otto of roses.

"Pipes, Goliath!" Rafael said gayly to a little negro with a silver collar (he spoke to him in his native tongue of Dongola); "and welcome to our snuggery, my Codlingsby. We are quieter here than in the front of the house, and I wanted to show you a picture. I'm proud of my pictures. That Leonardo came from Genoa, and was a gift to our father from my cousin, Marshal Manasseh: that Murillo was pawned to my uncle by Marie Antoinette before the flight to Varennes—the poor lady could not redeem the pledge, you know, and the picture remains with us. As for the Rafael, I suppose you are aware that he was one of our people. But what are you gazing at? Oh! my sister—I forgot. Miriam! this is the Lord Codlingsby."

She had been seated at an ivory pianoforte on a mother-of-pearl music-stool, trying a sonata of Herz. She rose when thus apostrophized. Miriam de Mendoza rose and greeted the stranger.

The Talmud relates that Adam had two wives—Zillah the dark beauty; Eva the fair one. The ringlets of Zillah were black; those of Eva were golden. The eyes of Zillah were night; those of Eva were morning. Codlingsby was fair—of the fair Saxon race of Hengist and Horsa—they called him Miss Codlingsby at school; but how much fairer was Miriam the Hebrew!

Her hair had that deep glowing tinge in it which has been the delight of all painters, and which, therefore, the vulgar sneer at. It was of burning auburn. Meandering over her fairest shoulders in twenty thousand minute ringlets, it hung to her waist and below it. A light blue velvet fillet clasped with a diamond aigrette (valued at two hundred thousand tomauns, and bought from Lieutenant Vicovich, who had received it from Dost Mahomed), with a simple bird of paradise, formed her head-gear. A sea-green cymar with short sleeves, displayed her exquisitely moulded arms to perfection, and was fastened by a girdle of emeralds over a yellow satin frock. Pink gauze trousers spangled with silver, and slippers of the same color as the band which clasped her ringlets (but so covered with pearls that the original hue of the charming little papoosh disappeared entirely) completed her costume. She had three necklaces on, each of which would have dowered a Princess—her fingers glistened with rings to their rosy tips, and priceless bracelets, bangles, and armlets wound round an arm that was whiter than the ivory grand piano on which it leaned.

As Miriam de Mendoza greeted the stranger, turning upon him the solemn welcome of her eyes, Codlingsby swooned almost in the brightness of her beauty. It was well she spoke; the sweet kind voice restored him to consciousness. Muttering a few words of incoherent recognition, he sank upon a sandalwood settee, as Goliath, the little slave, brought aromatic coffee in cups of opal, and alabaster spittoons, and pipes of the fragrant Gibelly.

"My lord's pipe is out," said Miriam with a smile, remarking the bewilderment of her guest—who in truth forgot to smoke—and taking up a thousand pound note from a bundle on the piano, she lighted it at the taper and proceeded to re-illumine the extinguished chibouk of Lord Codlingsby.


IV.

When Miriam, returning to the mother-of-pearl music-stool, at a signal from her brother, touched the silver and enamelled keys of the ivory piano, and began to sing, Lord Codlingsby felt as if he were listening at the gates of Paradise, or were hearing Jenny Lind.

"Lind is the name of the Hebrew race; so is Mendelssohn, the son of Almonds; so is Rosenthal, the Valley of the Roses: so is Lowe or Lewis or Lyons or Lion. The beautiful and the brave alike give cognizances to the ancient people: you Saxons call yourselves Brown, or Smith, or Rodgers," Rafael observed to his friend; and, drawing the instrument from his pocket, he accompanied his sister, in the most ravishing manner, on a little gold and jewelled harp, of the kind peculiar to his nation.

All the airs which the Hebrew maid selected were written by composers of her race; it was either a hymn by Rossini, a polacca by Braham, a delicious romance by Sloman, or a melody by Weber, that, thrilling on the strings of the instrument, wakened a harmony on the fibres of the heart; but she sang no other than the songs of her nation.

"Beautiful one! sing ever, sing always," Codlingsby thought. "I could sit at thy feet as under a green palm-tree, and fancy that Paradise-birds were singing in the boughs."

Rafael read his thoughts. "We have Saxon blood too in our veins," he said. "You smile! but it is even so. An ancestress of ours made a mesalliance in the reign of your King John. Her name was Rebecca, daughter of Isaac of York, and she married in Spain, whither she had fled to the Court of King Boabdil, Sir Wilfred of Ivanhoe; then a widower by the demise of his first lady, Rowena. The match was deemed a cruel insult amongst our people but Wilfred conformed, and was a Rabbi of some note at the synagogue of Cordova. We are descended from him lineally. It is the only blot upon the escutcheon of the Mendozas."

As they sat talking together, the music finished, and Miriam having retired (though her song and her beauty were still present to the soul of the stranger) at a signal from Mendoza, various messengers from the outer apartments came in to transact business with him.

First it was Mr. Aminadab, who kissed his foot, and brought papers to sign. "How is the house in Grosvenor Square, Aminadab; and is your son tired of his yacht yet?" Mendoza asked. "That is my twenty-fourth cashier," said Rafael to Codlingsby, when the obsequious clerk went away. "He is fond of display, and all my people may have what money they like."

Entered presently the Lord Bareacres, on the affair of his mortgage. The Lord Bareacres, strutting into the apartment with a haughty air, shrank back, nevertheless, with surprise on beholding the magnificence around him. "Little Mordecai," said Rafael to a little orange-boy, who came in at the heels of the noble, "take this gentleman out and let him have ten thousand pounds. I can't do more for you, my lord, than this—I'm busy. Good-by!" And Rafael waved his hand to the peer, and fell to smoking his narghilly.

A man with a square face, cat-like eyes, and a yellow moustache, came next. He had an hour-glass of a waist, and walked uneasily upon his high-heeled boots. "Tell your master that he shall have two millions more, but not another shilling," Rafael said. "That story about the five-and-twenty millions of ready money at Cronstadt is all bosh. They won't believe it in Europe. You understand me, Count Grogomoffski?"

"But his Imperial Majesty said four millions, and I shall get the knout unless—"

"Go and speak to Mr. Shadrach, in room Z 94, the fourth court," said Mendoza good-naturedly. "Leave me at peace, Count: don't you see it is Friday, and almost sunset?" The Calmuck envoy retired cringing, and left an odor of musk and candle-grease behind him.

An orange-man; an emissary from Lola Montes; a dealer in piping bullfinches; and a Cardinal in disguise, with a proposal for a new loan for the Pope, were heard by turns; and each, after a rapid colloquy in his own language, was dismissed by Rafael.

"The queen must come back from Aranjuez, or that king must be disposed of," Rafael exclaimed, as a yellow-faced ambassador from Spain, General the Duke of Olla Podrida, left him. "Which shall it be, my Codlingsby?" Codlingsby was about laughingly to answer—for indeed he was amazed to find all the affairs of the world represented here, and Holywell Street the centre of Europe—when three knocks of a peculiar nature were heard, and Mendoza starting up, said, "Ha! there are only four men in the world who know that signal." At once, and with a reverence quite distinct from his former nonchalant manner, he advanced towards the new-comer.

He was an old man—an old man evidently, too, of the Hebrew race—the light of his eyes was unfathomable—about his mouth there played an inscrutable smile. He had a cotton umbrella, and old trousers, and old boots, and an old wig, curling at the top like a rotten old pear.

He sat down, as if tired, in the first seat at hand, as Rafael made him the lowest reverence.

"I am tired," says he; "I have come in fifteen hours. I am ill at Neuilly," he added with a grin. "Get me some eau sucree, and tell me the news, Prince de Mendoza. These bread rows; this unpopularity of Guizot; this odious Spanish conspiracy against my darling Montpensier and daughter; this ferocity of Palmerston against Coletti, makes me quite ill. Give me your opinion, my dear duke. But ha! whom have we here?"

The august individual who had spoken, had used the Hebrew language to address Mendoza, and the Lord Codlingsby might easily have pleaded ignorance of that tongue. But he had been at Cambridge, where all the youth acquire it perfectly.

"SIRE," said he, "I will not disguise from you that I know the ancient tongue in which you speak. There are probably secrets between Mendoza and your Maj—"

"Hush!" said Rafael, leading him from the room. "Au revoir, dear Codlingsby. His Majesty is one of US," he whispered at the door; "so is the Pope of Rome; so is . . ."—a whisper concealed the rest.

"Gracious powers! is it so?" said Codlingsby, musing. He entered into Holywell Street. The sun was sinking.

"It is time," said he, "to go and fetch Armida to the Olympic."


PHIL FOGARTY

A TALE OF THE FIGHTING ONETY-ONETH

BY HARRY ROLLICKER

I.

The gabion was ours. After two hours' fighting we were in possession of the first embrasure, and made ourselves as comfortable as circumstances would admit. Jack Delamere, Tom Delancy, Jerry Blake, the Doctor, and myself, sat down under a pontoon, and our servants laid out a hasty supper on a tumbrel. Though Cambaceres had escaped me so provokingly after I cut him down, his spoils were mine; a cold fowl and a Bologna sausage were found in the Marshal's holsters; and in the haversack of a French private who lay a corpse on the glacis, we found a loaf of bread, his three days' ration. Instead of salt, we had gunpowder; and you may be sure, wherever the Doctor was, a flask of good brandy was behind him in his instrument-case. We sat down and made a soldier's supper. The Doctor pulled a few of the delicious fruit from the lemon-trees growing near (and round which the Carabineers and the 24th Leger had made a desperate rally), and punch was brewed in Jack Delamere's helmet.

"'Faith, it never had so much wit in it before," said the Doctor, as he ladled out the drink. We all roared with laughing, except the guardsman, who was as savage as a Turk at a christening.

"Buvez-en," said old Sawbones to our French prisoner; "ca vous fera du bien, mon vieux coq!" and the Colonel, whose wound had been just dressed, eagerly grasped at the proffered cup, and drained it with a health to the donors.

How strange are the chances of war! But half an hour before he and I were engaged in mortal combat, and our prisoner was all but my conqueror. Grappling with Cambaceres, whom I knocked from his horse, and was about to despatch, I felt a lunge behind, which luckily was parried by my sabretache; a herculean grasp was at the next instant at my throat—I was on the ground—my prisoner had escaped, and a gigantic warrior in the uniform of a colonel of the regiment of Artois glaring over me with pointed sword.

"Rends-toi, coquin!" said he.

"Allez an Diable!" said I: "a Fogarty never surrenders."

I thought of my poor mother and my sisters, at the old house in Killaloo—I felt the tip of his blade between my teeth—I breathed a prayer, and shut my eyes—when the tables were turned—the butt-end of Lanty Clancy's musket knocked the sword up and broke the arm that held it.

"Thonamoundiaoul nabochlish," said the French officer, with a curse in the purest Irish. It was lucky I stopped laughing time enough to bid Lanty hold his hand, for the honest fellow would else have brained my gallant adversary. We were the better friends for our combat, as what gallant hearts are not?

The breach was to be stormed at sunset, and like true soldiers we sat down to make the most of our time. The rogue of a Doctor took the liver-wing for his share—we gave the other to our guest, a prisoner; those scoundrels Jack Delamere and Tom Delaney took the legs—and, 'faith, poor I was put off with the Pope's nose and a bit of the back.

"How d'ye like his Holiness's FAYTURE?" said Jerry Blake.

"Anyhow you'll have a MERRY THOUGHT," cried the incorrigible Doctor, and all the party shrieked at the witticism.

"De mortuis nil nisi bonum," said Jack, holding up the drumstick clean.

"'Faith, there's not enough of it to make us CHICKEN-HEARTED, anyhow," said I; "come, boys, let's have a song."

"Here goes," said Tom Delaney, and sung the following lyric, of his own composition—

"Dear Jack, this white mug that with Guinness I fill,
And drink to the health of sweet Nan of the hill,
Was once Tommy Tosspot's, as jovial a sot,
As e'er drew a spigot, or drain'd a full pot—
In drinking all round 'twas his joy to surpass,
And with all merry tipplers he swigg'd off his glass.

"One morning in summer, while seated so snug,
In the porch of his garden, discussing his jug,
Stern Death, on a sudden, to Tom did appear,
And said, 'Honest Thomas, come take your last bier;'
We kneaded his clay in the shape of this can,
From which let us drink to the health of my Nan."

"Psha!" said the Doctor, "I've heard that song before; here's a new one for you, boys!" and Sawbones began, in a rich Corkagian voice—

"You've all heard of Larry O'Toole,
Of the beautiful town of Drumgoole;
He had but one eye,
To ogle ye by—
Oh, murther, but that was a jew'l!
A fool
He made of de girls, dis O'Toole.

"'Twas he was the boy didn't fail,
That tuck down pataties and mail;
He never would shrink
From any sthrong dthrink,
Was it whisky or Drogheda ale;
I'm bail
This Larry would swallow a pail.

"Oh, many a night at the bowl,
With Larry I've sot cheek by jowl;
He's gone to his rest,
Where there's dthrink of the best,

And so let us give his old sowl
A howl,
For twas he made the noggin to rowl."

I observed the French Colonel's eye glistened as he heard these well-known accents of his country but we were too well-bred to pretend to remark his emotion.

The sun was setting behind the mountains as our songs were finished, and each began to look out with some anxiety for the preconcerted signal, the rocket from Sir Hussey Vivian's quarters, which was to announce the recommencement of hostilities. It came just as the moon rose in her silver splendor, and ere the rocket-stick fell quivering to the earth at the feet of General Picton and Sir Lowry Cole, who were at their posts at the head of the storming-parties, nine hundred and ninety nine guns in position opened their fire from our batteries, which were answered by a tremendous cannonade from the fort.

"Who's going to dance?" said the Doctor: "the ball's begun. Ha! there goes poor Jack Delamere's head off! The ball chose a soft one, anyhow. Come here, Tim, till I mend your leg. Your wife has need only knit half as many stockings next year, Doolan my boy. Faix! there goes a big one had wellnigh stopped my talking: bedad! it has snuffed the feather off my cocked hat!"

In this way, with eighty-four-pounders roaring over us like hail, the undaunted little Doctor pursued his jokes and his duty. That he had a feeling heart, all who served with him knew, and none more so than Philip Fogarty, the humble writer of this tale of war.

Our embrasure was luckily bomb-proof, and the detachment of the Onety-oneth under my orders suffered comparatively little. "Be cool, boys," I said; "it will be hot enough work for you ere long." The honest fellows answered with an Irish cheer. I saw that it affected our prisoner.

"Countryman," said I, "I know you; but an Irishman was never a traitor."

"Taisez-vous!" said he, putting his finger to his lip. "C'est la fortune de la guerre: if ever you come to Paris, ask for the Marquis d' O'Mahony, and I may render you the hospitality which your tyrannous laws prevent me from exercising in the ancestral halls of my own race."

I shook him warmly by the hand as a tear bedimmed his eye. It was, then, the celebrated colonel of the Irish Brigade, created a Marquis by Napoleon on the field of Austerlitz!

"Marquis," said I, "the country which disowns you is proud of you; but—ha! here, if I mistake not, comes our signal to advance." And in fact, Captain Vandeleur, riding up through the shower of shot, asked for the commander of the detachment, and bade me hold myself in readiness to move as soon as the flank companies of the Ninety-ninth, and Sixty-sixth, and the Grenadier Brigade of the German Legion began to advance up the echelon. The devoted band soon arrived; Jack Bowser heading the Ninety-ninth (when was he away and a storming-party to the fore?), and the gallant Potztausend, with his Hanoverian veterans.

The second rocket flew up.

"Forward, Onety-oneth!" cried I, in a voice of thunder. "Killaloo boys, follow your captain!" and with a shrill hurray, that sounded above the tremendous fire from the fort, we sprung upon the steep; Bowser with the brave Ninety-ninth, and the bold Potztausend, keeping well up with us. We passed the demilune, we passed the culverin, bayoneting the artillerymen at their guns; we advanced across the two tremendous demilunes which flank the counterscarp, and prepared for the final spring upon the citadel. Soult I could see quite pale on the wall; and the scoundrel Cambaceres, who had been so nearly my prisoner that day, trembled as he cheered his men. "On, boys, on!" I hoarsely exclaimed. "Hurroo!" said the fighting Onety-oneth.

But there was a movement among the enemy. An officer, glittering with orders, and another in a gray coat and a cocked hat, came to the wall, and I recognized the Emperor Napoleon and the famous Joachim Murat.

"We are hardly pressed, methinks," Napoleon said sternly. "I must exercise my old trade as an artilleryman;" and Murat loaded, and the Emperor pointed the only hundred-and-twenty-four-pounder that had not been silenced by our fire.

"Hurray, Killaloo boys!" shouted I. The next moment a sensation of numbness and death seized me, and I lay like a corpse upon the rampart.


II.

"Hush!" said a voice, which I recognized to be that of the Marquis d' O'Mahony. "Heaven be praised, reason has returned to you. For six weeks those are the only sane words I have heard from you."

"Faix, and 'tis thrue for you, Colonel dear," cried another voice, with which I was even more familiar; 'twas that of my honest and gallant Lanty Clancy, who was blubbering at my bedside overjoyed at his master's recovery.

"O musha, Masther Phil agrah! but this will be the great day intirely, when I send off the news, which I would, barrin' I can't write, to the lady your mother and your sisters at Castle Fogarty; and 'tis his Riv'rence Father Luke will jump for joy thin, when he reads the letther! Six weeks ravin' and roarin' as bould as a lion, and as mad as Mick Malony's pig, that mistuck Mick's wig for a cabbage, and died of atin' it!"

"And have I then lost my senses?" I exclaimed feebly.

"Sure, didn't ye call me your beautiful Donna Anna only yesterday, and catch hould of me whiskers as if they were the Signora's jet-black ringlets?" Lanty cried.

At this moment, and blushing deeply, the most beautiful young creature I ever set my eyes upon, rose from a chair at the foot of the bed, and sailed out of the room.

"Confusion, you blundering rogue," I cried; "who is that lovely lady whom you frightened away by your impertinence? Donna Anna? Where am I?"

"You are in good hands, Philip," said the Colonel; "you are at my house in the Place Vendome, at Paris, of which I am the military Governor. You and Lanty were knocked down by the wind of the cannon-ball at Burgos. Do not be ashamed: 'twas the Emperor pointed the gun;" and the Colonel took off his hat as he mentioned the name darling to France. "When our troops returned from the sally in which your gallant storming party was driven back, you were found on the glacis, and I had you brought into the City. Your reason had left you, however, when you returned to life; but, unwilling to desert the son of my old friend, Philip Fogarty, who saved my life in '98, I brought you in my carriage to Paris."

"And many's the time you tried to jump out of the windy, Masther Phil," said Clancy.

"Brought you to Paris," resumed the Colonel, smiling; "where, by the soins of my friends Broussais, Esquirol, and Baron Larrey, you have been restored to health, thank heaven!"

"And that lovely angel who quitted the apartment?" I cried.

"That lovely angel is the Lady Blanche Sarsfield, my ward, a descendant of the gallant Lucan, and who may be, when she chooses, Madame la Marechale de Cambaceres, Duchess of Illyria."

"Why did you deliver the ruffian when he was in my grasp?" I cried.

"Why did Lanty deliver you when in mine?" the Colonel replied. "C'est la fortune de la guerre, mon garcon; but calm yourself, and take this potion which Blanche has prepared for you."

I drank the tisane eagerly when I heard whose fair hands had compounded it, and its effects were speedily beneficial to me, for I sank into a cool and refreshing slumber.

From that day I began to mend rapidly, with all the elasticity of youth's happy time. Blanche—the enchanting Blanche—ministered henceforth to me, for I would take no medicine but from her lily hand. And what were the effects? 'Faith, ere a month was past, the patient was over head and ears in love with the doctor; and as for Baron Larrey, and Broussais, and Esquirol, they were sent to the right-about. In a short time I was in a situation to do justice to the gigot aux navets, the boeuf aux cornichons, and the other delicious entremets of the Marquis's board, with an appetite that astonished some of the Frenchmen who frequented it.

"Wait till he's quite well, Miss," said Lanty, who waited always behind me. "'Faith! when he's in health, I'd back him to ate a cow, barrin' the horns and teel." I sent a decanter at the rogue's head, by way of answer to his impertinence.

Although the disgusting Cambaceres did his best to have my parole withdrawn from me, and to cause me to be sent to the English depot of prisoners at Verdun, the Marquis's interest with the Emperor prevailed, and I was allowed to remain at Paris, the happiest of prisoners, at the Colonel's hotel at the Place Vendome. I here had the opportunity (an opportunity not lost, I flatter myself, on a young fellow with the accomplishments of Philip Fogarty, Esq.) of mixing with the elite of French society, and meeting with many of the great, the beautiful, and the brave. Talleyrand was a frequent guest of the Marquis's. His bon-mots used to keep the table in a roar. Ney frequently took his chop with us; Murat, when in town, constantly dropt in for a cup of tea and friendly round game. Alas! who would have thought those two gallant heads would be so soon laid low? My wife has a pair of earrings which the latter, who always wore them, presented to her—but we are advancing matters. Anybody could see, "avec un demioeil," as the Prince of Benevento remarked, how affairs went between me and Blanche; but though she loathed him for his cruelties and the odiousness of his person, the brutal Cambaceres still pursued his designs upon her.

I recollect it was on St. Patrick's Day. My lovely friend had procured, from the gardens of the Empress Josephine, at Malmaison (whom we loved a thousand times more than her Austrian successor, a sandy-haired woman, between ourselves, with an odious squint), a quantity of shamrock wherewith to garnish the hotel, and all the Irish in Paris were invited to the national festival.

I and Prince Talleyrand danced a double hornpipe with Pauline Bonaparte and Madame de Stael; Marshal Soult went down a couple of sets with Madame Recamier; and Robespierre's widow—an excellent, gentle creature, quite unlike her husband—stood up with the Austrian ambassador. Besides, the famous artists Baron Gros, David and Nicholas Poussin, and Canova, who was in town making a statue of the Emperor for Leo X., and, in a word, all the celebrities of Paris—as my gifted countrywoman, the wild Irish girl, calls them—were assembled in the Marquis's elegant receiving-rooms.

At last a great outcry was raised for La Gigue Irlandaise! La Gigue Irlandaise! a dance which had made a fureur amongst the Parisians ever since the lovely Blanche Sarsfield had danced it. She stepped forward and took me for a partner, and amidst the bravoes of the crowd, in which stood Ney, Murat, Lannes, the Prince of Wagram, and the Austrian ambassador, we showed to the beau monde of the French capital, I flatter myself, a not unfavorable specimen of the dance of our country.

As I was cutting the double-shuffle, and toe-and-heeling it in the "rail" style, Blanche danced up to me, smiling, and said, "Be on your guard; I see Cambaceres talking to Fouche, the Duke of Otranto, about us; and when Otranto turns his eyes upon a man, they bode him no good."

"Cambaceres is jealous," said I. "I have it," says she; "I'll make him dance a turn with me." So, presently, as the music was going like mad all this time, I pretended fatigue from my late wounds, and sat down. The lovely Blanche went up smiling, and brought out Cambaceres as a second partner.

The Marshal is a lusty man, who makes desperate efforts to give himself a waist, and the effect of the exercise upon him was speedily visible. He puffed and snorted like a walrus, drops trickled down his purple face, while my lovely mischief of a Blanche went on dancing at treble quick, till she fairly danced him down.

"Who'll take the flure with me?" said the charming girl, animated by the sport.

"Faix, den, 'tis I, Lanty Clancy!" cried my rascal, who had been mad with excitement at the scene; and, stepping in with a whoop and a hurroo, he began to dance with such rapidity as made all present stare.

As the couple were footing it, there was a noise as of a rapid cavalcade traversing the Place Vendome, and stopping at the Marquis's door. A crowd appeared to mount the stair; the great doors of the reception-room were flung open, and two pages announced their Majesties the Emperor and the Empress. So engaged were Lanty and Blanche, that they never heard the tumult occasioned by the august approach.

It was indeed the Emperor, who, returning from the Theatre Francais, and seeing the Marquis's windows lighted up, proposed to the Empress to drop in on the party. He made signs to the musicians to continue: and the conqueror of Marengo and Friedland watched with interest the simple evolutions of two happy Irish people. Even the Empress smiled and, seeing this, all the courtiers, including Naples and Talleyrand, were delighted.

"Is not this a great day for Ireland?" said the Marquis, with a tear trickling down his noble face. "O Ireland! O my country! But no more of that. Go up, Phil, you divvle, and offer her Majesty the choice of punch or negus."

Among the young fellows with whom I was most intimate in Paris was Eugene Beauharnais, the son of the ill-used and unhappy Josephine by her former marriage with a French gentleman of good family. Having a smack of the old blood in him, Eugene's manners were much more refined than those of the new-fangled dignitaries of the Emperor's Court, where (for my knife and fork were regularly laid at the Tuileries) I have seen my poor friend Murat repeatedly mistake a fork for a toothpick, and the gallant Massena devour pease by means of his knife, in a way more innocent than graceful. Talleyrand, Eugene, and I used often to laugh at these eccentricities of our brave friends; who certainly did not shine in the drawing-room, however brilliant they were in the field of battle. The Emperor always asked me to take wine with him, and was full of kindness and attention.

"I like Eugene," he would say, pinching my ear confidentially, as his way was—"I like Eugene to keep company with such young fellows as you; you have manners; you have principles; my rogues from the camp have none. And I like you, Philip my boy," he added, "for being so attentive to my poor wife—the Empress Josephine, I mean." All these honors made my friends at the Marquis's very proud, and my enemies at Court crever with envy. Among these, the atrocious Cambaceres was not the least active and envenomed.

The cause of the many attentions which were paid to me, and which, like a vain coxcomb, I had chosen to attribute to my own personal amiability, soon was apparent. Having formed a good opinion of my gallantry from my conduct in various actions and forlorn hopes during the war, the Emperor was most anxious to attach me to his service. The Grand Cross of St. Louis, the title of Count, the command of a crack cavalry regiment, the l4me Chevaux Marins, were the bribes that were actually offered to me; and must I say it? Blanche, the lovely, the perfidious Blanche, was one of the agents employed to tempt me to commit this act of treason.

"Object to enter a foreign service!" she said, in reply to my refusal. "It is you, Philip, who are in a foreign service. The Irish nation is in exile, and in the territories of its French allies. Irish traitors are not here; they march alone under the accursed flag of the Saxon, whom the great Napoleon would have swept from the face of the earth, but for the fatal valor of Irish mercenaries! Accept this offer, and my heart, my hand, my all are yours. Refuse it, Philip, and we part."

"To wed the abominable Cambaceres!" I cried, stung with rage. "To wear a duchess's coronet, Blanche! Ha, ha! Mushrooms, instead of strawberry-leaves, should decorate the brows of the upstart French nobility. I shall withdraw my parole. I demand to be sent to prison—to be exchanged—to die—anything rather than be a traitor, and the tool of a traitress!" Taking up my hat, I left the room in a fury; and flinging open the door tumbled over Cambaceres, who was listening at the key-hole, and must have overheard every word of our conversation.

We tumbled over each other, as Blanche was shrieking with laughter at our mutual discomfiture. Her scorn only made me more mad; and, having spurs on, I began digging them into Cambaceres' fat sides as we rolled on the carpet, until the Marshal howled with rage and anger.

"This insult must be avenged with blood!" roared the Duke of Illyria.

"I have already drawn it," says I, "with my spurs."

"Malheur et malediction!" roared the Marshal.

"Hadn't you better settle your wig?" says I, offering it to him on the tip of my cane, "and we'll arrange time and place when you have put your jasey in order." I shall never forget the look of revenge which he cast at me, as I was thus turning him into ridicule before his mistress.

"Lady Blanche," I continued bitterly, "as you look to share the Duke's coronet, hadn't you better see to his wig?" and so saying, I cocked my hat, and walked out of the Marquis's place, whistling "Garryowen."

I knew my man would not be long in following me, and waited for him in the Place Vendome, where I luckily met Eugene too, who was looking at the picture-shop in the corner. I explained to him my affair in a twinkling. He at once agreed to go with me to the ground, and commended me, rather than otherwise, for refusing the offer which had been made to me. "I knew it would be so," he said, kindly; "I told my father you wouldn't. A man with the blood of the Fogarties, Phil my boy, doesn't wheel about like those fellows of yesterday." So, when Cambaceres came out, which he did presently, with a more furious air than before, I handed him at once over to Eugene, who begged him to name a friend, and an early hour for the meeting to take place.

"Can you make it before eleven, Phil?" said Beauharnais. "The Emperor reviews the troops in the Bois de Boulogne at that hour, and we might fight there handy before the review."

"Done!" said I. "I want of all things to see the newly-arrived Saxon cavalry manoeuvre:" on which Cambaceres, giving me a look, as much as to say, "See sights! Watch cavalry manoeuvres! Make your soul, and take measure for a coffin, my boy!" walked away, naming our mutual acquaintance, Marshal Ney, to Eugene, as his second in the business.

I had purchased from Murat a very fine Irish horse, Bugaboo, out of Smithereens, by Fadladeen, which ran into the French ranks at Salamanca, with poor Jack Clonakilty, of the 13th, dead, on the top of him. Bugaboo was too much and too ugly an animal for the King of Naples, who, though a showy horseman, was a bad rider across country; and I got the horse for a song. A wickeder and uglier brute never wore pig-skin; and I never put my leg over such a timber-jumper in my life. I rode the horse down to the Bois de Boulogne on the morning that the affair with Cambaceres was to come off, and Lanty held him as I went in, "sure to win," as they say in the ring.

Cambaceres was known to be the best shot in the French army; but I, who am a pretty good hand at a snipe, thought a man was bigger, and that I could wing him if I had a mind. As soon as Ney gave the word, we both fired: I felt a whiz past my left ear, and putting up my hand there, found a large piece of my whiskers gone; whereas at the same moment, and shrieking a horrible malediction, my adversary reeled and fell.

"Mon Dieu, il est mort!" cried Ney.

"Pas de tout," said Beauharnais. "Ecoute; il jure toujours."

And such, indeed, was the fact: the supposed dead man lay on the ground cursing most frightfully. We went up to him: he was blind with the loss of blood, and my ball had carried off the bridge of his nose. He recovered; but he was always called the Prince of Ponterotto in the French army, afterwards. The surgeon in attendance having taken charge of this unfortunate warrior, we rode off to the review where Ney and Eugene were on duty at the head of their respective divisions; and where, by the way, Cambaceres, as the French say, "se faisait desirer."

It was arranged that Cambaceres' division of six battalions and nine-and-twenty squadrons should execute a ricochet movement, supported by artillery in the intervals, and converging by different epaulements on the light infantry, that formed, as usual, the centre of the line. It was by this famous manoeuvre that at Arcola, at Montenotte, at Friedland, and subsequently at Mazagran, Suwaroff, Prince Charles, and General Castanos were defeated with such victorious slaughter: but it is a movement which, I need not tell every military man, requires the greatest delicacy of execution, and which, if it fails, plunges an army into confusion.

"Where is the Duke of Illyria?" Napoleon asked. "At the head of his division, no doubt," said Murat: at which Eugene, giving me an arch look, put his hand to his nose, and caused me almost to fall off my horse with laughter. Napoleon looked sternly at me; but at this moment the troops getting in motion, the celebrated manoeuvre began, and his Majesty's attention was taken off from my impudence.

Milhaud's Dragoons, their bands playing "Vive Henri Quatre," their cuirasses gleaming in the sunshine, moved upon their own centre from the left flank in the most brilliant order, while the Carbineers of Foy, and the Grenadiers of the Guard under Drouet d'Erlon, executed a carambolade on the right, with the precision which became those veteran troops; but the Chasseurs of the young guard, marching by twos instead of threes, bore consequently upon the Bavarian Uhlans (an ill-disciplined and ill-affected body), and then, falling back in disorder, became entangled with the artillery and the left centre of the line, and in one instant thirty thousand men were in inextricable confusion.

"Clubbed, by Jabers!" roared out Lanty Clancy. "I wish we could show 'em the Fighting Onety-oneth, Captain darling."

"Silence, fellow!" I exclaimed. I never saw the face of man express passion so vividly as now did the livid countenance of Napoleon. He tore off General Milhaud's epaulettes, which he flung into Foy's face. He glared about him wildly, like a demon, and shouted hoarsely for the Duke of Illyria. "He is wounded, Sire," said General Foy, wiping a tear from his eye, which was blackened by the force of the blow; "he was wounded an hour since in a duel, Sire, by a young English prisoner, Monsieur de Fogarty."

"Wounded! a marshal of France wounded! Where is the Englishman? Bring him out, and let a file of grenadiers—"

"Sire!" interposed Eugene.

"Let him be shot!" shrieked the Emperor, shaking his spyglass at me with the fury of a fiend.

This was too much. "Here goes!" said I, and rode slap at him.

There was a shriek of terror from the whole of the French army, and I should think at least forty thousand guns were levelled at me in an instant. But as the muskets were not loaded, and the cannon had only wadding in them, these facts, I presume, saved the life of Phil Fogarty from this discharge.

Knowing my horse, I put him at the Emperor's head, and Bugaboo went at it like a shot. He was riding his famous white Arab, and turned quite pale as I came up and went over the horse and the Emperor, scarcely brushing the cockade which he wore.

"Bravo!" said Murat, bursting into enthusiasm at the leap.

"Cut him down!" said Sieyes, once an Abbe, but now a gigantic Cuirassier; and he made a pass at me with his sword. But he little knew an Irishman on an Irish horse. Bugaboo cleared Sieyes, and fetched the monster a slap with his near hind hoof which sent him reeling from his saddle,—and away I went, with an army of a hundred and seventy-three thousand eight hundred men at my heels.

BARBAZURE

BY G. P. R. JEAMES, ESQ., ETC

I.

It was upon one of those balmy evenings of November, which are only known in the valleys of Languedoc and among the mountains of Alsace, that two cavaliers might have been perceived by the naked eye threading one of the rocky and romantic gorges that skirt the mountain-land between the Marne and the Garonne. The rosy tints of the declining luminary were gilding the peaks and crags which lined the path, through which the horsemen wound slowly; and as these eternal battlements with which Nature had hemmed in the ravine which our travellers trod, blushed with the last tints of the fading sunlight, the valley below was gray and darkling, and the hard and devious course was sombre in twilight. A few goats, hardly visible among the peaks, were cropping the scanty herbage here and there. The pipes of shepherds, calling in their flocks as they trooped homewards to their mountain villages, sent up plaintive echoes which moaned through those rocky and lonely steeps; the stars began to glimmer in the purple heavens spread serenely overhead and the faint crescent of the moon, which had peered for some time scarce visible in the azure, gleamed out more brilliantly at every moment, until it blazed as if in triumph at the sun's retreat. 'Tis a fair land that of France, a gentle, a green, and a beautiful; the home of arts and arms, of chivalry and romance, and (however sadly stained by the excesses of modern times) 'twas the unbought grace of nations once, and the seat of ancient renown and disciplined valor.

And of all that fair land of France, whose beauty is so bright and bravery is so famous, there is no spot greener or fairer than that one over which our travellers wended, and which stretches between the good towns of Vendemiaire and Nivose. 'Tis common now to a hundred thousand voyagers: the English tourist, with his chariot and his Harvey's Sauce, and his imperials; the bustling commis-voyageur on the roof of the rumbling diligence; the rapid malle-poste thundering over the chaussee at twelve miles an hour—pass the ground hourly and daily now: 'twas lonely and unfrequented at the end of that seventeenth century with which our story commences.

Along the darkening mountain-paths the two gentlemen (for such their outward bearing proclaimed them) caracoled together. The one, seemingly the younger of the twain, wore a flaunting feather in his barret-cap, and managed a prancing Andalusian palfrey that bounded and curveted gayly. A surcoat of peach-colored samite and a purfled doublet of vair bespoke him noble, as did his brilliant eye, his exquisitely chiselled nose, and his curling chestnut ringlets.

Youth was on his brow; his eyes were dark and dewy, like spring-violets; and spring-roses bloomed upon his cheek—roses, alas! that bloom and die with life's spring! Now bounding over a rock, now playfully whisking off with his riding rod a floweret in his path, Philibert de Coquelicot rode by his darker companion.

His comrade was mounted upon a destriere of the true Norman breed, that had first champed grass on the green pastures of Aquitaine. Thence through Berry, Picardy, and the Limousin, halting at many a city and commune, holding joust and tourney in many a castle and manor of Navarre, Poitou, and St. Germain l'Auxerrois, the warrior and his charger reached the lonely spot where now we find them.

The warrior who bestrode the noble beast was in sooth worthy of the steed which bore him. Both were caparisoned in the fullest trappings of feudal war. The arblast, the mangonel, the demiculverin, and the cuissart of the period, glittered upon the neck and chest of the war-steed; while the rider, with chamfron and catapult, with ban and arriere-ban, morion and tumbrel, battle-axe and rifflard, and the other appurtenances of ancient chivalry, rode stately on his steel-clad charger, himself a tower of steel. This mighty horseman was carried by his steed as lightly as the young springald by his Andalusian hackney.

"'Twas well done of thee, Philibert," said he of the proof-armor, "to ride forth so far to welcome thy cousin and companion in arms."

"Companion in battledore and shuttlecock, Romane de Clos-Vougeot!" replied the younger Cavalier. "When I was yet a page, thou wert a belted knight; and thou wert away to the Crusades ere ever my beard grew."

"I stood by Richard of England at the gates of Ascalon, and drew the spear from sainted King Louis in the tents of Damietta," the individual addressed as Romane replied. "Well-a-day! since thy beard grew, boy, (and marry 'tis yet a thin one,) I have broken a lance with Solyman at Rhodes, and smoked a chibouque with Saladin at Acre. But enough of this. Tell me of home—of our native valley—of my hearth, and my lady-mother, and my good chaplain—tell me of HER, Philibert," said the knight, executing a demivolt, in order to hide his emotion.

Philibert seemed uneasy, and to strive as though he would parry the question. "The castle stands on the rock," he said, "and the swallows still build in the battlements. The good chaplain still chants his vespers at morn, and snuffles his matins at even-song. The lady-mother still distributeth tracts, and knitteth Berlin linsey-woolsey. The tenants pay no better, and the lawyers dun as sorely, kinsman mine," he added with an arch look.

"But Fatima, Fatima, how fares she?" Romane continued. "Since Lammas was a twelvemonth, I hear nought of her; my letters are unanswered. The postman hath traversed our camp every day, and never brought me a billet. How is Fatima, Philibert de Coquelicot?"

"She is—well," Philibert replied; "her sister Anne is the fairest of the twain, though."

"Her sister Anne was a baby when I embarked for Egypt. A plague on sister Anne! Speak of Fatima, Philibert—my blue-eyed Fatima!"

"I say she is—well," answered his comrade gloomily.

"Is she dead? Is she ill? Hath she the measles? Nay, hath she had the small-pox, and lost her beauty? Speak; speak, boy!" cried the knight, wrought to agony.

"Her cheek is as red as her mother's, though the old Countess paints hers every day. Her foot is as light as a sparrow's, and her voice as sweet as a minstrel's dulcimer; but give me nathless the Lady Anne," cried Philibert; "give me the peerless Lady Anne! As soon as ever I have won spurs, I will ride all Christendom through, and proclaim her the Queen of Beauty. Ho, Lady Anne! Lady Anne!" and so saying—but evidently wishing to disguise some emotion, or conceal some tale his friend could ill brook to hear—the reckless damoiseau galloped wildly forward.

But swift as was his courser's pace, that of his companion's enormous charger was swifter. "Boy," said the elder, "thou hast ill tidings. I know it by thy glance. Speak: shall he who hath bearded grim Death in a thousand fields shame to face truth from a friend? Speak, in the name of heaven and good Saint Botibol. Romane de Clos-Vougeot will bear your tidings like a man!"

"Fatima is well," answered Philibert once again; "she hath had no measles: she lives and is still fair."

"Fair, ay, peerless fair; but what more, Philibert? Not false? By Saint Botibol, say not false," groaned the elder warrior.

"A month syne," Philibert replied, "she married the Baron de Barbazure."

With that scream which is so terrible in a strong man in agony, the brave knight Romane de Clos-Vougeot sank back at the words, and fell from his charger to the ground, a lifeless mass of steel.


II.

Like many another fabric of feudal war and splendor, the once vast and magnificent Castle of Barbazure is now a moss-grown ruin. The traveller of the present day, who wanders by the banks of the silvery Loire, and climbs the steep on which the magnificent edifice stood, can scarcely trace, among the shattered masses of ivy-covered masonry which lie among the lonely crags, even the skeleton of the proud and majestic palace stronghold of the Barons of Barbazure.

In the days of our tale its turrets and pinnacles rose as stately, and seemed (to the pride of sinful man!) as strong as the eternal rocks on which they stood. The three mullets on a gules wavy reversed, surmounted by the sinople couchant Or; the well-known cognizance of the house, blazed in gorgeous heraldry on a hundred banners, surmounting as many towers. The long lines of battlemented walls spread down the mountain to the Loire, and were defended by thousands of steel-clad serving-men. Four hundred knights and six times as many archers fought round the banner of Barbazure at Bouvines, Malplaquet, and Azincour. For his services at Fontenoy against the English, the heroic Charles Martel appointed the fourteenth Baron Hereditary Grand Bootjack of the kingdom of France; and for wealth, and for splendor, and for skill and fame in war, Raoul, the twenty-eighth Baron, was in no-wise inferior to his noble ancestors.

That the Baron Raoul levied toll upon the river and mail upon the shore; that he now and then ransomed a burgher, plundered a neighbor, or drew the fangs of a Jew; that he burned an enemy's castle with the wife and children within;—these were points for which the country knew and respected the stout Baron. When he returned from victory, he was sure to endow the Church with a part of his spoil, so that when he went forth to battle he was always accompanied by her blessing. Thus lived the Baron Raoul, the pride of the country in which he dwelt, an ornament to the Court, the Church, and his neighbors.

But in the midst of all his power and splendor there was a domestic grief which deeply afflicted the princely Barbazure. His lovely ladies died one after the other. No sooner was he married than he was a widower; in the course of eighteen years no less than nine bereavements had befallen the chieftain. So true it is, that if fortune is a parasite, grief is a republican, and visits the hall of the great and wealthy as it does the humbler tenements of the poor.

"Leave off deploring thy faithless, gad-about lover," said the Lady of Chacabacque to her daughter, the lovely Fatima, "and think how the noble Barbazure loves thee! Of all the damsels at the ball last night, he had eyes for thee and thy cousin only."

"I am sure my cousin hath no good looks to be proud of!" the admirable Fatima exclaimed, bridling up. "Not that I care for my Lord of Barbazure's looks. MY heart, dearest mother, is with him who is far away!"

"He danced with thee four galliards, nine quadrilles, and twenty-three corantoes, I think, child," the mother said, eluding her daughter's remark.

"Twenty-five," said lovely Fatima, casting her beautiful eyes to the ground. "Heigh-ho! but Romane danced them very well!"

"He had not the court air," the mother suggested.

"I don't wish to deny the beauty of the Lord of Burbazure's dancing, mamma," Fatima replied. "For a short, lusty man, 'tis wondrous how active he is; and in dignity the King's Grace himself could not surpass him."

"You were the noblest couple in the room, love," the lady cried.

"That pea-green doublet, slashed with orange-tawny, those ostrich plumes, blue, red, and yellow, those party-colored hose and pink shoon, became the noble baron wondrous well," Fatima acknowledged. "It must be confessed that, though middle-aged, he hath all the agility of youth. But alas, madam! The noble baron hath had nine wives already."

"And your cousin would give her eyes to become the tenth," the mother replied.

"My cousin give her eyes!" Fatima exclaimed. "It's not much, I'm sure, for she squints abominably." And thus the ladies prattled, as they rode home at night after the great ball at the house of the Baron of Barbazure.

The gentle reader, who has overheard their talk, will understand the doubts which pervaded the mind of the lovely Fatima, and the well-nurtured English maiden will participate in the divided feelings which rent her bosom. 'Tis true, that on his departure for the holy wars, Romane and Fatima were plighted to each other; but the folly of long engagements is proverbial; and though for many months the faithful and affectionate girl had looked in vain for news from him, her admirable parents had long spoken with repugnance of a match which must bring inevitable poverty to both parties. They had suffered, 'tis true, the engagement to subside, hostile as they ever were to it; but when on the death of the ninth lady of Barbazure, the noble baron remarked Fatima at the funeral, and rode home with her after the ceremony, her prudent parents saw how much wiser, better, happier for their child it would be to have for life a partner like the baron, than to wait the doubtful return of the penniless wanderer to whom she was plighted.

Ah! how beautiful and pure a being! how regardless of self! how true to duty! how obedient to parental command, is that earthly angel, a well-bred woman of genteel family! Instead of indulging in splenetic refusals or vain regrets for her absent lover, the exemplary Fatima at once signified to her excellent parents her willingness to obey their orders; though she had sorrows (and she declared them to be tremendous), the admirable being disguised them so well, that none knew they oppressed her. She said she would try to forget former ties, and (so strong in her mind was DUTY above every other feeling!—so strong may it be in every British maiden!) the lovely girl kept her promise. "My former engagements," she said, packing up Romane's letters and presents, (which, as the good knight was mortal poor, were in sooth of no great price)—"my former engagements I look upon as childish follies;—my affections are fixed where my dear parents graft them—on the noble, the princely, the polite Barbazure. 'Tis true he is not comely in feature, but the chaste and well-bred female knows how to despise the fleeting charms of form. 'Tis true he is old; but can woman be better employed than in tending her aged and sickly companion? That he has been married is likewise certain—but ah, my mother! who knows not that he must be a good and tender husband, who, nine times wedded, owns that, he cannot be happy without another partner?"

It was with these admirable sentiments the lovely Fatima proposed obedience to her parents' will, and consented to receive the magnificent marriage-gift presented to her by her gallant bridegroom.


III.

The old Countess of Chacabacque had made a score of vain attempts to see her hapless daughter. Ever, when she came, the porters grinned at her savagely through the grating of the portcullis of the vast embattled gate of the Castle of Barbazure, and rudely bade her begone. "The Lady of Barbazure sees nobody but her confessor, and keeps her chamber," was the invariable reply of the dogged functionaries to the entreaties of the agonized mother. And at length, so furious was he at her perpetual calls at his gate, that the angry Lord of Barbazure himself, who chanced to be at the postern, armed a cross-bow, and let fly an arblast at the crupper of the lady's palfrey, whereon she fled finally, screaming, and in terror. "I will aim at the rider next time!" howled the ferocious baron, "and not at the horse!" And those who knew his savage nature and his unrivalled skill as a bowman, knew that he would neither break his knightly promise nor miss his aim.

Since the fatal day when the Grand Duke of Burgundy gave his famous passage of arms at Nantes, and all the nobles of France were present at the joustings, it was remarked that the Barbazure's heart was changed towards his gentle and virtuous lady.

For the three first days of that famous festival, the redoubted Baron of Barbazure had kept the field against all the knights who entered. His lance bore everything down before it. The most famous champions of Europe, assembled at these joustings, had dropped, one by one, before this tremendous warrior. The prize of the tourney was destined to be his, and he was to be proclaimed bravest of the brave, as his lady was the fairest of the fair.

On the third day, however, as the sun was declining over the Vosges, and the shadows were lengthening over the plain where the warrior had obtained such triumphs;—after having overcome two hundred and thirteen knights of different nations, including the fiery Dunois, the intrepid Walter Manny, the spotless Bayard, and the undaunted Dugueselin, as the conqueror sat still erect on his charger, and the multitudes doubted whether ever another champion could be found to face him, three blasts of a trumpet were heard, faint at first, but at every moment ringing more clearly, until a knight in pink armor rode into the lists with his visor down, and riding a tremendous dun charger, which he managed to the admiration of all present.

The heralds asked him his name and quality.

"Call me," said he, in a hollow voice, "the Jilted Knight." What was it made the Lady of Barbazure tremble at his accents.

The knight refused to tell his name and qualities; but the companion who rode with him, the young and noble Philibert de Coquelicot, who was known and respected universally through the neighborhood, gave a warranty for the birth and noble degree of the Jilted Knight—and Raoul de Barbazure, yelling hoarsely for a two-hundred-and-fourteenth lance, shook the huge weapon in the air as though it were a reed, and prepared to encounter the intruder.

According to the wont of chivalry, and to keep the point of the spear from harm, the top of the unknown knight's lance was shielded with a bung, which the warrior removed; and galloping up to Barbazure's pavilion, over which his shield hung, touched that noble cognizance with the sharpened steel. A thrill of excitement ran through the assembly at this daring challenge to a combat a l'outrance. "Hast thou confessed, Sir Knight?" roared the Barbazure; "take thy ground, and look to thyself; for by heaven thy last hour is come!" "Poor youth, poor youth!" sighed the spectators; "he has called down his own fate." The next minute the signal was given, and as the simoom across the desert, the cataract down the rock, the shell from the howitzer, each warrior rushed from his goal.

"Thou wilt not slay so good a champion?" said the Grand Duke, as at the end of that terrific combat the knight in rose armor stood over his prostrate foe, whose helmet had rolled off when he was at length unhorsed, and whose bloodshot eyes glared unutterable hate and ferocity on his conqueror.

"Take thy life," said he who had styled himself the Jilted Knight; "thou hast taken all that was dear to me." And the sun setting, and no other warrior appearing to do battle against him, he was proclaimed the conqueror, and rode up to the duchess's balcony to receive the gold chain which was the reward of the victor. He raised his visor as the smiling princess guerdoned him—raised it, and gave ONE sad look towards the Lady Fatima at her side!

"Romane de Clos-Vougeot!" shrieked she, and fainted. The Baron of Barbazure heard the name as he writhed on the ground with his wound, and by his slighted honor, by his broken ribs, by his roused fury, he swore revenge; and the Lady Fatima, who had come to the tourney as a queen, returned to her castle as a prisoner.

(As it is impossible to give the whole of this remarkable novel, let it suffice to say briefly here, that in about a volume and a half, in which the descriptions of scenery, the account of the agonies of the baroness, kept on bread and water in her dungeon, and the general tone of morality, are all excellently worked out, the Baron de Barbazure resolves upon putting his wife to death by the hands of the public executioner.)

Two minutes before the clock struck noon, the savage baron was on the platform to inspect the preparation for the frightful ceremony of mid-day.

The block was laid forth—the hideous minister of vengeance, masked and in black, with the flaming glaive in his hand, was ready. The baron tried the edge of the blade with his finger, and asked the dreadful swordsman if his hand was sure? A nod was the reply of the man of blood. The weeping garrison and domestics shuddered and shrank from him. There was not one there but loved and pitied the gentle lady.

Pale, pale as a stone, she was brought from her dungeon. To all her lord's savage interrogatories, her reply had been, "I am innocent." To his threats of death, her answer was, "You are my lord; my life is in your hands, to take or to give." How few are the wives, in our day, who show such angelic meekness! It touched all hearts around her, save that of the implacable Barbazure! Even the Lady Blanche, (Fatima's cousin), whom he had promised to marry upon his faithless wife's demise, besought for her kinswoman's life, and a divorce; but Barbazure had vowed her death.

"Is there no pity, sir?" asked the chaplain who had attended her.

"No pity?" echoed the weeping serving-maid.

"Did I not aye say I would die for my lord?" said the gentle lady, and placed herself at the block.

Sir Raoul de Barbazure seized up the long ringlets of her raven hair. "Now!" shouted he to the executioner, with a stamp of his foot—"Now strike!"

The man (who knew his trade) advanced at once, and poised himself to deliver his blow: and making his flashing sword sing in the air, with one irresistible, rapid stroke, it sheared clean off the head of the furious, the bloodthirsty, the implacable Baron de Barbazure!

Thus he fell a victim to his own jealousy: and the agitation of the Lady Fatima may be imagined, when the executioner, flinging off his mask, knelt gracefully at her feet, and revealed to her the well-known features of Romane de Clos-Vougeot.

LORDS AND LIVERIES

BY THE AUTHORESS OF "DUKES AND DEJEUNERS," "HEARTS AND DIAMONDS," "MARCHIONESSES AND MILLINERS," ETC. ETC

I.

"Corbleu! What a lovely creature that was in the Fitzbattleaxe box to-night," said one of a group of young dandies who were leaning over the velvet-cushioned balconies of the "Coventry Club," smoking their full-flavored Cubas (from Hudson's) after the opera.

Everybody stared at such an exclamation of enthusiasm from the lips of the young Earl of Bagnigge, who was never heard to admire anything except a coulis de dindonneau a la St. Menehould, or a supreme de cochon en torticolis a la Piffarde; such as Champollion, the chef of the "Traveller's," only knows how to dress; or the bouquet of a flask of Medoc, of Carbonell's best quality; or a goutte of Marasquin, from the cellars of Briggs and Hobson.

Alured de Pentonville, eighteenth Earl of Bagnigge, Viscount Paon of Islington, Baron Pancras, Kingscross, and a Baronet, was, like too many of our young men of ton, utterly blase, although only in his twenty-fourth year. Blest, luckily, with a mother of excellent principles (who had imbued his young mind with that Morality which is so superior to all the vain pomps of the world!) it had not been always the young earl's lot to wear the coronet for which he now in sooth cared so little. His father, a captain of Britain's navy, struck down by the side of the gallant Collingwood in the Bay of Fundy, left little but his sword and spotless name to his young, lovely, and inconsolable widow, who passed the first years of her mourning in educating her child in an elegant though small cottage in one of the romantic marine villages of beautiful Devonshire. Her child! What a gush of consolation filled the widow's heart as she pressed him to it! How faithfully did she instil into his young bosom those principles which had been the pole-star of the existence of his gallant father!

In this secluded retreat, rank and wealth almost boundless found the widow and her boy. The seventeenth Earl—gallant and ardent, and in the prime of youth—went forth one day from the Eternal City to a steeple-chase in the Campagna. A mutilated corpse was brought back to his hotel in the Piazza di Spagna. Death, alas! is no respecter of the Nobility. That shattered form was all that remained of the fiery, the haughty, the wild, but the generous Altamont de Pentonville! Such, such is fate!

The admirable Emily de Pentonville trembled with all a mother's solicitude at the distinctions and honors which thus suddenly descended on her boy. She engaged an excellent clergyman of the Church of England to superintend his studies; to accompany him on foreign travel when the proper season arrived; to ward from him those dangers which dissipation always throws in the way of the noble, the idle, and the wealthy. But the Reverend Cyril Delaval died of the measles at Naples, and henceforth the young Earl of Bagnigge was without a guardian.

What was the consequence? That, at three-and-twenty, he was a cynic and an epicure. He had drained the cup of pleasure till it had palled in his unnerved hand. He had looked at the Pyramids without awe, at the Alps without reverence. He was unmoved by the sandy solitudes of the Desert as by the placid depths of Mediterranean's sea of blue. Bitter, bitter tears did Emily de Pentonville weep, when, on

Alured's return from the Continent, she beheld the awful change that dissipation had wrought in her beautiful, her blue-eyed, her perverted, her still beloved boy!

"Corpo di Bacco," he said, pitching the end of his cigar on to the red nose of the Countess of Delawaddymore's coachman—who, having deposited her fat ladyship at No. 236 Piccadilly, was driving the carriage to the stables, before commencing his evening at the "Fortune of War" public-house—"what a lovely creature that was! What eyes! what hair! Who knows her? Do you, mon cher prince?"

"E bellissima, certamente," said the Duca de Montepulciano, and stroked down his jetty moustache.

"Ein gar schones Madchen," said the Hereditary Grand Duke of Eulenschreckenstein, and turned up his carroty one.

"Elle n'est pas mal, ma foi!" said the Prince de Borodino, with a scowl on his darkling brows. "Mon Dieu, que ces cigarres sont mauvais!" he added as he too cast away his Cuba.

"Try one of my Pickwicks," said Franklin Fox, with a sneer, offering his gold etui to the young Frenchman; "they are some of Pontet's best, Prince. What, do you bear malice? Come, let us be friends," said the gay and careless young patrician; but a scowl on the part of the Frenchman was the only reply.

"Want to know who she is? Borodino knows who she is, Bagnigge," the wag went on.

Everybody crowded around Monsieur de Borodino thus apostrophized. The Marquis of Alicompayne, young De Boots of the Lifeguards, Tom Protocol of the Foreign Office; the gay young Peers, Farintosh, Poldoody, and the rest; and Bagnigge, for a wonder, not less eager than any one present.

"No, he will tell you nothing about her. Don't you see he has gone off in a fury!" Franklin Fox continued. "He has his reasons, ce cher prince: he will tell you nothing; but I will. You know that I am au mieux with the dear old duchess."

"They say Frank and she are engaged after the duke's death," cried Poldoody.

"I always thought Fwank was the duke's illicit gweatgwandson," drawled out De Boots.

"I heard that he doctored her Blenheim, and used to bring her wigs from Paris," cried that malicious Tom Protocol, whose mots are known in every diplomatic salon from Petersburg to Palermo.

"Burn her wigs and hang her poodle!" said Bagnigge. "Tell me about this girl, Franklin Fox."

"In the first place, she has five hundred thousand acres, in a ring fence in Norfolk; a county in Scotland, a castle in Wales, a villa at Richmond, a corner house in Belgrave Square, and eighty thousand a year in the three-per-cents."

"Apres?" said Bagnigge, still yawning.

"Secondly, Borodino lui fait la cour. They are cousins, her mother was an Armagnac of the emigration; the old Marshal, his father, married another sister. I believe he was footman in the family, before Napoleon princified him."

"No, no, he was second coachman," Tom Protocol good-naturedly interposed—"a cavalry officer, Frank, not an infantry man."

"'Faith you should have seen his fury (the young one's, I mean) when he found me in the duchess's room this evening, tete-a-tete with the heiress, who deigned to receive a bouquet from this hand."

"It cost me three guineas," poor Frank said, with a shrug and a sigh, "and that Covent Garden scoundrel gives no credit: but she took the flowers;—eh, Bagnigge?"

"And flung them to Alboni," the Peer replied, with a haughty sneer. And poor little Franklin Fox was compelled to own that she had.

The maitre d'hotel here announced that supper was served. It was remarked that even the coulis de dindonneau made no impression on Bagnigge that night.


II.

The sensation produced by the debut of Amethyst Pimlico at the court of the sovereign, and in the salons of the beau-monde, was such as has seldom been created by the appearance of any other beauty. The men were raving with love, and the women with jealousy. Her eyes, her beauty, her wit, her grace, her ton, caused a perfect fureur of admiration or envy.

Introduced by the Duchess of Fitzbattleaxe, along with her Grace's daughters, the Ladies Gwendoline and Gwinever Portcullis, the heiress's regal beauty quite flung her cousins' simple charms into the shade, and blazed with a splendor which caused all "minor lights" to twinkle faintly. Before a day the beau-monde, before a week even the vulgarians of the rest of the town, rang with the fame of her charms; and while the dandies and the beauties were raving about her, or tearing her to pieces in May Fair, even Mrs. Dobbs (who had been to the pit of the "Hoperer" in a green turban and a crumpled yellow satin) talked about the great HAIRESS to her D. in Bloomsbury Square.

Crowds went to Squab and Lynch's, in Long Acre, to examine the carriages building for her, so faultless, so splendid, so quiet, so odiously unostentatious and provokingly simple! Besides the ancestral services of argenterie and vaisselle plate, contained in a hundred and seventy-six plate-chests at Messrs. Childs', Rumble and Briggs prepared a gold service, and Garraway, of the Haymarket, a service of the Benvenuto Cellini pattern, which were the admiration of all London. Before a month it is a fact that the wretched haberdashers in the city exhibited the blue stocks, called "Heiress-killers, very chaste, two-and-six:" long before that, the monde had rushed to Madame Crinoline's, or sent couriers to Madame Marabou, at Paris, so as to have copies of her dresses; but, as the Mantuan bard observes, "Non cuivis contigit,"—every foot cannot accommodate itself to the chaussure of Cinderella.

With all this splendor, this worship, this beauty; with these cheers following her, and these crowds at her feet, was Amethyst happy? Ah, no! It is not under the necklace the most brilliant that Briggs and

Rumble can supply, it is not in Lynch's best cushioned chariot that the heart is most at ease. "Que je me ruinerai," says Fronsac in a letter to Bossuet, "si je savais ou acheter le bonheur!"

With all her riches, with all her splendor, Amethyst was wretched—wretched, because lonely; wretched, because her loving heart had nothing to cling to. Her splendid mansion was a convent; no male person even entered it, except Franklin Fox, (who counted for nothing,) and the duchess's family, her kinsman old Lord Humpington, his friend old Sir John Fogey, and her cousin, the odious, odious Borodino.

The Prince de Borodino declared openly that Amethyst was engaged to him. Crible de dettes, it is no wonder that he should choose such an opportunity to refaire sa fortune. He gave out that he would kill any man who should cast an eye on the heiress, and the monster kept his word. Major Grigg, of the Lifeguards, had already fallen by his hand at Ostend. The O'Toole, who had met her on the Rhine, had received a ball in his shoulder at Coblentz, and did not care to resume so dangerous a courtship. Borodino could snuff a bougie at a hundred and fifty yards. He could beat Bertrand or Alexander Dumas himself with the small-sword: he was the dragon that watched this pomme d'or, and very few persons were now inclined to face a champion si redoutable.

Over a salmi d'escargot at the "Coventry," the dandies whom we introduced in our last volume were assembled, there talking of the heiress; and her story was told by Franklin Fox to Lord Bagnigge, who, for a wonder, was interested in the tale. Borodino's pretensions were discussed, and the way in which the fair Amethyst was confined. Fitzbattleaxe House, in Belgrave Square, is—as everybody knows—the next mansion to that occupied by Amethyst. A communication was made between the two houses. She never went out except accompanied by the duchess's guard, which it was impossible to overcome.

"Impossible! Nothing's impossible," said Lord Bagnigge.

"I bet you what you like you don't get in," said the young Marquis of Martingale.

"I bet you a thousand ponies I stop a week in the heiress's house before the season's over," Lord Bagnigge replied with a yawn; and the bet was registered with shouts of applause.

But it seemed as if the Fates had determined against Lord Bagnigge, for the very next day, riding in the Park, his horse fell with him; he was carried home to his house with a fractured limb and a dislocated shoulder; and the doctor's bulletins pronounced him to be in the most dangerous state.

Martingale was a married man, and there was no danger of HIS riding by the Fitzbattleaxe carriage. A fortnight after the above events, his lordship was prancing by her Grace's great family coach, and chattering with Lady Gwinever about the strange wager.

"Do you know what a pony is, Lady Gwinever?" he asked. Her ladyship said yes: she had a cream-colored one at Castle Barbican; and stared when Lord Martingale announced that he should soon have a thousand ponies, worth five-and-twenty pounds each, which were all now kept at Coutts's. Then he explained the circumstances of the bet with Bagnigge. Parliament was to adjourn in ten days; the season would be over! Bagnigge was lying ill chez lui; and the five-and-twenty thousand were irrecoverably his. And he vowed he would buy Lord Binnacle's yacht—crew, captain, guns and all.

On returning home that night from Lady Polkimore's, Martingale found among the many billets upon the gold plateau in his antichambre, the following brief one, which made him start—

"DEAR MARTINGALE.—Don't be too sure of Binnacle's yacht. There are still ten days before the season is over; and my ponies may lie at Coutts's for some time to come.

"Yours,

"BAGNIGGE.

"P. S.—I write with my left hand; for my right is still splintered up from that confounded fall."


III.

The tall footman, number four, who had come in the place of John, cashiered, (for want of proper mollets, and because his hair did not take powder well,) had given great satisfaction to the under-butler, who reported well of him to his chief, who had mentioned his name with praise to the house-steward. He was so good-looking and well-spoken a young man, that the ladies in the housekeeper's room deigned to notice him more than once; nor was his popularity diminished on account of a quarrel in which he engaged with Monsieur Anatole, the enormous Walloon chasseur, who was one day found embracing Miss Flouncy, who waited on Amethyst's own maid. The very instant Miss Flouncy saw Mr. Jeames entering the Servants' Hall, where Monsieur Anatole was engaged in "aggravating" her, Miss Flouncy screamed: at the next moment the Belgian giant lay sprawling upon the carpet; and Jeames, standing over him, assumed so terrible a look, that the chasseur declined any further combat. The victory was made known to the house-steward himself, who, being a little partial to Miss Flouncy herself, complimented Jeames on his valor, and poured out a glass of Madeira in his own room.

Who was Jeames? He had come recommended by the Bagnigge people. He had lived, he said, in that family two years. "But where there was no ladies," he said, "a gentleman's hand was spiled for service;" and Jeames's was a very delicate hand; Miss Flouncy admired it very much, and of course he did not defile it by menial service: he had in a young man who called him sir, and did all the coarse work; and Jeames read the morning paper to the ladies; not spellingly and with hesitation, as many gentlemen do, but easily and elegantly, speaking off the longest words without a moment's difficulty. He could speak French, too, Miss Flouncy found, who was studying it under Mademoiselle Grande fille-de-chambre de confiance; for when she said to him, "Polly voo Fransy, Munseer Jeames?" he replied readily, "We, Mademaselle, j'ay passay boco de tong a Parry. Commong voo potty voo?" How Miss Flouncy admired him as he stood before her, the day after he had saved Miss Amethyst when the horses had run away with her in the Park!

Poor Flouncy, poor Flouncy! Jeames had been but a week in Amethyst's service, and already the gentle heart of the washing-girl was irrecoverably gone! Poor Flouncy! Poor Flouncy! he thought not of thee.

It happened thus. Miss Amethyst being engaged to drive with her cousin the prince in his phaeton, her own carriage was sent into the Park simply with her companion, who had charge of her little Fido, the dearest little spaniel in the world. Jeames and Frederick were behind the carriage with their long sticks and neat dark liveries; the horses were worth a thousand guineas each, the coachman a late lieutenant-colonel of cavalry: the whole ring could not boast a more elegant turn-out.

The prince drove his curricle, and had charge of his belle cousine. It may have been the red fezzes in the carriage of the Turkish ambassador which frightened the prince's grays, or Mrs. Champignon's new yellow liveries, which were flaunting in the Park, or hideous Lady Gorgon's preternatural ugliness, who passed in a low pony-carriage at the time, or the prince's own want of skill, finally; but certain it is that the horses took fright, dashed wildly along the mile, scattered equipages, pietons, dandies' cabs, and snobs' pheaytons. Amethyst was screaming; and the prince, deadly pale, had lost all presence of mind, as the curricle came rushing by the spot where Miss Amethyst's carriage stood.

"I'm blest," Frederick exclaimed to his companion, "if it ain't the prince a-drivin our missis! They'll be in the Serpingtine, or dashed to pieces, if they don't mind." And the runaway steeds at this instant came upon them as a whirlwind.

But if those steeds ran at a whirlwind pace, Jeames was swifter. To jump from behind, to bound after the rocking, reeling curricle, to jump into it, aided by the long stick which he carried and used as a leaping-pole, and to seize the reins out of the hands of the miserable Borodino, who shrieked piteously as the dauntless valet leapt on his toes and into his seat, was the work of an instant. In a few minutes the mad, swaying rush of the horses was reduced to a swift but steady gallop; presently into a canter, then a trot; until finally they pulled up smoking and trembling, but quite quiet, by the side of Amethyst's carriage, which came up at a rapid pace.

"Give me the reins, malappris! tu m'ecrases le corps, manant!" yelled the frantic nobleman, writhing underneath the intrepid charioteer.

"Tant pis pour toi, nigaud," was the reply. The lovely Amethyst of course had fainted; but she recovered as she was placed in her carriage, and rewarded her preserver with a celestial smile.

The rage, the fury, the maledictions of Borodino, as he saw the latter—a liveried menial—stoop gracefully forward and kiss Amethyst's hand, may be imagined rather than described. But Jeames heeded not his curses. Having placed his adored mistress in the carriage, he calmly resumed his station behind. Passion or danger seemed to have no impression upon that pale marble face.

Borodino went home furious; nor was his rage diminished, when, on coming to dinner that day, a recherche banquet served in the Frangipane best style, and requesting a supply of a puree a la bisque aux ecrevisses, the clumsy attendant who served him let fall the assiette of vermeille cisele, with its scalding contents, over the prince's chin, his Mechlin jabot, and the grand cordon of the Legion of honor which he wore.

"Infame," howled Borodino, "tu l'as fait expres!"

"Oui, je l'ai fait expres," said the man, with the most perfect Parisian accent. It was Jeames.

Such insolence of course could not be passed unnoticed even after the morning's service, and he was chassed on the spot. He had been but a week in the house.

The next month the newspapers contained a paragraph which may possibly elucidate the above mystery, and to the following effect:—

"Singular Wager.—One night, at the end of last season, the young and eccentric Earl of B-gn-gge laid a wager of twenty-five thousand pounds with a broken sporting patrician, the dashing Marquis of M-rt-ng-le, that he would pass a week under the roof of a celebrated and lovely young heiress, who lives not a hundred miles from B-lgr-ve Squ-re. The bet having been made, the earl pretended an illness, and having taken lessons from one of his lordship's own footmen (Mr. James Plush, whose name he also borrowed) in 'the MYSTERIES of the PROFESSION,' actually succeeded in making an entry into Miss P-ml-co's mansion, where he stopped one week exactly; having time to win his bet, and to save the life of the lady, whom we hear he is about to lead to the altar. He disarmed the Prince of Borodino in a duel fought on Calais sands—and, it is said, appeared at the C— club wearing his PLUSH COSTUME under a cloak, and displaying it as a proof that he had won his wager."

Such, indeed, were the circumstances. The young couple have not more than nine hundred thousand a year, but they live cheerfully, and manage to do good; and Emily de Pentonville, who adores her daughter-in-law and her little grandchildren, is blest in seeing her darling son enfin un homme range.

CRINOLINE

BY JE-MES PL-SH, ESQ

I.

I'm not at libbaty to divulj the reel names of the 2 Eroes of the igstrawny Tail which I am abowt to relait to those unlightnd paytrons of letarature and true connyshures of merrit—the great Brittish public—But I pledj my varacity that this singlar story of rewmantic love, absobbing pashn, and likewise of GENTEEL LIFE, is, in the main fax, TREW. The suckmstanzas I elude to, ocurd in the rain of our presnt Gratious Madjisty and her beluvd and roil Concert Prince Halbert.

Welthen. Some time in the seazen of 18—(mor I dar not rewheel) there arrived in this metropulus, per seknd class of the London and Dover Railway, an ellygant young foring gentleman, whom I shall danomminate Munseer Jools De Chacabac.

Having read through "The Vicker of Wackfield" in the same oridganal English tung in which this very harticle I write is wrote too, and halways been remarkyble, both at collidge and in the estamminy, for his aytred and orror of perfidgus Halbion, Munseer Jools was considered by the prapriretors of the newspaper in which he wrote, at Parris, the very man to come to this country, igsamin its manners and customs, cast an i upon the politticle and finalshle stat of the Hempire, and igspose the mackynations of the infyamous Palmerston, and the ebomminable Sir Pill—both enemies of France; as is every other Britten of that great, gloarus, libberal, and peasable country. In one word, Jools de Chacabac was a penny-a-liner.

"I will go see with my own I's," he said, "that infimus hiland of which the innabitants are shopkeepers, gorged with roast beef and treason. I will go and see the murderers of the Hirish, the pisoners of the Chynese, the villians who put the Hemperor to death in Saintyleany, the artful dodges who wish to smother Europe with their cotton, and can't sleep or rest heasy for henvy and hatred of the great inwinsable French nation. I will igsammin, face to face, these hotty insularies; I will pennytrate into the secrets of their Jessywhittickle cabinet, and beard Palmerston in his denn." When he jumpt on shor at

Foaxton (after having been tremenguously sick in the fourcabbing), he exclaimed, "Enfin je te tiens, Ile maudite! je te crache a la figure, vieille Angleterre! Je te foule a mes pieds an nom du monde outrage," and so proseaded to inwade the metropulus.

As he wisht to micks with the very chicest sosiaty, and git the best of infamation about this country, Munseer Jools of coarse went and lodgd in Lester Square—Lester Squarr, as he calls it—which, as he was infommed in the printed suckular presented to him by a very greasy but polite comishner at the Custumus Stares, was in the scenter of the town, contiggus to the Ouses of Parlyment, the prinsple theayters, the parx, St. Jams Pallice, and the Corts of Lor. "I can surwhey them all at one cut of the eye," Jools thought; "the Sovring, the infamus Ministers plotting the destruction of my immortial country; the business and pleasure of these pusprond Londoners and aristoxy; I can look round and see all." So he took a three-pair back in a French hotel, the "Hotel de l'Ail," kep by Monsieur Gigotot, Cranbourne Street, Lester Squarr, London.

In this otell there's a billiard-room on the first floor, and a tabble-doat at eighteenpence peredd at 5 o'clock; and the landlord, who kem into Jools's room smoaking a segar, told the young gent that the house was friquented by all the Brittish nobillaty, who reglar took their dinners there. "They can't ebide their own quiseen," he said. "You'll see what a dinner we'll serve you to-day." Jools wrote off to his paper—

"The members of the haughty and luxurious English aristocracy, like all the rest of the world, are obliged to fly to France for the indulgence of their luxuries. The nobles of England, quitting their homes, their wives, miladies and mistriss, so fair but so cold, dine universally at the tavern. That from which I write is frequented by Peel and Palmerston. I fremis to think that I may meet them at the board to-day."

Singlar to say, Peel and Palmerston didn't dine at the "Hotel de l'Ail" on that evening. "It's quite igstronnary they don't come," said Munseer de l'Ail.

"Peraps they're ingaged at some boxing-match or some combaw de cock," Munseer Jools sejested; and the landlord egreed that was very likely.

Instedd of English there was, however, plenty of foring sociaty, of every nation under the sun. Most of the noblemen were great hamatures of hale and porter. The tablecloth was marked over with brown suckles, made by the pewter-pots on that and the previous days.

"It is the usage here," wrote Jools to his newspaper, "among the Anglais of the fashonne to absorb immense quantities of ale and porter during their meals. These stupefying, but cheap, and not unpalatable liquors are served in shining pewter vessels. A mug of foaming hafanaf (so a certain sort of beer is called) was placed by the side of most of the convives. I was disappointed of seeing Sir Peel: he was engaged to a combat of cocks which occurs at Windsor."

Not one word of English was spoke during this dinner, excep when the gentlemen said "Garsong de l'afanaf," but Jool was very much pleased to meet the eleet of the foringers in town, and ask their opinion about the reel state of thinx. Was it likely that the bishops were to be turned out of the Chambre des Communes? Was it true that Lor Palmerston had boxed with Lor Broghamm in the House of Lords, until they were sepparayted by the Lor Maire? Who was the Lor Maire? Wasn't he Premier Minister? and wasn't the Archeveque de Cantorbery a Quaker? He got answers to these questions from the various gents round about during the dinner—which, he remarked, was very much like a French dinner, only dirtier. And he wrote off all the infamation he got to his newspaper.

"The Lord Maire, Lord Lansdowne, is Premier Ministre. His Grace has his dwelling in the City. The Archbishop of Cantabery is not turned Quaker, as some people stated. Quakers may not marry, nor sit in the Chamber of Peers. The minor bishops have seats in the House of Commons, where they are attacked by the bitter pleasantries of Lord Brougham. A boxer is in the house; he taught Palmerston the science of the pugilate, who conferred upon him the seat," &c. &c.

His writing hover, Jools came down and ad a gaym at pool with two Poles, a Bulgian, and 2 of his own countrymen. This being done amidst more hafanaf, without which nothink is done in England, and as there was no French play that night, he & the two French gents walked round and round Lester Squarr smoking segaws in the faces of other French gents who were smoaking 2. And they talked about the granjer of France and the perfidgusness of England, and looked at the aluminated pictur of Madame Wharton as Haryadney till bedtime. But befor he slep, he finished his letter you may be sure, and called it his "Fust Imprestiuns of Anglyterre."

"Mind and wake me early," he said to Boots, the ony Brittish subject in the "Hotel de l'Ail," and who therefore didn't understand him. "I wish to be at Smithfield at 6 hours to see THE MEN SELL THEIR WIVES." And the young roag fell asleep, thinking what sort of a one he'd buy.

This was the way Jools passed his days, and got infamation about Hengland and the Henglish—walking round and round Lester Squarr all day, and every day with the same company, occasionally dewussified by an Oprer Chorus-singer or a Jew or two, and every afternoon in the Quadrant admiring the genteal sosiaty there. Munseer Jools was not over well funnisht with pocket-money, and so his pleasure was of the gratis sort cheafly.

Well, one day as he and a friend was taking their turn among the aristoxy under the Quadrant—they were struck all of a heap by seeing—But, stop! who WAS Jools's friend? Here you have pictures of both—but the Istory of Jools's friend must be kep for another innings.

II.

Not fur from that knowble and cheerflie Squear which Munseer Jools de Chacabac had selacted for his eboad in London—not fur, I say, from Lester Squarr, is a rainje of bildings called Pipping's Buildings, leading to Blue Lion Court, leading to St. Martin's Lane. You know Pipping's Buildings by its greatest ornament, an am and beefouce (where Jools has often stood admiring the degstaraty of the carver a-cuttin the varous jints), and by the little fishmungur's, where you remark the mouldy lobsters, the fly-blown picklesammon, the playbills, and the gingybear bottles in the window—above all, by the "Constantinople" Divan, kep by the Misses Mordeky, and well known to every lover of "a prime sigaw and an exlent cup of reel Moky Coffy for 6d."

The Constantinople Divann is greatly used by the foring gents of Lester Squar. I never ad the good fortn to pass down Pipping's Buildings without seeing a haf a duzen of 'em on the threshole of the extablishment, giving the street an opperturnity of testing the odar of the Misses Mordeky's prime Avannas. Two or three mor may be visable inside, settn on the counter or the chestis, indulging in their fav'rit whead, the rich and spisy Pickwhick, the ripe Manilly, or the flagrant and arheumatic Qby.

"These Divanns are, as is very well known, the knightly resott of the young Henglish nobillaty. It is ear a young Pier, after an arjus day at the House of Commons, solazes himself with a glas of gin-and-water (the national beveridge), with cheerful conversation on the ewents of the day, or with an armless gaym of baggytell in the back-parlor."

So wrote at least our friend Jools to his newspaper, the Horriflam; and of this back-parlor and baggytell-bord, of this counter, of this "Constantinople" Divan, he became almost as reglar a frequenter as the plaster of Parish Turk who sits smoking a hookey between the two blue coffee-cups in the winder.

I have oftin, smokin my own shroot in silents in a corner of the Diwann, listened to Jools and his friends inwaying aginst Hingland, and boastin of their own immortial country. How they did go on about Wellintun, and what an arty contamp they ad for him!—how they used to prove that France was the Light, the Scenter-pint, the Igsample and hadmiration of the whole world! And though I scarcely take a French paper now-a-days (I lived in early days as groom in a French famly three years, and therefore knows the languidg), though, I say, you can't take up Jools's paper, the Orriflam, without readin that a minister has committed bribery and perjury, or that a littery man has committed perjury and murder, or that a Duke has stabbed his wife in fifty places, or some story equally horrible; yet for all that it's admiral to see how the French gents will swagger—how they will be the scenters of civilization—how they will be the Igsamples of Europ, and nothink shall prevent 'em—knowing they will have it, I say I listen, smokin my pip in silence. But to our tail.

Reglar every evening there came to the "Constantanople" a young gent etired in the igth of fashn; and indead presenting by the cleanlyness of his appearants and linning (which was generally a pink or blew shurt, with a cricketer or a dansuse pattern) rather a contrast to the dinjy and whistkcard sosaity of the Diwann. As for wiskars, this young mann had none beyond a little yellow tought to his chin, which you woodn notas, only he was always pulling at it. His statue was diminnative, but his coschume supubb, for he had the tippiest Jane boots, the ivoryheadest canes, the most gawjus scarlick Jonville ties, and the most Scotch-plaidest trowseys, of any customer of that establishment. He was univusaly called Milord.

"Que est ce jeune seigneur? Who is this young hurl who comes knightly to the 'Constantanople,' who is so proddigl of his gold (for indeed the young gent would frequinly propoase gininwater to the company), and who drinks so much gin?" asked Munseer Chacabac of a friend from the "Hotel de l'Ail."

"His name is Lord Yardham," answered that friend. "He never comes here but at night—and why?"

"Y?" igsclaimed Jools, istonisht.

"Why? because he is engaygd all day—and do you know where he is engaygd all day?"

"Where?" asked Jools.

"At the Foring Office—NOW do you begin to understand?"—Jools trembled.

He speaks of his uncle, the head of that office.—"Who IS the head of that offis?—Palmerston."

"The nephew of Palmerston!" said Jools, almost in a fit.

"Lor Yardham pretends not to speak French," the other went on. "He pretends he can only say wee and commong porty voo. Shallow humbug!—I have marked him during our conversations.—When we have spoken of the glory of France among the nations, I have seen his eye kindle, and his perfidious lip curl with rage. When they have discussed before him, the Imprudents! the affairs of Europe, and Raggybritchovich has shown us the next Circassian Campaign, or Sapousne has laid hare the plan of the Calabrian patriots for the next insurrection, I have marked this stranger—this Lor Yardham. He smokes, 'tis to conceal his countenance; he drinks gin, 'tis to hide his face in the goblet. And be sure, he carries every word of our conversation to the perfidious Palmerston, his uncle."

"I will beard him in his den," thought Jools. "I will meet him corps-a-corps—the tyrant of Europe shall suffer through his nephew, and I will shoot him as dead as Dujarrier."

When Lor Yardham came to the "Constantanople" that night, Jools i'd him savidgely from edd to foot, while Lord Yardham replied the same. It wasn't much for either to do—neyther being more than 4 foot ten hi—Jools was a grannydear in his company of the Nashnal Gard, and was as brayv as a lion.

"Ah, l'Angleterre, l'Angleterre, tu nous dois une revanche," said Jools, crossing his arms and grinding his teeth at Lord Yardham.

"Wee," said Lord Yardham; "wee."

"Delenda est Carthago!" howled out Jools.

"Oh, wee," said the Erl of Yardham, and at the same moment his glas of ginawater coming in, he took a drink, saying, "A voternsanty, Munseer:" and then he offered it like a man of fashn to Jools.

A light broak on Jools's mind as he igsepted the refreshmint. "Sapoase," he said, "instedd of slaughtering this nephew of the infamous Palmerston, I extract his secrets from him; suppose I pump him—suppose I unveil his schemes and send them to my paper? La France may hear the name of Jools de Chacabac, and the star of honor may glitter on my bosom."

So axepting Lord Yardham's cortasy, he returned it by ordering another glass of gin at his own expence, and they both drank it on the counter, where Jools talked of the affaers of Europ all night. To everything he said, the Earl of Yardham answered, "Wee, wee;" except at the end of the evening, when he squeeged his & and said, "Bong swore."

"There's nothing like goin amongst 'em to equire the reel pronounciation," his lordship said, as he let himself into his lodgings with his latch-key. "That was a very eloquent young gent at the 'Constantinople,' and I'll patronize him."

"Ah, perfide, je te demasquerai!" Jools remarked to himself as he went to bed in his "Hotel de l'Ail." And they met the next night, and from that heavning the young men were continyually together.

Well, one day, as they were walking in the Quadrant, Jools talking, and Lord Yardham saying, "Wee, wee," they were struck all of a heap by seeing—

But my paper is igshosted, and I must dixcribe what they sor in the nex number.

THE CASTLE OF THE ISLAND OF FOGO

The travler who pesews his dalitefle coarse through the fair rellum of Franse (as a great romantic landskippist and neamsack of mind would say) never chaumed his i's within a site more lovely, or vu'd a pallis more magniffiznt than that which was the buthplace of the Eroing of this Trew Tale. Phansy a country through whose werdant planes the selvery Garonne wines, like—like a benevvolent sarpent. In its plasid busum antient cassles, picturask willidges, and waving woods are reflected. Purple hills, crownd with inteak ruings; rivvilets babbling through gentle greenwoods; wight farm ouses, hevvy with hoverhanging vines, and from which the appy and peaseful okupier can cast his glans over goolden waving cornfealds, and M. Herald meddows in which the lazy cattle are graysinn; while the sheppard, tending his snoughy flox, wiles away the leisure mominx on his loot—these hoffer but a phaint pictur of the rurial felissaty in the midst of widge Crinoline and Hesteria de Viddlers were bawn.

Their Par, the Marcus de Viddlers, Shavilear of the Legend of Honor and of the Lion of Bulgum, the Golden Flease, Grand Cross of the Eflant and Castle, and of the Catinbagpipes of Hostria, Grand Chamberleng of the Crownd, and Major-Genaril of Hoss-Mareens, &c. &c. &c.—is the twenty-foth or fith Marquis that has bawn the Tittle; is disended lenyally from King Pipping, and has almost as antient a paddygree as any which the Ollywell Street frends of the Member of Buckinumsheer can supply.

His Marchyniss, the lovely & ecomplisht Emily de St. Cornichon, quitted this mortial spear very soon after she had presented her lord with the two little dawling Cherrybins above dixcribed, in whomb, after the loss of that angle his wife, the disconslit widderer found his only jy on huth. In all his emusemints they ecumpanied him; their edjacation was his sole bisniss; he atcheaved it with the assistnce of the ugliest and most lernid masters, and the most hidjus and egsimplary governices which money could procure. R, how must his peturnle art have bet, as these Budds, which he had nurrisht, bust into buty, and twined in blooming flagrance round his pirentle Busm!

The villidges all round his hancestral Alls blessed the Marcus and his lovely hoffsprig. Not one villidge in their naybrood but was edawned by their elygint benifisns, and where the inhabitnts weren't rendered appy. It was a pattern pheasantry. All the old men in the districk were wertuous & tockative, ad red stockins and i-eeled drab shoes, and beautiful snowy air. All the old women had peaked ats, and crooked cains, and chince gowns tucked into the pockits of their quiltid petticoats; they sat in pictarask porches, pretendin to spinn, while the lads and lassis of the villidges danst under the hellums. O, tis a noble sight to whitniss that of an appy pheasantry! Not one of those rustic wassals of the Ouse of Widdlers, but ad his air curled and his shirt-sheaves tied up with pink ribbing as he led to the macy dance some appy country gal, with a black velvit boddice and a redd or yaller petticoat, a hormylu cross on her neck, and a silver harrow in her air!

When the Marcus & ther young ladies came to the villidge it would have done the i's of the flanthropist good to see how all reseaved 'em! The little children scattered calico flowers on their path, the snowy-aired old men with red faces and rinkles took off their brown paper ats to slewt the noble Marcus. Young and old led them to a woodn bank painted to look like a bower of roses, and when they were sett down danst ballys before them. O 'twas a noble site to see the Marcus too, smilin ellygint with fethers in his edd and all his stars on, and the young Marchynisses with their ploomes, and trains, and little coronicks!

They lived in tremenjus splendor at home in their pyturnle alls, and had no end of pallises, willers, and town and country resadences; but their fayvorit resadence was called the Castle of the Island of Fogo.

Add I the penn of the hawther of a Codlingsby himself, I coodnt dixcribe the gawjusness of their aboad. They add twenty-four footmen in livery, besides a boy in codroys for the knives & shoes. They had nine meels aday—Shampayne and pineapples were served to each of the young ladies in bed before they got up. Was it Prawns, Sherry-cobblers, lobster-salids, or maids of honor, they had but to ring the bell and call for what they chose. They had two new dresses every day—one to ride out in the open carriage, and another to appear in the gardens of the Castle of the Island of Fogo, which were illuminated every night like Voxhall. The young noblemen of France were there ready to dance with them, and festif suppers concludid the jawyus night.

Thus they lived in ellygant ratirement until Missfortune bust upon this happy fammaly. Etached to his Princes and abommanating the ojus Lewyphlip, the Marcus was conspiring for the benefick of the helder branch of the Borebones—and what was the consquince?—One night a fleat presented itself round the Castle of the Island of Fogo—and skewering only a couple of chests of jewils, the Marcus and the two young ladies in disgyise, fled from that island of bliss. And whither fled they?—To England!—England the ome of the brave, the refuge of the world, where the pore slave never setts his foot but he is free!

Such was the ramantic tail which was told to 2 friends of ours by the Marcus de Viddlers himself, whose daughters, walking with their page from Ungerford Market (where they had been to purchis a paper of srimps for the umble supper of their noble father), Yardham and his equaintnce, Munseer Jools, had remarked and admired.

But how had those two young Erows become equainted with the noble Marcus?—That is a mistry we must elucydate in a futur vollam.

THE STARS AND STRIPES

THE AUTHOR OR "THE LAST OF THE MULLIGANS," "PILOT," ETC

I.

The King of France was walking on the terrace of Versailles; the fairest, not only of Queens, but of women, hung fondly on the Royal arm; while the children of France were indulging in their infantile hilarity in the alleys of the magnificent garden of Le Notre (from which Niblo's garden has been copied in our own Empire city of New York), and playing at leap-frog with their uncle, the Count of Provence; gaudy courtiers, emlazoned with orders, glittered in the groves, and murmured frivolous talk in the ears of high-bred beauty.

"Marie, my beloved," said the ruler of France, taking out his watch, "'tis time that the Minister of America should be here."

"Your Majesty should know the time," replied Marie Antoinette, archly, and in an Austrian accent; "is not my Royal Louis the first watchmaker in his empire?"

The King cast a pleased glance at his repeater, and kissed with courtly grace the fair hand of her who had made him the compliment. "My Lord Bishop of Autun," said he to Monsieur de Talleyrand Perigord, who followed the royal pair, in his quality of arch-chamberlain of the empire, "I pray you look through the gardens, and tell his Excellency Doctor Franklin that the King waits." The Bishop ran off, with more than youthful agility, to seek the United States' Minister. "These Republicans," he added, confidentially, and with something of a supercilious look, "are but rude courtiers, methinks."

"Nay," interposed the lovely Antoinette, "rude courtiers, Sire, they may be; but the world boasts not of more accomplished gentlemen. I have seen no grandee of Versailles that has the noble bearing of this American envoy and his suite. They have the refinement of the Old World, with all the simple elegance of the New. Though they have perfect dignity of manner, they have an engaging modesty which I have never seen equalled by the best of the proud English nobles with whom they wage war. I am told they speak their very language with a grace which the haughty Islanders who oppress them never attained. They are independent, yet never insolent; elegant, yet always respectful; and brave, but not in the least boastful."

"What! savages and all, Marie?" exclaimed Louis, laughing, and chucking the lovely Queen playfully under the royal chin. "But here comes Doctor Franklin, and your friend the Cacique with him." In fact, as the monarch spoke, the Minister of the United States made his appearance, followed by a gigantic warrior in the garb of his native woods.

Knowing his place as Minister of a sovereign state, (yielding even then in dignity to none, as it surpasses all now in dignity, in valor, in honesty, in strength, and civilization,) the Doctor nodded to the Queen of France, but kept his hat on as he faced the French monarch, and did not cease whittling the cane he carried in his hand.

"I was waiting for you, sir," the King said, peevishly, in spite of the alarmed pressure which the Queen gave his royal arm.

"The business of the Republic, sire, must take precedence even of your Majesty's wishes," replied Dr. Franklin. "When I was a poor printer's boy and ran errands, no lad could be more punctual than poor Ben Franklin; but all other things must yield to the service of the United States of North America. I have done. What would you, Sire?" and the intrepid republican eyed the monarch with a serene and easy dignity, which made the descendant of St. Louis feel ill at ease.

"I wished to—to say farewell to Tatua before his departure," said Louis XVI., looking rather awkward. "Approach, Tatua." And the gigantic Indian strode up, and stood undaunted before the first magistrate of the French nation: again the feeble monarch quailed before the terrible simplicity of the glance of the denizen of the primaeval forests.

The redoubted chief of the Nose-ring Indians was decorated in his war-paint, and in his top-knot was a peacock's feather, which had been given him out of the head-dress of the beautiful Princess of Lamballe. His nose, from which hung the ornament from which his ferocious tribe took its designation, was painted a light-blue, a circle of green and orange was drawn round each eye, while serpentine stripes of black, white, and vermilion alternately were smeared on his forehead, and descended over his cheek-bones to his chin. His manly chest was similarly tattooed and painted, and round his brawny neck and arms hung innumerable bracelets and necklaces of human teeth, extracted (one only from each skull) from the jaws of those who had fallen by the terrible tomahawk at his girdle. His moccasins, and his blanket, which was draped on his arm and fell in picturesque folds to his feet, were fringed with tufts of hair—the black, the gray, the auburn, the golden ringlet of beauty, the red lock from the forehead of the Scottish or the Northern soldier, the snowy tress of extreme old age, the flaxen down of infancy—all were there, dreadful reminiscences of the chief's triumphs in war. The warrior leaned on his enormous rifle, and faced the King.

"And it was with that carabine that you shot Wolfe in '57?" said Louis, eying the warrior and his weapon. "'Tis a clumsy lock, and methinks I could mend it," he added mentally.

"The chief of the French pale-faces speaks truth," Tatua said. "Tatua was a boy when he went first on the war-path with Montcalm."

"And shot a Wolfe at the first fire!" said the King.

"The English are braves, though their faces are white," replied the Indian. "Tatua shot the raging Wolfe of the English; but the other wolves caused the foxes to go to earth." A smile played round Dr. Franklin's lips, as he whittled his cane with more vigor than ever.

"I believe, your Excellency, Tatua has done good service elsewhere than at Quebec," the King said, appealing to the American Envoy: "at Bunker's Hill, at Brandywine, at York Island? Now that Lafayette and my brave Frenchmen are among you, your Excellency need have no fear but that the war will finish quickly—yes, yes, it will finish quickly. They will teach you discipline, and the way to conquer."

"King Louis of France," said the Envoy, clapping his hat down over his head, and putting his arms a-kimbo, "we have learned that from the British, to whom we are superior in everything: and I'd have your Majesty to know that in the art of whipping the world we have no need of any French lessons. If your reglars jine General Washington, 'tis to larn from HIM how Britishers are licked; for I'm blest if YU know the way yet."

Tatua said, "Ugh," and gave a rattle with the butt of his carabine, which made the timid monarch start; the eyes of the lovely Antoinette flashed fire, but it played round the head of the dauntless American Envoy harmless as the lightning which he knew how to conjure away.

The King fumbled in his pocket, and pulled out a Cross of the Order of the Bath. "Your Excellency wears no honor," the monarch said; "but Tatua, who is not a subject, only an ally, of the United States, may. Noble Tatua, I appoint you Knight Companion of my noble Order of the Bath. Wear this cross upon your breast in memory of Louis of France;" and the King held out the decoration to the Chief.

Up to that moment the Chief's countenance had been impassible. No look either of admiration or dislike had appeared upon that grim and war-painted visage. But now, as Louis spoke, Tatua's face assumed a glance of ineffable scorn, as, bending his head, he took the bauble.

"I will give it to one of my squaws," he said. "The papooses in my lodge will play with it. Come, Medecine, Tatua will go and drink fire-water;" and, shouldering his carabine, he turned his broad back without ceremony upon the monarch and his train, and disappeared down one of the walks of the garden. Franklin found him when his own interview with the French Chief Magistrate was over; being attracted to the spot where the Chief was, by the crack of his well-known rifle. He was laughing in his quiet way. He had shot the Colonel of the Swiss Guards through his cockade.

Three days afterwards, as the gallant frigate, the "Repudiator," was sailing out of Brest Harbor, the gigantic form of an Indian might be seen standing on the binnacle in conversation with Commodore Bowie, the commander of the noble ship. It was Tatua, the Chief of the Nose-rings.

II.

Leatherlegs and Tom Coxswain did not accompany Tatua when he went to the Parisian metropolis on a visit to the father of the French pale-faces. Neither the Legs nor the Sailor cared for the gayety and the crowd of cities; the stout mariner's home was in the puttock-shrouds of the old "Repudiator." The stern and simple trapper loved the sound of the waters better than the jargon of the French of the old country. "I can follow the talk of a Pawnee," he said, "or wag my jaw, if so be necessity bids me to speak, by a Sioux's council-fire and I can patter Canadian French with the hunters who come for peltries to Nachitoches or Thichimuchimachy; but from the tongue of a Frenchwoman, with white flour on her head, and war-paint on her face, the Lord deliver poor Natty Pumpo."

"Amen and amen!" said Tom Coxswain. "There was a woman in our aft-scuppers when I went a-whalin in the little 'Grampus'—and Lord love you, Pumpo, you poor land-swab, she WAS as pretty a craft as ever dowsed a tarpauling—there was a woman on board the 'Grampus,' who before we'd struck our first fish, or biled our first blubber, set the whole crew in a mutiny. I mind me of her now, Natty,—her eye was sich a piercer that you could see to steer by it in a Newfoundland fog; her nose stood out like the 'Grampus's' jibboom, and her woice, Lord love you, her woice sings in my ears even now:—it set the Captain a-quarrelin with the Mate, who was hanged in Boston harbor for harpoonin of his officer in Baffin's Bay;—it set me and Bob Bunting a-pouring broadsides into each other's old timbers, whereas me and Bob was worth all the women that ever shipped a hawser. It cost me three years' pay as I'd stowed away for the old mother, and might have cost me ever so much more, only bad luck to me, she went and married a little tailor out of Nantucket; and I've hated women and tailors ever since!" As he spoke, the hardy tar dashed a drop of brine from his tawny cheek, and once more betook himself to splice the taffrail.

Though the brave frigate lay off Havre de Grace, she was not idle. The gallant Bowie and his intrepid crew made repeated descents upon the enemy's seaboard. The coasts of Rutland and merry Leicestershire have still many a legend of fear to tell; and the children of the British fishermen tremble even now when they speak of the terrible "Repudiator." She was the first of the mighty American warships that have taught the domineering Briton to respect the valor of the Republic.

The novelist ever and anon finds himself forced to adopt the sterner tone of the historian, when describing deeds connected with his country's triumphs. It is well known that during the two months in which she lay off Havre, the "Repudiator" had brought more prizes into that port than had ever before been seen in the astonished French waters. Her actions with the "Dettingen" and the "Elector" frigates form part of our country's history; their defence—it may be said without prejudice to national vanity—was worthy of Britons and of the audacious foe they had to encounter; and it must be owned, that but for a happy fortune which presided on that day over the destinies of our country, the chance of the combat might have been in favor of the British vessels. It was not until the "Elector" blew up, at a quarter past three P.M., by a lucky shot which fell into her caboose, and communicated with the powder-magazine, that Commodore Bowie was enabled to lay himself on board the "Dettingen," which he carried sword in hand. Even when the American boarders had made their lodgment on the "Dettingen's" binnacle, it is possible that the battle would still have gone against us. The British were still seven to one; their carronades, loaded with marline-spikes, swept the gun-deck, of which we had possession, and decimated our little force; when a rifle-ball from the shrouds of the "Repudiator" shot Captain Mumford under the star of the Guelphic Order which he wore, and the Americans, with a shout, rushed up the companion to the quarter-deck, upon the astonished foe. Pike and cutlass did the rest of the bloody work. Rumford, the gigantic first-lieutenant of the "Dettingen," was cut down by Commodore Bowie's own sword, as they engaged hand to hand; and it was Tom Coxswain who tore down the British flag, after having slain the Englishman at the wheel. Peace be to the souls of the brave! The combat was honorable alike to the victor and the vanquished; and it never can be said that an American warrior depreciated a gallant foe. The bitterness of defeat was enough to the haughty islanders who had to suffer. The people of Herne Bay were lining the shore, near which the combat took place, and cruel must have been the pang to them when they saw the Stars and Stripes rise over the old flag of the Union, and the "Dettingen" fall down the river in tow of the Republican frigate.

Another action Bowie contemplated: the boldest and most daring perhaps ever imagined by seaman. It is this which has been so wrongly described by European annalists, and of which the British until now have maintained the most jealous secrecy.

Portsmouth Harbor was badly defended. Our intelligence in that town and arsenal gave us precise knowledge of the disposition of the troops, the forts, and the ships there; and it was determined to strike a blow which should shake the British power in its centre.

That a frigate of the size of the "Repudiator" should enter the harbor unnoticed, or could escape its guns unscathed, passed the notions of even American temerity. But upon the memorable 26th of June, 1782, the "Repudiator" sailed out of Havre Roads in a thick fog, under cover of which she entered and cast anchor in Bonchurch Bay, in the Isle of Wight. To surprise the Martello Tower and take the feeble garrison thereunder, was the work of Tom Coxswain and a few of his blue-jackets. The surprised garrison laid down their arms before him.

It was midnight before the boats of the ship, commanded by Lieutenant Bunker, pulled off from Bonchurch with muffled oars, and in another hour were off the Common Hard of Portsmouth, having passed the challenges of the "Thetis" and the "Amphion" frigates, and the "Polyanthus" brig.

There had been on that day great feasting and merriment on board the Flag-ship lying in the harbor. A banquet had been given in honor of the birthday of one of the princes of the royal line of the Guelphs—the reader knows the propensity of Britons when liquor is in plenty. All on board that royal ship were more or less overcome. The Flag-ship was plunged in a deathlike and drunken sleep. The very officer of the watch was intoxicated: he could not see the "Repudiator's" boats as they shot swiftly through the waters; nor had he time to challenge her seamen as they swarmed up the huge sides of the ship.

At the next moment Tom Coxswain stood at the wheel of the "Royal George"—the Briton who had guarded, a corpse at his feet. The hatches were down. The ship was in possession of the "Repudiator's" crew. They were busy in her rigging, bending her sails to carry her out of the harbor. The well-known heave of the men at the windlass woke up Kempenfelt in his state-cabin. We know, or rather do not know, the result; for who can tell by whom the lower-deck ports of the brave ship were opened, and how the haughty prisoners below sunk the ship and its conquerors rather than yield her as a prize to the Republic!

Only Tom Coxswain escaped of victors and vanquished. His tale was told to his Captain and to Congress, but Washington forbade its publication; and it was but lately that the faithful seaman told it to me, his grandson, on his hundred-and-fifteenth birthday.


A PLAN FOR A PRIZE NOVEL

IN A LETTER FROM THE EMINENT DRAMATIST BROWN TO THE EMINENT NOVELIST SNOOKS

"CAFE DES AVEUGLES

"My Dear Snooks,—I am on the look-out here for materials for original comedies such as those lately produced at your theatre; and, in the course of my studies, I have found something, my dear Snooks, which I think will suit your book. You are bringing, I see, your admirable novel, 'The Mysteries of May Fair,' to an end—(by the way, the scene, in the 200th number, between the Duke, his Grandmother, and the Jesuit Butler, is one of the most harrowing and exciting I ever read)—and, of course, you must turn your real genius to some other channel; and we may expect that your pen shall not be idle.

"The original plan I have to propose to you, then, is taken from the French, just like the original dramas above mentioned; and, indeed, I found it in the law report of the National newspaper, and a French literary gentleman, M. Emanuel Gonzales, has the credit of the invention. He and an advertisement agent fell out about a question of money, the affair was brought before the courts, and the little plot so got wind. But there is no reason why you should not take the plot and act on it yourself. You are a known man; the public relishes your works; anything bearing the name of Snooks is eagerly read by the masses; and though Messrs. Hookey, of Holywell Street, pay you handsomely, I make no doubt you would like to be rewarded at a still higher figure.

"Unless he writes with a purpose, you know, a novelist in our days is good for nothing. This one writes with a socialist purpose; that with a conservative purpose: this author or authoress with the most delicate skill insinuates Catholicism into you, and you find yourself all but a Papist in the third volume: another doctors you with Low Church remedies to work inwardly upon you, and which you swallow down unsuspiciously, as children do calomel in jelly. Fiction advocates all sorts of truth and causes—doesn't the delightful bard of the Minories find Moses in everything? M. Gonzales's plan, and the one which I recommend to my dear Snooks, simply was to write an advertisement novel. Look over The Times or the 'Directory,' walk down Regent Street or Fleet Street any day—see what houses advertise most, and put yourself into communication with their proprietors. With your rings, your chains, your studs, and the tip on your chin, I don't know any greater swell than Bob Snooks. Walk into the shops, I say, ask for the principal, and introduce yourself, saying, 'I am the great Snooks; I am the author of the "Mysteries of May Fair;" my weekly sale is 281,000; I am about to produce a new work called "The Palaces of Pimlico, or the Curse of the Court," describing and lashing fearlessly the vices of the aristocracy; this book will have a sale of at least 530,000; it will be on every table—in the boudoir of the pampered duke, as in the chamber of the honest artisan. The myriads of foreigners who are coming to London, and are anxious to know about our national manners, will purchase my book, and carry it to their distant homes. So, Mr. Taylor, or Mr. Haberdasher, or Mr. Jeweller, how much will you stand if I recommend you in my forthcoming novel?' You may make a noble income in this way, Snooks.

"For instance, suppose it is an upholsterer. What more easy, what more delightful, than the description of upholstery? As thus:—

"'Lady Emily was reclining on one of Down and Eider's voluptuous ottomans, the only couch on which Belgravian beauty now reposes, when Lord Bathershins entered, stepping noiselessly over one of Tomkins's elastic Axminster carpets. "Good heavens, my lord!" she said—and the lovely creature fainted. The Earl rushed to the mantel-piece, where he saw a flacon of Otto's eau-de-Cologne, and,' &c.

"Or say it's a cheap furniture-shop, and it may be brought in just as easily, as thus:—

"'We are poor, Eliza,' said Harry Hardhand, looking affectionately at his wife, 'but we have enough, love, have we not, for our humble wants? The rich and luxurious may go to Dillow's or Gobiggin's, but we can get our rooms comfortably furnished at Timmonson's for 20L.' And putting on her bonnet, and hanging affectionately on her husband, the stoker's pretty bride tripped gayly to the well-known mart, where Timmonson, within his usual affability, was ready to receive them.

"Then you might have a touch at the wine-merchant and purveyor. 'Where did you get this delicious claret, or pate de fois gras, or what you please?' said Count Blagowski to the gay young Sir Horace Swellmore. The voluptuous Bart answered, 'At So-and-So's, or So-and-So's.' The answer is obvious. You may furnish your cellar or your larder in this way. Begad, Snooks! I lick my lips at the very idea.

"Then, as to tailors, milliners, bootmakers, &c., how easy to get a word for them! Amranson, the tailor, waited upon Lord Paddington with an assortment of his unrivalled waistcoats, or clad in that simple but aristocratic style of which Schneider ALONE has the secret. Parvy Newcome really looked like a gentleman, and though corpulent and crooked, Schneider had managed to give him, &c. Don't you see what a stroke of business you might do in this way.

"The shoemaker.—Lady Fanny flew, rather than danced, across the ball-room; only a Sylphide, or Taglioni, or a lady chausseed by Chevillett of Bond Street could move in that fairy way; and

"The hairdresser.—'Count Barbarossa is seventy years of age,' said the Earl. 'I remember him at the Congress of Vienna, and he has not a single gray hair.' Wiggins laughed. 'My good Lord Baldock,' said the old wag, 'I saw Barbarossa's hair coming out of Ducroissant's shop, and under his valet's arm—ho! ho! ho!'—and the two bon-vivans chuckled as the Count passed by, talking with, &c. &c.

"The gunmaker.—'The antagonists faced each other; and undismayed before his gigantic enemy, Kilconnel raised his pistol. It was one of Clicker's manufacture, and Sir Marmaduke knew he could trust the maker and the weapon. "One, two, THREE," cried O'Tool, and the two pistols went off at that instant, and uttering a terrific curse, the Lifeguardsman,' &c.—A sentence of this nature from your pen, my dear Snooks, would, I should think, bring a case of pistols and a double-barrelled gun to your lodgings; and, though heaven forbid you should use such weapons, you might sell them, you know, and we could make merry with the proceeds.

"If my hint is of any use to you, it is quite at your service, dear Snooks; and should anything come of it, I hope you will remember your friend."

THE DIARY OF C. JEAMES DE LA PLUCHE, ESQ.

WITH HIS LETTERS

A LUCKY SPECULATOR

"Considerable sensation has been excited in the upper and lower circles in the West End, by a startling piece of good fortune which has befallen James Plush, Esq., lately footman in a respected family in Berkeley Square.

"One day last week, Mr. James waited upon his master, who is a banker in the City; and after a little blushing and hesitation, said he had saved a little money in service, was anxious to retire, and to invest his savings to advantage.

"His master (we believe we may mention, without offending delicacy, the well-known name of Sir George Flimsy, of the house of Flimsy, Diddler, and Flash,) smilingly asked Mr. James what was the amount of his savings, wondering considerably how, out of an income of thirty guineas—the main part of which he spent in bouquets, silk stockings, and perfumery—Mr. Plush could have managed to lay by anything.

"Mr. Plush, with some hesitation, said he had been SPECULATING IN RAILROADS, and stated his winnings to have been thirty thousand pounds. He had commenced his speculations with twenty, borrowed from a fellow-servant. He had dated his letters from the house in Berkeley Square, and humbly begged pardon of his master for not having instructed the Railway Secretaries who answered his applications to apply at the area-bell.

"Sir George, who was at breakfast, instantly rose, and shook Mr. P. by the hand; Lady Flimsy begged him to be seated, and partake of the breakfast which he had laid on the table; and has subsequently invited him to her grand dejeuner at Richmond, where it was observed that Miss Emily Flimsy, her beautiful and accomplished seventh daughter, paid the lucky gentleman MARKED ATTENTION.

"We hear it stated that Mr. P. is of a very ancient family (Hugo de la Pluche came over with the Conqueror); and the new brougham which he has started bears the ancient coat of his race.

"He has taken apartments in the Albany, and is a director of thirty-three railroads. He proposes to stand for Parliament at the next general election on decidedly conservative principles, which have always been the politics of his family.

"Report says, that even in his humble capacity Miss Emily Flimsy had remarked his high demeanor. Well, 'None but the brave,' say we, 'deserve the fair.'"—Morning Paper.

This announcement will explain the following lines, which have been put into our box* with a West End post-mark. If, as we believe, they are written by the young woman from whom the Millionnaire borrowed the sum on which he raised his fortune, what heart will not melt with sympathy at her tale, and pity the sorrows which she expresses in such artless language?

If it be not too late; if wealth have not rendered its possessor callous; if poor Maryanne BE STILL ALIVE; we trust, we trust, Mr. Plush will do her justice.

*The letter-box of Mr. Punch, in whose columns these papers were first published.*

"JEAMES OF BUCKLEY SQUARE.

"A HELIGY.

"Come all ye gents vot cleans the plate,
Come all ye ladies maids so fair—
Vile I a story vill relate
Of cruel Jeames of Buckley Square.
A tighter lad, it is confest,
Neer valked with powder in his air,
Or vore a nosegay in his breast,
Than andsum Jeames of Buckley Square.

"O Evns! it vas the best of sights,
Behind his Master's coach and pair,
To see our Jeames in red plush tights,
A driving hoff from Buckley Square.
He vel became his hagwilletts,
He cocked his at with SUCH a hair;
His calves and viskers VAS such pets,
That hall loved Jeames of Buckley Square.

"He pleased the hup-stairs folks as vell,
And o! I vithered vith despair,
Missis VOULD ring the parler bell,
And call up Jeames in Buckley Square.
Both beer and sperrits he abhord,
(Sperrits and beer I can't a bear,)
You would have thought he vas a lord
Down in our All in Buckley Square.

"Last year he visper'd 'Mary Ann,
Ven I've an under'd pound to spare,
To take a public is my plan,
And leave this hojous Buckley Square.'
O how my gentle heart did bound,
To think that I his name should bear.
'Dear Jeames.' says I, 'I've twenty pound;
And gev them him in Buckley Square.

"Our master vas a City gent,
His name's in railroads everywhere,

And lord, vot lots of letters vent
Betwigst his brokers and Buckley Square:
My Jeames it was the letters took,
And read them all, (I think it's fair,)
And took a leaf from Master's book,
As HOTHERS do in Buckley Square.

Encouraged with my twenty pound,
Of which poor I was unavare,
He wrote the Companies all round,
And signed hisself from Buckley Square.
And how John Porter used to grin,
As day by day, share after share,
Came railvay letters pouring in,
'J. Plush, Esquire, in Buckley Square.'

"Our servants' All was in a rage—
Scrip, stock, curves, gradients, bull and bear,
Vith butler, coachman, groom and page,
Vas all the talk in Buckley Square.
But O! imagine vot I felt
Last Vensday veek as ever were;
I gits a letter, which I spelt
'Miss M. A. Hoggins, Buckley Square.'

"He sent me back my money true—
He sent me back my lock of air,
And said, 'My dear, I bid ajew
To Mary Hann and Buckley Square.
Think not to marry, foolish Hann,
With people who your betters are;
James Plush is now a gentleman,
And you—a cook in Buckley Square.

"'I've thirty thousand guineas won,
In six short months, by genus rare;
You little thought what Jeames was on,
Poor Mary Hann, in Buckley Square.
I've thirty thousand guineas net,
Powder and plush I scorn to vear;
And so, Miss Mary Hann, forget
For hever Jeames, of Buckley Square.'"

The rest of the MS. is illegible, being literally washed away in a flood of tears.

A LETTER FROM "JEAMES, OF BUCKLEY SQUARE"

"Sir,—Has a reglar suscriber to your emusing paper, I beg leaf to state that I should never have done so, had I supposed that it was your abbit to igspose the mistaries of privit life, and to hinjer the delligit feelings of umble individyouals like myself, who have NO IDEER of being made the subject of newspaper criticism.

"I elude, sir, to the unjustafiable use which has been made of my name in your Journal, where both my muccantile speclations and the HINMOST PASHSN OF MY ART have been brot forrards in a ridicklus way for the public emusemint.

"What call, sir, has the public to inquire into the suckmstansies of my engagements with Miss Mary Hann Oggins, or to meddle with their rupsher? Why am I to be maid the hobjick of your REDICULE IN A DOGGRIL BALLIT impewted to her? I say IMPEWTED, because, in MY time at least, Mary Hann could only sign her + mark (has I've hoften witnist it for her when she paid hin at the Savings Bank), and has for SACRIFICING TO THE MEWSES and making POATRY, she was as HINCAPIBLE as Mr. Wakley himself.

"With respect to the ballit, my baleaf is, that it is wrote by a footman in a low famly, a pore retch who attempted to rivle me in my affections to Mary Hann—a feller not five foot six, and with no more calves to his legs than a donkey—who was always a-ritin (having been a doctor's boy) and who I nockt down with a pint of porter (as he well recklex) at the 3 Tuns Jerming Street, for daring to try to make a but of me. He has signed Miss H's name to his NONSINCE AND LIES: and you lay yourself hopen to a haction for libel for insutting them in your paper.

"It is false that I have treated Miss H. hill in HANY way. That I borrowed 20lb of her is TREW. But she confesses I paid it back. Can hall people say as much of the money THEY'VE lent or borrowed? No. And I not only paid it back, but giv her the andsomest pres'nts: WHICH I NEVER SHOULD HAVE ALLUDED TO, but for this attack. Fust, a silver thimble (which I found in Missus's work-box); secknd, a vollom of Byrom's poems; third, I halways brought her a glas of Curasore, when we ad a party, of which she was remarkable fond. I treated her to Hashley's twice, (and halways a srimp or a hoyster by the way,) and a THOWSND DELIGIT ATTENTIONS, which I sapose count for NOTHINK.

"Has for marridge. Haltered suckmstancies rendered it himpossable. I was gone into a new spear of life—mingling with my native aristoxy. I breathe no sallible of blame against Miss H., but his a hilliterit cookmaid fit to set at a fashnable table? Do young fellers of rank genrally marry out of the Kitching? If we cast our i's upon a low-born gal, I needn say it's only a tempory distraction, pore passy le tong. So much for HER claims upon me. Has for THAT BEEST OF A DOCTOR'S BOY he's unwuthy the notas of a Gentleman.

"That I've one thirty thousand lb, AND PRAPS MORE, I dont deny. Ow much has the Kilossus of Railroads one, I should like to know, and what was his cappitle? I hentered the market with 20lb, specklated Jewdicious, and ham what I ham. So may you be (if you have 20lb, and praps you haven't)—So may you be: if you choose to go in & win.

"I for my part am jusly PROWD of my suxess, and could give you a hundred instances of my gratatude. For igsample, the fust pair of hosses I bought (and a better pair of steppers I dafy you to see in hany curracle,) I crisn'd Hull and Selby, in grateful elusion to my transackshns in that railroad. My riding Cob I called very unhaptly my Dublin and Galway. He came down with me the other day, and I've jest sold him at 1/4 discount.

"At fust with prudence and modration I only kep two grooms for my stables, one of whom lickwise waited on me at table. I have now a confidenshle servant, a vally de shamber—He curls my air; inspex my accounts, and hansers my hinvitations to dinner. I call this Vally my TRENT VALLY, for it was the prophit I got from that exlent line, which injuiced me to ingage him.

"Besides my North British Plate and Breakfast equipidge—I have two handsom suvvices for dinner—the goold plate for Sundays, and the silver for common use. When I ave a great party, 'Trent,' I say to my man, 'we will have the London and Bummingham plate to-day (the goold), or else the Manchester and Leeds (the silver).' I bought them after realizing on the abuf lines, and if people suppose that the companys made me a presnt of the plate, how can I help it?

"In the sam way I say, 'Trent, bring us a bottle of Bristol amid Hexeter!' or, 'Put some Heastern Counties in hice!' HE knows what I mean: it's the wines I bought upon the hospicious tummination of my connexshn with those two railroads.

"So strong, indeed, as this abbit become, that being asked to stand Godfather to the youngest Miss Diddle last weak, I had her christened (provisionally) Rosamell—from the French line of which I am Director; and only the other day, finding myself rayther unwell, 'Doctor,' says I to Sir Jeames Clark, 'I've sent to consult you because my Midlands are out of horder; and I want you to send them up to a premium.' The Doctor lafd, and I beleave told the story subsquintly at Buckinum P-ll-s.

"But I will trouble you no father. My sole object in writing has been to CLEAR MY CARRATER—to show that I came by my money in a honrable way: that I'm not ashaymd of the manner in which I gayned it, and ham indeed grateful for my good fortune.

"To conclude, I have ad my podigree maid out at the Erald Hoffis (I don't mean the Morning Erald), and have took for my arms a Stagg. You are corrict in stating that I am of hancient Normin famly. This is more than Peal can say, to whomb I applied for a barnetcy; but the primmier being of low igstraction, natrally stickles for his horder. Consurvative though I be, I MAY CHANGE MY OPINIONS before the next Election, when I intend to hoffer myself as a Candydick for Parlymint.

"Meanwhile, I have the honor to be, Sir,

"Your most obeajnt Survnt,

"FITZ-JAMES DE LA PLUCHE."


THE DIARY

One day in the panic week, our friend Jeames called at our office, evidently in great perturbation of mind and disorder of dress. He had no flower in his button-hole; his yellow kid gloves were certainly two days old. He had not above three of the ten chains he usually sports, and his great coarse knotty-knuckled old hands were deprived of some dozen of the rubies, emeralds, and other cameos with which, since his elevation to fortune, the poor fellow has thought fit to adorn himself.

"How's scrip, Mr. Jeames?" said we pleasantly, greeting our esteemed contributor.

"Scrip be —," replied he, with an expression we cannot repeat, and a look of agony it is impossible to describe in print, and walked about the parlor whistling, humming, rattling his keys and coppers, and showing other signs of agitation. At last, "MR. PUNCH," says he, after a moment's hesitation, "I wish to speak to you on a pint of businiss. I wish to be paid for my contribewtions to your paper. Suckmstances is altered with me. I—I—in a word, CAN you lend me —L. for the account?"

He named the sum. It was one so great that we don't care to mention it here; but on receiving a cheque for the amount (on Messrs. Pump and Aldgate, our bankers,) tears came into the honest fellow's eyes. He squeezed our hand until he nearly wrung it off, and shouting to a cab, he plunged into it at our office-door, and was off to the City.

Returning to our study, we found he had left on our table an open pocket-book, of the contents of which (for the sake of safety) we took an inventory. It contained—three tavern-bills, paid; a tailor's ditto, unsettled; forty-nine allotments in different companies, twenty-six thousand seven hundred shares in all, of which the market value we take, on an average, to be 1/4 discount; and in an old bit of paper tied with pink ribbon a lock of chestnut hair, with the initials M. A. H.

In the diary of the pocket-book was a journal, jotted down by the proprietor from time to time. At first the entries are insignificant: as, for instance:—"3rd January—Our beer in the Suvnts' hall so PRECIOUS small at this Christmas time that I reely MUSS give warning, & wood, but for my dear Mary Hann. February 7—That broot Screw, the Butler, wanted to kis her, but my dear Mary Hann boxt his hold hears, & served him right. I DATEST Screw,"—and so forth. Then the diary relates to Stock Exchange operations, until we come to the time when, having achieved his successes, Mr. James quitted Berkeley Square and his livery, and began his life as a speculator and a gentleman upon town. It is from the latter part of his diary that we make the following

EXTRAX:—

"Wen I anounced in the Servnts All my axeshn of forting, and that by the exasize of my own talince and ingianiuty I had reerlized a summ of 20,000 lb. (it was only 5, but what's the use of a mann depreshiating the qualaty of his own mackyrel?)—wen I enounced my abrup intention to cut—you should have sean the sensation among hall the people! Cook wanted to know whether I woodn like a sweatbred, or the slise of the breast of a Cold Tucky. Screw, the butler, (womb I always detested as a hinsalant hoverbaring beest,) begged me to walk into the Hupper Servnts All, and try a glass of Shuperior Shatto Margo. Heven Visp, the coachmin, eld out his and, & said, 'Jeames, I hopes theres no quarraling betwigst you & me, & I'll stand a pot of beer with pleasure.'

"The sickofnts!—that wery Cook had split on me to the Housekeeper ony last week (catchin me priggin some cold tuttle soop, of which I'm remarkable fond). Has for the butler, I always EBOMMINATED him for his precious snears and imperence to all us Gents who woar livry (he never would sit in our parlor, fasooth, nor drink out of our mugs); and in regard of Visp—why, it was ony the day before the wulgar beest hoffered to fite me, and thretnd to give me a good iding if I refused. Gentlemen and ladies,' says I, as haughty as may be, 'there's nothink that I want for that I can't go for to buy with my hown money, and take at my lodgins in Halbany, letter Hex; if I'm ungry I've no need to refresh myself in the KITCHING.' And so saying, I took a dignified ajew of these minnial domestics; and ascending to my epartment in the 4 pair back, brushed the powder out of my air, and taking off those hojous livries for hever, put on a new soot, made for me by Cullin of St. Jeames Street, and which fitted my manly figger as tight as whacks.

"There was ONE pusson in the house with womb I was rayther anxious to evoid a persnal leave-taking—Mary Hann Oggins, I mean—for my art is natural tender, and I can't abide seeing a pore gal in pane. I'd given her previous the infamation of my departure—doing the ansom thing by her at the same time—paying her back 20 lb., which she'd lent me 6 months before: and paying her back not only the interest, but I gave her an andsome pair of scissars and a silver thimbil, by way of boanus. 'Mary Hann,' says I, 'suckimstancies has haltered our rellatif positions in life. I quit the Servnts Hall for ever, (for has for your marrying a person in my rank, that, my dear, is hall gammin,) and so I wish you a good-by, my good gal, and if you want to better yourself, halways refer to me.'

"Mary Hann didn't hanser my speech (which I think was remarkable kind), but looked at me in the face quite wild like, and bust into somethink betwigst a laugh & a cry, and fell down with her ed on the kitching dresser, where she lay until her young Missis rang the dressing-room bell. Would you bleave it? She left the thimbil & things, & my check for 20lb. 10s., on the tabil when she went to hanser the bell. And now I heard her sobbing and vimpering in her own room nex but one to mine, vith the dore open, peraps expecting I should come in and say good-by. But, as soon as I was dressed, I cut down stairs, hony desiring Frederick my fellow-servnt, to fetch me a cabb, and requesting permission to take leaf of my lady & the famly before my departure."

"How Miss Hemly did hogle me to be sure! Her ladyship told me what a sweet gal she was—hamiable, fond of poetry, plays the gitter. Then she hasked me if I liked blond bewties and haubin hair. Haubin, indeed! I don't like carrits! as it must be confest Miss Hemly's his—and has for a BLOND BUTY, she has pink I's like a Halbino, and her face looks as if it were dipt in a brann mash. How she squeeged my & as she went away!

"Mary Hann now HAS haubin air, and a cumplexion like roses and hivory, and I's as blew as Evin.

"I gev Frederick two and six for fetchin the cabb—been resolved to hact the gentleman in hall things. How he stared!"

"25th.—I am now director of forty-seven hadvantageous lines, and have past hall day in the Citty. Although I've hate or nine new soots of close, and Mr. Cullin fits me heligant, yet I fansy they hall reckonise me. Conshns whispers to me, 'Jeams, you'r hony a footman in disguise hafter all.'"

"28th.—Been to the Hopra. Music tol lol. That Lablash is a wopper at singing. I coodn make out why some people called out 'Bravo,' some 'Bravar,' and some 'Bravee.' 'Bravee, Lablash,' says I, at which heverybody laft.

"I'm in my new stall. I've had new cushings put in, and my harms in goold on the back. I'm dressed hall in black, excep a gold waistcoat and dimind studds in the embriderd busom of my shameese. I wear a Camallia Jiponiky in my button-ole, and have a double-barreld opera-glas, so big, that I make Timmins, my secnd man, bring it in the other cabb.

"What an igstronry exabishn that Pawdy Carter is! If those four gals are faries, Tellioni is sutnly the fairy Queend. She can do all that they can do, and somethink they can't. There's an indiscrible grace about her, and Carlotty, my sweet Carlotty, she sets my art in flams.

"Ow that Miss Hemly was noddin and winkin at me out of their box on the fourth tear?

"What linx i's she must av. As if I could mount up there!

"P.S.—Talking of MOUNTING HUP! the St. Helena's walked up 4 per cent this very day."

"2nd July.—Rode my bay oss Desperation in the park. There was me, Lord George Ringwood (Lord Cinqbar's son), Lord Ballybunnion, Honorable Capting Trap, & sevral hother young swells. Sir John's carridge there in coarse. Miss Hemly lets fall her booky as I pass, and I'm obleged to get hoff and pick it hup, & get splashed up to the his. The gettin on hossback agin is halways the juice & hall. Just as I was on, Desperation begins a porring the hair with his 4 feet, and sinks down so on his anches, that I'm blest if I didn't slip hoff agin over his tail, at which Ballybunnion & the hother chaps rord with lafter.

"As Bally has istates in Queen's County, I've put him on the St. Helena direction. We call it the 'Great St. Helena Napoleon Junction,' from Jamestown to Longwood. The French are taking it hup heagerly."

"6th July.—Dined to-day at the London Tavin with one of the Welsh bords of Direction I'm hon. The Cwrwmwrw & Plmwyddlywm, with tunnils through Snowding and Plinlimming.

"Great nashnallity of course. Ap Shinkin in the chair, Ap Llwydd in the vice; Welsh mutton for dinner; Welsh iron knives & forks; Welsh rabbit after dinner; and a Welsh harper, be hanged to him: he went strummint on his hojous hinstrument, and played a toon piguliarly disagreeble to me.

"It was PORE MARY HANN. The clarrit holmost choaked me as I tried it, and I very nearly wep myself as I thought of her bewtifle blue i's. Why HAM I always thinking about that gal? Sasiety is sasiety, it's lors is irresistabl. Has a man of rank I can't marry a serving-made. What would Cinqbar and Ballybunnion say?

"P.S.—I don't like the way that Cinqbars has of borroing money, & halways making me pay the bill. Seven pound six at the 'Shipp,' Grinnidge, which I don't grudge it, for Derbyshire's brown Ock is the best in Urup; nine pound three at the 'Trafflygar,' and seventeen pound sixteen and nine at the 'Star and Garter,' Richmond, with the Countess St. Emilion & the Baroness Frontignac. Not one word of French could I speak, and in consquince had nothink to do but to make myself halmost sick with heating hices and desert, while the hothers were chattering and parlyvooing.

"Ha! I remember going to Grinnidge once with Mary Hann, when we were more happy (after a walk in the park, where we ad one gingy-beer betwigst us), more appy with tea and a simple srimp than with hall this splender!"—

"July 24.—My first-floor apartmince in Halbiny is now kimpletely and chasely furnished—the droring-room with yellow satting and silver for the chairs and sophies—hemrall green tabbinet curtings with pink velvet & goold borders and fringes; a light blue Haxminster Carpit, embroydered with tulips; tables, secritaires, cunsoles, &c., as handsome as goold can make them, and candle-sticks and shandalers of the purest Hormolew.

"The Dining-room furniture is all HOAK, British Hoak; round igspanding table, like a trick in a Pantimime, iccommadating any number from 8 to 24—to which it is my wish to restrict my parties. Curtings crimsing damask, Chairs crimsing myrocky. Portricks of my favorite great men decorats the wall—namely, the Duke of Wellington. There's four of his Grace. For I've remarked that if you wish to pass for a man of weight and considdration you should holways praise and quote him. I have a valluble one lickwise of my Queend, and 2 of Prince Halbert—has a Field Martial and halso as a privat Gent. I despise the vulgar SNEARS that are daily hullered aginst that Igsolted Pottentat. Betwigxt the Prins & the Duke hangs me, in the Uniform of the Cinqbar Malitia, of which Cinqbars has made me Capting.

"The Libery is not yet done.

"But the Bedd-roomb is the Jem of the whole. If you could but see it! such a Bedworr! Ive a Shyval Dressing Glass festooned with Walanseens Lace, and lighted up of evenings with rose-colored tapers. Goold dressing-case and twilet of Dresding Cheny. My bed white and gold with curtings of pink and silver brocayd held up a top by a goold Qpid who seems always a smilin angillicly hon me, has I lay with my Ed on my piller hall sarounded with the finest Mechlin. I have a own man, a yuth under him, 2 groombs, and a fimmale for the House. I've 7 osses: in cors if I hunt this winter I must increase my ixtablishment.

"N.B. Heverythink looking well in the City. St. Helenas, 12 pm.; Madagascars, 9 5/8; Saffron Hill and Rookery Junction, 24; and the new lines in prospick equily incouraging.

"People phansy it's hall gaiety and pleasure the life of us fashnabble gents about townd—But I can tell 'em it's not hall goold that glitters. They don't know our momints of hagony, hour ours of studdy and reflecshun. They little think when they see Jeames de la Pluche, Exquire, worling round in a walce at Halmax with Lady Hann, or lazaly stepping a kidrill with Lady Jane, poring helegant nothinx into the Countess's hear at dinner, or gallopin his hoss Desperation hover the exorcisin ground in the Park,—they little think that leader of the tong, seaminkly so reckliss, is a careworn mann! and yet so it is.

"Imprymus. I've been ableged to get up all the ecomplishments at double quick, & to apply myself with treemenjuous energy.

"First,—in horder to give myself a hideer of what a gentleman reely is, I've read the novvle of 'Pelham' six times, and am to go through it 4 times mor.

"I practis ridin and the acquirement of 'a steady and & a sure seat across Country' assijuously 4 times a week, at the Hippydrum Riding Grounds. Many's the tumbil I've ad, and the aking boans I've suffered from, though I was grinnin in the Park or laffin at the Opra.

"Every morning from 6 till 9, the innabitance of Halbany may have been surprised to hear the sounds of music ishuing from the apartmince of Jeames de la Pluche, Exquire, Letter Hex. It's my dancing-master. From six to nine we have walces and polkies—at nine, 'mangtiang & depotment,' as he calls it & the manner of hentering a room, complimenting the ost and ostess & compotting yourself at table. At nine I henter from my dressing-room (has to a party), I make my bow—my master (he's a Marquis in France, and ad misfortins, being connected with young Lewy Nepoleum) reseaves me—I hadwance—speak abowt the weather & the toppix of the day in an elegant & cussory manner. Brekfst is enounced by Fitzwarren, my mann—we precede to the festive bord—complimence is igschanged with the manner of drinking wind, addressing your neighbor, employing your napking & finger-glas, &c. And then we fall to brekfst, when I prommiss you the Marquis don't eat like a commoner. He says I'm gettn on very well—soon I shall be able to inwite people to brekfst, like Mr. Mills, my rivle in Halbany; Mr. Macauly, (who wrote that sweet book of ballets, 'The Lays of Hancient Rum;') & the great Mr. Rodgers himself.

"The above was wrote some weeks back. I HAVE given brekfst sins then, reglar Deshunys. I have ad Earls and Ycounts—Barnits as many as I chose: and the pick of the Railway world, of which I form a member. Last Sunday was a grand Fate. I had the Eleet of my friends: the display was sumptious; the company reshershy. Everything that Dellixy could suggest was provided by Gunter. I had a Countiss on my right & (the Countess of Wigglesbury, that loveliest and most dashing of Staggs, who may be called the Railway Queend, as my friend George H— is the Railway King,) on my left the Lady Blanche Bluenose, Prince Towrowski, the great Sir Huddlestone Fuddlestone from the North, and a skoar of the fust of the fashn. I was in my GLOARY—the dear Countess and Lady Blanche was dying with lauffing at my joax and fun—I was keeping the whole table in a roar—when there came a ring at my door-bell, and sudnly Fitzwarren, my man, henters with an air of constanation. 'Theres somebody at the door,' says he in a visper.

"'Oh, it's that dear Lady Hemily,' says I, 'and that lazy raskle of a husband of hers. Trot them in, Fitzwarren,' (for you see by this time I had adopted quite the manners and hease of the arristoxy.)—And so, going out, with a look of wonder he returned presently, enouncing Mr. & Mrs. Blodder.

"I turned gashly pail. The table—the guests—the Countiss—Towrouski, and the rest, weald round & round before my hagitated I's. IT WAS MY GRANDMOTHER AND Huncle Bill. She is a washerwoman at Healing Common, and he—he keeps a wegetable donkey-cart.

"Y, Y hadn't John, the tiger, igscluded them? He had tried. But the unconscious, though worthy creeters, advanced in spite of him, Huncle Bill bringing in the old lady grinning on his harm!

"Phansy my feelinx."

"Immagin when these unfortnat members of my famly hentered the room: you may phansy the ixtonnishment of the nobil company presnt. Old Grann looked round the room quite estounded by its horiental splender, and huncle Bill (pulling off his phantail, & seluting the company as respeckfly as his wulgar natur would alow) says—'Crikey, Jeames, you've got a better birth here than you ad where you were in the plush and powder line.' 'Try a few of them plovers hegs, sir,' I says, whishing, I'm asheamed to say, that somethink would choke huncle B—; 'and I hope, mam, now you've ad the kindniss to wisit me, a little refreshment won't be out of your way.'

"This I said, detummind to put a good fase on the matter: and because in herly times I'd reseaved a great deal of kindniss from the hold lady, which I should be a roag to forgit. She paid for my schooling; she got up my fine linning gratis; shes given me many & many a lb; and manys the time in appy appy days when me and Maryhann has taken tea. But never mind THAT. 'Mam,' says I, 'you must be tired hafter your walk.'

"'Walk? Nonsince, Jeames,' says she; 'it's Saturday, & I came in, in THE CART.' 'Black or green tea, maam?' says Fitzwarren, intarupting her. And I will say the feller showed his nouce & good breeding in this difficklt momink; for he'd halready silenced huncle Bill, whose mouth was now full of muffinx, am, Blowny sausag, Perrigole pie, and other dellixies.

"'Wouldn't you like a little SOMETHINK in your tea, Mam,' says that sly wagg Cinqbars. 'HE knows what I likes,' replies the hawfle hold Lady, pinting to me, (which I knew it very well, having often seen her take a glass of hojous gin along with her Bohee), and so I was ableeged to horder Fitzwarren to bring round the licures, and to help my unfortnit rellatif to a bumper of Ollands. She tost it hoff to the elth of the company, giving a smack with her lipps after she'd emtied the glas, which very nearly caused me to phaint with hagny. But, luckaly for me, she didn't igspose herself much farther: for when Cinqbars was pressing her to take another glas, I cried out, 'Don't, my lord,' on which old Grann hearing him edressed by his title, cried out, 'A Lord! o law!' and got up and made him a cutsy, and coodnt be peswaded to speak another word. The presents of the noble gent heavidently made her uneezy.

"The Countiss on my right and had shownt symtms of ixtream disgust at the beayvior of my relations, and having called for her carridg, got up to leave the room, with the most dignified hair. I, of coarse, rose to conduct her to her weakle. Ah, what a contrast it was! There it stood, with stars and garters hall hover the pannels; the footmin in peach-colored tites; the hosses worth 3 hundred apiece;—and there stood the horrid LINNEN-CART, with 'Mary Blodder, Laundress, Ealing, Middlesex,' wrote on the bord, and waiting till my abandind old parint should come out.

"Cinqbars insisted upon helping her in. Sir Huddlestone Fuddlestone, the great Barnet from the North, who, great as he is, is as stewpid as a howl, looked on, hardly trusting his goggle I's as they witnessed the sean. But little lively good naterd Lady Kitty Quickset, who was going away with the Countiss, held her little & out of the carridge to me and said, 'Mr. De la Pluche, you are a much better man than I took you to be. Though her Ladyship IS horrified, & though your Grandmother DID take gin for breakfast, don't give her up. No one ever came to harm yet for honoring their father & mother.'

"And this was a sort of consolation to me, and I observed that all the good fellers thought none the wuss of me. Cinqbars said I was a trump for sticking up for the old washerwoman; Lord George Gills said she should have his linning; and so they cut their joax, and I let them. But it was a great releaf to my mind when the cart drove hoff.

"There was one pint which my Grandmother observed, and which, I muss say, I thought lickwise: 'Ho, Jeames,' says she, 'hall those fine ladies in sattns and velvets is very well, but there's not one of em can hold a candle to Mary Hann.'"

"Railway Spec is going on phamusly. You should see how polite they har at my bankers now! Sir Paul Pump Aldgate, & Company. They bow me out of the back parlor as if I was a Nybobb. Every body says I'm worth half a millium. The number of lines they're putting me upon is inkumseavable. I've put Fitzwarren, my man, upon several. Reginald Fitzwarren, Esquire, looks splendid in a perspectus; and the raskle owns that he has made two thowsnd.

"How the ladies, & men too, foller and flatter me! If I go into Lady Binsis hopra box, she makes room for me, who ever is there, and cries out, 'O do make room for that dear creature!' And she complyments me on my taste in musick, or my new Broom-oss, or the phansy of my weskit, and always ends by asking me for some shares. Old Lord Bareacres, as stiff as a poaker, as prowd as loosyfer, as poor as Joab—even he condysends to be sivvle to the great De la Pluche, and begged me at Harthur's, lately, in his sollom, pompus way, 'to faver him with five minutes' conversation.' I knew what was coming—application for shares—put him down on my private list. Would'nt mind the Scrag End Junction passing through Bareacres—hoped I'd come down and shoot there.

"I gave the old humbugg a few shares out of my own pocket. 'There, old Pride,' says I, 'I like to see you down on your knees to a footman. There, old Pompossaty! Take fifty pound; I like to see you come cringing and begging for it.' Whenever I see him in a VERY public place, I take my change for my money. I digg him in the ribbs, or slap his padded old shoulders. I call him, 'Bareacres, my old buck!' and I see him wince. It does my art good.

"I'm in low sperits. A disagreeable insadent has just occurred. Lady Pump, the banker's wife, asked me to dinner. I sat on her right, of course, with an uncommon gal ner me, with whom I was getting on in my fassanating way—full of lacy ally (as the Marquis says) and easy plesntry. Old Pump, from the end of the table, asked me to drink shampane; and on turning to tak the glass I saw Charles Wackles (with womb I'd been imployed at Colonel Spurriers' house) grinning over his shoulder at the butler.

"The beest reckonised me. Has I was putting on my palto in the hall, he came up again: 'HOW DY DOO, Jeames?' says he, in a findish visper. 'Just come out here, Chawles,' says I, 'I've a word for you, my old boy.' So I beckoned him into Portland Place, with my pus in my hand, as if I was going to give him a sovaring.

"'I think you said "Jeames," Chawles,' says I, 'and grind at me at dinner?'

"'Why, sir.' says he, 'we're old friends, you know.'

"'Take that for old friendship then,' says I, and I gave him just one on the noas, which sent him down on the pavemint as if he'd been shot. And mounting myjesticly into my cabb, I left the rest of the grinning scoundrills to pick him up, & droav to the Clubb."

"Have this day kimpleated a little efair with my friend George, Earl Bareacres, which I trust will be to the advantidge both of self & that noble gent. Adjining the Bareacre proppaty is a small piece of land of about 100 acres, called Squallop Hill, igseeding advantageous for the cultivation of sheep, which have been found to have a pickewlear fine flaviour from the natur of the grass, tyme, heather, and other hodarefarus plants which grows on that mounting in the places where the rox and stones don't prevent them. Thistles here is also remarkable fine, and the land is also devided hoff by luxurient Stone Hedges—much more usefle and ickonomicle than your quickset or any of that rubbishing sort of timber: indeed the sile is of that fine natur, that timber refuses to grow there altogether. I gave Bareacres 50L. an acre for this land (the igsact premium of my St. Helena Shares)—a very handsom price for land which never yielded two shillings an acre; and very convenient to his Lordship I know, who had a bill coming due at his Bankers which he had given them. James de la Pluche, Esquire, is thus for the fust time a landed propriator—or rayther, I should say, is about to reshume the rank & dignity in the country which his Hancestors so long occupied.

"I have caused one of our inginears to make me a plann of the Squallop Estate, Diddlesexshire, the property of &c. &c., bordered on the North by Lord Bareacres' Country; on the West by Sir Granby Growler; on the South by the Hotion. An Arkytect & Survare, a young feller of great emagination, womb we have employed to make a survey of the Great Caffranan line, has built me a beautiful Villar (on paper), Plushton Hall, Diddlesex, the seat of I de la P., Esquire. The house is reprasented a handsome Itallian Structer, imbusmd in woods, and circumwented by beautiful gardings. Theres a lake in front with boatsful of nobillaty and musitions floting on its placid sufface—and a curricle is a driving up to the grand hentrance, and me in it, with Mrs., or perhaps Lady Hangelana de la Pluche. I speak adwisedly. I

MAY be going to form a noble kinexion. I may be (by marridge) going to unight my family once more with Harrystoxy, from which misfortn has for some sentries separated us. I have dreams of that sort.

"I've sean sevral times in a dalitifle vishn a SERTING ERL, standing in a hattitude of bennydiction, and rattafying my union with a serting butifle young lady, his daughter. Phansy Mr. or Sir Jeames and lady Hangelina de la Pluche! Ho! what will the old washywoman, my grandmother, say? She may sell her mangle then, and shall too by my honor as a Gent."

"As for Squallop Hill, its not to be emadgind that I was going to give 5000 lb. for a bleak mounting like that, unless I had some ideer in vew. Ham I not a Director of the Grand Diddlesex? Don't Squallop lie amediately betwigst Old Bone House, Single Gloster, and Scrag End, through which cities our line passes? I will have 400,000 lb. for that mounting, or my name is not Jeames. I have arranged a little barging too for my friend the Erl. The line will pass through a hangle of Bareacre Park. He shall have a good compensation I promis you; and then I shall get back the 3000 I lent him. His banker's acount, I fear, is in a horrid state."

[The Diary now for several days contains particulars of no interest to the public:—Memoranda of City dinners—meetings of Directors—fashionable parties in which Mr. Jeames figures, and nearly always by the side of his new friend, Lord Bareacres, whose "pompossaty," as previously described, seems to have almost entirely subsided.]

We then come to the following:—

"With a prowd and thankfle Art, I copy off this morning's Gayzett the following news:—

"'Commission signed by the Lord Lieutenant of the County of Diddlesex.

"'JAMES AUGUSTUS DE LA PLUCHE, Esquire, to be Deputy Lieutenant.'"

"'North Diddlesex Regiment of Yeomanry Cavalry.

"'James Augustus de la Pluche, Esquire, to be Captain, vice Blowhard, promoted.'"

"And his it so? Ham I indeed a landed propriator—a Deppaty Leftnant—a Capting? May I hatend the Cort of my Sovring? and dror a sayber in my country's defens? I wish the French WOOD land, and me at the head of my squadring on my hoss Desparation. How I'd extonish 'em! How the gals will stare when they see me in youniform! How Mary Hann would—but nonsince! I'm halways thinking of that pore gal. She's left Sir John's. She couldn't abear to stay after I went, I've heerd say. I hope she's got a good place. Any sumn of money that would sett her up in bisniss, or make her comfarable, I'd come down with like a mann. I told my granmother so, who sees her, and rode down to Healing on porpose on Desparation to leave a five lb. noat in an anvylope. But she's sent it back, sealed with a thimbill."

Tuesday.—Reseaved the folliong letter from Lord B—, rellatiff to my presntation at Cort and the Youniform I shall wear on that hospicious seramony:—

"'MY DEAR DE LA PLUCHE,—I THINK you had better be presented as a Deputy Lieutenant. As for the Diddlesex Yeomanry, I hardly know what the uniform is now. The last time we were out was in 1803, when the Prince of Wales reviewed us, and when we wore French gray jackets, leathers, red morocco boots, crimson pelisses, brass helmets with leopard-skin and a white plume, and the regulation pig-tail of eighteen inches. That dress will hardly answer at present, and must be modified, of coarse. We were called the White Feathers, in those days. For my part, I decidedly recommend the Deputy Lieutenant.

"'I shall be happy to present you at the Levee and at the Drawing-room. Lady Bareacres will be in town for the 13th, with Angelina, who will be presented on that day. My wife has heard much of you, and is anxious to make your acquaintance.

"'All my people are backward with their rents: for heaven's sake, my dear fellow, lend me five hundred and oblige

"'Yours, very gratefully,

"'BAREACRES.'

"Note.—Bareacres may press me about the Depity Leftnant; but I'M for the cavvlery."

"Jewly will always be a sacrid anniwussary with me. It was in that month that I became persnally ecquaintid with my Prins and my gracious Sovarink.

"Long before the hospitious event acurd, you may imadgin that my busm was in no triffling flutter. Sleaplis of nights, I past them thinking of the great ewent—or if igsosted natur DID clothes my highlids—the eyedear of my waking thoughts pevaded my slummers. Corts, Erls, presntations, Goldstix, gracious Sovarinx mengling in my dreembs unceasnly. I blush to say it (for humin prisumpshn never surely igseeded that of my wicked wickid vishn), one night I actially dremt that Her R. H. the Princess Hallis was grown up, and that there was a Cabinit Counsel to detummin whether her & was to be bestoad on me or the Prins of Sax-Muffinhausen-Pumpenstein, a young Prooshn or Germing zion of nobillaty. I ask umly parding for this hordacious ideer.

"I said, in my fommer remarx, that I had detummined to be presented to the notus of my reveared Sovaring in a melintary coschewm. The Court-shoots in which Sivillians attend a Levy are so uncomming like the—the—livries (ojous wud! I 8 to put it down) I used to wear before entering sosiaty, that I couldn't abide the notium of wearing one. My detummination was fumly fixt to apeer as a Yominry Cavilry Hoffiser, in the galleant youniform of the North Diddlesex Huzzas.

"Has that redgmint had not been out sins 1803, I thought myself quite hotherized to make such halterations in the youniform as shuited the presnt time and my metured and elygint taste. Pig-tales was out of the question. Tites I was detummind to mintain. My legg is praps the finist pint about me, and I was risolved not to hide it under a booshle.

"I phixt on scarlit tites, then, imbridered with goold, as I have seen Widdicomb wear them at Hashleys when me and Mary Hann used to go there. Ninety-six guineas worth of rich goold lace and cord did I have myhandering hall hover those shoperb inagspressables.

"Yellow marocky Heshn boots, red eels, goold spurs and goold tassels as bigg as belpulls.

"Jackit—French gray and silver oringe fasings & cuphs, according to the old patn; belt, green and goold, tight round my pusn, & settin hoff the cemetry of my figgar NOT DISADVINTAJUSLY.

"A huzza paleese of pupple velvit & sable fir. A sayber of Demaskus steal, and a sabertash (in which I kep my Odiclone and imbridered pocket ankercher), kimpleat my acooterments, which, without vannaty, was, I flatter myself, UNEAK.

"But the crownding triumph was my hat. I couldnt wear a cock At. The huzzahs dont use 'em. I wouldnt wear the hojous old brass Elmet & Leppardskin. I choas a hat which is dear to the memry of hevery Brittn; an at which was inwented by my Feeld Marshle and adord Prins; an At which VULGAR PREJIDIS & JOAKING has in vane etempted to run down. I chose the HALBERT AT. I didn't tell Bareacres of this egsabishn of loilty, intending to SURPRISE him. The white ploom of the West Diddlesex Yomingry I fixt on the topp of this Shacko, where it spread hout like a shaving-brush.

"You may be sure that befor the fatle day arrived, I didnt niglect to practus my part well; and had sevral REHUSTLES, as they say.

"This was the way. I used to dress myself in my full togs. I made Fitzwarren, my boddy servnt, stand at the dor, and figger as the Lord in Waiting. I put Mrs. Bloker, my laundress, in my grand harm chair to reprasent the horgust pusn of my Sovring; Frederick, my secknd man, standing on her left, in the hattatude of an illustrus Prins Consort. Hall the Candles were lighted. 'Captain de la Pluche, presented by Herl Bareacres,' Fitzwarren, my man, igsclaimed, as adwancing I made obasins to the Thrown. Nealin on one nee, I cast a glans of unhuttarable loilty towards the British Crownd, then stepping gracefully hup, (my Dimascus Simiter WOULD git betwigst my ligs, in so doink, which at fust was wery disagreeble)—rising hup grasefly, I say, I flung a look of manly but respeckfl hommitch tords my Prins, and then ellygntly ritreated backards out of the Roil Presents. I kep my 4 suvnts hup for 4 hours at this gaym the night before my presntation, and yet I was the fust to be hup with the sunrice. I COODNT sleep that night. By abowt six o'clock in the morning I was drest in my full uniform; and I didnt know how to pass the interveaning hours.

"'My Granmother hasnt seen me in full phigg,' says I. 'It will rejoice that pore old sole to behold one of her race so suxesfle in life. Has I ave read in the novle of "Kennleworth," that the Herl goes down in Cort dress and extoneshes Hamy Robsart, I will go down in all my splender and astownd my old washywoman of a Granmother.' To make this detummination; to horder my Broom; to knock down Frederick the groomb for delaying to bring it; was with me the wuck of a momint. The next sor as galliant a cavyleer as hever rode in a cabb, skowering the road to Healing.

"I arrived at the well-known cottitch. My huncle was habsent with the cart; but the dor of the humble eboad stood hopen, and I passed through the little garding where the close was hanging out to dry. My snowy ploom was ableeged to bend under the lowly porch, as I hentered the apartmint.

"There was a smell of tea there—there's always a smell of tea there—the old lady was at her Bohee as usual. I advanced tords her; but ha! phansy my extonishment when I sor Mary Hann!

"I halmost faintid with himotion. 'Ho, Jeames!' (she has said to me subsquintly) 'mortial mann never looked so bewtifle as you did when you arrived on the day of the Levy. You were no longer mortial, you were diwine!'

"R! what little Justas the hartist has done to my mannly etractions in the groce carriketure he's made of me." *

"Nothing, perhaps, ever created so great a sensashun as my hentrance to St. Jeames's, on the day of the Levy. The Tuckish Hambasdor himself was not so much remarked as my shuperb turn out.

"As a Millentary man, and a North Diddlesex Huzza, I was resolved to come to the ground on HOSSBACK. I had Desparation phigd out as a charger, and got 4 Melentery dresses from Ollywell Street, in which I drest my 2 men (Fitzwarren, hout of livry, woodnt stand it,) and 2 fellers from Rimles, where my hosses stand at livry. I rode up St. Jeames's Street, with my 4 Hadycongs—the people huzzaying—the gals waving their hankerchers, as if I were a Foring Prins—hall the winders crowdid to see me pass.

"The guard must have taken me for a Hempror at least, when I came, for the drums beat, and the guard turned out and seluted me with presented harms.

"What a momink of triumth it was! I sprung myjestickly from Desperation. I gav the rains to one of my horderlies, and, salewting the crowd, I past into the presnts of my Most Gracious Mrs.

"You, peraps, may igspect that I should narrait at lenth the suckmstanzas of my hawjince with the British Crown. But I am not one who would gratafy IMPUTTNINT CURAIOSATY. Rispect for our reckonized instatewtions is my fust quallaty. I, for one, will dye rallying round my Thrown.

"Suffise it to say, when I stood in the Horgust Presnts,—when I sor on the right & of my Himperial Sovring that Most Gracious Prins, to admire womb has been the chief Objick of my life, my busum was seased with an imotium which my Penn rifewses to dixcribe—my trembling knees halmost rifused their hoffis—I reckleck nothing mor until I was found phainting in the harms of the Lord Chamberling. Sir Robert Peal apnd to be standing by (I knew our wuthy Primmier by Punch's pictures of him, igspecially his ligs), and he was conwussing with a man of womb I shall say nothink, but that he is a hero of 100 fites, AND HEVERY FITE HE FIT HE ONE. Nead I say that I elude to Harthur of Wellingting? I introjuiced myself to these Jents, and intend to improve the equaintance, and peraps ast Guvmint for a Barnetcy.

"But there was ANOTHER pusn womb on this droring-room I fust had the inagspressable dalite to beold. This was that Star of fashing, that Sinecure of neighboring i's, as Milting observes, the ecomplisht Lady Hangelina Thistlewood, daughter of my exlent frend, John George Godfrey de Bullion Thistlewood, Earl of Bareacres, Baron Southdown, in the Peeridge of the United Kingdom, Baron Haggismore, in Scotland, K.T., Lord Leftnant of the County of Diddlesex, &c. &c. This young lady was with her Noble Ma, when I was kinducted tords her. And surely never lighted on this hearth a more delightfle vishn. In that gallixy of Bewty the Lady Hangelina was the fairest Star—in that reath of Loveliness the sweetest Rosebud! Pore Mary Hann, my Art's young affeckshns had been senterd on thee; but like water through a sivv, her immidge disappeared in a momink, and left me intransd in the presnts of Hangelina.

"Lady Bareacres made me a myjestick bow—a grand and hawfle pusnage her Ladyship is, with a Roming Nose, and an enawmus ploom of Hostridge phethers; the fare Hangelina smiled with a sweetness perfickly bewhildring, and said, 'O, Mr. De la Pluche, I'm so delighted to make your acquaintance. I have often heard of you.'

"'Who,' says I, 'has mentioned my insiggnifficknt igsistance to the fair Lady Hangelina? kel bonure igstrame poor mwaw!' (For you see I've not studdied 'Pelham' for nothink, and have lunt a few French phraces, without which no Gent of fashn speaks now.)

"'O,' replies my lady, 'it was Papa first; and then a very, VERY old friend of yours.'

"'Whose name is,' says I, pusht on by my stoopid curawsaty—

"'Hoggins—Mary Ann Hoggins'—ansurred my lady (laffing phit to splitt her little sides). 'She is my maid, Mr. De la Pluche, and I'm afraid you are a very sad, sad person.'

"'A mere baggytell,' says I. 'In fommer days I WAS equainted with that young woman; but haltered suckmstancies have sepparated us for hever, and mong cure is irratreevably perdew elsewhere.'

"'Do tell me all about it. Who is it? When was it? We are all dying to know."

"'Since about two minnits, and the Ladys name begins with a HA,' says I, looking her tendarly in the face, and conjring up hall the fassanations of my smile.

"'Mr. De la Pluche,' here said a gentleman in whiskers and mistashes standing by, 'hadn't you better take your spurs out of the Countess of Bareacres' train?'—'Never mind Mamma's train' (said Lady Hangelina): 'this is the great Mr. De la Pluche, who is to make all our fortunes—yours too. Mr. de la Pluche, let me present you to Captain George Silvertop,'—The Capting bent just one jint of his back very slitely; I retund his stare with equill hottiness. 'Go and see for Lady Bareacres' carridge, George,' says his Lordship; and vispers to me, 'a cousin of ours—a poor relation.' So I took no notis of the feller when he came back, nor in my subsquint visits to Hill Street, where it seems a knife and fork was laid reglar for this shabby Capting."

"Thusday Night.—O Hangelina, Hangelina, my pashn for you hogments daily! I've bean with her two the Hopra. I sent her a bewtifle Camellia Jyponiky from Covn Garding, with a request she would wear it in her raving Air. I woar another in my butnole. Evns, what was my sattusfackshn as I leant hover her chair, and igsammined the house with my glas!

"She was as sulky and silent as pawsble, however—would scarcely speek; although I kijoled her with a thowsnd little plesntries. I spose it was because that wulgar raskle Silvertop WOOD stay in the box. As if he didn't know (Lady B.'s as deaf as a poast and counts for nothink) that people SOMETIMES like a tatytaty."

"Friday.—I was sleepless all night. I gave went to my feelings in the folloring lines—there's a hair out of Balfe's Hopera that she's fond of. I edapted them to that mellady.

"She was in the droring-room alone with Lady B. She was wobbling at the pyanna as I hentered. I flung the convasation upon mewsick; said I sung myself (I've ad lesns lately of Signor Twankydillo); and, on her rekwesting me to faver her with somethink, I bust out with my pom:

"'WHEN MOONLIKE OER THE HAZURE SEAS.

"'When moonlike ore the hazure seas

In soft effulgence swells,
When silver jews and balmy breaze
Bend down the Lily's bells;
When calm and deap, the rosy sleap
Has lapt your soal in dreems,
R Hangeline! R lady mine!
Dost thou remember Jeames?


"'I mark thee in the Marble All,
Where Englands loveliest shine—
I say the fairest of them hall
Is Lady Hangeline.
My soul, in desolate eclipse,
With recollection teems—
And then I hask, with weeping lips
Dost thou remember Jeames?


"'Away! I may not tell thee hall
This soughring heart endures—
There is a lonely sperrit-call
That Sorrow never cures;
There is a little, little Star,
That still above me beams;
It is the Star of Hope—but ar!
Dost thou remember Jeames?'

"When I came to the last words, 'Dost thou remember Je-e-e-ams?' I threw such an igspresshn of unuttrable tenderniss into the shake at the hend, that Hangelina could bare it no more. A bust of uncumtrollable emotium seized her. She put her ankercher to her face and left the room. I heard her laffing and sobbing histerickly in the bedwor.

"O Hangelina—My adord one, My Arts joy!" . . .

"BAREACRES, me, the ladies of the famly, with their sweet Southdown, B's eldest son, and George Silvertop, the shabby Capting (who seems to git leaf from his ridgmint whenhever he likes,) have beene down into Diddlesex for a few days, enjying the spawts of the feald there.

"Never having done much in the gunning line (since when a hinnasent boy, me and Jim Cox used to go out at Healing, and shoot sparrers in the Edges with a pistle)—I was reyther dowtfle as to my suxes as a shot, and practusd for some days at a stoughd bird in a shooting gallery, which a chap histed up and down with a string. I sugseaded in itting the hannimle pretty well. I bought Awker's 'Shooting-Guide,' two double-guns at Mantings, and selected from the French prints of fashn the most gawjus and ellygant sportting ebillyment. A lite blue velvet and goold cap, woar very much on one hear, a cravatt of yaller & green imbroidered satting, a weskit of the McGrigger plaid, & a jacket of the McWhirter tartn, (with large, motherapurl butns, engraved with coaches & osses, and sporting subjix,) high leather gayters, and marocky shooting shoes, was the simple hellymence of my costewm, and I flatter myself set hoff my figger in rayther a fayverable way. I took down none of my own pusnal istablishmint except Fitzwarren, my hone mann, and my grooms, with Desparation and my curricle osses, and the Fourgong containing my dressing-case and close.

"I was heverywhere introjuiced in the county as the great Railroad Cappitlist, who was to make Diddlesex the most prawsperous districk of the hempire. The squires prest forrards to welcome the new comer amongst 'em; and we had a Hagricultural Meating of the Bareacres tenantry, where I made a speech droring tears from heavery i. It was in compliment to a layborer who had brought up sixteen children, and lived sixty years on the istate on seven bobb a week. I am not prowd, though I know my station. I shook hands with that mann in lavinder kidd gloves. I told him that the purshuit of hagriculture wos the noblist hockupations of humannaty: I spoke of the yoming of Hengland, who (under the command of my hancisters) had conquered at Hadjincourt & Cressy; and I gave him a pair of new velveteen inagspressables, with two and six in each pocket, as a reward for three score years of labor. Fitzwarren, my man, brought them forrards on a satting cushing. Has I sat down defning chears selewted the horator; the band struck up 'The Good Old English Gentleman.' I looked to the ladies galry; my Hangelina waived her ankasher and kissd her &; and I sor in the distans that pore Mary Hann efected evidently to tears by my ellaquints."

"What an adwance that gal has made since she's been in Lady Hangelina's company! Sins she wears her young lady's igsploded gownds and retired caps and ribbings, there's an ellygance abowt her which is puffickly admarable; and which, haddid to her own natral bewty & sweetniss, creates in my boozum serting sensatiums . . . Shor! I MUSTN'T give way to fealinx unwuthy of a member of the aristoxy. What can she be to me but a mear recklection—a vishn of former ears?

"I'm blest if I didn mistake her for Hangelina herself yesterday. I met her in the grand Collydore of Bareacres Castle. I sor a lady in a melumcolly hattatude gacing outawinder at the setting sun, which was eluminating the fair parx and gardings of the ancient demean.

"'Bewchus Lady Hangelina,' says I—'A penny for your Ladyship's thought,' says I.

"'Ho, Jeames! Ho, Mr. De la Pluche!' hansered a well-known vice, with a haxnt of sadnis which went to my art. 'YOU know what my thoughts are, well enough. I was thinking of happy, happy old times, when both of us were poo—poo—oor,' says Mary Hann, busting out in a phit of crying, a thing I can't ebide. I took her and tried to cumft her: I pinted out the diffrents of our sitawashns; igsplained to her that proppaty has its jewties as well as its previletches, and that MY juty clearly was to marry into a noble family. I kep on talking to her (she sobbing and going hon hall the time) till Lady Hangelina herself came up—'The real Siming Pewer,' as they say in the play.

"There they stood together—them two young women. I don't know which is the ansamest. I coodn help comparing them; and I coodnt help comparing myself to a certing Hannimle I've read of, that found it difficklt to make a choice betwigst 2 Bundles of A."

"That ungrateful beest Fitzwarren—my oan man—a feller I've maid a fortune for—a feller I give 100 lb. per hannum to!—a low bred Wallydyshamber! HE must be thinking of falling in love too! and treating me to his imperence.

"He's a great big athlatic feller—six foot i, with a pair of black whiskers like air-brushes—with a look of a Colonel in the harmy—a dangerous pawmpus-spoken raskle I warrunt you. I was coming ome from shuiting this hafternoon—and passing through Lady Hangelina's flour-garding, who should I see in the summerouse, but Mary Hann pretending to em an ankyshr and Mr. Fitzwarren paying his cort to her?

"'You may as well have me, Mary Hann,' says he. 'I've saved money. We'll take a public-house and I'll make a lady of you. I'm not a purse-proud ungrateful fellow like Jeames—who's such a snob ['such a SNOB' was his very words!) that I'm ashamed to wait on him—who's the laughing stock of all the gentry and the housekeeper's room too—try a MAN,' says he—'don't be taking on about such a humbug as Jeames.'

"Here young Joe the keaper's sun, who was carrying my bagg, bust out a laffing thereby causing Mr. Fitwarren to turn round and intarupt this polite convasation.

"I was in such a rayge. 'Quit the building, Mary Hann,' says I to the young woman—and you, Mr. Fitzwarren, have the goodness to remain.'

"'I give you warning,' roars he, looking black, blue, yaller—all the colors of the ranebo.

"'Take off your coat, you imperent, hungrateful scoundrl,' says I.

"'It's not your livery,' says he.

"'Peraps you'll understand me, when I take off my own,' says I, unbuttoning the motherapurls of the MacWhirter tartn. 'Take my jackit, Joe,' says I to the boy,—and put myself in a hattitude about which there was NO MISTAYK.

"He's 2 stone heavier than me—and knows the use of his ands as well as most men; but in a fite, BLOOD'S EVERYTHINK: the Snobb can't stand before the gentleman; and I should have killed him, I've little doubt, but they came and stopt the fite betwigst us before we'd had more than 2 rounds.

"I punisht the raskle tremenjusly in that time, though; and I'm writing this in my own sittn-room, not being able to come down to dinner on account of a black-eye I've got, which is sweld up and disfiggrs me dreadfl."

"On account of the hoffle black i which I reseaved in my rangcounter with the hinfimus Fitzwarren, I kep my roomb for sevral days, with the rose-colored curtings of the apartmint closed, so as to form an agreeable twilike; and a light-bloo sattin shayd over the injard pheacher. My woons was thus made to become me as much as pawsable; and (has the Poick well observes 'Nun but the Brayv desuvs the Fare') I cumsoled myself in the sasiaty of the ladies for my tempory disfiggarment.

"It was Mary Hann who summind the House and put an end to my phisticoughs with Fitzwarren. I licked him and bare him no mallis: but of corse I dismist the imperent scoundrill from my suvvis, apinting Adolphus, my page, to his post of confidenshle Valley.

"Mary Hann and her young and lovely Mrs. kep paying me continyoul visits during my retiremint. Lady Hangelina was halways sending me messidges by her: while my exlent friend, Lady Bareacres (on the contry) was always sending me toakns of affeckshn by Hangelina. Now it was a coolin hi-lotium, inwented by herself, that her Ladyship would perscribe—then, agin, it would be a booky of flowers (my favrit polly hanthuses, pellagoniums, and jyponikys), which none but the fair &s of Hangelina could dispose about the chamber of the hinvyleed. Ho! those dear mothers! when they wish to find a chans for a galliant young feller, or to ixtablish their dear gals in life, what awpertunities they WILL give a man! You'd have phansied I was so hill (on account of my black hi), that I couldnt live exsep upon chicking and spoon-meat, and jellies, and blemonges, and that I coudnt eat the latter dellixies (which I ebomminate onternoo, prefurring a cut of beaf or muttn to hall the kickpshaws of France), unless Hangelina brought them. I et 'em, and sacrafised myself for her dear sayk.

"I may stayt here that in privit convasations with old Lord B. and his son, I had mayd my proposals for Hangelina, and was axepted, and hoped soon to be made the appiest gent in Hengland.

"'You must break the matter gently to her,' said her hexlent father. 'You have my warmest wishes, my dear Mr. De la Pluche, and those of my Lady Bareacres; but I am not—not quite certain about Lady Angelina's feelings. Girls are wild and romantic. They do not see the necessity of prudent establishments, and I have never yet been able to make Angelina understand the embarrassments of her family. These silly creatures prate about love and a cottage, and despise advantages which wiser heads than theirs know how to estimate.'

"'Do you mean that she aint fassanated by me?' says I, bursting out at this outrayjus ideer.

"'She WILL be, my dear sir. You have already pleased her,—your admirable manners must succeed in captivating her, and a fond father's wishes will be crowned on the day in which you enter our family.'

"'Recklect, gents,' says I to the 2 lords,—'a barging's a barging—I'll pay hoff Southdown's Jews, when I'm his brother. As a STRAYNGER'—(this I said in a sarcastickle toan)—'I wouldn't take such a LIBBATY. When I'm your suninlor I'll treble the valyou of your estayt. I'll make your incumbrinces as right as a trivit, and restor the ouse of Bareacres to its herly splender. But a pig in a poak is not the way of transacting bisniss imployed by Jeames De la Pluche, Esquire.'

"And I had a right to speak in this way. I was one of the greatest scrip-holders in Hengland; and calclated on a kilossle fortune. All my shares were rising immence. Every poast brot me noose that I was sevral thowsands richer than the day befor. I was detummind not to reerlize till the proper time, and then to buy istates; to found a new family of Delapluches, and to alie myself with the aristoxy of my country.

"These pints I represented to pore Mary Hann hover and hover agin. 'If you'd been Lady Hangelina, my dear gal,' says I, 'I would have married you: and why don't I? Because my dooty prewents me. I'm a marter to dooty; and you, my pore gal, must cumsole yorself with that ideer.'

"There seemed to be a consperracy, too, between that Silvertop and Lady Hangelina to drive me to the same pint. 'What a plucky fellow you were, Pluche,' says he (he was rayther more familiar than I liked), 'in your fight with Fitzwarren—to engage a man of twice your strength and science, though you were sure to be beaten' (this is an etroashous folsood: I should have finnisht Fitz in 10 minnits), 'for the sake of poor Mary Hann! That's a generous fellow. I like to see a man risen to eminence like you, having his heart in the right place. When is to be the marriage, my boy?'

"'Capting S.' says I, 'my marridge consunns your most umble servnt a precious sight more than you;'—and I gev him to understand I didn't want him to put in HIS ore—I wasn't afrayd of his whiskers, I prommis you, Capting as he was. I'm a British Lion, I am as brayv as Bonypert, Hannible, or Holiver Crummle, and would face bagnits as well as any Evy drigoon of 'em all.

"Lady Hangelina, too, igspawstulated in her hartfl way. 'Mr. De la Pluche (seshee), why, why press this point? You can't suppose that you will be happy with a person like me?'

"'I adoar you, charming gal!' says I. 'Never, never go to say any such thing.'

"'You adored Mary Ann first,' answers her ladyship; 'you can't keep your eyes off her now. If any man courts her you grow so jealous that you begin beating him. You will break the girl's heart if you don't marry her, and perhaps some one else's—but you don't mind THAT.'

"'Break yours, you adoarible creature! I'd die first! And as for Mary Hann, she will git over it; people's arts aint broakn so easy. Once for all, suckmstances is changed betwigst me and er. It's a pang to part with her' (says I, my fine hi's filling with tears), 'but part from her I must.'

"It was curius to remark abowt that singlar gal, Lady Hangelina, that melumcolly as she was when she was talking to me, and ever so disml—yet she kep on laffing every minute like the juice and all.

"'What a sacrifice!' says she; 'it's like Napoleon giving up Josephine. What anguish it must cause to your susceptible heart!'

"'It does,' says I—'Hagnies!' (Another laff.)

"'And if—if I don't accept you—you will invade the States of the Emperor, my papa, and I am to be made the sacrifice and the occasion of peace between you!'

"'I don't know what you're eluding to about Joseyfeen and Hemperors your Pas; but I know that your Pa's estate is over hedaneers morgidged; that if some one don't elp him, he's no better than an old pawper; that he owes me a lot of money; and that I'm the man that can sell him up hoss & foot; or set him up agen—THAT'S what I know, Lady Hangelina,' says I, with a hair as much as to say, 'Put THAT in your ladyship's pipe and smoke it.'

"And so I left her, and nex day a serting fashnable paper enounced—

"'MARRIAGE IN HIGH LIFE.—We hear that a matrimonial union is on the tapis between a gentleman who has made a colossal fortune in the Railway World, and the only daughter of a noble earl, whose estates are situated in D–ddles-x. An early day is fixed for this interesting event.'"

"Contry to my expigtations (but when or ow can we reckn upon the fealinx of wimming?) Mary Hann didn't seem to be much efected by the hideer of my marridge with Hangelinar. I was rayther disapinted peraps that the fickle young gal reckumsiled herself so easy to give me hup, for we Gents are creechers of vannaty after all, as well as those of the hopsit secks; and betwigst you and me there WAS mominx, when I almost wisht that I'd been borne a Myommidn or Turk, when the Lor would have permitted me to marry both these sweet beinx, whereas I was now condemd to be appy with ony one.

"Meanwild everythink went on very agreeable betwigst me and my defianced bride. When we came back to town I kemishnd Mr. Showery the great Hoctionear to look out for a town maushing sootable for a gent of my qualaty. I got from the Erald Hoffis (not the Mawning Erald—no, no, I'm not such a Mough as to go THERE for ackrit infamation) an account of my famly, my harms and pedigry.

"I hordered in Long Hacre, three splendid equipidges, on which my arms and my adord wife's was drawn & quartered; and I got portricks of me and her paynted by the sellabrated Mr. Shalloon, being resolved to be the gentleman in all things, and knowing that my character as a man of fashn wasn't compleat unless I sat to that dixtinguished Hartist. My likenis I presented to Hangelina. It's not considered flattring—and though SHE parted with it, as you will hear, mighty willingly, there's ONE young lady (a thousand times handsomer) that values it as the happle of her hi.

"Would any man beleave that this picture was soald at my sale for about a twenty-fifth part of what it cost me? It was bought in by Maryhann, though: 'O dear Jeames,' says she, often (kissing of it & pressing it to her art), 'it isn't ansum enough for you, and hasn't got your angellick smile and the igspreshn of your dear dear i's.'

"Hangelina's pictur was kindly presented to me by Countess B., her mamma, though of coarse I paid for it. It was engraved for the 'Book of Bewty' the same year.

"With such a perfusion of ringlits I should scarcely have known her—but the ands, feat, and i's, was very like. She was painted in a gitar supposed to be singing one of my little melladies; and her brother Southdown, who is one of the New England poits, wrote the follering stanzys about her:—

"LINES UPON MY SISTER'S PORTRAIT.

"BY THE LORD SOUTHDOWN.

"The castle towers of Bareacres are fair upon the lea,
Where the cliffs of bonny Diddlesex rise up from out the sea:
I stood upon the donjon keep and view'd the country o'er,
 I saw the lands of Bareacres for fifty miles or more.
I stood upon the donjon keep—it is a sacred place,—
Where floated for eight hundred years the banner of my race;
Argent, a dexter sinople, and gules an azure field,
There ne'er was nobler cognizance on knightly warrior's shield.

"The first time England saw the shield 'twas round a Norman neck,
On board a ship from Valery, King William was on deck.
A Norman lance the colors wore, in Hastings' fatal fray—St.
Willibald for Bareacres! 'twas double gules that day!
O Heaven and sweet St. Willibald! in many a battle since
A loyal-hearted Bareacres has ridden by his Prince!
At Acre with Plantagenet, with Edward at Poitiers,
The pennon of the Bareacres was foremost on the spears!

"'Twas pleasant in the battle-shock to hear our war-cry ringing:
O grant me, sweet St. Willibald, to listen to such singing!
Three hundred steel-clad gentlemen, we drove the foe before us,
And thirty score of British bows kept twanging to the chorus!
O knights, my noble ancestors! and shall I never hear
Saint Willibald for Bareacres through battle ringing clear?

I'd cut me off this strong right hand a single hour to ride,
And strike a blow for Bareacres, my fathers, at your side!

"Dash down, dash down, yon Mandolin, beloved sister mine!
Those blushing lips may never sing the glories of our line:
Our ancient castles echo to the clumsy feet of churls,
The spinning Jenny houses in the mansion of our Earls.
Sing not, sing not, my Angeline! in days so base and vile,
'Twere sinful to be happy, 'twere sacrilege to smile.
I'll hie me to my lonely hall, and by its cheerless hob
I'll muse on other days, and wish—and wish I were.—A SNOB."

"All young Hengland, I'm told, considers the poim bewtifle. They're always writing about battleaxis and shivvlery, these young chaps; but the ideer of Southdown in a shoot of armer, and his cuttin hoff his 'strong right hand,' is rayther too good; the feller is about 5 fit hi,—as ricketty as a babby, with a vaist like a gal; and though he may have the art and curridge of a Bengal tyger, I'd back my smallest cab-boy to lick him,—that is, if I AD a cab-boy. But io! MY cab-days is over.

"Be still my hagnizing Art! I now am about to hunfoald the dark payges of the Istry of my life!"

"My friends! you've seen me ither in the full kerear of Fortn, prawsprus but not hover prowd of my prawsperraty; not dizzy though mounted on the haypix of Good Luck—feasting hall the great (like the Good Old Henglish Gent in the song, which he has been my moddle and igsample through life), but not forgitting the small—No, my beayvior to my granmother at Healing shows that. I bot her a new donkey cart (what the French call a cart-blansh) and a handsome set of peggs for anging up her linning, and treated Huncle Bill to a new shoot of close, which he ordered in St. Jeames's Street, much to the estonishment of my Snyder there, namely an olliffgreen velvyteen jackit and smalclose, and a crimsn plush weskoat with glas-buttns. These pints of genarawsaty in my disposishn I never should have eluded to, but to show that I am naturally of a noble sort, and have that kind of galliant carridge which is equel to either good or bad forting.

"What was the substns of my last chapter? In that everythink was prepayred for my marridge—the consent of the parents of my Hangelina was gaynd, the lovely gal herself was ready (as I thought) to be led to Himing's halter—the trooso was hordered—the wedding dressis were being phitted hon—a weddinkake weighing half a tunn was a gettn reddy by Mesurs Gunter of Buckley Square; there was such an account for Shantilly and Honiton laces as would have staggerd hennyboddy (I know they did the Commissioner when I came hup for my Stiffikit), and has for Injar-shawls I bawt a dozen sich fine ones as never was given away—no not by Hiss Iness the Injan Prins Juggernaut Tygore. The juils (a pearl and dimind shoot) were from the establishmint of Mysurs Storr and Mortimer. The honey-moon I intended to pass in a continentle excussion, and was in treaty for the ouse at Halberd-gate (hopsit Mr. Hudson's) as my town-house. I waited to cumclude the putchis untle the Share-Markit which was rayther deprest (oing I think not so much to the atax of the misrable Times as to the prodidjus flams of the Morning Erald) was restored to its elthy toan. I wasn't goin to part with scrip which was 20 primmium at 2 or 3: and bein confidnt that the Markit would rally, had bought very largely for the two or three new accounts.

"This will explane to those unfortnight traydsmen to womb I gayv orders for a large igstent ow it was that I couldn't pay their accounts. I am the soal of onour—but no gent can pay when he has no money—it's not MY fault if that old screw Lady Bareacres cabbidged three hundred yards of lace, and kep back 4 of the biggest diminds and seven of the largist Injar Shawls—it's not MY fault if the tradespeople didn git their goods back, and that Lady B. declared they were LOST. I began the world afresh with the close on my back, and thirteen and six in money, concealing nothink, giving up heverythink, Onist and undismayed, and though beat, with pluck in me still, and ready to begin agin.

"Well—it was the day before that apinted for my Unium. The 'Ringdove' steamer was lying at Dover ready to carry us hoff. The Bridle apartmince had been hordered at Salt Hill, and subsquintly at Balong sur Mare—the very table cloth was laid for the weddn brexfst in Ill Street, and the Bride's Right Reverend Huncle, the Lord Bishop of Bullocksmithy, had arrived to sellabrayt our unium. All the papers were full of it. Crowds of the fashnable world went to see the trooso, and admire the Carridges in Long Hacre. Our travleng charrat (light bloo lined with pink satting, and vermillium and goold weals) was the hadmaration of all for quiet ellygns. We were to travel only 4, viz. me, my lady, my vally, and Mary Hann as famdyshamber to my Hangelina. Far from oposing our match, this worthy gal had quite givn into it of late, and laught and joakt, and enjoyd our plans for the fewter igseedinkly.

"I'd left my lovely Bride very gay the night before—aving a multachewd of bisniss on, and Stockbrokers' and bankers' accounts to settle: atsettrey atsettrey. It was layt before I got these in horder: my sleap was feavrish, as most mens is when they are going to be marrid or to be hanged. I took my chocklit in bed about one: tride on my wedding close, and found as ushle that they became me exeedingly.

"One thing distubbed my mind—two weskts had been sent home. A blush-white satting and gold, and a kinary colored tabbinet imbridered in silver: which should I wear on the hospicious day? This hadgitated and perplext me a good deal. I detummined to go down to Hill Street and cumsult the Lady whose wishis were henceforth to be my HALLINALL; and wear whichever SHE phixt on.

"There was a great bussel and distubbans in the Hall in Ill Street: which I etribyouted to the eproaching event. The old porter stared meost uncommon when I kem in—the footman who was to enounce me laft I thought—I was going up stairs—

"'Her ladyship's not—not at HOME,' says the man; 'and my lady's hill in bed.'

"'Git lunch,' says I, 'I'll wait till Lady Hangelina returns.'

"At this the feller loox at me for a momint with his cheex blown out like a bladder, and then busts out in a reglar guffau! the porter jined in it, the impident old raskle: and Thomas says, slapping his and on his thy, without the least respect—I say, Huffy, old boy! ISN'T this a good un?'

"'Wadyermean, you infunnle scoundrel,' says I, 'hollaring and laffing at me?'

"'Oh, here's Miss Mary Hann coming up,' says Thomas, 'ask HER'—and indeed there came my little Mary Hann tripping down the stairs—her &s in her pockits; and when she saw me, SHE began to blush and look hod & then to grin too.

"'In the name of Imperence,' says I, rushing on Thomas, and collaring him fit to throttle him—'no raskle of a flunky shall insult ME,' and I sent him staggerin up aginst the porter, and both of 'em into the hall-chair with a flopp—when Mary Hann, jumping down, says, 'O James! O Mr. Plush! read this'—and she pulled out a billy doo.

"I reckanized the and-writing of Hangelina."

"Deseatful Hangelina's billy ran as follows:—

"'I had all along hoped that you would have relinquished pretensions which you must have seen were so disagreeable to me; and have spared me the painful necessity of the step which I am compelled to take. For a long time I could not believe my parents were serious in wishing to sacrifice me, but have in vain entreated them to spare me. I cannot undergo the shame and misery of a union with you. To the very last hour I remonstrated in vain, and only now anticipate by a few hours, my departure from a home from which they themselves were about to expel me.

"'When you receive this, I shall be united to the person to whom, as you are aware, my heart was given long ago. My parents are already informed of the step I have taken. And I have my own honor to consult, even before their benefit: they will forgive me, I hope and feel, before long.

"'As for yourself, may I not hope that time will calm your exquisite feelings too? I leave Mary Ann behind me to console you. She admires you as you deserve to be admired, and with a constancy which I entreat you to try and imitate. Do, my dear Mr. Plush, try—for the sake of your sincere friend and admirer, A.

"'P.S. I leave the wedding-dresses behind for her: the diamonds are beautiful, and will become Mrs. Plush admirably.'

"This was hall!—Confewshn! And there stood the footmen sniggerin, and that hojus Mary Hann half a cryin, half a laffing at me! 'Who has she gone hoff with?' rors I; and Mary Hann (smiling with one hi) just touched the top of one of the Johns' canes who was goin out with the noats to put hoff the brekfst. It was Silvertop then!

"I bust out of the house in a stayt of diamoniacal igsitement!

"The stoary of that ilorpmint I have no art to tell. Here it is from the Morning Tatler newspaper:—

"ELOPEMENT IN HIGH LIFE.

"THE ONLY AUTHENTIC ACCOUNT.

"The neighborhood of Berkeley Square, and the whole fashionable world, has been thrown into a state of the most painful excitement by an event which has just placed a noble family in great perplexity and affliction.

"It has long been known among the select nobility and gentry that a marriage was on the tapis between the only daughter of a Noble Earl, and a Gentleman whose rapid fortunes in the railway world have been the theme of general remark. Yesterday's paper, it was supposed, in all human probability would have contained an account of the marriage of James De la Pl-che, Esq., and the Lady Angelina —, daughter of the Right honorable the Earl of B-re-cres. The preparations for this ceremony were complete: we had the pleasure of inspecting the rich trousseau (prepared by Miss Twiddler, of Pall Mall); the magnificent jewels from the establishment of Messrs. Storr and Mortimer; the elegant marriage cake, which, already cut up and portioned, is, alas! not destined to be eaten by the friends of Mr. De la Pl-che; the superb carriages, and magnificent liveries, which had been provided in a style of the most lavish yet tasteful sumptuosity. The Right Reverend the Lord Bishop of Bullocksmithy had arrived in town to celebrate the nuptials, and is staying at Mivart's. What must have been the feelings of that venerable prelate, what those of the agonized and noble parents of the Lady Angelina—when it was discovered, on the day previous to the wedding, that her Ladyship had fled the paternal mansion! To the venerable Bishop the news of his noble niece's departure might have been fatal: we have it from the waiters of Mivart's that his Lordship was about to indulge in the refreshment of turtle soup when the news was brought to him; immediate apoplexy was apprehended; but Mr. Macann, the celebrated surgeon of Westminster, was luckily passing through Bond Street at the time, and being promptly called in, bled and relieved the exemplary patient. His Lordship will return to the Palace, Bullocksmithy, tomorrow.

"The frantic agonies of the Right Honorable the Earl of Bareacres can be imagined by every paternal heart. Far be it from us to disturb—impossible is it for us to describe their noble sorrow. Our reporters have made inquiries every ten minutes at the Earl's mansion in Hill Street, regarding the health of the Noble Peer and his incomparable Countess. They have been received with a rudeness which we deplore but pardon. One was threatened with a cane; another, in the pursuit of his official inquiries, was saluted with a pail of water; a third gentleman was menaced in a pugilistic manner by his Lordship's porter; but being of an Irish nation, a man of spirit and sinew, and Master of Arts of Trinity College, Dublin, the gentleman of our establishment confronted the menial, and having severely beaten him, retired to a neighboring hotel much frequented by the domestics of the surrounding nobility, and there obtained what we believe to be the most accurate particulars of this extraordinary occurrence.

"George Frederick Jennings, third footman in the establishment of Lord Bareacres, stated to our employe as follows:—Lady Angelina had been promised to Mr. De la Pluche for near six weeks. She never could abide that gentleman. He was the laughter of all the servants' hall. Previous to his elevation he had himself been engaged in a domestic capacity. At that period he had offered marriage to Mary Ann Hoggins, who was living in the quality of ladies'-maid in the family where Mr. De la P. was employed. Miss Hoggins became subsequently lady's-maid to Lady Angelina—the elopement was arranged between those two. It was Miss Hoggins who delivered the note which informed the bereaved Mr. Plush of his loss.

"Samuel Buttons, page to the Right honorable the Earl of Bareacres, was ordered on Friday afternoon at eleven o'clock to fetch a cabriolet from the stand in Davies Street. He selected the cab No. 19,796, driven by George Gregory Macarty, a one-eyed man from Clonakilty, in the neighborhood of Cork, Ireland (of whom more anon), and waited, according to his instructions, at the corner of Berkeley Square with his vehicle. His young lady, accompanied by her maid, Miss Mary Ann Hoggins, carrying a band-box, presently arrived, and entered the cab with the box: what were the contents of that box we have never been able to ascertain. On asking her Ladyship whether he should order the cab to drive in any particular direction, he was told to drive to Madame Crinoline's, the eminent milliner in Cavendish Square. On requesting to know whether he should accompany her Ladyship, Buttons was peremptorily ordered by Miss Hoggins to go about his business.

"Having now his clue, our reporter instantly went in search of cab 19,796, or rather the driver of that vehicle, who was discovered with no small difficulty at his residence, Whetstone Park, Lincoln's Inn Fields, where he lives with his family of nine children. Having received two sovereigns, instead doubtless of two shillings (his regular fare, by the way, would have been only one-and-eightpence), Macarty had not gone out with the cab for the two last days, passing them in a state of almost ceaseless intoxication. His replies were very incoherent in answer to the queries of our reporter; and, had not that gentleman himself been a compatriot, it is probable he would have refused altogether to satisfy the curiosity of the public.

"At Madame Crinoline's, Miss Hoggins quitted the carriage, and A GENTLEMAN entered it. Macarty describes him as a very CLEVER gentleman (meaning tall) with black moustaches, Oxford-gray trousers, and black hat and a pea-coat. He drove the couple TO THE EUSTON SQUARE STATION, and there left them. How he employed his time subsequently we have stated.

"At the Euston Square Station, the gentleman of our establishment learned from Frederick Corduroy, a porter there, that a gentleman answering the above description had taken places to Derby. We have despatched a confidential gentleman thither, by a special train, and shall give his report in a second edition.

"SECOND EDITION.

"(From our Reporter.)

"NEWCASTLE, Monday.

"I am just arrived at this ancient town, at the 'Elephant and Cucumber Hotel.' A party travelling under the name of MR. AND MRS. JONES, the gentleman wearing moustaches, and having with them a blue band-box, arrived by the train two hours before me, and have posted onwards to SCOTLAND. I have ordered four horses, and write this on the hind boot, as they are putting to.

"THIRD EDITION.

"GRETNA GREEN, Monday Evening.

"The mystery is at length solved. This afternoon, at four o'clock, the Hymeneal Blacksmith, of Gretna Green, celebrated the marriage between George Granby Silvertop, Esq., a Lieutenant in the 150th Hussars, third son of General John Silvertop, of Silvertop Hall, Yorkshire, and Lady Emily Silvertop, daughter of the late sister of the present Earl of Bareacres, and the Lady Angelina Amelia Arethusa Anaconda Alexandrina Alicompania Annemaria Antoinetta, daughter of the last-named Earl Bareacres.

(Here follows a long extract from the Marriage Service in the Book of Common Prayer, which was not read on the occasion, and need not be repeated here.)

"After the ceremony, the young couple partook of a slight refreshment of sherry and water—the former the Captain pronounced to be execrable; and, having myself tasted some glasses from the VERY SAME BOTTLE with which the young and noble pair were served, I must say I think the Captain was rather hard upon mine host of the 'Bagpipes Hotel and Posting-House,' whence they instantly proceeded. I follow them as soon as the horses have fed.

"FOURTH EDITION.

"SHAMEFUL TREATMENT OF OUR REPORTER.

"WHISTLEBINKIE, N. B. Monday, Midnight.

"I arrived at this romantic little villa about two hours after the newly married couple, whose progress I have the honor to trace, reached Whistlebinkie. They have taken up their residence at the 'Cairngorm Arms'—mine is at the other hostelry, the 'Clachan of Whistlebinkie.'

"On driving up to the 'Cairngorm Arms,' I found a gentleman of military appearance standing at the doer, and occupied seemingly in smoking a cigar. It was very dark as I descended from my carriage, and the gentleman in question exclaimed, 'Is it you, Southdown my boy? You have come too late; unless you are come to have some supper;' or words to that effect. I explained that I was not the Lord Viscount Southdown, and politely apprised Captain Silvertop (for I justly concluded the individual before me could be no other) of his mistake.

"'Who the deuce' (the Captain used a stronger term) 'are you, then?' said Mr. Silvertop. 'Are you Baggs and Tapewell, my uncle's attorneys? If you are, you have come too late for the fair.'

"I briefly explained that I was not Baggs and Tapewell, but that my name was J—ms, and that I was a gentleman connected with the establishment of the Morning Tatler newspaper.

"'And what has brought you here, Mr. Morning Tatler?' asked my interlocutor, rather roughly. My answer was frank—that the disappearance of a noble lady from the house of her friends had caused the greatest excitement in the metropolis, and that my employers were anxious to give the public every particular regarding an event so singular.

"'And do you mean to say, sir, that you have dogged me all the way from London, and that my family affairs are to be published for the readers of the Morning Tatler newspaper? The Morning Tatter be —(the Captain here gave utterance to an oath which I shall not repeat) and you too, sir; you unpudent meddling scoundrel.'

"'Scoundrel, sir!' said I. 'Yes,' replied the irate gentleman, seizing me rudely by the collar—and he would have choked me, but that my blue satin stock and false collar gave way, and were left in the hands of this GENTLEMAN. 'Help, landlord!' I loudly exclaimed, adding, I believe, 'murder,' and other exclamations of alarm. In vain I appealed to the crowd, which by this time was pretty considerable; they and the unfeeling post-boys only burst into laughter, and called out, 'Give it him, Captain.' A struggle ensued, in which I have no doubt I should have had the better, but that the Captain, joining suddenly in the general and indecent hilarity, which was doubled when I fell down, stopped and said, 'Well, Jims, I won't fight on my marriage-day. Go into the tap, Jims, and order a glass of brandy-and-water at my expense—and mind I don't see your face to-morrow morning, or I'll make it more ugly than it is.'

"With these gross expressions and a cheer from the crowd, Mr. Silvertop entered the inn. I need not say that I did not partake of his hospitality, and that personally I despise his insults. I make them known that they may call down the indignation of the body of which I am a member, and throw myself on the sympathy of the public, as a gentleman shamefully assaulted and insulted in the discharge of a public duty."

"Thus you've sean how the flower of my affeckshns was tawn out of my busm, and my art was left bleading. Hangelina! I forgive thee. Mace thou be appy! If ever artfelt prayer for others wheel awailed on i, the beink on womb you trampled addresses those subblygations to Evn in your be1/2!

"I went home like a maniack, after hearing the announcement of Hangelina's departur. She'd been gone twenty hours when I heard the fatle noose. Purshoot was vain. Suppose I DID kitch her up, they were married, and what could we do? This sensable remark I made to Earl Bareacres, when that distragted nobleman igspawstulated with me. Er who was to have been my mother-in-lor, the Countiss, I never from that momink sor agin. My presnts, troosoes, juels, &c., were sent back—with the igsepshn of the diminds and Cashmear shawl, which her Ladyship COODN'T FIND. Ony it was whispered that at the nex buthday she was seen with a shawl IGSACKLY OF THE SAME PATTN. Let er keep it.

"Southdown was phurius. He came to me hafter the ewent, and wanted me adwance 50 lb., so that he might purshew his fewgitif sister—but I wasn't to be ad with that sort of chaugh—there was no more money for THAT famly. So he went away, and gave huttrance to his feelinx in a poem, which appeared (price 2 guineas) in the Bel Assombly.

"All the juilers, manchumakers, lacemen, coch bilders, apolstrers, hors dealers, and weddencake makers came pawring in with their bills, haggravating feelings already woondid beyond enjurants. That madniss didn't seaze me that night was a mussy. Fever, fewry, and rayge rack'd my hagnized braind, and drove sleap from my throbbink ilids. Hall night I follered Hangelinar in imadganation along the North Road. I wented cusses & mallydickshuns on the hinfamus Silvertop. I kickd and rord in my unhuttarable whoe! I seazed my pillar: I pitcht into it: pummld it, strangled it. Ha har! I thought it was Silvertop writhing in my Jint grasp; and taw the hordayshis villing lim from lim in the terrible strenth of my despare! . . . Let me drop a cutting over the memries of that night. When my boddy-suvnt came with my ot water in the mawning, the livid copse in the charnill was not payler than the gashly De la Pluche!

"'Give me the Share-list, Mandeville,' I micanickly igsclaimed. I had not perused it for the past 3 days, my etention being engayged elseware. Hevns & huth!—what was it I red there? What was it that made me spring outabed as if sumbady had given me cold pig?—I red Rewin in that Share-list—the Pannick was in full hoparation!

"Shall I describe that kitastrafy with which hall Hengland is familliar? My & rifewses to cronnicle the misfortns which lassarated my bleeding art in Hoctober last. On the fust of Hawgust where was I? Director of twenty-three Companies; older of scrip hall at a primmium, and worth at least a quarter of a millium. On Lord Mare's day my Saint Helenas quotid at 14 pm, were down at 1/2 discount; my Central Ichaboes at 3/8 discount; my Table Mounting & Hottentot Grand Trunk, no where; my Bathershins and Derrynane Beg, of which I'd bought 2000 for the account at 17 primmium, down to nix; my Juan Fernandez, my Great Central Oregons, prostrit. There was a momint when I thought I shouldn't be alive to write my own tail!"

(Here follow in Mr. Plush's MS. about twenty-four pages of railroad calculations, which we pretermit.)

"Those beests, Pump & Aldgate, once so cringing and umble, wrote me a threaten letter because I overdrew my account three-and-sixence: woodn't advance me five thousand on 25,000 worth of scrip; kep me waiting 2 hours when I asked to see the house; and then sent out Spout, the jewnior partner, saying they wouldn't discount my paper, and implawed me to clothes my account. I did: I paid the three-and-six balliance, and never sor 'em mor.

"The market fell daily. The Rewin grew wusser and wusser. Hagnies, Hagnies! it wasn't in the city aloan my misfortns came upon me. They beerded me in my own ome. The biddle who kips watch at the Halbany wodn keep misfortn out of my chambers; and Mrs. Twiddler, of Pall Mall, and Mr. Hunx, of Long

Acre, put egsicution into my apartmince, and swep off every stick of my furniture. 'Wardrobe & furniture of a man of fashion.' What an adwertisement George Robins DID make of it; and what a crowd was collected to laff at the prospick of my ruing! My chice plait; my seller of wine; my picturs—that of myself included (it was Maryhann, bless her! that bought it, unbeknown to me); all—all went to the ammer. That brootle Fitzwarren, my ex-vally, womb I met, fimilliarly slapt me on the sholder, and said, 'Jeames, my boy, you'd best go into suvvis aginn.'

"I DID go into suvvis—the wust of all suvvices—I went into the Queen's Bench Prison, and lay there a misrabble captif for 6 mortial weeks. Misrabble shall I say? no, not misrabble altogether; there was sunlike in the dunjing of the prospre prisner. I had visitors. A cart used to drive hup to the prizn gates of Saturdays; a washywoman's cart, with a fat old lady in it, and a young one. Who was that young one? Every one who has an art can gess, it was my blue-eyed blushing hangel of a Mary Hann! 'Shall we take him out in the linnen-basket, grandmamma?' Mary Hann said. Bless her, she'd already learned to say grandmamma quite natral: but I didn't go out that way; I went out by the door a whitewashed man. Ho, what a feast there was at Healing the day I came out! I'd thirteen shillings left when I'd bought the gold ring. I wasn't proud. I turned the mangle for three weeks; and then Uncle Bill said, 'Well, there IS some good in the feller;' and it was agreed that we should marry."

The Plush manuscript finishes here: it is many weeks since we saw the accomplished writer, and we have only just learned his fate. We are happy to state that it is a comfortable and almost a prosperous one.

The Honorable and Right Reverend Lionel Thistlewood, Lord Bishop of Bullocksmithy, was mentioned as the uncle of Lady Angelina Silvertop. Her elopement with her cousin caused deep emotion to the venerable prelate: he returned to the palace at Bullocksmithy, of which he had been for thirty years the episcopal ornament, and where he married three wives, who lie buried in his Cathedral Church of St. Boniface, Bullocksmithy.

The admirable man has rejoined those whom he loved. As he was preparing a charge to his clergy in his study after dinner, the Lord Bishop fell suddenly down in a fit of apoplexy; his butler, bringing in his accustomed dish of devilled kidneys for supper, discovered the venerable form extended on the Turkey carpet with a glass of Madeira in his hand; but life was extinct: and surgical aid was therefore not particularly useful.

All the late prelate's wives had fortunes, which the admirable man increased by thrift, the judicious sale of leases which fell in during his episcopacy, &c. He left three hundred thousand pounds—divided between his nephew and niece—not a greater sum than has been left by several deceased Irish prelates.

What Lord Southdown has done with his share we are not called upon to state. He has composed an epitaph to the Martyr of Bullocksmithy, which does him infinite credit. But we are happy to state that Lady Angelina Silvertop presented five hundred pounds to her faithful and affectionate servant, Mary Ann Hoggins, on her marriage with Mr. James Plush, to whom her Ladyship also made a handsome present—namely, the lease, good-will, and fixtures of the "Wheel of Fortune" public-house, near Shepherd's Market, May Fair: a house greatly frequented by all the nobility's footmen, doing a genteel stroke of business in the neighborhood, and where, as we have heard, the "Butlers' Club" is held.

Here Mr. Plush lives happy in a blooming and interesting wife: reconciled to a middle sphere of life, as he was to a humbler and a higher one before. He has shaved off his whiskers, and accommodates himself to an apron with perfect good humor. A gentleman connected with this establishment dined at the "Wheel of Fortune" the other day, and collected the above particulars. Mr. Plush blushed rather, as he brought in the first dish, and told his story very modestly over a pint of excellent port. He had only one thing in life to complain of, he said—that a witless version of his adventures had been produced at the Princess's theatre, "without with your leaf or by your leaf," as he expressed it. "Has for the rest," the worthy fellow said, "I'm appy—praps betwixt you and me I'm in my proper spear. I enjy my glass of beer or port (with your elth & my suvvice to you, sir,) quite as much as my clarrit in my prawsprus days. I've a good busniss, which is likely to be better. If a man can't be appy with such a wife as my Mary Hann, he's a beest: and when a christening takes place in our famly, will you give my complments to MR. PUNCH, and ask him to be godfather."

## LETTERS OF JEAMES

### JEAMES ON TIME BARGINGS

"Peraps at this present momink of Railway Hagetation and unsafety the follying little istory of a young friend of mine may hact as an olesome warning to hother week and hirresolute young gents.

"Young Frederick Timmins was the horphan son of a respectable cludgyman in the West of Hengland. Hadopted by his uncle, Colonel T—, of the Hoss-Mareens, and regardless of expence, this young man was sent to Heaton Collidge, and subsiquintly to Hoxford, where he was very nearly being Senior Rangler. He came to London to study for the lor. His prospix was bright indead; and he lived in a secknd flore in Jerming Street, having a ginteal inkum of two hundred lbs. per hannum.

"With this andsum enuity it may be supposed that Frederick wanted for nothink. Nor did he. He was a moral and well-educated young man, who took care of his close; pollisht his hone tea-party boots; cleaned his kidd-gloves with injer rubber; and, when not invited to dine out, took his meals reglar at the Hoxford and Cambridge Club—where (unless somebody treated him) he was never known to igseed his alf-pint of Marsally Wine.

"Merrits and vuttues such as his coodnt long pass unperseavd in the world. Admitted to the most fashnabble parties, it wasn't long befor sevral of the young ladies viewed him with a favorable i; one, ixpecially, the lovely Miss Hemily Mulligatawney, daughter of the Heast-Injar Derector of that name. As she was the richest gal of all the season, of corse Frederick fell in love with her. His haspirations were on the pint of being crowndid with success; and it was agreed that as soon as he was called to the bar, when he would sutnly be apinted a Judge, or a revising barrister, or Lord Chanslor, he should lead her to the halter.

"What life could be more desirable than Frederick's? He gave up his mornings to perfeshnl studdy, under Mr. Bluebag, the heminent pleader; he devoted his hevenings to helegant sosiaty at his Clubb, or with his hadord Hemily. He had no cares; no detts; no egstravigancies; he never was known to ride in a cabb, unless one of his tip-top friends lent it him; to go to a theayter unless he got a horder; or to henter a tavern or smoke a cigar. If prosperraty was hever chocked out, it was for that young man.

"But SUCKMSTANCES arose. Fatle suckmstances for pore Frederick Timmins. The Railway Hoperations began.

"For some time, immerst in lor and love, in the hardent hoccupations of his cheembers, or the sweet sosiaty of his Hemily, Frederick took no note of railroads. He did not reckonize the jigantic revalution which with hiron strides was a walkin over the country. But they began to be talked of even in HIS quiat haunts. Heven in the Hoxford and Cambridge Clubb, fellers were a speculatin. Tom Thumper (of Brasen Nose) cleared four thousand lb.; Bob Bullock (of Hexeter), who had lost all his proppaty gambling, had set himself up again; and Jack Deuceace, who had won it, had won a small istate besides by lucky specklations in the Share Markit.

"HEVERY BODY WON. 'Why shouldn't I?' thought pore Fred; and having saved 100 lb., he began a writin for shares—using, like an ickonominicle feller as he was, the Clubb paper to a prodigious igstent. All the Railroad directors, his friends, helped him to shares—the allottments came tumbling in—he took the primmiums by fifties and hundreds a day. His desk was cramd full of bank notes: his brane world with igsitement.

"He gave up going to the Temple, and might now be seen hall day about Capel Court. He took no more hinterest in lor; but his whole talk was of railroad lines. His desk at Mr. Bluebag's was filled full of prospectisises, and that legal gent wrote to Fred's uncle, to say he feared he was neglectin his bisniss.

"Alass! he WAS neglectin it, and all his sober and industerous habits. He begann to give dinners, and thought nothin of partys to Greenwich or Richmond. He didn't see his Hemily near so often: although the hawdacious and misguided young man might have done so much more heasily now than before: for now he kep a Broom!

"But there's a tumminus to hevery Railway. Fred's was approachin: in an evil hour he began making TIME-BARGINGS. Let this be a warning to all young fellers, and Fred's huntimely hend hoperate on them in a moral pint of vu!

"You all know under what favrabble suckemstanses the Great Hafrican Line, the Grand Niger Junction, or Gold Coast and Timbuctoo (Provishnal) Hatmospheric Railway came out four weeks ago: deposit ninepence per share of 20L. (six elephant's teeth, twelve tons of palm-oil, or four healthy niggers, African currency)—the shares of this helegeble investment rose to 1, 2, 3, in the Markit. A happy man was Fred when, after paying down 100 ninepences (3L. 15s.), he sold his shares for 250L. He gave a dinner at the 'Star and Garter' that very day. I promise you there was no Marsally THERE.

"Nex day they were up at 3 1/4. This put Fred in a rage: they rose to 5, he was in a fewry. 'What an ass I was to sell,' said he, 'when all this money was to be won!'

"'And so you WERE an Ass,' said his partiklar friend, Colonel Claw, K.X.R., a director of the line, 'a double-eared Ass. My dear fellow, the shares will be at 15 next week. Will you give me your solemn word of honor not to breathe to mortal man what I am going to tell you?'

"'Honor bright,' says Fred.

"'HUDSON HAS JOINED THE LINE.' Fred didn't say a word more, but went tumbling down to the City in his Broom. You know the state of the streets. Claw WENT BY WATER.

"'Buy me one thousand Hafricans for the 30th,' cries Fred, busting into his broker's; and they were done for him at 4 7/8.

"Can't you guess the rest? Haven't you seen the Share List? which says:—

"'Great Africans, paid 9d.; price 1/4 par.'

"And that's what came of my pore dear friend Timmins's time-barging.

"What'll become of him I can't say; for nobody has seen him since. His lodgins in Jerming Street is to let. His brokers in vain deplores his absence. His Uncle has declared his marriage with his housekeeper; and the Morning Erald (that emusing print) has a paragraf yesterday in the fashnabble news, headed 'Marriage in High Life.—The rich and beautiful Miss Mulligatawney, of Portland Place, is to be speedily united to Colonel Claw, K.X.R.'

"JEAMES."


JEAMES ON THE GAUGE QUESTION

"You will scarcely praps reckonize in this little skitch* the haltered linimints of I, with woos face the reders of your valluble mislny were once fimiliar,—the unfortnt Jeames de la Pluche, fomly so selabrated in the fashnabble suckles, now the pore Jeames Plush, landlord of the 'Wheel of Fortune' public house. Yes, that is me; that is my haypun which I wear as becomes a publican—those is the checkers which hornymint the pillows of my dor. I am like the Romin Genral, St. Cenatus, equal to any emudgency of Fortun. I, who have drunk Shampang in my time, aint now abov droring a pint of Small Bier. As for my wife—that Angel—I've not ventured to depigt HER. Fansy her a sittn in the Bar, smiling like a sunflower and, ho, dear Punch! happy in nussing a deer little darlint totsywotsy of a Jeames, with my air to a curl, and my i's to a T!

* This refers to an illustrated edition of the work.

"I never thought I should have been injuiced to write anything but a Bill agin, much less to edress you on Railway Subjix—which with all my sole I ABAW. Railway letters, obbligations to pay hup, ginteal inquirys as to my Salissator's name, &c. &c., I dispize and scorn artily. But as a man, an usbnd, a father, and a freebon Brittn, my jewty compels me to come forwoods, and igspress my opinion upon that NASHNAL NEWSANCE—the break of Gage.

"An interesting ewent in a noble family with which I once very nearly had the honor of being kinected, acurd a few weex sins, when the Lady Angelina S—, daughter of the Earl of B—cres, presented the gallant Capting, her usband, with a Son & hair. Nothink would satasfy her Ladyship but that her old and attacht famdyshamber, my wife Mary Hann Plush, should be presnt upon this hospicious occasion. Captain S—was not jellus of me on account of my former attachment to his Lady. I cunsented that my Mary Hann should attend her, and me, my wife, and our dear babby acawdingly set out for our noable frend's residence, Honeymoon Lodge, near Cheltenham.

"Sick of all Railroads myself, I wisht to poast it in a Chay and 4, but Mary Hann, with the hobstenacy of her Sex, was bent upon Railroad travelling, and I yealded, like all husbinds. We set out by the Great Westn, in an eavle Hour.

"We didnt take much luggitch—my wife's things in the ushal bandboxes—mine in a potmancho. Our dear little James Angelo's (called so in complament to his noble Godmamma) craddle, and a small supply of a few 100 weight of Topsanbawtems, Farinashious food, and Lady's fingers, for that dear child, who is now 6 months old, with a PERDIDGUS APPATITE. Likewise we were charged with a bran new Medsan chest for my lady, from Skivary & Morris, containing enough Rewbub, Daffy's Alixir, Godfrey's cawdle, with a few score of parsles for Lady Hangelina's family and owsehold: about 2000 spessymins of Babby linning from Mrs. Flummary's in Regent Street, a Chayny Cresning bowl from old Lady Bareacres (big enough to immus a Halderman), & a case marked 'Glass,' from her ladyship's meddicle man, which were stowed away together; had to this an ormylew Cradle, with rose-colored Satting & Pink lace hangings, held up by a gold tuttle-dove, &c. We had, ingluding James Hangelo's rattle & my umbrellow, 73 packidges in all.

"We got on very well as far as Swindon, where, in the Splendid Refreshment room, there was a galaxy of lovely gals in cottn velvet spencers, who serves out the soop, and 1 of whom maid an impresshn upon this Art which I shoodn't like Mary Hann to know—and here, to our infaint disgust, we changed carridges. I forgot to say that we were in the seeknd class, having with us James Hangelo, and 23 other light harticles.

"Fust inconveniance: and almost as bad as break of gage. I cast my hi upon the gal in cottn velvet, and wanted some soop, of coarse; but seasing up James Hangelo (who was layin his dear little pors on an Am Sangwidg) and seeing my igspresshn of hi—'James,' says Mary Hann, 'instead of looking at that young lady—and not so VERY young neither—be pleased to look to our packidges, & place them in the other carridge.' I did so with an evy Art. I eranged them 23 articles in the opsit carridg, only missing my umberella & baby's rattle; and jest as I came back for my baysn of soop, the beast of a bell rings, the whizzling injians proclayms the time of our departure,—& farewell soop and cottn velvet. Mary Hann was sulky. She said it was my losing the umberella. If it had been a COTTON VELVET UMBERELLA I could have understood. James Hangelo sittn on my knee was evidently unwell; without his coral: & for 20 miles that blessid babby kep up a rawring, which caused all the passingers to simpithize with him igseedingly.

"We arrive at Gloster, and there fansy my disgust at bein ableeged to undergo another change of carridges! Fansy me holding up moughs, tippits, cloaks, and baskits, and James Hangelo rawring still like mad, and pretending to shuperintend the carrying over of our luggage from the broad gage to the narrow gage. 'Mary Hann,' says I, rot to desperation, 'I shall throttle this darling if he goes on.' 'Do,' says she—'and GO INTO THE REFRESHMENT room,' says she—a snatchin the babby out of my arms. Do go,' says she, youre not fit to look after luggage,' and she began lulling James Hangelo to sleep with one hi, while she looked after the packets with the other. Now, Sir! if you please, mind that packet!—pretty darling—easy with that box, Sir, its glass—pooooty poppet—where's the deal case, marked arrowroot, No. 24?' she cried, reading out of a list she had.—And poor little James went to sleep. The porters were bundling and carting the various harticles with no more ceremony than if each package had been of cannonball.

"At last—bang goes a package marked 'Glass,' and containing the Chayny bowl and Lady Bareacres' mixture, into a large white bandbox, with a crash and a smash. 'It's My Lady's box from Crinoline's!' cries

Mary Hann; and she puts down the child on the bench, and rushes forward to inspect the dammidge. You could hear the Chayny bowls clinking inside; and Lady B.'s mixture (which had the igsack smell of cherry brandy) was dribbling out over the smashed bandbox containing a white child's cloak, trimmed with Blown lace and lined with white satting.

"As James was asleep, and I was by this time uncommon hungry, I thought I WOULD go into the Refreshment Room and just take a little soup; so I wrapped him up in his cloak and laid him by his mamma, and went off. There's not near such good attendance as at Swindon.

"We took our places in the carriage in the dark, both of us covered with a pile of packages, and Mary Hann so sulky that she would not speak for some minutes. At last she spoke out—

"'Have you all the small parcels?'

"'Twenty-three in all,' says I.

"'Then give me baby.'

"'Give you what?' says I.

"'Give me baby.'

"'What, haven't y-y-yoooo got him?' says I.

"O Mussy! You should have heard her sreak! WE'D LEFT HIM ON THE LEDGE AT GLOSTER.

"It all came of the break of gage."


MR. JEAMES AGAIN

"Dear Mr. Punch,—As newmarus inquiries have been maid both at my privit ressddence, 'The Wheel of Fortune Otel,' and at your Hoffis, regarding the fate of that dear babby, James Hangelo, whose primmiture dissappearnts caused such hagnies to his distracted parents, I must begg, dear sir, the permission to ockupy a part of your valuble collams once more, and hease the public mind about my blessid boy.

"Wictims of that nashnal cuss, the Broken Gage, me and Mrs. Plush was left in the train to Cheltenham, soughring from that most disgreeble of complaints, a halmost BROKEN ART. The skreems of Mrs. Jeames might be said almost to out-Y the squeel of the dying, as we rusht into that fashnable Spaw, and my pore Mary Hann found it was not Baby, but Bundles I had in my lapp.

"When the Old Dowidger Lady Bareacres, who was waiting heagerly at the train, herd that owing to that abawminable Brake of Gage the luggitch, her Ladyship's Cherrybrandy box, the cradle for Lady Hangelina's baby, the lace, crockary and chany, was rejuiced to one immortal smash; the old cat howld at me and pore dear Mary Hann, as if it was huss, and not the infunnle Brake of Gage, was to blame; and as if we ad no misfortns of our hown to deplaw. She bust out about my stupid imparence; called Mary

Hann a good for nothink creecher, and wep, and abewsd, and took on about her broken Chayny Bowl, a great deal mor than she did about a dear little Christian child. 'Don't talk to me abowt your bratt of a babby' (seshe); 'where's my bowl?—where's my medsan?—where's my bewtiffle Pint lace?—All in rewing through your stupiddaty, you brute, you!'

"'Bring your haction against the Great Western, Maam,' says I, quite riled by this crewel and unfealing hold wixen. 'Ask the pawters at Gloster, why your goods is spiled—it's not the fust time they've been asked the question. Git the gage haltered against the nex time you send for MEDSAN and meanwild buy some at the "Plow"—they keep it very good and strong there, I'll be bound. Has for us, WE'RE a going back to the cussid station at Gloster, in such of our blessid child.'

"'You don't mean to say, young woman,' seshe, 'that you're not going to Lady Hangelina: what's her dear boy to do? who's to nuss it?'

"'YOU nuss it, Maam,' says I. 'Me and Mary Hann return this momint by the Fly.' And so (whishing her a suckastic ajew) Mrs. Jeames and I lep into a one oss weakle, and told the driver to go like mad back to Gloster.

"I can't describe my pore gals hagny juring our ride. She sat in the carridge as silent as a milestone, and as madd as a march Air. When we got to Gloster she sprang hout of it as wild as a Tigris, and rusht to the station, up to the fatle Bench.

"'My child, my child,' shreex she, in a hoss, hot voice. 'Where's my infant? a little bewtifle child, with blue eyes,—dear Mr. Policeman, give it me—a thousand guineas for it.'

"'Faix, Mam,' says the man, a Hirishman, 'and the divvle a babby have I seen this day except thirteen of my own—and you're welcome to any one of THEM, and kindly.'

"'As if HIS babby was equal to ours,' as my darling Mary Hann said, afterwards. All the station was scrouging round us by this time—pawters & clarx and refreshmint people and all. 'What's this year row about that there babby?' at last says the Inspector, stepping hup. I thought my wife was going to jump into his harms. 'Have you got him?' says she.

"'Was it a child in a blue cloak?' says he.

"'And blue eyse!' says my wife.

"'I put a label on him and sent him on to Bristol; he's there by this time. The Guard of the Mail took him and put him into a letter-box,' says he: 'he went 20 minutes ago. We found him on the broad gauge line, and sent him on by it, in course,' says he. 'And it'll be a caution to you, young woman, for the future, to label your children along with the rest of your luggage.'

"If my piguniary means had been such as ONCE they was, you may emadgine I'd have ad a speshle train and been hoff like smoak. As it was, we was obliged to wait 4 mortial hours for the next train (4 ears they seemed to us), and then away we went.

"'My boy! my little boy!' says poor choking Mary Hann, when we got there. 'A parcel in a blue cloak?' says the man. 'No body claimed him here, and so we sent him back by the mail. An Irish nurse here gave him some supper, and he's at Paddington by this time. Yes,' says he, looking at the clock, 'he's been there these ten minutes.'

"But seeing my poor wife's distracted histarricle state, this good-naterd man says, 'I think, my dear, there's a way to ease your mind. We'll know in five minutes how he is.'

"'Sir,' says she, 'don't make sport of me.'

"'No, my dear, we'll TELEGRAPH him.'

"And he began hopparating on that singlar and ingenus elecktricle inwention, which aniliates time, and carries intellagence in the twinkling of a peg-post.

"'I'll ask,' says he, 'for child marked G. W. 273.'

"Back comes the telegraph with the sign, 'All right.'

"'Ask what he's doing, sir,' says my wife, quite amazed. Back comes the answer in a Jiffy—

"'C. R. Y. I. N. G.'

"This caused all the bystanders to laugh excep my pore Mary Hann, who pull'd a very sad face.

"The good-naterd feller presently said, 'he'd have another trile;' and what d'ye think was the answer? I'm blest if it wasn't—

"'P. A. P.'

"He was eating pap! There's for you—there's a rogue for you—there's a March of Intaleck! Mary Hann smiled now for the fust time. 'He'll sleep now,' says she. And she sat down with a full hart.

"If hever that good-naterd Shooperintendent comes to London, HE need never ask for his skore at the 'Wheel of Fortune Otel,' I promise you—where me and my wife and James Hangelo now is; and where only yesterday a gent came in and drew this pictur* of us in our bar.

* This refers to an illustrated edition of the work.

"And if they go on breaking gages; and if the child, the most precious luggidge of the Henglishman, is to be bundled about this year way, why it won't be for want of warning, both from Professor Harris, the Commission, and from

"My dear Mr. Punch's obeajent servant,

"JEAMES PLUSH."

CHAPTER I

"TRUTH IS STRANGE, STRANGER THAN FICTION."

I think it but right that in making my appearance before the public I should at once acquaint them with my titles and name. My card, as I leave it at the houses of the nobility, my friends, is as follows:—

MAJOR GOLIAH O'GRADY GAHAGAN, H.E.I.C.S.,

Commanding Battalion of Irregular Horse,

AHMEDNUGGAR.

Seeing, I say, this simple visiting ticket, the world will avoid any of those awkward mistakes as to my person, which have been so frequent of late. There has been no end to the blunders regarding this humble title of mine, and the confusion thereby created. When I published my volume of poems, for instance, the Morning Post newspaper remarked "that the Lyrics of the Heart, by Miss Gahagan, may be ranked among the sweetest flowrets of the present spring season." The Quarterly Review, commenting upon my Observations on the "Pons Asinorum" (4to. London, 1836), called me "Doctor Gahagan," and so on. It was time to put an end to these mistakes, and I have taken the above simple remedy.

I was urged to it by a very exalted personage. Dining in August last at the palace of the T-lr-es at Paris, the lovely young Duch-ss of Orl—ns (who, though she does not speak English, understands it as well as I do,) said to me in the softest Teutonic, "Lieber Herr Major, haben sie den Ahmednuggarischen-jager-battalion gelassen?" "Warum denn?" said I, quite astonished at her R—l H—ss's question. The P—cess then spoke of some trifle from my pen, which was simply signed Goliah Gahagan.

There was, unluckily, a dead silence as H. R. H. put this question.

"Comment donc?" said H. M. Lo-is Ph-l-ppe, looking gravely at Count Mole; "le cher Major a quitte l'armee! Nicolas donc sera maitre de l'Inde!" H. M— and the Pr. M-n-ster pursued their conversation in a low tone, and left me, as may be imagined in a dreadful state of confusion. I blushed and stuttered, and murmured out a few incoherent words to explain—but it would not do—I could not recover my equanimity during the course of the dinner and while endeavoring to help an English Duke, my neighbor, to poulet a l'Austerlitz, fairly sent seven mushrooms and three large greasy croutes over his whiskers and shirt-frill. Another laugh at my expense. "Ah! M. le Major," said the Q— of the B-lg—ns, archly, "vous n'aurez jamais votre brevet de Colonel." Her M—y's joke will be better understood when I state that his Grace is the brother of a Minister.

I am not at liberty to violate the sanctity of private life, by mentioning the names of the parties concerned in this little anecdote. I only wish to have it understood that I am a gentleman, and live at least in DECENT society. Verbum sat.

But to be serious. I am obliged always to write the name of Goliah in full, to distinguish me from my brother, Gregory Gahagan, who was also a Major (in the King's service), and whom I killed in a duel, as the public most likely knows. Poor Greg! a very trivial dispute was the cause of our quarrel, which never would have originated but for the similarity of our names. The circumstance was this: I had been lucky enough to render the Nawaub of Lucknow some trifling service (in the notorious affair of Choprasjee Muckjee), and his Highness sent down a gold toothpick-case directed to Captain G. Gahagan, which I of course thought was for me: my brother madly claimed it; we fought, and the consequence was, that in about three minutes he received a slash in the right side (cut 6), which effectually did his business:—he was a good swordsman enough—I was THE BEST in the universe. The most ridiculous part of the affair is, that the toothpick-case was his, after all—he had left it on the Nawaub's table at tiffin. I can't conceive what madness prompted him to fight about such a paltry bauble; he had much better have yielded it at once, when he saw I was determined to have it. From this slight specimen of my adventures, the reader will perceive that my life has been one of no ordinary interest; and, in fact, I may say that I have led a more remarkable life than any man in the service—I have been at more pitched battles, led more forlorn hopes, had more success among the fair sex, drunk harder, read more, and been a handsomer man than any officer now serving her Majesty.

When I at first went to India in 1802, I was a raw cornet of seventeen, with blazing red hair, six feet four in height, athletic at all kinds of exercises, owing money to my tailor and everybody else who would trust me, possessing an Irish brogue, and my full pay of 120L. a year. I need not say that with all these advantages I did that which a number of clever fellows have done before me—I fell in love, and proposed to marry immediately.

But how to overcome the difficulty?—It is true that I loved Julia Jowler—loved her to madness; but her father intended her for a Member of Council at least, and not for a beggarly Irish ensign. It was, however, my fate to make the passage to India (on board of the "Samuel Snob" East Indiaman, Captain Duffy,) with this lovely creature, and my misfortune instantaneously to fall in love with her. We were not out of the Channel before I adored her, worshipped the deck which she trod upon, kissed a thousand times the cuddy-chair on which she used to sit. The same madness fell on every man in the ship. The two mates fought about her at the Cape; the surgeon, a sober, pious Scotchman, from disappointed affection, took so dreadfully to drinking as to threaten spontaneous combustion; and old Colonel Lilywhite, carrying his wife and seven daughters to Bengal, swore that he would have a divorce from Mrs. L., and made an attempt at suicide; the captain himself told me, with tears in his eyes, that he hated his hitherto-adored Mrs. Duffy, although he had had nineteen children by her.

We used to call her the witch—there was magic in her beauty and in her voice. I was spell-bound when I looked at her, and stark staring mad when she looked at me! O lustrous black eyes!—O glossy night-black ringlets!—O lips!—O dainty frocks of white muslin!—O tiny kid slippers!—though old and gouty, Gahagan sees you still! I recollect, off Ascension, she looked at me in her particular way one day at dinner, just as I happened to be blowing on a piece of scalding hot green fat. I was stupefied at once—I thrust the entire morsel (about half a pound) into my mouth. I made no attempt to swallow, or to masticate it, but left it there for many minutes, burning, burning! I had no skin to my palate for seven weeks after, and lived on rice-water during the rest of the voyage. The anecdote is trivial, but it shows the power of Julia Jowler over me.

The writers of marine novels have so exhausted the subject of storms, shipwrecks, mutinies, engagements, sea-sickness, and so forth, that (although I have experienced each of these in many varieties) I think it quite unnecessary to recount such trifling adventures; suffice it to say, that during our five months' trajet, my mad passion for Julia daily increased; so did the captain's and the surgeon's; so did Colonel Lilywhite's; so did the doctor's, the mate's—that of most part of the passengers, and a considerable number of the crew. For myself, I swore—ensign as I was—I would win her for my wife; I vowed that I would make her glorious with my sword—that as soon as I had made a favorable impression on my commanding officer (which I did not doubt to create), I would lay open to him the state of my affections, and demand his daughter's hand. With such sentimental outpourings did our voyage continue and conclude.

We landed at the Sunderbunds on a grilling hot day in December, 1802, and then for the moment Julia and I separated. She was carried off to her papa's arms in a palanquin, surrounded by at least forty hookahbadars; whilst the poor cornet, attended but by two dandies and a solitary beasty (by which unnatural name these blackamoors are called), made his way humbly to join the regiment at head-quarters.

The —th Regiment of Bengal Cavalry, then under the command of Lieut.-Colonel Julius Jowler, C.B., was known throughout Asia and Europe by the proud title of the Bundelcund Invincibles—so great was its character for bravery, so remarkable were its services in that delightful district of India. Major Sir George Gutch was next in command, and Tom Thrupp, as kind a fellow as ever ran a Mahratta through the body, was second Major. We were on the eve of that remarkable war which was speedily to spread throughout the whole of India, to call forth the valor of a Wellesley, and the indomitable gallantry of a Gahagan; which was illustrated by our victories at Ahmednuggar (where I was the first over the barricade at the storming of the Pettah); at Argaum, where I slew with my own sword twenty-three matchlock-men, and cut a dromedary in two; and by that terrible day of Assaye, where Wellesley would have been beaten but for me—me alone: I headed nineteen charges of cavalry, took (aided by only four men of my own troop) seventeen field-pieces, killing the scoundrelly French artillerymen; on that day I had eleven elephants shot under me, and carried away Scindiah's nose-ring with a pistol-ball. Wellesley is a Duke and a Marshal, I but a simple Major of Irregulars. Such is fortune and war! But my feelings carry me away from my narrative, which had better proceed with more order.

On arriving, I say, at our barracks at Dum Dum, I for the first time put on the beautiful uniform of the Invincibles: a light blue swallow-tailed jacket with silver lace and wings, ornamented with about 3,000 sugar-loaf buttons, rhubarb-colored leather inexpressibles (tights), and red morocco boots with silver spurs and tassels, set off to admiration the handsome persons of the officers of our corps. We wore powder in those days; and a regulation pigtail of seventeen inches, a brass helmet surrounded by leopard-skin with a bearskin top and a horsetail feather, gave the head a fierce and chivalrous appearance, which is far more easily imagined than described.

Attired in this magnificent costume, I first presented myself before Colonel Jowler. He was habited in a manner precisely similar, but not being more than five feet in height, and weighing at least fifteen stone, the dress he wore did not become him quite so much as slimmer and taller men. Flanked by his tall Majors, Thrupp and Gutch, he looked like a stumpy skittle-ball between two attenuated skittles. The plump little Colonel received me with vast cordiality, and I speedily became a prime favorite with himself and the other officers of the corps. Jowler was the most hospitable of men; and gratifying my appetite and my love together, I continually partook of his dinners, and feasted on the sweet presence of Julia.

I can see now, what I would not and could not perceive in those early days, that this Miss Jowler—on whom I had lavished my first and warmest love, whom I had endowed with all perfection and purity—was no better than a little impudent flirt, who played with my feelings, because during the monotony of a sea-voyage she had no other toy to play with; and who deserted others for me, and me for others, just as her whim or her interest might guide her. She had not been three weeks at head-quarters when half the regiment was in love with her. Each and all of the candidates had some favor to boast of, or some encouraging hopes on which to build. It was the scene of the "Samuel Snob" over again, only heightened in interest by a number of duels. The following list will give the reader a notion of some of them:—

1. Cornet Gahagan . . Ensign Hicks, of the Sappers and Miners. Hicks received a ball in his jaw, and was half choked by a quantity of carroty whisker forced down his throat with the ball.

2. Capt. Macgillicuddy, B.N.I., . . Cornet Gahagan. I was run through the body, but the sword passed between the ribs, and injured me very slightly.

3. Capt. Macgillicuddy, B.N.I., . . Mr. Mulligatawny, B.C.S., Deputy-Assistant Vice Sub-Controller of the Boggleywollah Indigo grounds, Ramgolly branch.

Macgillicuddy should have stuck to sword's-play, and he might have come off in his second duel as well as in his first; as it was, the civilian placed a ball and a part of Mac's gold repeater in his stomach. A remarkable circumstance attended this shot, an account of which I sent home to the "Philosophical Transactions:" the surgeon had extracted the ball, and was going off, thinking that all was well, when the gold repeater struck thirteen in poor Macgillicuddy's abdomen. I suppose that the works must have been disarranged in some way by the bullet, for the repeater was one of Barraud's, never known to fail before, and the circumstance occurred at SEVEN o'clock.*

*So admirable are the performances of these watches, which will stand in any climate, that I repeatedly heard poor Macgillicuddy relate the following fact. The hours, as it is known, count in Italy from one to twenty-four: the day Mac landed at Naples his repeater rung the Italian hours, from one to twenty-four; as soon as he crossed the Alps it only sounded as usual.—G. O'G. G.*

I could continue, almost ad infinitum, an account of the wars which this Helen occasioned, but the above three specimens will, I should think, satisfy the peaceful reader. I delight not in scenes of blood, heaven knows, but I was compelled in the course of a few weeks, and for the sake of this one woman, to fight nine duels myself, and I know that four times as many more took place concerning her.

I forgot to say that Jowler's wife was a half-caste woman, who had been born and bred entirely in India, and whom the Colonel had married from the house of her mother, a native. There were some singular rumors abroad regarding this latter lady's history: it was reported that she was the daughter of a native Rajah, and had been carried off by a poor English subaltern in Lord Clive's time. The young man was killed very soon after, and left his child with its mother. The black Prince forgave his daughter and bequeathed to her a handsome sum of money. I suppose that it was on this account that Jowler married Mrs. J., a creature who had not, I do believe, a Christian name, or a single Christian quality: she was a hideous, bloated, yellow creature, with a beard, black teeth, and red eyes: she was fat, lying, ugly, and stingy—she hated and was hated by all the world, and by her jolly husband as devoutly as by any other. She did not pass a month in the year with him, but spent most of her time with her native friends. I wonder how she could have given birth to so lovely a creature as her daughter. This woman was of course with the Colonel when Julia arrived, and the spice of the devil in her daughter's composition was most carefully nourished and fed by her. If Julia had been a flirt before, she was a downright jilt now; she set the whole cantonment by the ears; she made wives jealous and husbands miserable; she caused all those duels of which I have discoursed already, and yet such was the fascination of THE WITCH that I still thought her an angel. I made court to the nasty mother in order to be near the daughter; and I listened untiringly to Jowler's interminable dull stories, because I was occupied all the time in watching the graceful movements of Miss Julia.

But the trumpet of war was soon ringing in our ears; and on the battle-field Gahagan is a man! The Bundelcund Invincibles received orders to march, and Jowler, Hector-like, donned his helmet and prepared to part from his Andromache. And now arose his perplexity: what must be done with his daughter, his Julia? He knew his wife's peculiarities of living, and did not much care to trust his daughter to her keeping; but in vain he tried to find her an asylum among the respectable ladies of his regiment. Lady Gutch offered to receive her, but would have nothing to do with Mrs. Jowler; the surgeon's wife, Mrs. Sawbone, would have neither mother nor daughter; there was no help for it, Julia and her mother must have a house together, and Jowler knew that his wife would fill it with her odious blackamoor friends.

I could not, however, go forth satisfied to the campaign until I learned from Julia my fate. I watched twenty opportunities to see her alone, and wandered about the Colonel's bungalow as an informer does about a public-house, marking the incomings and the outgoings of the family, and longing to seize the moment when Miss Jowler, unbiassed by her mother or her papa, might listen, perhaps, to my eloquence, and melt at the tale of my love.

But it would not do—old Jowler seemed to have taken all of a sudden to such a fit of domesticity, that there was no finding him out of doors, and his rhubarb-colored wife (I believe that her skin gave the first idea of our regimental breeches), who before had been gadding ceaselessly abroad, and poking her broad nose into every menage in the cantonment, stopped faithfully at home with her spouse. My only chance was to beard the old couple in their den, and ask them at once for their cub.

So I called one day at tiffin:—old Jowler was always happy to have my company at this meal; it amused him, he said, to see me drink Hodgson's pale ale (I drank two hundred and thirty-four dozen the first year I was in Bengal)—and it was no small piece of fun, certainly, to see old Mrs. Jowler attack the currie-bhaut;—she was exactly the color of it, as I have had already the honor to remark, and she swallowed the mixture with a gusto which was never equalled, except by my poor friend Dando apropos d'huitres. She consumed the first three platefuls with a fork and spoon, like a Christian; but as she warmed to her work, the old hag would throw away her silver implements, and dragging the dishes towards her, go to work with her hands, flip the rice into her mouth with her fingers, and stow away a quantity of eatables sufficient for a sepoy company. But why do I diverge from the main point of my story?

Julia, then, Jowler, and Mrs. J. were at luncheon: the dear girl was in the act to sabler a glass of Hodgson as I entered. "How do you do, Mr. Gagin?" said the old hag, leeringly. "Eat a bit o' currie-bhaut,"—and she thrust the dish towards me, securing a heap as it passed. "What! Gagy my boy, how do, how do?" said the fat Colonel. "What! run through the body?—got well again—have some Hodgson—run through your body too!"—and at this, I may say, coarse joke (alluding to the fact that in these hot climates the ale oozes out as it were from the pores of the skin) old Jowler laughed: a host of swarthy chobdars, kitmatgars, sices, consomahs, and bobbychies laughed too, as they provided me, unasked, with the grateful fluid. Swallowing six tumblers of it, I paused nervously for a moment, and then said—

"Bobbachy, consomah, ballybaloo hoga."

The black ruffians took the hint and retired.

"Colonel and Mrs. Jowler," said I solemnly, "we are alone; and you, Miss Jowler, you are alone too; that is—I mean—I take this opportunity to—(another glass of ale, if you please)—to express, once for all, before departing on a dangerous campaign"—(Julia turned pale)—"before entering, I say, upon a war which may stretch in the dust my high-raised hopes and me, to express my hopes while life still remains to me, and to declare in the face of heaven, earth, and Colonel Jowler, that I love you, Julia!" The Colonel, astonished, let fall a steel fork, which stuck quivering for some minutes in the calf of my leg; but I heeded not the paltry interruption. "Yes, by yon bright heaven," continued I, "I love you, Julia! I respect my commander, I esteem your excellent and beauteous mother; tell me, before I leave you, if I may hope for a return of my affection. Say that you love me, and I will do such deeds in this coming war as shall make you proud of the name of your Gahagan."

The old woman, as I delivered these touching words, stared, snapped, and ground her teeth, like an enraged monkey. Julia was now red, now white; the Colonel stretched forward, took the fork out of the calf of my leg, wiped it, and then seized a bundle of letters which I had remarked by his side.

"A cornet!" said he, in a voice choking with emotion; "a pitiful, beggarly Irish cornet aspire to the hand of Julia Jowler! Gag, Gahagan, are you mad, or laughing at us? Look at these letters, young man—at these letters, I say—one hundred and twenty-four epistles from every part of India (not including one from the Governor-General, and six from his brother, Colonel Wellesley,)—one hundred and twenty-four proposals for the hand of Miss Jowler! Cornet Gahagan," he continued, "I wish to think well of you: you are the bravest, the most modest, and, perhaps, the handsomest man in our corps; but you have not got a single rupee. You ask me for Julia, and you do not possess even an anna!"—(Here the old rogue grinned, as if he had made a capital pun).—"No, no," said he, waxing good-natured; "Gagy, my boy, it is nonsense! Julia, love, retire with your mamma; this silly young gentleman will remain and smoke a pipe with me."

I took one; it was the bitterest chillum I ever smoked in my life.

I am not going to give here an account of my military services; they will appear in my great national autobiography, in forty volumes, which I am now preparing for the press. I was with my regiment in all Wellesley's brilliant campaigns; then taking dawk, I travelled across the country north-eastward, and had the honor of fighting by the side of Lord Lake at Laswaree, Deeg, Furruckabad, Futtyghur, and Bhurtpore: but I will not boast of my actions—the military man knows them, MY SOVEREIGN appreciates them. If asked who was the bravest man of the Indian army, there is not an officer belonging to it who would not cry at once, GAHAGAN. The fact is, I was desperate: I cared not for life, deprived of Julia Jowler.

With Julia's stony looks ever before my eyes, her father's stern refusal in my ears, I did not care, at the close of the campaign, again to seek her company or to press my suit. We were eighteen months on service, marching and countermarching, and fighting almost every other day: to the world I did not seem altered; but the world only saw the face, and not the seared and blighted heart within me. My valor, always desperate, now reached to a pitch of cruelty; I tortured my grooms and grass-cutters for the most trifling offence or error,—I never in action spared a man,—I sheared off three hundred and nine heads in the course of that single campaign.

Some influence, equally melancholy, seemed to have fallen upon poor old Jowler. About six months after we had left Dum Dum, he received a parcel of letters from Benares (whither his wife had retired with her daughter), and so deeply did they seem to weigh upon his spirits, that he ordered eleven men of his regiment to be flogged within two days; but it was against the blacks that he chiefly turned his wrath. Our fellows, in the heat and hurry of the campaign, were in the habit of dealing rather roughly with their prisoners, to extract treasure from them: they used to pull their nails out by the root, to boil them in kedgeree pots, to flog them and dress their wounds with cayenne pepper, and so on. Jowler, when he heard of these proceedings, which before had always justly exasperated him (he was a humane and kind little man), used now to smile fiercely and say, "D— the black scoundrels! Serve them right, serve them right!"

One day, about a couple of miles in advance of the column, I had been on a foraging-party with a few dragoons, and was returning peaceably to camp, when of a sudden a troop of Mahrattas burst on us from a neighboring mango-tope, in which they had been hidden: in an instant three of my men's saddles were empty, and I was left with but seven more to make head against at least thirty of these vagabond black horsemen. I never saw in my life a nobler figure than the leader of the troop—mounted on a splendid black Arab: he was as tall, very nearly, as myself; he wore a steel cap and a shirt of mail, and carried a beautiful French carbine, which had already done execution upon two of my men. I saw that our only chance of safety lay in the destruction of this man. I shouted to him in a voice of thunder (in the Hindustanee tongue of course), "Stop, dog, if you dare, and encounter a man!"

In reply his lance came whirling in the air over my head, and mortally transfixed poor Foggarty of ours, who was behind me. Grinding my teeth and swearing horribly, I drew that scimitar which never yet failed its blow,* and rushed at the Indian. He came down at full gallop, his own sword making ten thousand gleaming circles in the air, shrieking his cry of battle.

*In my affair with Macgillicuddy, I was fool enough to go out with small-swords—miserable weapons only fit for tailors.—G. O'G. G.*

The contest did not last an instant. With my first blow I cut off his sword-arm at the wrist; my second I levelled at his head. I said that he wore a steel cap, with a gilt iron spike of six inches, and a hood of chain mail. I rose in my stirrups and delivered "ST. GEORGE;" my sword caught the spike exactly on the point, split it sheer in two, cut crashing through the steel cap and hood, and was only stopped by a ruby which he wore in his back-plate. His head, cut clean in two between the eyebrows and nostrils, even between the two front teeth, fell one side on each shoulder, and he galloped on till his horse was stopped by my men, who were not a little amused at the feat.

As I had expected, the remaining ruffians fled on seeing their leader's fate. I took home his helmet by way of curiosity, and we made a single prisoner, who was instantly carried before old Jowler.

We asked the prisoner the name of the leader of the troop; he said it was Chowder Loll.

"Chowder Loll!" shrieked Colonel Jowler. "O fate! thy hand is here!" He rushed wildly into his tent—the next day applied for leave of absence. Gutch took the command of the regiment, and I saw him no more for some time.

As I had distinguished myself not a little during the war, General Lake sent me up with despatches to Calcutta, where Lord Wellesley received me with the greatest distinction. Fancy my surprise, on going to a ball at Government House, to meet my old friend Jowler; my trembling, blushing, thrilling delight, when I saw Julia by his side!

Jowler seemed to blush too when he beheld me. I thought of my former passages with his daughter. "Gagy my boy," says he, shaking hands, "glad to see you. Old friend, Julia—come to tiffin—Hodgson's pale—brave fellow Gagy." Julia did not speak, but she turned ashy pale, and fixed upon me her awful eyes! I fainted almost, and uttered some incoherent words. Julia took my hand, gazed at me still, and said, "Come!" Need I say I went?

I will not go over the pale ale and currie-bhaut again; but this I know, that in half an hour I was as much in love as I ever had been: and that in three weeks I—yes, I—was the accepted lover of Julia! I did not pause to ask where were the one hundred and twenty-four offers? why I, refused before, should be accepted now? I only felt that I loved her, and was happy!

One night, one memorable night, I could not sleep, and, with a lover's pardonable passion, wandered solitary through the city of palaces until I came to the house which contained my Julia. I peeped into the compound—all was still; I looked into the veranda—all was dark, except a light—yes, one light—and it was in Julia's chamber! My heart throbbed almost to stilling. I would—I WOULD advance, if but to gaze upon her for a moment, and to bless her as she slept. I DID look, I DID advance; and, O heaven! I saw a lamp burning, Mrs. Jow. in a nightdress, with a very dark baby in her arms, and Julia looking tenderly at an ayah, who was nursing another.

"Oh, mamma," said Julia, "what would that fool Gahagan say if he knew all?"

"HE DOES KNOW ALL!" shouted I, springing forward, and tearing down the tatties from the window. Mrs. Jow. ran shrieking out of the room, Julia fainted, the cursed black children squalled, and their d—d nurse fell on her knees, gabbling some infernal jargon of Hindustanee. Old Jowler at this juncture entered with a candle and a drawn sword.

"Liar! scoundrel! deceiver!" shouted I. "Turn, ruffian, and defend yourself!" But old Jowler, when he saw me, only whistled, looked at his lifeless daughter, and slowly left the room.

Why continue the tale? I need not now account for Jowler's gloom on receiving his letters from Benares—for his exclamation upon the death of the Indian chief—for his desire to marry his daughter: the woman I was wooing was no longer Miss Julia Jowler, she was Mrs. Chowder Loll!

CHAPTER II

ALLYGHUR AND LASWAREE

I sat down to write gravely and sadly, for (since the appearance of some of my adventures in a monthly magazine) unprincipled men have endeavored to rob me of the only good I possess, to question the statements that I make, and, themselves without a spark of honor or good feeling, to steal from me that which is my sole wealth—my character as a teller of THE TRUTH.

The reader will understand that it is to the illiberal strictures of a profligate press I now allude; among the London journalists, none (luckily for themselves) have dared to question the veracity of my statements: they know me, and they know that I am IN LONDON. If I can use the pen, I can also wield a more manly and terrible weapon, and would answer their contradictions with my sword! No gold or gems adorn the hilt of that war-worn scimitar; but there is blood upon the blade—the blood of the enemies of my country, and the maligners of my honest fame. There are others, however—the disgrace of a disgraceful trade—who, borrowing from distance a despicable courage, have ventured to assail me. The infamous editors of the Kelso Champion, the Bungay Beacon, the Tipperary Argus, and the Stoke Pogis Sentinel, and other dastardly organs of the provincial press, have, although differing in politics, agreed upon this one point, and with a scoundrelly unanimity, vented a flood of abuse upon the revelations made by me.

They say that I have assailed private characters, and wilfully perverted history to blacken the reputation of public men. I ask, was any one of these men in Bengal in the year 1803? Was any single conductor of any one of these paltry prints ever in Bundelcund or the Rohilla country? Does this EXQUISITE Tipperary scribe know the difference between Hurrygurrybang and Burrumtollah? Not he! and because, forsooth, in those strange and distant lands strange circumstances have taken place, it is insinuated that the relater is a liar: nay, that the very places themselves have no existence but in my imagination. Fools!—but I will not waste my anger upon them, and proceed to recount some other portions of my personal history.

It is, I presume, a fact which even THESE scribbling assassins will not venture to deny, that before the commencement of the campaign against Scindiah, the English General formed a camp at Kanouge on the Jumna, where he exercised that brilliant little army which was speedily to perform such wonders in the Dooab. It will be as well to give a slight account of the causes of a war which was speedily to rage through some of the fairest portions of the Indian continent.

Shah Allum, the son of Shah Lollum, the descendant by the female line of Nadir Shah (that celebrated Toorkomaun adventurer, who had wellnigh hurled Bajazet and Selim the Second from the throne of Bagdad)—Shah Allum, I say, although nominally the Emperor of Delhi, was in reality the slave of the various warlike chieftains who lorded it by turns over the country and the sovereign, until conquered and slain by some more successful rebel. Chowder Loll Masolgee, Zubberdust Khan, Dowsunt Row Scindiah, and the celebrated Bobbachy Jung Bahawder, had held for a time complete mastery in Delhi. The second of these, a ruthless Afghan soldier, had abruptly entered the capital; nor was he ejected from it until he had seized upon the principal jewels, and likewise put out the eyes of the last of the unfortunate family of Afrasiab. Scindiah came to the rescue of the sightless Shah Allum, and though he destroyed his oppressor, only increased his slavery; holding him in as painful a bondage as he had suffered under the tyrannous Afghan.

As long as these heroes were battling among themselves, or as long rather as it appeared that they had any strength to fight a battle, the British Government, ever anxious to see its enemies by the ears, by no means interfered in the contest. But the French Revolution broke out, and a host of starving sans-culottes appeared among the various Indian States, seeking for military service, and inflaming the minds of the various native princes against the British East India Company. A number of these entered into Scindiah's ranks: one of them, Perron, was commander of his army; and though that chief was as yet quite engaged in his hereditary quarrel with Jeswunt Row Holkar, and never thought of an invasion of the British territory, the Company all of a sudden discovered that Shah Allum, his sovereign, was shamefully ill-used, and determined to re-establish the ancient splendor of his throne.

Of course it was sheer benevolence for poor Shah Allum that prompted our governors to take these kindly measures in his favor. I don't know how it happened that, at the end of the war, the poor Shah was not a whit better off than at the beginning; and that though Holkar was beaten, and Scindiah annihilated, Shah Allum was much such a puppet as before. Somehow, in the hurry and confusion of this struggle, the oyster remained with the British Government, who had so kindly offered to dress it for the Emperor, while his Majesty was obliged to be contented with the shell.

The force encamped at Kanouge bore the title of the Grand Army of the Ganges and the Jumna; it consisted of eleven regiments of cavalry and twelve battalions of infantry, and was commanded by General Lake in person.

Well, on the 1st of September we stormed Perron's camp at Allyghur; on the fourth we took that fortress by assault; and as my name was mentioned in general orders, I may as well quote the Commander-in-Chief's words regarding me—they will spare me the trouble of composing my own eulogium:—

"The Commander-in-Chief is proud thus publicly to declare his high sense of the gallantry of Lieutenant Gahagan, of the — cavalry. In the storming of the fortress, although unprovided with a single ladder, and accompanied but by a few brave men, Lieutenant Gahagan succeeded in escalading the inner and fourteenth wall of the place. Fourteen ditches lined with sword-blades and poisoned chevaux-de-frise, fourteen walls bristling with innumerable artillery and as smooth as looking-glasses, were in turn triumphantly passed by that enterprising officer. His course was to be traced by the heaps of slaughtered enemies lying thick upon the platforms; and alas! by the corpses of most of the gallant men who followed him!—when at length he effected his lodgment, and the dastardly enemy, who dared not to confront him with arms, let loose upon him the tigers and lions of Scindiah's menagerie. This meritorious officer destroyed, with his own hand, four of the largest and most ferocious animals, and the rest, awed by the indomitable majesty of BRITISH VALOR, shrank back to their dens. Thomas Higgory, a private, and Runty Goss, havildar, were the only two who remained out of the nine hundred who followed Lieutenant Gahagan. Honor to them! honor and tears for the brave men who perished on that awful day!"

I have copied this, word for word, from the Bengal Hurkaru of September 24, 1803: and anybody who has the slightest doubt as to the statement, may refer to the paper itself.

And here I must pause to give thanks to Fortune, which so marvellously preserved me, Sergeant-Major Higgory, and Runty Goss. Were I to say that any valor of ours had carried us unhurt through this tremendous combat, the reader would laugh me to scorn. No: though my narrative is extraordinary, it is nevertheless authentic; and never, never would I sacrifice truth for the mere sake of effect. The fact is this:—the citadel of Allyghur is situated upon a rock, about a thousand feet above the level of the sea, and is surrounded by fourteen walls, as his Excellency was good enough to remark in his despatch. A man who would mount these without scaling-ladders, is an ass; he who would SAY he mounted them without such assistance, is a liar and a knave. We HAD scaling-ladders at the commencement of the assault, although it was quite impossible to carry them beyond the first line of batteries. Mounted on them, however, as our troops were falling thick about me, I saw that we must ignominiously retreat, unless some other help could be found for our brave fellows to escalade the next wall. It was about seventy feet high. I instantly turned the guns of wall A on wall B, and peppered the latter so as to make, not a breach, but a scaling place; the men mounting in the holes made by the shot. By this simple stratagem, I managed to pass each successive barrier—for to ascend a wall which the General was pleased to call "as smooth as glass" is an absurd impossibility: I seek to achieve none such:—

"I dare do all that may become a man,

Who dares do more, is neither more nor less."

Of course, had the enemy's guns been commonly well served, not one of us would ever have been alive out of the three; but whether it was owing to fright, or to the excessive smoke caused by so many pieces of artillery, arrive we did. On the platforms, too, our work was not quite so difficult as might be imagined—killing these fellows was sheer butchery. As soon as we appeared, they all turned and fled helter-skelter, and the reader may judge of their courage by the fact that out of about seven hundred men killed by us, only forty had wounds in front, the rest being bayoneted as they ran.

And beyond all other pieces of good fortune was the very letting out of these tigers; which was the dernier ressort of Bournonville, the second commandant of the fort. I had observed this man (conspicuous for a tri-colored scarf which he wore) upon every one of the walls as we stormed them, and running away the very first among the fugitives. He had all the keys of the gates; and in his tremor, as he opened the menagerie portal, left the whole bunch in the door, which I seized when the animals were overcome. Runty Goss then opened them one by one, our troops entered, and the victorious standard of my country floated on the walls of Allyghur!

When the General, accompanied by his staff; entered the last line of fortifications, the brave old man raised me from the dead rhinoceros on which I was seated, and pressed me to his breast. But the excitement which had borne me through the fatigues and perils of that fearful day failed all of a sudden, and I wept like a child upon his shoulder.

Promotion, in our army, goes unluckily by seniority; nor is it in the power of the General-in-Chief to advance a Caesar, if he finds him in the capacity of a subaltern: MY reward for the above exploit was, therefore, not very rich. His Excellency had a favorite horn snuff-box (for, though exalted in station, he was in his habits most simple): of this, and about a quarter of an ounce of high-dried Welsh, which he always took, he made me a present, saying, in front of the line, "Accept this, Mr. Gahagan, as a token of respect from the first to the bravest officer in the army."

Calculating the snuff to be worth a halfpenny, I should say that fourpence was about the value of this gift: but it has at least this good effect—it serves to convince any person who doubts my story, that the facts of it are really true. I have left it at the office of my publisher, along with the extract from the Bengal Hurkaru, and anybody may examine both by applying in the counting-house of Mr. Cunningham.* That once popular expression, or proverb, "are you up to snuff?" arose out of the above circumstance; for the officers of my corps, none of whom, except myself, had ventured on the storming-party, used to twit me about this modest reward for my labors. Never mind! when they want me to storm a fort AGAIN, I shall know better.

* The Major certainly offered to leave an old snuff-box at Mr. Cunningham's office; but it contained no extract from a newspaper, and does not QUITE prove that he killed a rhinoceros and stormed fourteen intrenchments at the siege of Allyghur.

Well, immediately after the capture of this important fortress, Perron, who had been the life and soul of Scindiah's army, came in to us, with his family and treasure, and was passed over to the French settlements at Chandernagur. Bourquien took his command, and against him we now moved. The morning of the 11th of September found us upon the plains of Delhi.

It was a burning hot day, and we were all refreshing ourselves after the morning's march, when I, who was on the advanced piquet along with O'Gawler of the King's Dragoons, was made aware of the enemy's neighborhood in a very singular manner. O'Gawler and I were seated under a little canopy of horse-cloths, which we had formed to shelter us from the intolerable heat of the sun, and were discussing with great delight a few Manilla cheroots, and a stone jar of the most exquisite, cool, weak, refreshing sangaree. We had been playing cards the night before, and O'Gawler had lost to me seven hundred rupees. I emptied the last of the sangaree into the two pint tumblers out of which we were drinking, and holding mine up, said, "Here's better luck to you next time, O'Gawler!"

As I spoke the words—whish!—a cannon-ball cut the tumbler clean out of my hand, and plumped into poor O'Gawler's stomach. It settled him completely, and of course I never got my seven hundred rupees. Such are the uncertainties of war!

To strap on my sabre and my accoutrements—to mount my Arab charger—to drink off what O'Gawler had left of the sangaree—and to gallop to the General, was the work of a moment. I found him as comfortably at tiffin as if he were at his own house in London.

"General," said I, as soon as I got into his paijamahs (or tent), "you must leave your lunch if you want to fight the enemy."

"The enemy—psha! Mr. Gahagan, the enemy is on the other side of the river."

"I can only tell your Excellency that the enemy's guns will hardly carry five miles, and that Cornet O'Gawler was this moment shot dead at my side with a cannon-ball."

"Ha! is it so?" said his Excellency, rising, and laying down the drumstick of a grilled chicken. "Gentlemen, remember that the eyes of Europe are upon us, and follow me!"

Each aide-de-camp started from table and seized his cocked hat; each British heart beat high at the thoughts of the coming melee. We mounted our horses and galloped swiftly after the brave old General; I not the last in the train, upon my famous black charger.

It was perfectly true, the enemy were posted in force within three miles of our camp, and from a hillock in the advance to which we galloped, we were enabled with our telescopes to see the whole of his imposing line. Nothing can better describe it than this:—

_____  ...............................A    .      .      .      .

—A is the enemy, and the dots represent the hundred and twenty pieces of artillery which defended his line. He was, moreover, intrenched; and a wide morass in his front gave him an additional security.

His Excellency for a moment surveyed the line, and then said, turning round to one of his aides-de-camp, "Order up Major-General Tinkler and the cavalry."

"HERE, does your Excellency mean?" said the aide-de-camp, surprised, for the enemy had perceived us, and the cannon-balls were flying about as thick as peas.

"HERE, sir!" said the old General, stamping with his foot in a passion, and the A.D.C. shrugged his shoulders and galloped away. In five minutes we heard the trumpets in our camp, and in twenty more the greater part of the cavalry had joined us.

Up they came, five thousand men, their standards flapping in the air, their long line of polished jack-boots gleaming in the golden sunlight. "And now we are here," said Major-General Sir Theophilus Tinkler, "what next?" "Oh, damn it," said the Commander-in-Chief, "charge, charge—nothing like charging—galloping—guns—rascally black scoundrels—charge, charge!" And then turning round to me (perhaps he was glad to change the conversation), he said, "Lieutenant Gahagan, you will stay with me."

And well for him I did, for I do not hesitate to say that the battle WAS GAINED BY ME. I do not mean to insult the reader by pretending that any personal exertions of mine turned the day,—that I killed, for instance, a regiment of cavalry or swallowed a battery of guns,—such absurd tales would disgrace both the hearer and the teller. I, as is well known, never say a single word which cannot be proved, and hate more than all other vices the absurd sin of egotism; I simply mean that my ADVICE to the General, at a quarter past two o'clock in the afternoon of that day, won this great triumph for the British army.

Gleig, Mill, and Thorn have all told the tale of this war, though somehow they have omitted all mention of the hero of it. General Lake, for the victory of that day, became Lord Lake of Laswaree. Laswaree! and who, forsooth, was the real conqueror of Laswaree? I can lay my hand upon my heart and say that I was. If any proof is wanting of the fact, let me give it at once, and from the highest military testimony in the world—I mean that of the Emperor Napoleon.

In the month of March, 1817, I was passenger on board the "Prince Regent," Captain Harris, which touched at St. Helena on its passage from Calcutta to England. In company with the other officers on board the ship, I paid my respects to the illustrious exile of Longwood, who received us in his garden, where he was walking about, in a nankeen dress and a large broad-brimmed straw-hat, with General Montholon, Count Las Casas, and his son Emanuel, then a little boy; who I dare say does not recollect me, but who nevertheless played with my sword-knot and the tassels of my Hessian boots during the whole of our interview with his Imperial Majesty.

Our names were read out (in a pretty accent, by the way!) by General Montholon, and the Emperor, as each was pronounced, made a bow to the owner of it, but did not vouchsafe a word. At last Montholon came to mine. The Emperor looked me at once in the face, took his hands out of his pockets, put them behind his back, and coming up to me smiling, pronounced the following words:—

"Assaye, Delhi, Deeg, Futtyghur?"

I blushed, and taking off my hat with a bow, said—"Sire, c'est moi."

"Parbleu! je le savais bien," said the Emperor, holding out his snuff-box. "En usez-vous, Major?" I took a large pinch (which, with the honor of speaking to so great a man, brought the tears into my eyes), and he continued as nearly as possible in the following words:—

"Sir, you are known; you come of an heroic nation. Your third brother, the Chef de Bataillon, Count Godfrey Gahagan, was in my Irish brigade."

Gahagan.—"Sire, it is true. He and my countrymen in your Majesty's service stood under the green flag in the breach of Burgos, and beat Wellington back. It was the only time, as your Majesty knows, that Irishmen and Englishmen were beaten in that war."

Napoleon (looking as if he would say, "D--your candor, Major Gahagan").—"Well, well; it was so. Your brother was a Count, and died a General in my service."

Gahagan.—"He was found lying upon the bodies of nine-and-twenty Cossacks at Borodino. They were all dead, and bore the Gahagan mark."

Napoleon (to Montholon).—"C'est vrai, Montholon: je vous donne ma parole d'honneur la plus sacree, que c'est vrai. Ils ne sont pas d'autres, ces terribles Ga'gans. You must know that Monsieur gained the battle of Delhi as certainly as I did that of Austerlitz. In this way:—Ce belitre de Lor Lake, after calling up his cavalry, and placing them in front of Holkar's batteries, qui balayaient la plaine, was for charging the enemy's batteries with his horse, who would have been ecrases, mitrailles, foudroyes to a man but for the cunning of ce grand rogue que vous voyez."

Montholon.—"Coquin de Major, va!"

Napoleon.—"Montholon! tais-toi. When Lord Lake, with his great bull-headed English obstinacy, saw the facheuse position into which he had brought his troops, he was for dying on the spot, and would infallibly have done so—and the loss of his army would have been the ruin of the East India Company—and the ruin of the English East India Company would have established my empire (bah! it was a republic then!) in the East—but that the man before us, Lieutenant Goliah Gahagan, was riding at the side of General Lake."

Montholon (with an accent of despair and fury).—"Gredin! cent mille tonnerres de Dieu!"

Napoleon (benignantly).—"Calme-toi, mon fidele ami. What will you? It was fate. Gahagan, at the critical period of the battle, or rather slaughter (for the English had not slain a man of the enemy), advised a retreat."

Montholon. "Le lache! Un Francais meurt, mais il ne recule jamais."

Napoleon.—"STUPIDE! Don't you see WHY the retreat was ordered?—don't you know that it was a feint on the part of Gahagan to draw Holkar from his impregnable intrenchments? Don't you know that the ignorant Indian fell into the snare, and issuing from behind the cover of his guns, came down with his cavalry on the plains in pursuit of Lake and his dragoons? Then it was that the Englishmen turned upon him; the hardy children of the north swept down his feeble horsemen, bore them back to their guns, which were useless, entered Holkar's intrenchments along with his troops, sabred the artillerymen at their pieces, and won the battle of Delhi!"

As the Emperor spoke, his pale cheek glowed red, his eye flashed fire, his deep clear voice rung as of old when he pointed out the enemy from beneath the shadow of the Pyramids, or rallied his regiments to the charge upon the death-strewn plain of Wagram. I have had many a proud moment in my life, but never such a proud one as this; and I would readily pardon the word "coward," as applied to me by Montholon, in consideration of the testimony which his master bore in my favor.

"Major," said the Emperor to me in conclusion, "why had I not such a man as you in my service? I would have made you a Prince and a Marshal!" and here he fell into a reverie, of which I knew and respected the purport. He was thinking, doubtless, that I might have retrieved his fortunes; and indeed I have very little doubt that I might.

Very soon after, coffee was brought by Monsieur Marchand, Napoleon's valet-de-chambre, and after partaking of that beverage, and talking upon the politics of the day, the Emperor withdrew, leaving me deeply impressed by the condescension he had shown in this remarkable interview.

CHAPTER III

A PEEP INTO SPAIN—ACCOUNT OF THE ORIGIN AND SERVICES OF THE AHMEDNUGGAR IRREGULARS.

HEAD QUARTERS, MORELLA, Sept. 16, 1838

I have been here for some months, along with my young friend Cabrera: and in the hurry and bustle of war—daily on guard and in the batteries for sixteen hours out of the twenty-four, with fourteen severe wounds and seven musket-balls in my body—it may be imagined that I have had little time to think about the publication of my memoirs. Inter arma silent leges—in the midst of fighting be hanged to writing! as the poet says; and I never would have bothered myself with a pen, had not common gratitude incited me to throw off a few pages.

Along with Oraa's troops, who have of late been beleaguering this place, there was a young Milesian gentleman, Mr. Toone O'Connor Emmett Fitzgerald Sheeny, by name, a law student, and member of Gray's Inn, and what he called Bay Ah of Trinity College, Dublin. Mr. Sheeny was with the Queen's people, not in a military capacity, but as representative of an English journal; to which, for a trifling weekly remuneration, he was in the habit of transmitting accounts of the movements of the belligerents, and his own opinion of the politics of Spain. Receiving, for the discharge of his duty, a couple of guineas a week from the proprietors of the journal in question, he was enabled, as I need scarcely say, to make such a show in Oraa's camp as only a Christino general officer, or at the very least a colonel of a regiment, can afford to keep up.

In the famous sortie which we made upon the twenty-third, I was of course among the foremost in the melee, and found myself, after a good deal of slaughtering (which it would be as disagreeable as useless to describe here), in the court of a small inn or podesta, which had been made the head-quarters of several Queenite officers during the siege. The pesatero or landlord of the inn had been despatched by my brave chapel-churies, with his fine family of children—the officers quartered in the podesta had of course bolted; but one man remained, and my fellows were on the point of cutting him into ten thousand pieces with their borachios, when I arrived in the room time enough to prevent the catastrophe. Seeing before me an individual in the costume of a civilian—a white hat, a light blue satin cravat, embroidered with butterflies and other quadrupeds, a green coat and brass buttons, and a pair of blue plaid trousers, I recognized at once a countryman, and interposed to save his life.

In an agonized brogue the unhappy young man was saying all that he could to induce the chapel-churies to give up their intention of slaughtering him; but it is very little likely that his protestations would have had any effect upon them, had not I appeared in the room, and shouted to the ruffians to hold their hand.

Seeing a general officer before them (I have the honor to hold that rank in the service of his Catholic Majesty), and moreover one six feet four in height, and armed with that terrible cabecilla (a sword so called, because it is five feet long) which is so well known among the Spanish armies—seeing, I say, this figure, the fellows retired, exclaiming, "Adios, corpo di bacco, nosotros," and so on, clearly proving (by their words) that they would, if they dared, have immolated the victim whom I had thus rescued from their fury. "Villains!" shouted I, hearing them grumble, "away! quit the apartment!" Each man, sulkily sheathing his sombrero, obeyed, and quitted the camarilla.

It was then that Mr. Sheeny detailed to me the particulars to which I have briefly adverted; and, informing me at the same time that he had a family in England who would feel obliged to me for his release, and that his most intimate friend the English ambassador would move heaven and earth to revenge his fall, he directed my attention to a portmanteau passably well filled, which he hoped would satisfy the cupidity of my troops. I said, though with much regret, that I must subject his person to a search; and hence arose the circumstance which has called for what I fear you will consider a somewhat tedious explanation. I found upon Mr. Sheeny's person three sovereigns in English money (which I have to this day), and singularly enough a copy of The New Monthly Magazine, containing a portion of my adventures. It was a toss-up whether I should let the poor young man be shot or no, but this little circumstance saved his life. The gratified vanity of authorship induced me to accept his portmanteau and valuables, and to allow the poor wretch to go free. I put the Magazine in my coat-pocket, and left him and the podesta.

The men, to my surprise, had quitted the building, and it was full time for me to follow; for I found our sallying party, after committing dreadful ravages in Oraa's lines, were in full retreat upon the fort, hotly pressed by a superior force of the enemy. I am pretty well known and respected by the men of both parties in Spain (indeed I served for some months on the Queen's side before I came over to Don Carlos); and, as it is my maxim never to give quarter, I never expect to receive it when taken myself. On issuing from the podesta with Sheeny's portmanteau and my sword in my hand, I was a little disgusted and annoyed to see our own men in a pretty good column retreating at double-quick, and about four hundred yards beyond me, up the hill leading to the fort; while on my left hand, and at only a hundred yards, a troop of the Queenite lancers were clattering along the road.

I had got into the very middle of the road before I made this discovery, so that the fellows had a full sight of me, and whiz! came a bullet by my left whisker before I could say Jack Robinson. I looked round—there were seventy of the accursed malvados at the least, and within, as I said, a hundred yards. Were I to say that I stopped to fight seventy men, you would write me down a fool or a liar: no, sir, I did not fight, I ran away.

I am six feet four—my figure is as well known in the Spanish army as that of the Count de Luchana, or my fierce little friend Cabrera himself. "GAHAGAN!" shouted out half a dozen scoundrelly voices, and fifty more shots came rattling after me. I was running—running as the brave stag before the hounds—running as I have done a great number of times before in my life, when there was no help for it but a race.

After I had run about five hundred yards, I saw that I had gained nearly three upon our column in front, and that likewise the Christino horsemen were left behind some hundred yards more; with the exception of three, who were fearfully near me. The first was an officer without a lance; he had fired both his pistols at me, and was twenty yards in advance of his comrades; there was a similar distance between the two lancers who rode behind him. I determined then to wait for No. 1, and as he came up delivered cut 3 at his horse's near leg—off it flew, and down, as I expected, went horse and man. I had hardly time to pass my sword through my prostrate enemy, when No. 2 was upon me. If I could but get that fellow's horse, thought I, I am safe; and I executed at once the plan which I hoped was to effect my rescue.

I had, as I said, left the podesta with Sheeny's portmanteau, and, unwilling to part with some of the articles it contained—some shirts, a bottle of whiskey, a few cakes of Windsor soap, &c. &c.,—I had carried it thus far on my shoulders, but now was compelled to sacrifice it malgre moi. As the lancer came up, I dropped my sword from my right hand, and hurled the portmanteau at his head, with aim so true, that he fell back on his saddle like a sack, and thus when the horse galloped up to me, I had no difficulty in dismounting the rider: the whiskey-bottle struck him over his right eye, and he was completely stunned. To dash him from the saddle and spring myself into it, was the work of a moment; indeed, the two combats had taken place in about a fifth part of the time which it has taken the reader to peruse the description. But in the rapidity of the last encounter, and the mounting of my enemy's horse, I had committed a very absurd oversight—I was scampering away WITHOUT MY SWORD! What was I to do?—to scamper on, to be sure, and trust to the legs of my horse for safety!

The lancer behind me gained on me every moment, and I could hear his horrid laugh as he neared me. I leaned forward jockey-fashion in my saddle, and kicked, and urged, and flogged with my hand, but all in vain. Closer—closer—the point of his lance was within two feet of my back. Ah! ah! he delivered the point, and fancy my agony when I felt it enter—through exactly fifty-nine pages of the New Monthly Magazine. Had it not been for that Magazine, I should have been impaled without a shadow of a doubt. Was I wrong in feeling gratitude? Had I not cause to continue my contributions to that periodical?

When I got safe into Morella, along with the tail of the sallying party, I was for the first time made acquainted with the ridiculous result of the lancer's thrust (as he delivered his lance, I must tell you that a ball came whiz over my head from our fellows, and entering at his nose, put a stop to HIS lancing for the future). I hastened to Cabrera's quarter, and related to him some of my adventures during the day.

"But, General," said he, "you are standing. I beg you chiudete l'uscio (take a chair)."

I did so, and then for the first time was aware that there was some foreign substance in the tail of my coat, which prevented my sitting at ease. I drew out the Magazine which I had seized, and there, to my wonder, DISCOVERED THE CHRISTINO LANCE twisted up like a fish-hook, or a pastoral crook.

"Ha! ha! ha!" said Cabrera (who is a notorious wag).

"Valdepenas madrilenos," growled out Tristany.

"By my cachuca di caballero (upon my honor as a gentleman)," shrieked out Ros d'Eroles, convulsed with laughter, "I will send it to the Bishop of Leon for a crozier."

"Gahagan has CONSECRATED it," giggled out Ramon Cabrera; and so they went on with their muchacas for an hour or more. But, when they heard that the means of my salvation from the lance of the scoundrelly Christino had been the Magazine containing my own history, their laugh was changed into wonder. I read them (speaking Spanish more fluently than English) every word of my story. "But how is this?" said Cabrera. "You surely have other adventures to relate?"

"Excellent Sir," said I, "I have;" and that very evening, as we sat over our cups of tertullia (sangaree), I continued my narrative in nearly the following words:—

"I left off in the very middle of the battle of Delhi, which ended, as everybody knows, in the complete triumph of the British arms. But who gained the battle? Lord Lake is called Viscount Lake of Delhi and Laswaree, while Major Gaha—nonsense, never mind HIM, never mind the charge he executed when, sabre in hand, he leaped the six-foot wall in the mouth of the roaring cannon, over the heads of the gleaming pikes; when, with one hand seizing the sacred peishcush, or fish—which was the banner always borne before Scindiah,—he, with his good sword, cut off the trunk of the famous white elephant, which, shrieking with agony, plunged madly into the Mahratta ranks, followed by his giant brethren, tossing, like chaff before the wind, the affrighted kitmatgars. He, meanwhile, now plunging into the midst of a battalion of consomahs, now cleaving to the chine a screaming and ferocious bobbachee,* rushed on, like the simoom across the red Zaharan plain, killing with his own hand, a hundred and forty-thr—but never mind—'ALONE HE DID IT;' sufficient be it for him, however, that the victory was won: he cares not for the empty honors which were awarded to more fortunate men!

* The double-jointed camel of Bactria, which the classic reader may recollect is mentioned by Suidas (in his Commentary on the Flight of Darius), is so called by the Mahrattas.

"We marched after the battle to Delhi, where poor blind old Shah Allum received us, and bestowed all kinds of honors and titles on our General. As each of the officers passed before him, the Shah did not fail to remark my person,* and was told my name.

* There is some trifling inconsistency on the Major's part. Shah Allum was notoriously blind: how, then, could he have seen Gahagan? The thing is manifestly impossible.

"Lord Lake whispered to him my exploits, and the old man was so delighted with the account of my victory over the elephant (whose trunk I use to this day), that he said, 'Let him be called GUJPUTI,' or the lord of elephants; and Gujputi was the name by which I was afterwards familiarly known among the natives,—the men, that is. The women had a softer appellation for me, and called me 'Mushook,' or charmer.

"Well, I shall not describe Delhi, which is doubtless well known to the reader; nor the siege of Agra, to which place we went from Delhi; nor the terrible day at Laswaree, which went nigh to finish the war. Suffice it to say that we were victorious, and that I was wounded; as I have invariably been in the two hundred and four occasions when I have found myself in action. One point, however, became in the course of this campaign QUITE evident—THAT SOMETHING MUST BE DONE FOR GAHAGAN. The country cried shame, the King's troops grumbled, the sepoys openly murmured that their Gujputi was only a lieutenant, when he had performed such signal services. What was to be done? Lord Wellesley was in an evident quandary. 'Gahagan,' wrote he, 'to be a subaltern is evidently not your fate—YOU WERE BORN FOR COMMAND; but Lake and General Wellesley are good officers, they cannot be turned out—I must make a post for you. What say you, my dear fellow, to a corps of IRREGULAR HORSE?'

"It was thus that the famous corps of AHMEDNUGGAR IRREGULARS had its origin; a guerilla force, it is true, but one which will long be remembered in the annals of our Indian campaigns.

"As the commander of this regiment, I was allowed to settle the uniform of the corps, as well as to select recruits. These were not wanting as soon as my appointment was made known, but came flocking to my standard a great deal faster than to the regular corps in the Company's service. I had European officers, of course, to command them, and a few of my countrymen as sergeants; the rest were all natives, whom I chose of the strongest and bravest men in India; chiefly Pitans, Afghans, Hurrumzadehs, and Calliawns: for these are well known to be the most warlike districts of our Indian territory.

"When on parade and in full uniform we made a singular and noble appearance. I was always fond of dress; and, in this instance, gave a carte blanche to my taste, and invented the most splendid costume that ever perhaps decorated a soldier. I am, as I have stated already, six feet four inches in height, and of matchless symmetry and proportion. My hair and beard are of the most brilliant auburn, so bright as scarcely to be distinguished at a distance from scarlet. My eyes are bright blue, overshadowed by bushy eyebrows of the color of my hair, and a terrific gash of the deepest purple, which goes over the forehead, the eyelid, and the cheek, and finishes at the ear, gives my face a more strictly military appearance than can be conceived. When I have been drinking (as is pretty often the case) this gash becomes ruby bright, and as I have another which took off a piece of my under-lip, and shows five of my front teeth, I leave you to imagine that 'seldom lighted on the earth' (as the monster Burke remarked of one of his unhappy victims), 'a more extraordinary vision.' I improved these natural advantages; and, while in cantonment during the hot winds at Chittybobbary, allowed my hair to grow very long, as did my beard, which reached to my waist. It took me two hours daily to curl my hair in ten thousand little cork-screw ringlets, which waved over my shoulders, and to get my moustaches well round to the corners of my eyelids. I dressed in loose scarlet trousers and red morocco boots, a scarlet jacket, and a shawl of the same color round my waist; a scarlet turban three feet high, and decorated with a tuft of the scarlet feathers of the flamingo, formed my head-dress, and I did not allow myself a single ornament, except a small silver skull and crossbones in front of my turban. Two brace of pistols, a Malay creese, and a tulwar, sharp on both sides, and very nearly six feet in length, completed this elegant costume. My two flags were each surmounted with a red skull and cross-bones, and ornamented, one with a black, and the other with a red beard (of enormous length, taken from men slain in battle by me). On one flag were of course the arms of John Company; on the other, an image of myself bestriding a prostrate elephant, with the simple word, 'Gujputi' written underneath in the Nagaree, Persian, and Sanscrit characters. I rode my black horse, and looked, by the immortal gods, like Mars. To me might be applied the words which were written concerning handsome General Webb, in Marlborough's time:—

"'To noble danger he conducts the way,
His great example all his troop obey,
Before the front the Major sternly rides,
With such an air as Mars to battle strides.
Propitious heaven must sure a hero save
Like Paris handsome, and like Hector brave!'

"My officers (Captains Biggs and Mackanulty, Lieutenants Glogger, Pappendick, Stuffle, &c., &c.) were dressed exactly in the same way, but in yellow; and the men were similarly equipped, but in black. I have seen many regiments since, and many ferocious-looking men, but the Ahmednuggar Irregulars were more dreadful to the view than any set of ruffians on which I ever set eyes. I would to heaven that the Czar of Muscovy had passed through Cabool and Lahore, and that I with my old Ahmednuggars stood on a fair field to meet him! Bless you, bless you, my swart companions in victory! through the mist of twenty years I hear the booming of your war-cry, and mark the glitter of your scimitars as ye rage in the thickest of the battle!*

*I do not wish to brag of my style of writing, or to pretend that my genius as a writer has not been equalled in former times; but if, in the works of Byron, Scott, Goethe, or Victor Hugo, the reader can find a more beautiful sentence than the above, I will be obliged to him, that is all—I simply say, I WILL BE OBLIGED TO HIM.—G. O'G. G., M. H. E. I. C. S., C. I. H. A.*

"But away with melancholy reminiscences. You may fancy what a figure the Irregulars cut on a field-day—a line of five hundred black-faced, black-dressed, black-horsed, black-bearded men—Biggs, Glogger, and the other officers in yellow, galloping about the field like flashes of lightning; myself enlightening them, red, solitary, and majestic, like yon glorious orb in heaven.

"There are very few men, I presume, who have not heard of Holkar's sudden and gallant incursion into the Dooab, in the year 1804, when we thought that the victory of Laswaree and the brilliant success at Deeg had completely finished him. Taking ten thousand horse he broke up his camp at Palimbang; and the first thing General Lake heard of him was, that he was at Putna, then at Rumpooge, then at Doncaradam—he was, in fact, in the very heart of our territory.

"The unfortunate part of the affair was this:—His Excellency, despising the Mahratta chieftain, had allowed him to advance about two thousand miles in his front, and knew not in the slightest degree where to lay hold on him. Was he at Hazarubaug? was he at Bogly Gunge? nobody knew, and for a considerable period the movements of Lake's cavalry were quite ambiguous, uncertain, promiscuous, and undetermined.

"Such, briefly, was the state of affairs in October, 1804. At the beginning of that month I had been wounded (a trifling scratch, cutting off my left upper eyelid, a bit of my cheek, and my under lip), and I was obliged to leave Biggs in command of my Irregulars, whilst I retired for my wounds to an English station at Furruckabad, alias Futtyghur—it is, as every twopenny postman knows, at the apex of the Dooab. We have there a cantonment, and thither I went for the mere sake of the surgeon and the sticking-plaster.

"Furruckabad, then, is divided into two districts or towns: the lower Cotwal, inhabited by the natives, and the upper (which is fortified slightly, and has all along been called Futtyghur, meaning in Hindoostanee 'the-favorite-resort-of-the-white-faced-Feringhees-near the-mango-tope-consecrated-to Ram') occupied by Europeans. (It is astonishing, by the way, how comprehensive that language is, and how much can be conveyed in one or two of the commonest phrases.)

"Biggs, then, and my men were playing all sorts of wondrous pranks with Lord Lake's army, whilst I was detained an unwilling prisoner of health at Futtyghur.

"An unwilling prisoner, however, I should not say. The cantonment at Futtyghur contained that which would have made ANY man a happy slave. Woman, lovely woman, was there in abundance and variety! The fact is, that when the campaign commenced in 1803, the ladies of the army all congregated to this place, where they were left, as it was supposed, in safety. I might, like Homer, relate the names and qualities of all. I may at least mention SOME whose memory is still most dear to me. There was—

"Mrs. Major-General Bulcher, wife of Bulcher of the infantry.

"Miss Bulcher.

"Miss BELINDA BULCHER (whose name I beg the printer to place in large capitals.)

"Mrs. Colonel Vandegobbleschroy.

"Mrs. Major Macan and the four Misses Macan.

"The Honorable Mrs. Burgoo, Mrs. Flix, Hicks, Wicks, and many more too numerous to mention. The flower of our camp was, however, collected there, and the last words of Lord Lake to me, as I left him, were, 'Gahagan, I commit those women to your charge. Guard them with your life, watch over them with your honor, defend them with the matchless power of your indomitable arm.'

"Futtyghur is, as I have said, a European station, and the pretty air of the bungalows, amid the clustering topes of mango-trees, has often ere this excited the admiration of the tourist and sketcher. On the brow of a hill—the Burrumpooter river rolls majestically at its base; and no spot, in a word, can be conceived more exquisitely arranged, both by art and nature, as a favorite residence of the British fair. Mrs. Bulcher, Mrs. Vandegobbleschroy, and the other married ladies above mentioned, had each of them delightful bungalows and gardens in the place, and between one cottage and another my time passed as delightfully as can the hours of any man who is away from his darling occupation of war.

"I was the commandant of the fort. It is a little insignificant pettah, defended simply by a couple of gabions, a very ordinary counterscarp, and a bomb-proof embrasure. On the top of this my flag was planted, and the small garrison of forty men only were comfortably barracked off in the case-mates within. A surgeon and two chaplains (there were besides three reverend gentlemen of amateur missions, who lived in the town,) completed, as I may say, the garrison of our little fortalice, which I was left to defend and to command.

"On the night of the first of November, in the year 1804, I had invited Mrs. Major-General Bulcher and her daughters, Mrs. Vandegobbleschroy, and, indeed, all the ladies in the cantonment, to a little festival in honor of the recovery of my health, of the commencement of the shooting season, and indeed as a farewell visit, for it was my intention to take dawk the very next morning and return to my regiment. The three amateur missionaries whom I have mentioned, and some ladies in the cantonment of very rigid religious principles, refused to appear at my little party. They had better never have been born than have done as they did: as you shall hear.

"We had been dancing merrily all night, and the supper (chiefly of the delicate condor, the luscious adjutant, and other birds of a similar kind, which I had shot in the course of the day) had been duly feted by every lady and gentleman present; when I took an opportunity to retire on the ramparts, with the interesting and lovely Belinda Bulcher. I was occupied, as the French say, in conter-ing fleurettes to this sweet young creature, when, all of a sudden, a rocket was seen whizzing through the air, and a strong light was visible in the valley below the little fort.

"'What, fireworks! Captain Gahagan,' said Belinda; 'this is too gallant.'

"'Indeed, my dear Miss Bulcher,' said I, 'they are fireworks of which I have no idea: perhaps our friends the missionaries—'

"'Look, look!' said Belinda, trembling, and clutching tightly hold of my arm: 'what do I see? yes—no—yes! it is—OUR BUNGALOW IS IN FLAMES!'

"It was true, the spacious bungalow occupied by Mrs. Major-General was at that moment seen a prey to the devouring element—another and another succeeded it—seven bungalows, before I could almost ejaculate the name of Jack Robinson, were seen blazing brightly in the black midnight air!

"I seized my night-glass, and looking towards the spot where the conflagration raged, what was my astonishment to see thousands of black forms dancing round the fires; whilst by their lights I could observe columns after columns of Indian horse, arriving and taking up their ground in the very middle of the open square or tank, round which the bungalows were built!

"'Ho, warder!' shouted I (while the frightened and trembling Belinda clung closer to my side, and pressed the stalwart arm that encircled her waist), 'down with the drawbridge! see that your masolgees' (small tumbrels which are used in place of large artillery) 'be well loaded: you, sepoys, hasten and man the ravelin! you, choprasees, put out the lights in the embrasures! we shall have warm work of it to-night, or my name is not Goliah Gahagan.'

"The ladies, the guests (to the number of eighty-three), the sepoys, choprasees, masolgees, and so on, had all crowded on the platform at the sound of my shouting, and dreadful was the consternation, shrill the screaming, occasioned by my words. The men stood irresolute and mute with terror! the women, trembling, knew scarcely whither to fly for refuge. 'Who are yonder ruffians?' said I. A hundred voices yelped in reply—some said the Pindarees, some said the Mahrattas, some vowed it was Scindiah, and others declared it was Holkar—no one knew.

"'Is there any one here,' said I, 'who will venture to reconnoitre yonder troops?' There was a dead pause.

"'A thousand tomauns to the man who will bring me news of yonder army!' again I repeated. Still a dead silence. The fact was that Scindiah and Holkar both were so notorious for their cruelty, that no one dared venture to face the danger. Oh for fifty of my brave Abmednuggarees!' thought I.

"'Gentlemen,' said I, 'I see it—you are cowards—none of you dare encounter the chance even of death. It is an encouraging prospect: know you not that the ruffian Holkar, if it be he, will with the morrow's dawn beleaguer our little fort, and throw thousands of men against our walls? know you not that, if we are taken, there is no quarter, no hope; death for us—and worse than death for these lovely ones assembled here?' Here the ladies shrieked and raised a howl as I have heard the jackals on a summer's evening. Belinda, my dear Belinda! flung both her arms round me, and sobbed on my shoulder (or in my waistcoat-pocket rather, for the little witch could reach no higher).

"'Captain Gahagan,' sobbed she, 'GO—GO—GOGGLE—IAH!'

"'My soul's adored!' replied I.

"'Swear to me one thing.'

"'I swear.'

"'That if—that if—the nasty, horrid, odious black Mah-ra-a-a-attahs take the fort, you will put me out of their power.'

"I clasped the dear girl to my heart, and swore upon my sword that, rather than she should incur the risk of dishonors she should perish by my own hand. This comforted her; and her mother, Mrs. Major-General Bulcher, and her elder sister, who had not until now known a word of our attachment, (indeed, but for these extraordinary circumstances, it is probable that we ourselves should never have discovered it,) were under these painful circumstances made aware of my beloved Belinda's partiality for me. Having communicated thus her wish of self-destruction, I thought her example a touching and excellent one, and proposed to all the ladies that they should follow it, and that at the entry of the enemy into the fort, and at a signal given by me, they should one and all make away with themselves. Fancy my disgust when, after making this proposition, not one of the ladies chose to accede to it, and received it with the same chilling denial that my former proposal to the garrison had met with.

"In the midst of this hurry and confusion, as if purposely to add to it, a trumpet was heard at the gate of the fort, and one of the sentinels came running to me, saying that a Mahratta soldier was before the gate with a flag of truce!

"I went down, rightly conjecturing, as it turned out, that the party, whoever they might be, had no artillery; and received at the point of my sword a scroll, of which the following is a translation:—

"'TO GOLIAH GAHAGAN GUJPUTI.

"'LORD OF ELEPHANTS, SIR,—I have the honor to inform you that I arrived before this place at eight o'clock P.M. with ten thousand cavalry under my orders. I have burned, since my arrival, seventeen bungalows in Furruckabad and Futtyghur, and have likewise been under the painful necessity of putting to death three clergymen (mollahs), and seven English officers, whom I found in the village; the women have been transferred to safe keeping in the harems of my officers and myself.

"'As I know your courage and talents, I shall be very happy if you will surrender the fortress, and take service as a major-general (hookahbadar) in my army. Should my proposal not meet with your assent, I beg leave to state that to-morrow I shall storm the fort, and on taking it, shall put to death every male in the garrison, and every female above twenty years of age. For yourself I shall reserve a punishment, which for novelty and exquisite torture has, I flatter myself, hardly ever been exceeded. Awaiting the favor of a reply, I am, Sir,

"'Your very obedient servant,

"'JESWUNT ROW HOLKAR.

"'CAMP BEFORE FUTTYGHUR, Sept. 1, 1804.

"'R. S. V. P.'

"The officer who had brought this precious epistle (it is astonishing how Holkar had aped the forms of English correspondence), an enormous Pitan soldier, with a shirt of mail, and a steel cap and cape, round which his turban wound, was leaning against the gate on his matchlock, and whistling a national melody.

I read the letter, and saw at once there was no time to be lost. That man, thought I, must never go back to Holkar. Were he to attack us now before we were prepared, the fort would be his in half an hour.

"Tying my white pocket-handkerchief to a stick, I flung open the gate and advanced to the officer; he was standing, I said, on the little bridge across the moat. I made him a low salaam, after the fashion of the country, and, as he bent forward to return the compliment, I am sorry to say, I plunged forward, gave him a violent blow on the head, which deprived him of all sensation, and then dragged him within the wall, raising the drawbridge after me.

"I bore the body into my own apartment: there, swift as thought, I stripped him of his turban, cammerbund, peijammahs, and papooshes, and, putting them on myself, determined to go forth and reconnoitre the enemy."

Here I was obliged to stop, for Cabrera, Ros d'Eroles, and the rest of the staff, were sound asleep! What I did in my reconnaisance, and how I defended the fort of Futtyghur, I shall have the honor of telling on another occasion.


CHAPTER IV

THE INDIAN CAMP—THE SORTIE FROM THE FORT

HEAD-QUARTERS, MORELLA, Oct. 3, 1838

It is a balmy night. I hear the merry jingle of the tambourine, and the cheery voices of the girls and peasants, as they dance beneath my casement, under the shadow of the clustering vines. The laugh and song pass gayly round, and even at this distance I can distinguish the elegant form of Ramon Cabrera, as he whispers gay nothings in the ears of the Andalusian girls, or joins in the thrilling chorus of Riego's hymn, which is ever and anon vociferated by the enthusiastic soldiery of Carlos Quinto. I am alone, in the most inaccessible and most bomb-proof tower of our little fortalice; the large casements are open—the wind, as it enters, whispers in my ear its odorous recollections of the orange grove and the myrtle bower. My torch (a branch of the fragrant cedar-tree) flares and flickers in the midnight breeze, and disperses its scent and burning splinters on my scroll and the desk where I write—meet implements for a soldier's authorship!—it is CARTRIDGE paper over which my pen runs so glibly, and a yawning barrel of gunpowder forms my rough writing-table. Around me, below me, above me, all—all is peace! I think, as I sit here so lonely, on my country, England! and muse over the sweet and bitter recollections of my early days! Let me resume my narrative, at the point where (interrupted by the authoritative summons of war) I paused on the last occasion.

I left off, I think—(for I am a thousand miles away from proof-sheets as I write, and, were I not writing the simple TRUTH, must contradict myself a thousand times in the course of my tale)—I think, I say, that I left off at that period of my story, when, Holkar being before Futtyghur, and I in command of that fortress, I had just been compelled to make away with his messenger; and, dressed in the fallen Indian's accoutrements, went forth to reconnoitre the force, and, if possible, to learn the intentions of the enemy. However much my figure might have resembled that of the Pitan, and, disguised in his armor, might have deceived the lynx-eyed Mahrattas, into whose camp I was about to plunge, it was evident that a single glance at my fair face and auburn beard would have undeceived the dullest blockhead in

Holkar's army. Seizing, then, a bottle of Burgess's walnut catsup, I dyed my face and my hands, and, with the simple aid of a flask of Warren's jet, I made my hair and beard as black as ebony. The Indian's helmet and chain hood covered likewise a great part of my face and I hoped thus, with luck, impudence, and a complete command of all the Eastern dialects and languages, from Burmah to Afghanistan, to pass scot-free through this somewhat dangerous ordeal.

I had not the word of the night, it is true—but I trusted to good fortune for that, and passed boldly out of the fortress, bearing the flag of truce as before; I had scarcely passed on a couple of hundred yards, when lo! a party of Indian horsemen, armed like him I had just overcome, trotted towards me. One was leading a noble white charger, and no sooner did he see me than, dismounting from his own horse, and giving the rein to a companion, he advanced to meet me with the charger; a second fellow likewise dismounted and followed the first; one held the bridle of the horse, while the other (with a multitude of salaams, aleikums, and other genuflexions), held the jewelled stirrup, and kneeling, waited until I should mount.

I took the hint at once: the Indian who had come up to the fort was a great man—that was evident; I walked on with a majestic air, gathered up the velvet reins, and sprung into the magnificent high-peaked saddle. "Buk, buk," said I. "It is good. In the name of the forty-nine Imaums, let us ride on." And the whole party set off at a brisk trot, I keeping silence, and thinking with no little trepidation of what I was about to encounter.

As we rode along, I heard two of the men commenting upon my unusual silence (for I suppose, I—that is the Indian—was a talkative officer). "The lips of the Bahawder are closed," said one. "Where are those birds of Paradise, his long-tailed words? they are imprisoned between the golden bars of his teeth!"

"Kush," said his companion, "be quiet! Bobbachy Bahawder has seen the dreadful Feringhee, Gahagan Khan Gujputi, the elephant-lord, whose sword reaps the harvest of death; there is but one champion who can wear the papooshes of the elephant-slayer—it is Bobbachy Bahawder!"

"You speak truly, Puneeree Muckun, the Bahawder ruminates on the words of the unbeliever: he is an ostrich, and hatches the eggs of his thoughts."

"Bekhusm! on my nose be it! May the young birds, his actions, be strong and swift in flight."

"May they DIGEST IRON!" said Puneeree Muckun, who was evidently a wag in his way.

"O-ho!" thought I, as suddenly the light flashed upon me. "It was, then, the famous Bobbachy Bahawder, whom I overcame just now! and he is the man destined to stand in my slippers, is he?" and I was at that very moment standing in his own! Such are the chances and changes that fall to the lot of the soldier!

I suppose everybody—everybody who has been in India, at least—has heard the name of Bobbachy Bahawder: it is derived from the two Hindustanee words—bobbachy, general; bahawder, artilleryman. He had entered into Holkar's service in the latter capacity, and had, by his merit and his undaunted bravery in action, attained the dignity of the peacock's feather, which is only granted to noblemen of the first class; he was married, moreover, to one of Holkar's innumerable daughters: a match which, according to the Chronique Scandaleuse, brought more of honor than of pleasure to the poor Bobbachy. Gallant as he was in the field, it was said that in the harem he was the veriest craven alive, completely subjugated by his ugly and odious wife. In all matters of importance the late Bahawder had been consulted by his prince, who had, as it appears, (knowing my character, and not caring to do anything rash in his attack upon so formidable an enemy,) sent forward the unfortunate Pitan to reconnoitre the fort; he was to have done yet more, as I learned from the attendant Puneeree Muckun, who was, I soon found out, an old favorite with the Bobbachy—doubtless on account of his honesty and love of repartee.

"The Bahawder's lips are closed," said he, at last, trotting up to me; "has he not a word for old Puneeree Muckun?"

"Bismillah, mashallah, barikallah," said I; which means, "My good friend, what I have seen is not worth the trouble of relation, and fills my bosom with the darkest forebodings."

"You could not then see the Gujputi alone, and stab him with your dagger?"

[Here was a pretty conspiracy!] "No, I saw him, but not alone; his people were always with him."

"Hurrumzadeh! it is a pity; we waited but the sound of your jogree (whistle), and straightway would have galloped up and seized upon every man, woman, and child in the fort: however, there are but a dozen men in the garrison, and they have not provision for two days—they must yield; and then hurrah for the moon-faces! Mashallah! I am told the soldiers who first get in are to have their pick. How my old woman, Rotee Muckun, will be surprised when I bring home a couple of Feringhee wives,—ha! ha!"

"Fool!" said I, "be still!—twelve men in the garrison! there are twelve hundred! Gahagan himself is as good as a thousand men; and as for food, I saw with my own eyes five hundred bullocks grazing in the court-yard as I entered." This WAS a bouncer, I confess; but my object was to deceive Puneeree Muckun, and give him as high a notion as possible of the capabilities of defence which the besieged had.

"Pooch, pooch," murmured the men; "it is a wonder of a fortress: we shall never be able to take it until our guns come up."

There was hope then! they had no battering-train. Ere this arrived, I trusted that Lord Lake would hear of our plight, and march down to rescue us. Thus occupied in thought and conversation, we rode on until the advanced sentinel challenged us, when old Puneeree gave the word, and we passed on into the centre of Holkar's camp.

It was a strange—a stirring sight! The camp-fires were lighted; and round them—eating, reposing, talking, looking at the merry steps of the dancing-girls, or listening to the stories of some Dhol Baut (or Indian improvisatore) were thousands of dusky soldiery. The camels and horses were picketed under the banyan-trees, on which the ripe mango fruit was growing, and offered them an excellent food. Towards the spot which the golden fish and royal purdahs, floating in the wind, designated as the tent of Holkar, led an immense avenue—of elephants! the finest street, indeed, I ever saw. Each of the monstrous animals had a castle on its back, armed with Mauritanian archers and the celebrated Persian matchlock-men: it was the feeding time of these royal brutes, and the grooms were observed bringing immense toffungs, or baskets, filled with pine-apples, plantains, bandannas, Indian corn, and cocoa-nuts, which grow luxuriantly at all seasons of the year. We passed down this extraordinary avenue—no less than three hundred and eighty-eight tails did I count on each side—each tail appertaining to an elephant twenty-five feet high—each elephant having a two-storied castle on its back—each castle containing sleeping and eating rooms for the twelve men that formed its garrison, and were keeping watch on the roof—each roof bearing a flag-staff twenty feet long on its top, the crescent glittering with a thousand gems, and round it the imperial standard,—each standard of silk velvet and cloth-of-gold, bearing the well-known device of Holkar, argent an or gules, between a sinople of the first, a chevron, truncated, wavy. I took nine of these myself in the course of a very short time after, and shall be happy, when I come to England, to show them to any gentleman who has a curiosity that way. Through this gorgeous scene our little cavalcade passed, and at last we arrived at the quarters occupied by Holkar.

That celebrated chieftain's tents and followers were gathered round one of the British bungalows which had escaped the flames, and which he occupied during the siege. When I entered the large room where he sat, I found him in the midst of a council of war; his chief generals and viziers seated round him, each smoking his hookah, as is the common way with these black fellows, before, at, and after breakfast, dinner, supper, and bedtime. There was such a cloud raised by their smoke you could hardly see a yard before you—another piece of good luck for me—as it diminished the chances of my detection. When, with the ordinary ceremonies, the kitmatgars and consomahs had explained to the prince that Bobbachy Bahawder, the right eye of the Sun of the universe (as the ignorant heathens called me), had arrived from his mission, Holkar immediately summoned me to the maidaun, or elevated platform, on which he was seated in a luxurious easy-chair, and I, instantly taking off my slippers, falling on my knees, and beating my head against the ground ninety-nine times, proceeded, still on my knees, a hundred and twenty feet through the room, and then up the twenty steps which led to his maidaun—a silly, painful, and disgusting ceremony, which can only be considered as a relic of barbarian darkness, which tears the knees and shins to pieces, let alone the pantaloons. I recommend anybody who goes to India, with the prospect of entering the service of the native rajahs, to recollect my advice and have them WELL-WADDED.

Well, the right eye of the Sun of the universe scrambled as well as he could up the steps of the maidaun (on which in rows, smoking, as I have said, the musnuds or general officers were seated), and I arrived within speaking-distance of Holkar, who instantly asked me the success of my mission. The impetuous old man thereon poured out a multitude of questions: "How many men are there in the fort?" said he; "how many women? Is it victualled? Have they ammunition? Did you see Gahagan Sahib, the commander? did you kill him?"

All these questions Jeswunt Row Holkar puffed out with so many whiffs of tobacco.

Taking a chillum myself, and raising about me such a cloud that, upon my honor as a gentleman, no man at three yards' distance could perceive anything of me except the pillar of smoke in which I was encompassed, I told Holkar, in Oriental language of course, the best tale I could with regard to the fort.

"Sir" said I, "to answer your last question first—that dreadful Gujputi I have seen—and he is alive: he is eight feet, nearly, in height; he can eat a bullock daily (of which he has seven hundred at present in the compound, and swears that during the siege he will content himself with only three a week): he has lost in battle his left eye; and what is the consequence? O Ram Gunge" (O thou-with-the-eye-as-bright-as-morning and-with-beard-as-black-as-night), "Goliah Gujputi—NEVER SLEEPS!"

"Ah, you Ghorumsaug (you thief of the world)," said the Prince Vizier, Saadut Alee Beg Bimbukchee—"it's joking you are;"—and there was a universal buzz through the room at the announcement of this bouncer.

"By the hundred and eleven incarnations of Vishnu," said I, solemnly, (an oath which no Indian was ever known to break,) "I swear that so it is: so at least he told me, and I have good cause to know his power. Gujputi is an enchanter: he is leagued with devils; he is invulnerable. Look," said I, unsheathing my dagger—and every eye turned instantly towards me—"thrice did I stab him with this steel—in the back, once—twice right through the heart; but he only laughed me to scorn, and bade me tell Holkar that the steel was not yet forged which was to inflict an injury upon him."

I never saw a man in such a rage as Holkar was when I gave him this somewhat imprudent message.

"Ah, lily-livered rogue!" shouted he out to me, "milk-blooded unbeliever! pale-faced miscreant! lives he after insulting thy master in thy presence! In the name of the prophet, I spit on thee, defy thee, abhor thee, degrade thee! Take that, thou liar of the universe! and that—and that—and that!"

Such are the frightful excesses of barbaric minds! every time this old man said, "Take that," he flung some article near him at the head of the undaunted Gahagan—his dagger, his sword, his carbine, his richly ornamented pistols, his turban covered with jewels, worth a hundred thousand crores of rupees—finally, his hookah, snake mouthpiece, silver-bell, chillum and all—which went hissing over my head, and flattening into a jelly the nose of the Grand Vizier.

"Yock muzzee! my nose is off;" said the old man, mildly. "Will you have my life, O Holkar? it is thine likewise!" and no other word of complaint escaped his lips.

Of all these missiles, though a pistol and carbine had gone off as the ferocious Indian flung them at my head, and the naked scimitar fiercely but unadroitly thrown, had lopped off the limbs of one or two of the musnuds as they sat trembling on their omrahs, yet, strange to say, not a single weapon had hurt me. When the hubbub ceased, and the unlucky wretches who had been the victims of this fit of rage had been removed, Holkar's good humor somewhat returned, and he allowed me to continue my account of the fort; which I did, not taking the slightest notice of his burst of impatience: as indeed it would have been the height of impoliteness to have done for such accidents happened many times in the day.

"It is well that the Bobbachy has returned," snuffled out the poor Grand Vizier, after I had explained to the Council the extraordinary means of defence possessed by the garrison. "Your star is bright, O Bahawder! for this very night we had resolved upon an escalade of the fort, and we had sworn to put every one of the infidel garrison to the edge of the sword."

"But you have no battering train," said I.

"Bah! we have a couple of ninety-six pounders, quite sufficient to blow the gates open; and then, hey for a charge!" said Loll Mahommed, a general of cavalry, who was a rival of Bobbachy's, and contradicted, therefore, every word I said. "In the name of Juggernaut, why wait for the heavy artillery? Have we not swords? Have we not hearts? Mashallah! Let cravens stay with Bobbachy, all true men will follow Loll Mahommed! Allahhumdillah, Bismillah, Barikallah?" * and drawing his scimitar, he waved it over his head, and shouted out his cry of battle. It was repeated by many of the other omrahs; the sound of their cheers was carried into the camp, and caught up by the men; the camels began to cry, the horses to prance and neigh, the eight hundred elephants set up a scream, the trumpeters and drummers clanged away at their instruments. I never heard such a din before or after. How I trembled for my little garrison when I heard the enthusiastic cries of this innumerable host!

There was but one way for it. "Sir," said I, addressing Holkar, "go out to-night and you go to certain death. Loll Mahommed has not seen the fort as I have. Pass the gate if you please, and for what? to fall before the fire of a hundred pieces of artillery; to storm another gate, and then another, and then to be blown up, with Gahagan's garrison in the citadel. Who talks of courage? Were I not in your august presence, O star of the faithful, I would crop Loll Mahommed's nose from his face, and wear his ears as an ornament in my own pugree! Who is there here that knows not the difference between yonder yellow-skinned coward and Gahagan Khan Guj—I mean Bobbachy Bahawder? I am ready to fight one, two, three, or twenty of them, at broad-sword, small-sword, single-stick, with fists if you please. By the holy piper, fighting is like mate and dthrink to Ga—to Bobbachy, I mane—whoop! come on, you divvle, and I'll bate the skin off your ugly bones."

This speech had very nearly proved fatal to me, for when I am agitated, I involuntarily adopt some of the phraseology peculiar to my own country; which is so un-eastern, that, had there been any suspicion as to my real character, detection must indubitably have ensued. As it was, Holkar perceived nothing, but instantaneously stopped the dispute. Loll Mahommed, however, evidently suspected something, for, as Holkar, with a voice of thunder, shouted out, "Tomasha (silence)," Loll sprang forward and gasped out—

"My lord! my lord I this is not Bob—"

But he could say no more. "Gag the slave!" screamed out Holkar, stamping with fury: and a turban was instantly twisted round the poor devil's jaws. "Ho, furoshes! carry out Loll Mahommed Khan, give him a hundred dozen on the soles of his feet, set him upon a white donkey, and carry him round the camp, with an inscription before him: 'This is the way that Holkar rewards the talkative.'"

I breathed again; and ever as I heard each whack of the bamboo falling on Loll Mahommed's feet, I felt peace returning to my mind, and thanked my stars that I was delivered of this danger.

"Vizier," said Holkar, who enjoyed Loll's roars amazingly, "I owe you a reparation for your nose: kiss the hand of your prince, O Saadut Alee Beg Bimbukchee! be from this day forth Zoheir u Dowlut!"

The good old man's eyes filled with tears. "I can bear thy severity, O Prince," said he; "I cannot bear thy love. Was it not an honor that your Highness did me just now when you condescended to pass over the bridge of your slave's nose?"

The phrase was by all voices pronounced to be very poetical. The Vizier retired, crowned with his new honors, to bed. Holkar was in high good humor.

"Bobbachy," said he, "thou, too, must pardon me. A propos, I have news for thee. Your wife, the incomparable Puttee Rooge," (white and red rose,) has arrived in camp."

"My WIFE, my lord!" said I, aghast.

"Our daughter, the light of thine eyes! Go, my son; I see thou art wild with joy. The Princess's tents are set up close by mine, and I know thou longest to join her."

My wife? Here was a complication truly!


CHAPTER V

THE ISSUE OF MY INTERVIEW WITH MY WIFE

I found Puneeree Muckun, with the rest of my attendants, waiting at the gate, and they immediately conducted me to my own tents in the neighborhood. I have been in many dangerous predicaments before that time and since, but I don't care to deny that I felt in the present instance such a throbbing of the heart as I never have experienced when leading a forlorn hope, or marching up to a battery.

As soon as I entered the tents a host of menials sprang forward, some to ease me of my armor, some to offer me refreshments, some with hookahs, attar of roses (in great quart-bottles), and the thousand delicacies of Eastern life. I motioned them away. "I will wear my armor," said I; "I shall go forth to-night; carry my duty to the princess, and say I grieve that to-night I have not the time to see her. Spread me a couch here, and bring me supper here: a jar of Persian wine well cooled, a lamb stuffed with pistachio-nuts, a pillaw of a couple of turkeys, a curried kid—anything. Begone! Give me a pipe; leave me alone, and tell me when the meal is ready."

I thought by these means to put off the fair Puttee Rooge, and hoped to be able to escape without subjecting myself to the examination of her curious eyes. After smoking for a while, an attendant came to tell me that my supper was prepared in the inner apartment of the tent (I suppose that the reader, if he be possessed of the commonest intelligence, knows that the tents of the Indian grandees are made of the finest Cashmere shawls, and contain a dozen rooms at least, with carpets, chimneys, and sash-windows complete). I entered, I say, into an inner chamber, and there began with my fingers to devour my meal in the Oriental fashion, taking, every now and then, a pull from the wine-jar, which was cooling deliciously in another jar of snow.

I was just in the act of despatching the last morsel of a most savory stewed lamb and rice, which had formed my meal, when I heard a scuffle of feet, a shrill clatter of female voices, and, the curtain being flung open, in marched a lady accompanied by twelve slaves, with moon faces and slim waists, lovely as the houris in Paradise.

The lady herself, to do her justice, was as great a contrast to her attendants as could possibly be: she was crooked, old, of the complexion of molasses, and rendered a thousand times more ugly by the tawdry dress and the blazing jewels with which she was covered. A line of yellow chalk drawn from her forehead to the tip of her nose (which was further ornamented by an immense glittering nose-ring), her eyelids painted bright red, and a large dab of the same color on her chin, showed she was not of the Mussulman, but the Brahmin faith—and of a very high caste; you could see that by her eyes. My mind was instantaneously made up as to my line of action.

The male attendants had of course quitted the apartment, as they heard the well-known sound of her voice. It would have been death to them to have remained and looked in her face. The females ranged themselves round their mistress, as she squatted down opposite to me.

"And is this," said she, "a welcome, O Khan! after six months' absence, for the most unfortunate and loving wife in all the world? Is this lamb, O glutton! half so tender as thy spouse? Is this wine, O sot! half so sweet as her looks?"

I saw the storm was brewing—her slaves, to whom she turned, kept up a kind of chorus:—

"Oh, the faithless one!" cried they. "Oh, the rascal, the false one, who has no eye for beauty, and no heart for love, like the Khanum's!"

"A lamb is not so sweet as love," said I gravely: "but a lamb has a good temper; a wine-cup is not so intoxicating as a woman—but a wine-cup has NO TONGUE, O Khanum Gee!" and again I dipped my nose in the soul-refreshing jar.

The sweet Puttee Rooge was not, however, to be put off by my repartees; she and her maidens recommenced their chorus, and chattered and stormed until I lost all patience.

"Retire, friends," said I, "and leave me in peace."

"Stir, on your peril!" cried the Khanum.

So, seeing there was no help for it but violence, I drew out my pistols, cocked them, and said, "O houris! these pistols contain each two balls: the daughter of Holkar bears a sacred life for me—but for you!—by all the saints of Hindustan, four of ye shall die if ye stay a moment longer in my presence!" This was enough; the ladies gave a shriek, and skurried out of the apartment like a covey of partridges on the wing.

Now, then, was the time for action. My wife, or rather Bobbachy's wife, sat still, a little flurried by the unusual ferocity which her lord had displayed in her presence. I seized her hand and, gripping it close, whispered in her ear, to which I put the other pistol:—"O Khanum, listen and scream not; the moment you scream, you die!" She was completely beaten: she turned as pale as a woman could in her situation, and said, "Speak, Bobbachy Bahawder, I am dumb."

"Woman," said I, taking off my helmet, and removing the chain cape which had covered almost the whole of my face—"I AM NOT THY HUSBAND—I am the slaver of elephants, the world renowned GAHAGAN!"

As I said this, and as the long ringlets of red hair fell over my shoulders (contrasting strangely with my dyed face and beard), I formed one of the finest pictures that can possibly be conceived, and I recommend it as a subject to Mr. Heath, for the next "Book of Beauty."

"Wretch!" said she, "what wouldst thou?"

"You black-faced fiend," said I, "raise but your voice, and you are dead!"

"And afterwards," said she, "do you suppose that YOU can escape? The torments of hell are not so terrible as the tortures that Holkar will invent for thee."

"Tortures, madam?" answered I, coolly. "Fiddlesticks! You will neither betray me, nor will I be put to the torture: on the contrary, you will give me your best jewels and facilitate my escape to the fort. Don't grind your teeth and swear at me. Listen, madam : you know this dress and these arms;—they are the arms of your husband, Bobbachy Bahawder—MY PRISONER. He now lies in yonder fort, and if I do not return before daylight, at SUNRISE HE DIES: and then, when they send his corpse back to Holkar, what will you, HIS WIDOW, do?"

"Oh!" said she, shuddering, "spare me, spare me!"

"I'll tell you what you will do. You will have the pleasure of dying along with him—of BEING ROASTED, madam: an agonizing death, from which your father cannot save you, to which he will be the first man to condemn and conduct you. Ha! I see we understand each other, and you will give me over the cash-box and jewels." And so saying I threw myself back with the calmest air imaginable, flinging the pistols over to her. "Light me a pipe, my love," said I, "and then go and hand me over the dollars; do you hear?" You see I had her in my power—up a tree, as the Americans say, and she very humbly lighted my pipe for me, and then departed for the goods I spoke about.

What a thing is luck! If Loll Mahommed had not been made to take that ride round the camp, I should infallibly have been lost.

My supper, my quarrel with the princess, and my pipe afterwards, had occupied a couple of hours of my time. The princess returned from her quest, and brought with her the box, containing valuables to the amount of about three millions sterling. (I was cheated of them afterwards, but have the box still, a plain deal one.) I was just about to take my departure, when a tremendous knocking, shouting, and screaming was heard at the entrance of the tent. It was Holkar himself, accompanied by that cursed Loll Mahommed, who, after his punishment, found his master restored to good humor, and had communicated to him his firm conviction that I was an impostor.

"Ho, Begum," shouted he, in the ante-room (for he and his people could not enter the women's apartments), "speak, O my daughter! is your husband returned?"

"Speak, madam," said I, "or REMEMBER THE ROASTING."

"He is, papa," said the Begum.

"Are you sure? Ho! ho! ho!" (the old ruffian was laughing outside)—"are you sure it is?—Ha! aha!—HE-E-E!"

"Indeed it is he, and no other. I pray you, father, to go, and to pass no more such shameless jests on your daughter. Have I ever seen the face of any other man?" And hereat she began to weep as if her heart would break—the deceitful minx!

Holkar's laugh was instantly turned to fury. "Oh, you liar and eternal thief!" said he, turning round (as I presume, for I could only hear) to Loll Mahommed, "to make your prince eat such monstrous dirt as this! Furoshes, seize this man. I dismiss him from my service, I degrade him from his rank, I appropriate to myself all his property: and hark ye, furoshes, GIVE HIM A HUNDRED DOZEN MORE!"

Again I heard the whacks of the bamboos, and peace flowed into my soul.

Just as morn began to break, two figures were seen to approach the little fortress of Futtyghur: one was a woman wrapped closely in a veil, the other a warrior, remarkable for the size and manly beauty of his form, who carried in his hand a deal box of considerable size. The warrior at the gate gave the word and was admitted, the woman returned slowly to the Indian camp. Her name was Puttee Rooge; his was—

G. O'G. G., M. H. E. I. C. S., C. I. H. A.

CHAPTER VI

FAMINE IN THE GARRISON

Thus my dangers for the night being overcome, I hastened with my precious box into my own apartment, which communicated with another, where I had left my prisoner, with a guard to report if he should recover, and to prevent his escape. My servant, Ghorumsaug, was one of the guard. I called him, and the fellow came, looking very much confused and frightened, as it seemed, at my appearance.

"Why, Ghorumsaug," said I, "what makes thee look so pale, fellow?" (he was as white as a sheet.) "It is thy master, dost thou not remember him?" The man had seen me dress myself in the Pitan's clothes, but was not present when I had blacked my face and beard in the manner I have described.

"O Bramah, Vishnu, and Mahomet!" cried the faithful fellow, "and do I see my dear master disguised in this way? For heaven's sake let me rid you of this odious black paint; for what will the ladies say in the ball-room, if the beautiful Feringhee should appear amongst them with his roses turned into coal?"

I am still one of the finest men in Europe, and at the time of which I write, when only two-and-twenty, I confess I WAS a little vain of my personal appearance, and not very willing to appear before my dear Belinda disguised like a blackamoor. I allowed Ghorumsaug to divest me of the heathenish armor and habiliments which I wore; and having, with a world of scrubbing and trouble, divested my face and beard of their black tinge, I put on my own becoming uniform, and hastened to wait on the ladies; hastened, I say,—although delayed would have been the better word, for the operation of bleaching lasted at least two hours.

"How is the prisoner, Ghorumsaug?" said I, before leaving my apartment.

"He has recovered from the blow which the Lion dealt him; two men and myself watch over him; and Macgillicuddy Sahib (the second in command) has just been the rounds, and has seen that all was secure."

I bade Ghorumsaug help me to put away my chest of treasure (my exultation in taking it was so great that I could not help informing him of its contents); and this done, I despatched him to his post near the prisoner, while I prepared to sally forth and pay my respects to the fair creatures under my protection. "What good after all have I done," thought I to myself, "in this expedition which I had so rashly undertaken?" I had seen the renowned Holkar, I had been in the heart of his camp; I knew the disposition of his troops, that there were eleven thousand of them, and that he only waited for his guns to make a regular attack on the fort. I had seen Puttee Rooge; I had robbed her (I say ROBBED her, and I don't care what the reader or any other man may think of the act) of a deal box, containing jewels to the amount of three millions sterling, the property of herself and husband.

Three millions in money and jewels! And what the deuce were money and jewels to me or to my poor garrison? Could my adorable Miss Bulcher eat a fricassee of diamonds, or, Cleopatra-like, melt down pearls to her tea? Could I, careless as I am about food, with a stomach that would digest anything—(once, in Spain, I ate the leg of a horse during a famine, and was so eager to swallow this morsel that I bolted the shoe, as well as the hoof, and never felt the slightest inconvenience from either,)—could I, I say, expect to live long and well upon a ragout of rupees, or a dish of stewed emeralds and rubies? With all the wealth of Croesus before me I felt melancholy; and would have paid cheerfully its weight in carats for a good honest round of boiled beef. Wealth, wealth, what art thou? What is gold?—Soft metal. What are diamonds?—Shining tinsel. The great wealth-winners, the only fame-achievers, the sole objects worthy of a soldier's consideration, are beefsteaks, gunpowder, and cold iron.

The two latter means of competency we possessed; I had in my own apartments a small store of gunpowder (keeping it under my own bed, with a candle burning for fear of accidents); I had 14 pieces of artillery (4 long 48's and 4 carronades, 5 howitzers, and a long brass mortar, for grape, which I had taken myself at the battle of Assaye), and muskets for ten times my force. My garrison, as I have told the reader in a previous number, consisted of 40 men, two chaplains, and a surgeon; add to these my guests, 83 in number, of whom nine only were gentlemen (in tights, powder, pigtails, and silk stockings, who had come out merely for a dance, and found themselves in for a siege). Such were our numbers:—

| | |
|---|---|
| Ladies | 74 |
| Troops and artillerymen | 40 |
| Other non-combatants | 11 |
| MAJOR-GEN. O'G. GAHAGAN | 1000 |
| | — |
| | 1,125 |

I count myself good for a thousand, for so I was regularly rated in the army: with this great benefit to it, that I only consumed as much as an ordinary mortal. We were then, as far as the victuals went, 126 mouths; as combatants we numbered 1,040 gallant men, with 12 guns and a fort, against Holkar and his 12,000. No such alarming odds, if—

IF!—ay, there was the rub—IF we had SHOT, as well as powder for our guns; IF we had not only MEN but MEAT. Of the former commodity we had only three rounds for each piece. Of the latter, upon my sacred honor, to feed 126 souls, we had but

Two drumsticks of fowls, and a bone of ham.
Fourteen bottles of ginger-beer.
Of soda-water, four ditto.
Two bottles of fine Spanish olives.
Raspberry cream—the remainder of two dishes.
Seven macaroons, lying in the puddle of a demolished trifle.
Half a drum of best Turkey figs.
Some bits of broken bread; two Dutch cheeses (whole); the crust of an old Stilton; and about an ounce of almonds and raisins.

Three ham-sandwiches, and a pot of currant-jelly, and 197 bottles of brandy, rum, madeira, pale ale (my private stock); a couple of hard eggs for a salad, and a flask of Florence oil.

This was the provision for the whole garrison! The men after supper had seized upon the relics of the repast, as they were carried off from the table; and these were the miserable remnants I found and counted on my return, taking good care to lock the door of the supper-room, and treasure what little sustenance still remained in it.

When I appeared in the saloon, now lighted up by the morning sun, I not only caused a sensation myself, but felt one in my own bosom, which was of the most painful description. Oh, my reader! may you never behold such a sight as that which presented itself: eighty-three men and women in ball-dresses; the former with their lank powdered locks streaming over their faces; the latter with faded flowers, uncurled wigs, smudged rouge, blear eyes, draggling feathers, rumpled satins—each more desperately melancholy and hideous than the other—each, except my beloved Belinda Bulcher, whose raven ringlets never having been in curl, could of course never go OUT of curl; whose cheek, pale as the lily, could, as it may naturally be supposed, grow no paler; whose neck and beauteous arms, dazzling as alabaster, needed no pearl-powder, and therefore, as I need not state, did not suffer because the pearl-powder had come off. Joy (deft link-boy!) lit his lamps in each of her eyes as I entered. As if I had been her sun, her spring, lo! blushing roses mantled in her cheek! Seventy-three ladies, as I entered, opened their fire upon me, and stunned me with cross-questions, regarding my adventures in the camp—SHE, as she saw me, gave a faint scream, (the sweetest, sure, that ever gurgled through the throat of a woman!) then started up—then made as if she would sit down—then moved backwards—then tottered forwards—then tumbled into my—Psha! why recall, why attempt to describe that delicious—that passionate greeting of two young hearts? What was the surrounding crowd to US? What cared we for the sneers of the men, the titters of the jealous women, the shrill "Upon my word!" of the elder Miss Bulcher, and the loud expostulations of Belinda's mamma? The brave girl loved me, and wept in my arms. "Goliah! my Goliah!" said she, "my brave, my beautiful, THOU art returned, and hope comes back with thee. Oh! who can tell the anguish of my soul, during this dreadful, dreadful night!" Other similar ejaculations of love and joy she uttered; and if I HAD perilled life in her service, if I DID believe that hope of escape there was none, so exquisite was the moment of our meeting, that I forgot all else in this overwhelming joy!

[The Major's description of this meeting, which lasted at the very most not ten seconds, occupies thirteen pages of writing. We have been compelled to dock off twelve and a half; for the whole passage, though highly creditable to his feelings, might possibly be tedious to the reader.]

As I said, the ladies and gentlemen were inclined to sneer, and were giggling audibly. I led the dear girl to a chair, and, scowling round with a tremendous fierceness, which those who know me know I can sometimes put on, I shouted out, "Hark ye men and women—I am this lady's truest knight—her husband I hope one day to be. I am commander, too, in this fort—the enemy is without it; another word of mockery—another glance of scorn—and, by heaven, I will hurl every man and woman from the battlements, a prey to the ruffianly Holkar!" This quieted them. I am a man of my word, and none of them stirred or looked disrespectfully from that moment.

It was now MY turn to make THEM look foolish. Mrs. Vandegobbleschroy (whose unfailing appetite is pretty well known to every person who has been in India) cried, "Well, Captain Gahagan, your ball has been so pleasant, and the supper was despatched so long ago, that myself and the ladies would be very glad of a little breakfast." And Mrs. Van giggled as if she had made a very witty and reasonable speech. "Oh! breakfast, breakfast by all means," said the rest; "we really are dying for a warm cup of tea."

"Is it bohay tay or souchong tay that you'd like, ladies?" says I.

"Nonsense, you silly man; any tea you like," said fat Mrs. Van.

"What do you say, then, to some prime GUNPOWDER?" Of course they said it was the very thing.

"And do you like hot rowls or cowld—muffins or crumpets—fresh butter or salt? And you, gentlemen, what do you say to some ilegant divvled-kidneys for yourselves, and just a trifle of grilled turkeys, and a couple of hundthred new-laid eggs for the ladies?"

"Pooh, pooh! be it as you will, my dear fellow," answered they all.

"But stop," says I. "O ladies, O ladies: O gentlemen, gentlemen, that you should ever have come to the quarters of Goliah Gahagan, and he been without—"

"What?" said they, in a breath.

"Alas I alas! I have not got a single stick of chocolate in the whole house."

"Well, well, we can do without it."

"Or a single pound of coffee."

"Never mind; let that pass too." (Mrs. Van and the rest were beginning to look alarmed.)

"And about the kidneys—now I remember, the black divvles outside the fort have seized upon all the sheep; and how are we to have kidneys without them?" (Here there was a slight o—o—o!)

"And with regard to the milk and crame, it may be remarked that the cows are likewise in pawn, and not a single drop can be had for money or love: but we can beat up eggs, you know, in the tay, which will be just as good."

"Oh! just as good."

"Only the divvle's in the luck, there's not a fresh egg to be had—no, nor a fresh chicken," continued I, "nor a stale one either; nor a tayspoonful of souchong, nor a thimbleful of bohay; nor the laste taste in life of butther, salt or fresh; nor hot rowls or cowld!"

"In the name of heaven!" said Mrs. Van, growing very pale, "what is there, then?"

"Ladies and gentlemen, I'll tell you what there is now," shouted I. "There's

"Two drumsticks of fowls, and a bone of ham. Fourteen bottles of ginger-beer," &c. &c. &c.

And I went through the whole list of eatables as before, ending with the ham-sandwiches and the pot of jelly.

"Law! Mr. Gahagan," said Mrs. Colonel Vandegobbleschroy, "give me the ham-sandwiches—I must manage to breakfast off them."

And you should have heard the pretty to-do there was at this modest proposition! Of course I did not accede to it—why should I? I was the commander of the fort, and intended to keep these three very sandwiches for the use of myself and my dear Belinda. "Ladies," said I, "there are in this fort one hundred and twenty-six souls, and this is all the food which is to last us during the siege. Meat there is none—of drink there is a tolerable quantity; and at one o'clock punctually, a glass of wine and one olive shall be served out to each woman: the men will receive two glasses, and an olive and a fig—and this must be your food during the siege. Lord Lake cannot be absent more than three days; and if he be—why, still there is a chance—why do I say a chance?—a CERTAINTY of escaping from the hands of these ruffians."

"Oh, name it, name it, dear Captain Gahagan!" screeched the whole covey at a breath.

"It lies," answered I, "in the POWDER MAGAZINE. I will blow this fort, and all it contains, to atoms, ere it becomes the prey of Holkar."

The women, at this, raised a squeal that might have been heard in Holkar's camp, and fainted in different directions; but my dear Belinda whispered in my ear, "Well done, thou noble knight! bravely said, my heart's Goliah!" I felt I was right: I could have blown her up twenty times for the luxury of that single moment! "And now, ladies," said I, "I must leave you. The two chaplains will remain with you to administer professional consolation—the other gentlemen will follow me up stairs to the ramparts, where I shall find plenty of work for them."

CHAPTER VII

THE ESCAPE

Loth as they were, these gentlemen had nothing for it but to obey, and they accordingly followed me to the ramparts, where I proceeded to review my men. The fort, in my absence, had been left in command of Lieutenant Macgillicuddy, a countryman of my own (with whom, as may be seen in an early chapter of my memoirs, I had an affair of honor); and the prisoner Bobbachy Bahawder, whom I had only stunned, never wishing to kill him, had been left in charge of that officer. Three of the garrison (one of them a man of the Ahmednuggar Irregulars, my own body-servant, Ghorumsaug above named,) were appointed to watch the captive by turns, and never leave him out of their sight. The lieutenant was instructed to look to them and to their prisoner, and as Bobbachy was severely injured by the blow which I had given him, and was, moreover, bound hand and foot, and gagged smartly with cords, I considered myself sure of his person.

Macgillicuddy did not make his appearance when I reviewed my little force, and the three havildars were likewise absent: this did not surprise me, as I had told them not to leave their prisoner; but desirous to speak with the lieutenant, I despatched a messenger to him, and ordered him to appear immediately.

The messenger came back; he was looking ghastly pale: he whispered some information into my ear, which instantly caused me to hasten to the apartments where I had caused Bobbachy Bahawder to be confined.

The men had fled;—Bobbachy had fled; and in his place, fancy my astonishment when I found—with a rope cutting his naturally wide mouth almost into his ears—with a dreadful sabre-cut across his forehead—with his legs tied over his head, and his arms tied between his legs—my unhappy, my attached friend—Mortimer Macgillicuddy!

He had been in this position for about three hours—it was the very position in which I had caused Bobbachy Bahawder to be placed—an attitude uncomfortable, it is true, but one which renders escape impossible, unless treason aid the prisoner.

I restored the lieutenant to his natural erect position: I poured half a bottle of whiskey down the immensely enlarged orifice of his mouth, and when he had been released, he informed me of the circumstances that had taken place.

Fool that I was! idiot!—upon my return to the fort, to have been anxious about my personal appearance, and to have spent a couple of hours in removing the artificial blackening from my beard and complexion, instead of going to examine my prisoner—when his escape would have been prevented. O foppery, foppery!—it was that cursed love of personal appearance which had led me to forget my duty to my general, my country, my monarch, and my own honor!

Thus it was that the escape took place:—My own fellow of the Irregulars, whom I had summoned to dress me, performed the operation to my satisfaction, invested me with the elegant uniform of my corps, and removed the Pitan's disguise, which I had taken from the back of the prostrate Bobbachy Bahawder. What did the rogue do next?—Why, he carried back the dress to the Bobbachy—he put it, once more, on its right owner; he and his infernal black companions (who had been won over by the Bobbachy with promises of enormous reward), gagged Macgillicuddy, who was going the rounds, and then marched with the Indian coolly up to the outer gate, and gave the word. The sentinel, thinking it was myself, who had first come in, and was as likely to go out again,—(indeed my rascally valet said that Gahagan Sahib was about to go out with him and his two companions to reconnoitre,)—opened the gates, and off they went!

This accounted for the confusion of my valet when I entered!—and for the scoundrel's speech, that the lieutenant had JUST BEEN THE ROUNDS;—he HAD, poor fellow, and had been seized and bound in this cruel way. The three men, with their liberated prisoner, had just been on the point of escape, when my arrival disconcerted them: I had changed the guard at the gate (whom they had won over likewise); and yet, although they had overcome poor Mac, and although they were ready for the start, they had positively no means for effecting their escape, until I was ass enough to put means in their way. Fool! fool! thrice besotted fool that I was, to think of my own silly person when I should have been occupied solely with my public duty.

From Macgillicuddy's incoherent accounts, as he was gasping from the effects of the gag and the whiskey he had taken to revive him, and from my own subsequent observations, I learned this sad story.

A sudden and painful thought struck me—my precious box!—I rushed back, I found that box—I have it still. Opening it, there, where I had left ingots, sacks of bright tomauns, kopeks and rupees, strings of diamonds as big as ducks' eggs, rubies as red as the lips of my Belinda, countless strings of pearls, amethysts, emeralds, piles upon piles of bank-notes—I found—a piece of paper! with a few lines in the Sanscrit language, which are thus, word for word, translated:

"EPIGRAM.

"(On disappointing a certain Major.)

"The conquering Lion return'd with his prey,
And safe in his cavern he set it,
The sly little fox stole the booty away;
And, as he escaped, to the lion did say,
'AHA! don't you wish you may get it?'"

Confusion! Oh, how my blood boiled as I read these cutting lines. I stamped,—I swore,—I don't know to what insane lengths my rage might have carried me, had not at this moment a soldier rushed in, screaming, "The enemy, the enemy!"


CHAPTER VIII

THE CAPTIVE

It was high time, indeed, that I should make my appearance. Waving my sword with one hand, and seizing my telescope with the other, I at once frightened and examined the enemy. Well they knew when they saw that flamingo-plume floating in the breeze—that awful figure standing in the breach—that waving war-sword sparkling in the sky—well, I say, they knew the name of the humble individual who owned the sword, the plume, and the figure. The ruffians were mustered in front, the cavalry behind. The flags were flying, the drums, gongs, tambourines, violoncellos, and other instruments of Eastern music, raised in the air a strange, barbaric melody; the officers (yatabals), mounted on white dromedaries, were seen galloping to and fro, carrying to the advancing hosts the orders of Holkar.

You see that two sides of the fort of Futtyghur (rising as it does on a rock that is almost perpendicular) are defended by the Burrumpooter river, two hundred feet deep at this point, and a thousand yards wide, so that I had no fear about them attacking me in THAT quarter. My guns, therefore (with their six-and-thirty miserable charges of shot) were dragged round to the point at which I conceived Holkar would be most likely to attack me. I was in a situation that I did not dare to fire, except at such times as I could kill a hundred men by a single discharge of a cannon; so the attacking party marched and marched, very strongly, about a mile and a half off, the elephants marching without receiving the slightest damage from us, until they had come to within four hundred yards of our walls (the rogues knew all the secrets of our weakness, through the betrayal of the dastardly Ghorumsaug, or they never would have ventured so near). At that distance—it was about the spot where the Futtyghur hill began gradually to rise—the invading force stopped; the elephants drew up in a line, at right angles with our wall (the fools! they thought they should expose themselves too much by taking a position parallel to it);

the cavalry halted too, and—after the deuce's own flourish of trumpets and banging of gongs, to be sure,—somebody, in a flame-colored satin-dress, with an immense jewel blazing in his pugree (that looked through my telescope like a small but very bright planet), got up from the back of one of the very biggest elephants, and began a speech.

The elephants were, as I said, in a line formed with admirable precision, about three hundred of them. The following little diagram will explain matters:—

```
                                              _G
                                             /
         . . . . . . . . . . . . . . . . .   /
                     E                       /
                                             /
                                            /
                                           |  F
```

E is the line of elephants. F is the wall of the fort. G a gun in the fort. NOW the reader will see what I did.

The elephants were standing, their trunks waggling to and fro gracefully before them; and I, with superhuman skill and activity, brought the gun G (a devilish long brass gun) to bear upon them. I pointed it myself; bang! it went, and what was the consequence? Why, this:—

```
                    X
    ─────────────────────────────          |_G
         . . . . . . . . . . . . . . . . .  /
                     E                      /
                                            /
                                           /
                                          |  F
```

F is the fort, as before. G is the gun, as before. E, the elephants, as we have previously seen them. What then is X? X IS THE LINE TAKEN BY THE BALL FIRED FROM G, which took off ONE HUNDRED AND THIRTY-FOUR elephants' trunks, and only spent itself in the tusk of a very old animal, that stood the hundred and thirty-fifth.

I say that such a shot was never fired before or since; that a gun was never pointed in such a way. Suppose I had been a common man, and contented myself with firing bang at the head of the first animal? An ass would have done it, prided himself had he hit his mark, and what would have been the consequence? Why, that the ball might have killed two elephants and wounded a third; but here, probably, it would have stopped, and done no further mischief. The TRUNK was the place at which to aim; there are no bones there; and away, consequently, went the bullet, shearing, as I have said, through one hundred and thirty-five proboscbes. Heavens! what a howl there was when the shot took effect! What a sudden stoppage of Holkar's speech! What a hideous snorting of elephants! What a rush backwards was made by the whole army, as if some demon was pursuing them!

Away they went. No sooner did I see them in full retreat, than, rushing forward myself, I shouted to my men, "My friends, yonder lies your dinner!" We flung open the gates—we tore down to the spot where the elephants had fallen: seven of them were killed; and of those that escaped to die of their hideous wounds elsewhere, most had left their trunks behind them. A great quantity of them we seized; and I myself, cutting up with my scimitar a couple of the fallen animals, as a butcher would a calf, motioned to the men to take the pieces back to the fort, where barbacued elephant was served round for dinner, instead of the miserable allowance of an olive and a glass of wine, which I had promised to my female friends, in my speech to them. The animal reserved for the ladies was a young white one—the fattest and tenderest I ever ate, in my life: they are very fair eating, but the flesh has an India-rubber flavor, which, until one is accustomed to it, is unpalatable.

It was well that I had obtained this supply, for, during my absence on the works, Mrs. Vandegobbleschroy and one or two others had forced their way into the supper-room, and devoured every morsel of the garrison larder, with the exception of the cheeses, the olives, and the wine, which were locked up in my own apartment, before which stood a sentinel. Disgusting Mrs. Van! When I heard of her gluttony, I had almost a mind to eat HER. However, we made a very comfortable dinner off the barbacued steaks, and when everybody had done, had the comfort of knowing that there was enough for one meal more.

The next day, as I expected, the enemy attacked us in great force, attempting to escalade the fort; but by the help of my guns, and my good sword, by the distinguished bravery of Lieutenant Macgillicuddy and the rest of the garrison, we beat this attack off completely, the enemy sustaining a loss of seven hundred men. We were victorious; but when another attack was made, what were we to do? We had still a little powder left, but had fired off all the shot, stones, iron-bars, &c. in the garrison! On this day, too, we devoured the last morsel of our food: I shall never forget Mrs. Vandegobbleschroy's despairing look, as I saw her sitting alone, attempting to make some impression on the little white elephant's roasted tail.

The third day the attack was repeated. The resources of genius are never at an end. Yesterday I had no ammunition; to-day, I discovered charges sufficient for two guns, and two swivels, which were much longer, but had bores of about blunderbuss size.

This time my friend Loll Mahommed, who had received, as the reader may remember, such a bastinadoing for my sake, headed the attack. The poor wretch could not walk, but he was carried in an open palanquin, and came on waving his sword, and cursing horribly in his Hindustan jargon. Behind him came troops of matchlock-men, who picked off every one of our men who showed their noses above the ramparts: and a great host of blackamoors with scaling-ladders, bundles to fill the ditch, fascines, gabions, culverins, demilunes, counterscarps, and all the other appurtenances of offensive war.

On they came: my guns and men were ready for them. You will ask how my pieces were loaded? I answer, that though my garrison were without food, I knew my duty as an officer, and had put the two Dutch cheeses into the two guns, and had crammed the contents of a bottle of olives into each swivel.

They advanced,—whish! went one of the Dutch cheeses,—bang! went the other. Alas! they did little execution. In their first contact with an opposing body, they certainly floored it but they became at once like so much Welsh-rabbit, and did no execution beyond the man whom they struck down.

"Hogree, pogree, wongree-fum (praise to Allah and the forty-nine Imaums!)" shouted out the ferocious Loll Mahommed when he saw the failure of my shot. "Onward, sons of the Prophet! the infidel has no more ammunition. A hundred thousand lakhs of rupees to the man who brings me Gahagan's head!"

His men set up a shout, and rushed forward—he, to do him justice, was at the very head, urging on his own palanquin-bearers, and poking them with the tip of his scimitar. They came panting up the hill: I was black with rage, but it was the cold, concentrated rage of despair. "Macgillicuddy," said I, calling that faithful officer, "you know where the barrels of powder are?" He did. "You know the use to make of them?" He did. He grasped my hand. "Goliah," said he, "farewell! I swear that the fort shall be in atoms, as soon as yonder unbelievers have carried it. Oh, my poor mother!" added the gallant youth, as sighing, yet fearless, he retired to his post.

I gave one thought to my blessed, my beautiful Belinda, and then, stepping into the front, took down one of the swivels;—a shower of matchlock balls came whizzing round my head. I did not heed them.

I took the swivel, and aimed coolly. Loll Mahommed, his palanquin, and his men, were now not above two hundred yards from the fort. Loll was straight before me, gesticulating and shouting to his men. I fired—bang! ! !

I aimed so true, that one hundred and seventeen best Spanish olives were lodged in a lump in the face of the unhappy Loll Mahommed. The wretch, uttering a yell the most hideous and unearthly I ever heard, fell back dead; the frightened bearers flung down the palanquin and ran—the whole host ran as one man: their screams might be heard for leagues. "Tomasha, tomasha," they cried, "it is enchantment!" Away they fled, and the victory a third time was ours. Soon as the fight was done, I flew back to my Belinda. We had eaten nothing for twenty-four hours, but I forgot hunger in the thought of once more beholding HER!

The sweet soul turned towards me with a sickly smile as I entered, and almost fainted in my arms; but alas! it was not love which caused in her bosom an emotion so strong—it was hunger! "Oh! my Goliah," whispered she, "for three days I have not tasted food—I could not eat that horrid elephant yesterday; but now—oh! heaven! . . . ." She could say no more, but sank almost lifeless on my shoulder. I administered to her a trifling dram of rum, which revived her for a moment, and then rushed down stairs, determined that if it were a piece of my own leg, she should still have something to satisfy her hunger. Luckily I remembered that three or four elephants were still lying in the field, having been killed by us in the first action, two days before. Necessity, thought I, has no law; my adorable girl must eat elephant, until she can get something better.

I rushed into the court where the men were, for the most part, assembled. "Men," said I, "our larder is empty; we must fill it as we did the day before yesterday. Who will follow Gahagan on a foraging party?" I expected that, as on former occasions, every man would offer to accompany me.

To my astonishment, not a soul moved—a murmur arose among the troops; and at last one of the oldest and bravest came forward.

"Captain," he said, "it is of no use; we cannot feed upon elephants for ever; we have not a grain of powder left, and must give up the fort when the attack is made to-morrow. We may as well be prisoners now as then, and we won't go elephant-hunting any more."

"Ruffian!" I said, "he who first talks of surrender, dies!" and I cut him down. "Is there any one else who wishes to speak?"

No one stirred.

"Cowards! miserable cowards!" shouted I; "what, you dare not move for fear of death, at the hands of those wretches who even now fled before your arms—what, do I say YOUR arms?—before MINE!—alone I did it; and as alone I routed the foe, alone I will victual the fortress! Ho! open the gate!"

I rushed out; not a single man would follow. The bodies of the elephants that we had killed still lay on the ground where they had fallen, about four hundred yards from the fort. I descended calmly the hill, a very steep one, and coming to the spot, took my pick of the animals, choosing a tolerably small and plump one, of about thirteen feet high, which the vultures had respected. I threw this animal over my shoulders, and made for the fort.

As I marched up the acclivity, whiz—piff—whir! came the balls over my head; and pitter-patter, pitter-patter! they fell on the body of the elephant like drops of rain. The enemy were behind me; I knew it, and quickened my pace. I heard the gallop of their horse: they came nearer, nearer; I was within a hundred yards of the fort—seventy—fifty! I strained every nerve; I panted with the superhuman exertion—I ran—could a man run very fast with such a tremendous weight on his shoulders?

Up came the enemy; fifty horsemen were shouting and screaming at my tail. O heaven! five yards more—one moment—and I am saved! It is done—I strain the last strain—I make the last step—I fling forward my precious burden into the gate opened wide to receive me and it, and—I fall! The gate thunders to, and I am left ON THE OUTSIDE! Fifty knives are gleaming before my bloodshot eyes—fifty black hands are at my throat, when a voice exclaims, "Stop!—kill him not, it is Gujputi!" A film came over my eyes—exhausted nature would bear no more.

CHAPTER IX

SURPRISE OF FUTTYGHUR

When I awoke from the trance into which I had fallen, I found myself in a bath, surrounded by innumerable black faces; and a Hindoo pothukoor (whence our word apothecary) feeling my pulse and looking at me with an air of sagacity.

"Where am I?" I exclaimed, looking round and examining the strange faces, and the strange apartment which met my view. "Bekhusm!" said the apothecary. "Silence! Gahagan Sahib is in the hands of those who know his valor, and will save his life."

"Know my valor, slave? Of course you do," said I; "but the fort—the garrison—the elephant—Belinda, my love—my darling—Macgillicuddy—the scoundrelly mutineers—the deal bo—. . . ."

I could say no more; the painful recollections pressed so heavily upon my poor shattered mind and frame, that both failed once more. I fainted again, and I know not how long I lay insensible.

Again, however, I came to my senses: the pothukoor applied restoratives, and after a slumber of some hours I awoke, much refreshed. I had no wound; my repeated swoons had been brought on (as indeed well they might) by my gigantic efforts in carrying the elephant up a steep hill a quarter of a mile in length. Walking, the task is bad enough: but running, it is the deuce; and I would recommend any of my readers who may be disposed to try and carry a dead elephant, never, on any account, to go a pace of more than five miles an hour.

Scarcely was I awake, when I heard the clash of arms at my door (plainly indicating that sentinels were posted there), and a single old gentleman, richly habited, entered the room. Did my eyes deceive me? I had surely seen him before. No—yes—no—yes—it WAS he: the snowy white beard, the mild eyes, the nose flattened to a jelly, and level with the rest of the venerable face, proclaimed him at once to be—Saadut Alee Beg Bimbukchee, Holkar's prime vizier; whose nose, as the reader may recollect, his Highness had flattened with his kaleawn during my interview with him in the Pitan's disguise. I now knew my fate but too well—I was in the hands of Holkar.

Saadut Alee Beg Bimbukchee slowly advanced towards me, and with a mild air of benevolence, which distinguished that excellent man (he was torn to pieces by wild horses the year after, on account of a difference with Holkar), he came to my bedside, and taking gently my hand, said, "Life and death, my son, are not ours. Strength is deceitful, valor is unavailing, fame is only wind—the nightingale sings of the rose all night—where is the rose in the morning? Booch, booch! it is withered by a frost. The rose makes remarks regarding the nightingale, and where is that delightful song-bird? Penabekhoda, he is netted, plucked, spitted, and roasted! Who knows how misfortune comes? It has come to Gahagan Gujputi!"

"It is well," said I, stoutly, and in the Malay language. "Gahagan Gujputi will bear it like a man."

"No doubt—like a wise man and a brave one; but there is no lane so long to which there is not a turning, no night so black to which there comes not a morning. Icy winter is followed by merry spring-time—grief is often succeeded by joy."

"Interpret, O riddler!" said I; "Gahagan Khan is no reader of puzzles—no prating mollah. Gujputi loves not words, but swords."

"Listen, then, O Gujputi: you are in Holkar's power."

"I know it."

"You will die by the most horrible tortures to-morrow morning."

"I dare say."

"They will tear your teeth from your jaws, your nails from your fingers, and your eyes from your head."

"Very possibly."

"They will flay you alive, and then burn you."

"Well; they can't do any more."

"They will seize upon every man and woman in yonder fort,"—it was not then taken!—"and repeat upon them the same tortures."

"Ha! Belinda! Speak—how can all this be avoided?"

"Listen. Gahagan loves the moon-face called Belinda."

"He does, Vizier, to distraction."

"Of what rank is he in the Koompani's army?"

"A captain."

"A miserable captain—oh shame! Of what creed is he?"

"I am an Irishman, and a Catholic."

"But he has not been very particular about his religious duties?"

"Alas, no."

"He has not been to his mosque for these twelve years?"

"'Tis too true."

"Hearken now, Gahagan Khan. His Highness Prince Holkar has sent me to thee. You shall have the moon-face for your wife—your second wife, that is;—the first shall be the incomparable Puttee Rooge, who loves you to madness;—with Puttee Rooge, who is the wife, you shall have the wealth and rank of Bobbachy Bahawder, of whom his Highness intends to get rid. You shall be second in command of his Highness's forces. Look, here is his commission signed with the celestial seal, and attested by the sacred names of the forty-nine Imaums. You have but to renounce your religion and your service, and all these rewards are yours."

He produced a parchment, signed as he said, and gave it to me (it was beautifully written in Indian ink: I had it for fourteen years, but a rascally valet, seeing it very dirty, WASHED it, forsooth, and washed off every bit of the writing). I took it calmly, and said, "This is a tempting offer. O Vizier, how long wilt thou give me to consider of it?"

After a long parley, he allowed me six hours, when I promised to give him an answer. My mind, however, was made up—as soon as he was gone, I threw myself on the sofa and fell asleep.

At the end of the six hours the Vizier came back: two people were with him; one, by his martial appearance, I knew to be Holkar, the other I did not recognize. It was about midnight.

"Have you considered?" said the Vizier as he came to my couch.

"I have," said I, sitting up,—I could not stand, for my legs were tied, and my arms fixed in a neat pair of steel handcuffs. "I have," said I, "unbelieving dogs! I have. Do you think to pervert a Christian gentleman from his faith and honor? Ruffian blackamoors! do your worst; heap tortures on this body, they cannot last long. Tear me to pieces: after you have torn me into a certain number of pieces, I shall not feel it; and if I did, if each torture could last a life, if each limb were to feel the agonies of a whole body, what then? I would bear all—all—all—all—all—ALL!" My breast heaved—my form dilated—my eye flashed as I spoke these words. "Tyrants!" said I, "dulce et decorum est pro patria mori." Having thus clinched the argument, I was silent.

The venerable Grand Vizier turned away; I saw a tear trickling down his cheeks.

"What a constancy," said he. "Oh, that such beauty and such bravery should be doomed so soon to quit the earth!"

His tall companion only sneered and said, "AND BELINDA—?"

"Ha!" said I, "ruffian, be still!—heaven will protect her spotless innocence. Holkar, I know thee, and thou knowest ME too! Who, with his single sword, destroyed thy armies? Who, with his pistol, cleft in twain thy nose-ring? Who slew thy generals? Who slew thy elephants? Three hundred mighty beasts went forth to battle: of these I slew one hundred and thirty-five! Dog, coward, ruffian, tyrant, unbeliever! Gahagan hates thee, spurns thee, spits on thee!"

Holkar, as I made these uncomplimentary remarks, gave a scream of rage, and, drawing his scimitar, rushed on to despatch me at once (it was the very thing I wished for), when the third person sprang forward, and seizing his arm, cried—

"Papa! oh, save him!" It was Puttee Rooge! "Remember," continued she, "his misfortunes—remember, oh, remember my—love!"—and here she blushed, and putting one finger into her mouth, and banging down her head, looked the very picture of modest affection.

Holkar sulkily sheathed his scimitar, and muttered, "'Tis better as it is; had I killed him now, I had spared him the torture. None of this shameless fooling, Puttee Rooge," continued the tyrant, dragging her away. "Captain Gahagan dies three hours from hence." Puttee Rooge gave one scream and fainted—her father and the Vizier carried her off between them; nor was I loth to part with her, for, with all her love, she was as ugly as the deuce.

They were gone—my fate was decided. I had but three hours more of life: so I flung myself again on the sofa, and fell profoundly asleep. As it may happen to any of my readers to be in the same situation, and to be hanged themselves, let me earnestly entreat them to adopt this plan of going to sleep, which I for my part have repeatedly found to be successful. It saves unnecessary annoyance, it passes away a great deal of unpleasant time, and it prepares one to meet like a man the coming catastrophe.

Three o'clock came: the sun was at this time making his appearance in the heavens, and with it came the guards, who were appointed to conduct me to the torture. I woke, rose, was carried out, and was set on the very white donkey on which Loll Mahommed was conducted through the camp after he was bastinadoed. Bobbachy Bahawder rode behind me, restored to his rank and state; troops of cavalry hemmed us in on all sides; my ass was conducted by the common executioner: a crier went forward, shouting out, "Make way for the destroyer of the faithful—he goes to bear the punishment of his crimes." We came to the fatal plain: it was the very spot whence I had borne away the elephant, and in full sight of the fort. I looked towards it. Thank heaven! King George's banner waved on it still—a crowd were gathered on the walls—the men, the dastards who had deserted me—and women, too. Among the latter I thought I distinguished ONE who—O gods! the thought turned me sick—I trembled and looked pale for the first time.

"He trembles! he turns pale," shouted out Bobbachy Bahawder, ferociously exulting over his conquered enemy.

"Dog!" shouted I—(I was sitting with my head to the donkey's tail, and so looked the Bobbachy full in the face)—"not so pale as you looked when I felled you with this arm—not so pale as your women looked when I entered your harem!" Completely chop-fallen, the Indian ruffian was silent: at any rate, I had done for HIM.

We arrived at the place of execution. A stake, a couple of feet thick and eight high, was driven in the grass: round the stake, about seven feet from the ground, was an iron ring, to which were attached two fetters; in these my wrists were placed. Two or three executioners stood near, with strange-looking instruments: others were blowing at a fire, over which was a caldron, and in the embers were stuck other prongs and instruments of iron.

The crier came forward and read my sentence. It was the same in effect as that which had been hinted to me the day previous by the Grand Vizier. I confess I was too agitated to catch every word that was spoken.

Holkar himself, on a tall dromedary, was at a little distance. The Grand Vizier came up to me—it was his duty to stand by, and see the punishment performed. "It is yet time!" said he.

I nodded my head, but did not answer.

The Vizier cast up to heaven a look of inexpressible anguish, and with a voice choking with emotion, said, "EXECUTIONER—DO—YOUR—DUTY!"

The horrid man advanced—he whispered sulkily in the ears of the Grand Vizier, "Guggly ka ghee, hum khedgeree," said he, "the oil does not boil yet—wait one minute." The assistants blew, the fire blazed, the oil was heated. The Vizier drew a few feet aside: taking a large ladle full of the boiling liquid, he advanced—

"Whish! bang, bang! pop!" the executioner was dead at my feet, shot through the head; the ladle of scalding oil had been dashed in the face of the unhappy Grand Vizier, who lay on the plain, howling. "Whish! bang! pop! Hurrah!—charge!—forwards!—cut them down!—no quarter!"

I saw—yes, no, yes, no, yes!—I saw regiment upon regiment of galloping British horsemen riding over the ranks of the flying natives. First of the host, I recognized, O heaven! my AHMEDNUGGAR IRREGULARS! On came the gallant line of black steeds and horsemen, swift, swift before them rode my officers in yellow—Glogger, Pappendick, and Stuffle; their sabres gleamed in the sun, their voices rung in the air. "Damn them!" they cried, "give it them, boys!" A strength supernatural thrilled through my veins at that delicious music: by one tremendous effort, I wrested the post from its foundation, five feet in the ground. I could not release my hands from the fetters, it is true; but, grasping the beam tightly, I sprung forward—with one blow I levelled the five executioners in the midst of the fire, their fall upsetting the scalding oil-can; with the next, I swept the bearers of Bobbachy's palanquin off their legs; with the third, I caught that chief himself in the small of the back, and sent him flying on to the sabres of my advancing soldiers!

The next minute, Glogger and Stuffle were in my arms, Pappendick leading on the Irregulars. Friend and foe in that wild chase had swept far away. We were alone; I was freed from my immense bar; and ten minutes afterwards, when Lord Lake trotted up with his staff, he found me sitting on it.

"Look at Gahagan," said his lordship. "Gentlemen, did I not tell you we should be sure to find him AT HIS POST?"

The gallant old nobleman rode on: and this was the famous BATTLE OF FURRUCKABAD, OR SURPRISE OF FUTTYGHUR, fought on the 17th of November, 1804.

About a month afterwards, the following announcement appeared in the Boggleywollah Hurkaru and other Indian papers:—"Married, on the 25th of December, at Futtyghur, by the Rev. Dr. Snorter, Captain Goliah O'Grady Gahagan, Commanding Irregular Horse, Abmednuggar, to Belinda, second daughter of Major-General Bulcher, C.B. His Excellency the Commander-in-Chief gave away the bride; and after a splendid dejeune, the happy pair set off to pass the Mango season at Hurrygurrybang. Venus must recollect, however, that Mars must not ALWAYS be at her side. The Irregulars are nothing without their leader."

Such was the paragraph—such the event—the happiest in the existence of

G. O'G. G., M. H. E. I. C. S., C. I. H. A.


A LEGEND OF THE RHINE

CHAPTER I

SIR LUDWIG OF HOMBOURG

It was in the good old days of chivalry, when every mountain that bathes its shadow in the Rhine had its castle: not inhabited, as now, by a few rats and owls, nor covered with moss and wallflowers, and funguses, and creeping ivy. No, no! where the ivy now clusters there grew strong portcullis and bars of steel; where the wallflower now quivers in the rampart there were silken banners embroidered with wonderful heraldry; men-at-arms marched where now you shall only see a bank of moss or a hideous black champignon; and in place of the rats and owlets, I warrant me there were ladies and knights to revel in the great halls, and to feast, and to dance, and to make love there. They are passed away:—those old knights and ladies: their golden hair first changed to silver, and then the silver dropped off and disappeared for ever; their elegant legs, so slim and active in the dance, became swollen and gouty, and then, from being swollen and gouty, dwindled down to bare bone-shanks; the roses left their cheeks, and then their cheeks disappeared, and left their skulls, and then their skulls powdered into dust, and all sign of them was gone. And as it was with them, so shall it be with us. Ho, seneschal! fill me a cup of liquor! put sugar in it, good fellow—yea, and a little hot water; a very little, for my soul is sad, as I think of those days and knights of old.

They, too, have revelled and feasted, and where are they?—gone?—nay, not altogether gone; for doth not the eye catch glimpses of them as they walk yonder in the gray limbo of romance, shining faintly in their coats of steel, wandering by the side of long-haired ladies, with long-tailed gowns that little pages carry? Yes! one sees them: the poet sees them still in the far-off Cloudland, and hears the ring of their clarions as they hasten to battle or tourney—and the dim echoes of their lutes chanting of love and fair ladies! Gracious privilege of poesy! It is as the Dervish's collyrium to the eyes, and causes them to see treasures that to the sight of donkeys are invisible. Blessed treasures of fancy! I would not change ye—no, not for many donkey-loads of gold. . . . Fill again, jolly seneschal, thou brave wag; chalk me up the produce on the hostel door—surely the spirits of old are mixed up in the wondrous liquor, and gentle visions of bygone princes and princesses look blandly down on us from the cloudy perfume of the pipe. Do you know in what year the fairies left the Rhine?—long before Murray's "Guide-Book" was wrote—long before squat steamboats, with snorting funnels, came paddling down the stream. Do you not know that once upon a time the appearance of eleven thousand British virgins was considered at Cologne as a wonder? Now there come twenty thousand such annually, accompanied by their ladies'-maids. But of them we will say no more—let us back to those who went before them.

Many, many hundred thousand years ago, and at the exact period when chivalry was in full bloom, there occurred a little history upon the banks of the Rhine, which has been already written in a book, and hence must be positively true. 'Tis a story of knights and ladies—of love and battle, and virtue rewarded; a story of princes and noble lords, moreover: the best of company. Gentles, an ye will, ye shall hear it. Fair dames and damsels, may your loves be as happy as those of the heroine of this romaunt.

On the cold and rainy evening of Thursday, the 26th of October, in the year previously indicated, such travellers as might have chanced to be abroad in that bitter night, might have remarked a fellow-wayfarer journeying on the road from Oberwinter to Godesberg. He was a man not tall in stature, but of the most athletic proportions, and Time, which had browned and furrowed his cheek and sprinkled his locks with gray, declared pretty clearly that He must have been acquainted with the warrior for some fifty good years. He was armed in mail, and rode a powerful and active battle-horse, which (though the way the pair had come that day was long and weary indeed,) yet supported the warrior, his armor and luggage, with seeming ease. As it was in a friend's country, the knight did not think fit to wear his heavy destrier, or helmet, which hung at his saddlebow over his portmanteau. Both were marked with the coronet of a count; and from the crown which surmounted the helmet, rose the crest of his knightly race, an arm proper lifting a naked sword.

At his right hand, and convenient to the warrior's grasp, hung his mangonel or mace—a terrific weapon which had shattered the brains of many a turbaned soldan; while over his broad and ample chest there fell the triangular shield of the period, whereon were emblazoned his arms—argent, a gules wavy, on a saltire reversed of the second: the latter device was awarded for a daring exploit before Ascalon, by the Emperor Maximilian, and a reference to the German Peerage of that day, or a knowledge of high families which every gentleman then possessed, would have sufficed to show at once that the rider we have described was of the noble house of Hombourg. It was, in fact, the gallant knight Sir Ludwig of Hombourg: his rank as a count, and chamberlain of the Emperor of Austria, was marked by the cap of maintenance with the peacock's feather which he wore (when not armed for battle), and his princely blood was denoted by the oiled silk umbrella which he carried (a very meet protection against the pitiless storm), and which, as it is known, in the middle ages, none but princes were justified in using. A bag, fastened with a brazen padlock, and made of the costly produce of the Persian looms (then extremely rare in Europe), told that he had travelled in Eastern climes. This, too, was evident from the inscription writ on card or parchment, and sewed on the bag. It first ran "Count Ludwig de Hombourg, Jerusalem;" but the name of the Holy City had been dashed out with the pen, and that of "Godesberg" substituted. So far indeed had the cavalier travelled!—and it is needless to state that the bag in question contained such remaining articles of the toilet as the high-born noble deemed unnecessary to place in his valise.

"By Saint Bugo of Katzenellenbogen!" said the good knight, shivering, "'tis colder here than at Damascus! Marry, I am so hungry I could eat one of Saladin's camels. Shall I be at Godesberg in time for dinner?" And taking out his horologe (which hung in a small side-pocket of his embroidered surcoat), the crusader consoled himself by finding that it was but seven of the night, and that he would reach Godesberg ere the warder had sounded the second gong.

His opinion was borne out by the result. His good steed, which could trot at a pinch fourteen leagues in the hour, brought him to this famous castle, just as the warder was giving the first welcome signal which told that the princely family of Count Karl, Margrave of Godesberg, were about to prepare for their usual repast at eight o'clock. Crowds of pages and horse-keepers were in the court, when, the portcullis being raised, and amidst the respectful salutes of the sentinels, the most ancient friend of the house of Godesberg entered into its castle-yard. The under-butler stepped forward to take his bridle-rein. "Welcome, Sir Count, from the Holy Land!" exclaimed the faithful old man. "Welcome, Sir Count, from the Holy Land!" cried the rest of the servants in the hall. A stable was speedily found for the Count's horse, Streithengst, and it was not before the gallant soldier had seen that true animal well cared for, that he entered the castle itself, and was conducted to his chamber. Wax-candles burning bright on the mantel, flowers in china vases, every variety of soap, and a flask of the precious essence manufactured at the neighboring city of Cologne, were displayed on his toilet-table; a cheering fire "crackled on the hearth," and showed that the good knight's coming had been looked and cared for. The serving-maidens, bringing him hot water for his ablutions, smiling asked, "Would he have his couch warmed at eve?" One might have been sure from their blushes that the tough old soldier made an arch reply. The family tonsor came to know whether the noble Count had need of his skill. "By Saint Bugo," said the knight, as seated in an easy settle by the fire, the tonsor rid his chin of its stubby growth, and lightly passed the tongs and pomatum through "the sable silver" of his hair,—"By Saint Bugo, this is better than my dungeon at Grand Cairo. How is my godson Otto, master barber; and the lady countess, his mother; and the noble Count Karl, my dear brother-in-arms?"

"They are well," said the tonsor, with a sigh.

"By Saint Bugo, I'm glad on't; but why that sigh?"

"Things are not as they have been with my good lord," answered the hairdresser, "ever since Count Gottfried's arrival."

"He here!" roared Sir Ludwig. "Good never came where Gottfried was!" and the while he donned a pair of silken hose, that showed admirably the proportions of his lower limbs, and exchanged his coat of mail for the spotless vest and black surcoat collared with velvet of Genoa, which was the fitting costume for "knight in ladye's bower," the knight entered into a conversation with the barber, who explained to him, with the usual garrulousness of his tribe, what was the present position of the noble family of Godesberg.

This will be narrated in the next chapter.

## CHAPTER II

## THE GODESBERGERS

'Tis needless to state that the gallant warrior Ludwig of Hombourg found in the bosom of his friend's family a cordial welcome. The brother-in-arms of the Margrave Karl, he was the esteemed friend of the Margravine, the exalted and beautiful Theodora of Boppum, and (albeit no theologian, and although the first princes of Christendom coveted such an honor,) he was selected to stand as sponsor for the Margrave's son Otto, the only child of his house.

It was now seventeen years since the Count and Countess had been united: and although heaven had not blessed their couch with more than one child, it may be said of that one that it was a prize, and that surely never lighted on the earth a more delightful vision. When Count Ludwig, hastening to the holy wars, had quitted his beloved godchild, he had left him a boy; he now found him, as the latter rushed into his arms, grown to be one of the finest young men in Germany: tall and excessively graceful in proportion, with the blush of health mantling upon his cheek, that was likewise adorned with the first down of manhood, and with magnificent golden ringlets, such as a Rowland might envy, curling over his brow and his shoulders. His eyes alternately beamed with the fire of daring, or melted with the moist glance of benevolence. Well might a mother be proud of such a boy. Well might the brave Ludwig exclaim, as he clasped the youth to his breast, "By St. Bugo of Katzenellenbogen, Otto, thou art fit to be one of Coeur de Lion's grenadiers!" and it was the fact: the "Childe" of Godesberg measured six feet three.

He was habited for the evening meal in the costly, though simple attire of the nobleman of the period—and his costume a good deal resembled that of the old knight whose toilet we have just described; with the difference of color, however. The pourpoint worn by young Otto of Godesberg was of blue, handsomely decorated with buttons of carved and embossed gold; his haut-de-chausses, or leggings, were of the stuff of Nanquin, then brought by the Lombard argosies at an immense price from China. The neighboring country of Holland had supplied his wrists and bosom with the most costly laces; and thus attired, with an opera-hat placed on one side of his head, ornamented with a single flower, (that brilliant one, the tulip,) the boy rushed into his godfather's dressing-room, and warned him that the banquet was ready.

It was indeed: a frown had gathered on the dark brows of the Lady Theodora, and her bosom heaved with an emotion akin to indignation; for she feared lest the soups in the refectory and the splendid fish now smoking there were getting cold: she feared not for herself, but for her lord's sake. "Godesberg," whispered she to Count Ludwig, as trembling on his arm they descended from the drawing-room, "Godesberg is sadly changed of late."

"By St. Bugo!" said the burly knight, starting, "these are the very words the barber spake."

The lady heaved a sigh, and placed herself before the soup-tureen. For some time the good Knight Ludwig of Hombourg was too much occupied in ladling out the forced-meat balls and rich calves' head of which the delicious pottage was formed (in ladling them out, did we say? ay, marry, and in eating them, too,) to look at his brother-in-arms at the bottom of the table, where he sat with his son on his left hand, and the Baron Gottfried on his right.

The Margrave was INDEED changed. "By St. Bugo," whispered Ludwig to the Countess, "your husband is as surly as a bear that hath been wounded o' the head." Tears falling into her soup-plate were her only reply. The soup, the turbot, the haunch of mutton, Count Ludwig remarked that the Margrave sent all away untasted.

"The boteler will serve ye with wine, Hombourg," said the Margrave gloomily from the end of the table: not even an invitation to drink! how different was this from the old times!

But when in compliance with this order the boteler proceeded to hand round the mantling vintage of the Cape to the assembled party, and to fill young Otto's goblet, (which the latter held up with the eagerness of youth,) the Margrave's rage knew no bounds. He rushed at his son; he dashed the wine-cup over his spotless vest: and giving him three or four heavy blows which would have knocked down a bonassus, but only caused the young Childe to blush: "YOU take wine!" roared out the Margrave; "YOU dare to help yourself! Who time d-v-l gave YOU leave to help yourself?" and the terrible blows were reiterated over the delicate ears of the boy.

"Ludwig! Ludwig!" shrieked the Margravine.

"Hold your prate, madam," roared the Prince. "By St. Buffo, mayn't a father beat his own child?"

"HIS OWN CHILD!" repeated the Margrave with a burst, almost a shriek of indescribable agony. "Ah, what did I say?"

Sir Ludwig looked about him in amaze; Sir Gottfried (at the Margrave's right hand) smiled ghastily; the young Otto was too much agitated by the recent conflict to wear any expression but that of extreme discomfiture; but the poor Margravine turned her head aside and blushed, red almost as the lobster which flanked the turbot before her.

In those rude old times, 'tis known such table quarrels were by no means unusual amongst gallant knights; and Ludwig, who had oft seen the Margrave cast a leg of mutton at an offending servitor, or empty a sauce-boat in the direction of the Margravine, thought this was but one of the usual outbreaks of his worthy though irascible friend, and wisely determined to change the converse.

"How is my friend," said he, "the good knight, Sir Hildebrandt?"

"By Saint Buffo, this is too much!" screamed the Margrave, and actually rushed from time room.

"By Saint Bugo," said his friend, "gallant knights, gentle sirs, what ails my good Lord Margave?"

"Perhaps his nose bleeds," said Gottfried, with a sneer.

"Ah, my kind friend," said the Margravine with uncontrollable emotion, "I fear some of you have passed from the frying-pan into the fire." And making the signal of departure to the ladies, they rose and retired to coffee in the drawing-room.

The Margrave presently came back again, somewhat more collected than he had been. "Otto," he said sternly, "go join the ladies: it becomes not a young boy to remain in the company of gallant knights after dinner." The noble Childe with manifest unwillingness quitted the room, and the Margrave, taking his lady's place at the head of the table, whispered to Sir Ludwig, "Hildebrandt will be here to-night to an evening-party, given in honor of your return from Palestine. My good friend—my true friend—my old companion in arms, Sir Gottfried! you had best see that the fiddlers be not drunk, and that the crumpets be gotten ready." Sir Gottfried, obsequiously taking his patron's hint, bowed and left the room.

"You shall know all soon, dear Ludwig," said the Margrave, with a heart-rending look. "You marked Gottfried, who left the room anon?"

"I did."

"You look incredulous concerning his worth; but I tell thee, Ludwig, that yonder Gottfried is a good fellow, and my fast friend. Why should he not be! He is my near relation, heir to my property: should I" (here the Margrave's countenance assumed its former expression of excruciating agony),—"SHOULD I HAVE NO SON."

"But I never saw the boy in better health," replied Sir Ludwig.

"Nevertheless,—ha! ha!—it may chance that I shall soon have no son."

The Margrave had crushed many a cup of wine during dinner, and Sir Ludwig thought naturally that his gallant friend had drunken rather deeply. He proceeded in this respect to imitate him; for the stern soldier of those days neither shrunk before the Paynim nor the punch-bowl: and many a rousing night had our crusader enjoyed in Syria with lion-hearted Richard; with his coadjutor, Godfrey of Bouillon; nay, with the dauntless Saladin himself.

"You knew Gottfried in Palestine?" asked the Margrave.

"I did."

"Why did ye not greet him then, as ancient comrades should, with the warm grasp of friendship? It is not because Sir Gottfried is poor? You know well that he is of race as noble as thine own, my early friend!"

"I care not for his race nor for his poverty," replied the blunt crusader. "What says the Minnesinger? 'Marry, that the rank is but the stamp of the guinea; the man is the gold.' And I tell thee, Karl of Godesberg, that yonder Gottfried is base metal."

"By Saint Buffo, thou beliest him, dear Ludwig."

"By Saint Bugo, dear Karl, I say sooth. The fellow was known i' the camp of the crusaders—disreputably known. Ere he joined us in Palestine, he had sojourned in Constantinople, and learned the arts of the Greek. He is a cogger of dice, I tell thee—a chanter of horseflesh. He won five thousand marks from bluff Richard of England the night before the storming of Ascalon, and I caught him with false trumps in his pocket. He warranted a bay mare to Conrad of Mont Serrat, and the rogue had fired her."

"Ha! mean ye that Sir Gottfried is a LEG?" cried Sir Karl, knitting his brows. "Now, by my blessed patron, Saint Buffo of Bonn, had any other but Ludwig of Hombourg so said, I would have cloven him from skull to chine."

"By Saint Bugo of Katzenellenbogen, I will prove my words on Sir Gottfried's body—not on thine, old brother-in-arms. And to do the knave justice, he is a good lance. Holy Bugo! but he did good service at Acre! But his character was such that, spite of his bravery, he was dismissed the army; nor even allowed to sell his captain's commission."

"I have heard of it," said the Margrave; "Gottfried hath told me of it. 'Twas about some silly quarrel over the wine-cup—a mere silly jape, believe me. Hugo de Brodenel would have no black bottle on the board. Gottfried was wroth, and to say sooth, flung the black bottle at the county's head. Hence his dismission and abrupt return. But you know not," continued the Margrave, with a heavy sigh, "of what use that worthy Gottfried has been to me. He has uncloaked a traitor to me."

"Not YET," answered Hombourg, satirically.

"By Saint Buffo! a deep-dyed dastard! a dangerous, damnable traitor!—a nest of traitors. Hildebranndt is a traitor—Otto is a traitor—and Theodora (O heaven!) she—she is ANOTHER." The old Prince burst into tears at the word, and was almost choked with emotion.

"What means this passion, dear friend?" cried Sir Ludwig, seriously alarmed.

"Mark, Ludwig! mark Hildebrandt and Theodora together: mark Hildebrandt and OTTO together. Like, like I tell thee as two peas. O holy saints, that I should be born to suffer this!—to have all my affections wrenched out of my bosom, and to be left alone in my old age! But, hark! the guests are arriving. An ye will not empty another flask of claret, let us join the ladyes i' the withdrawing chamber. When there, mark HILDEBRANDT AND OTTO!"


CHAPTER III

THE FESTIVAL

The festival was indeed begun. Coming on horseback, or in their caroches, knights and ladies of the highest rank were assembled in the grand saloon of Godesberg, which was splendidly illuminated to receive them. Servitors, in rich liveries, (they were attired in doublets of the sky-blue broadcloth of Ypres, and hose of the richest yellow sammit—the colors of the house of Godesberg,) bore about various refreshments on trays of silver—cakes, baked in the oven, and swimming in melted butter; manchets of bread, smeared with the same delicious condiment, and carved so thin that you might have expected them to take wing and fly to the ceiling; coffee, introduced by Peter the Hermit, after his excursion into Arabia, and tea such as only Bohemia could produce, circulated amidst the festive throng, and were eagerly devoured by the guests. The Margrave's gloom was unheeded by them—how little indeed is the smiling crowd aware of the pangs that are lurking in the breasts of those who bid them to the feast! The Margravine was pale; but woman knows how to deceive; she was more than ordinarily courteous to her friends, and laughed, though the laugh was hollow, and talked, though the talk was loathsome to her.

"The two are together," said the Margrave, clutching his friend's shoulder. "NOW LOOK!"

Sir Ludwig turned towards a quadrille, and there, sure enough, were Sir Hildebrandt and young Otto standing side by side in the dance. Two eggs were not more like! The reason of the Margrave's horrid suspicion at once flashed across his friend's mind.

"'Tis clear as the staff of a pike," said the poor Margrave, mournfully. "Come, brother, away from the scene; let us go play a game at cribbage!" and retiring to the Margravine's boudoir, the two warriors sat down to the game.

But though 'tis an interesting one, and though the Margrave won, yet he could not keep his attention on the cards: so agitated was his mind by the dreadful secret which weighed upon it. In the midst of their play, the obsequious Gottfried came to whisper a word in his patron's ear, which threw the latter into such a fury, that apoplexy was apprehended by the two lookers-on. But the Margrave mastered his emotion. "AT WHAT TIME, did you say?" said he to Gottfried.

"At daybreak, at the outer gate."

"I will be there."

"AND SO WILL I TOO," thought Count Ludwig, the good Knight of Hombourg.


CHAPTER IV

THE FLIGHT

How often does man, proud man, make calculations for the future, and think he can bend stern fate to his will! Alas, we are but creatures in its hands! How many a slip between the lip and the lifted wine-cup! How often, though seemingly with a choice of couches to repose upon, do we find ourselves dashed to earth; and then we are fain to say the grapes are sour, because we cannot attain them; or worse, to yield to anger in consequence of our own fault. Sir Ludwig, the Hombourger, was NOT AT THE OUTER GATE at daybreak.

He slept until ten of the clock. The previous night's potations had been heavy, the day's journey had been long and rough. The knight slept as a soldier would, to whom a featherbed is a rarity, and who wakes not till he hears the blast of the reveille.

He looked up as he woke. At his bedside sat the Margrave. He had been there for hours watching his slumbering comrade. Watching?—no, not watching, but awake by his side, brooding over thoughts unutterably bitter—over feelings inexpressibly wretched.

"What's o'clock?" was the first natural exclamation of the Hombourger.

"I believe it is five o'clock," said his friend. It was ten. It might have been twelve, two, half-past four, twenty minutes to six, the Margrave would still have said, "I BELIEVE IT IS FIVE O'CLOCK." The wretched take no count of time: it flies with unequal pinions, indeed, for THEM.

"Is breakfast over?" inquired the crusader.

"Ask the butler," said the Margrave, nodding his head wildly, rolling his eyes wildly, smiling wildly.

"Gracious Bugo!" said the Knight of Hombourg, "what has ailed thee, my friend? It is ten o'clock by my horologe. Your regular hour is nine. You are not—no, by heavens! you are not shaved! You wear the tights and silken hose of last evening's banquet. Your collar is all rumpled—'tis that of yesterday. YOU HAVE NOT BEEN TO BED! What has chanced, brother of mine: what has chanced?"

"A common chance, Louis of Hombourg," said the Margrave: "one that chances every day. A false woman, a false friend, a broken heart. THIS has chanced. I have not been to bed."

"What mean ye?" cried Count Ludwig, deeply affected. "A false friend? I am not a false friend. A false woman? Surely the lovely Theodora, your wife—"

"I have no wife, Louis, now; I have no wife and no son."

In accents broken by grief, the Margrave explained what had occurred. Gottfried's information was but too correct. There was a CAUSE for the likeness between Otto and Sir Hildebrandt: a fatal cause! Hildebrandt and Theodora had met at dawn at the outer gate. The Margrave had seen them. They walked long together; they embraced. Ah! how the husband's, the father's, feelings were harrowed at that embrace! They parted; and then the Margrave, coming forward, coldly signified to his lady that she was to retire to a convent for life, and gave orders that the boy should be sent too, to take the vows at a monastery.

Both sentences had been executed. Otto, in a boat, and guarded by a company of his father's men-at-arms, was on the river going towards Cologne, to the monastery of Saint Buffo there. The Lady Theodora, under the guard of Sir Gottfried and an attendant, were on their way to the convent of Nonnenwerth, which many of our readers have seen—the beautiful Green Island Convent, laved by the bright waters of the Rhine!

"What road did Gottfried take?" asked the Knight of Hombourg, grinding his teeth.

"You cannot overtake him," said the Margrave. "My good Gottfried, he is my only comfort now: he is my kinsman, and shall be my heir. He will be back anon."

"Will he so?" thought Sir Ludwig. "I will ask him a few questions ere he return." And springing from his couch, he began forthwith to put on his usual morning dress of complete armor; and, after a hasty ablution, donned, not his cap of maintenance, but his helmet of battle. He rang the bell violently.

"A cup of coffee, straight," said he, to the servitor who answered the summons; "bid the cook pack me a sausage and bread in paper, and the groom saddle Streithengst; we have far to ride."

The various orders were obeyed. The horse was brought; the refreshments disposed of; the clattering steps of the departing steed were heard in the court-yard; but the Margrave took no notice of his friend, and sat, plunged in silent grief, quite motionless by the empty bedside.

## CHAPTER V

THE TRAITOR'S DOOM

The Hombourger led his horse down the winding path which conducts from the hill and castle of Godesberg into the beautiful green plain below. Who has not seen that lovely plain, and who that has seen it has not loved it? A thousand sunny vineyards and cornfields stretch around in peaceful luxuriance; the mighty Rhine floats by it in silver magnificence, and on the opposite bank rise the seven mountains robed in majestic purple, the monarchs of the royal scene.

A pleasing poet, Lord Byron, in describing this very scene, has mentioned that "peasant girls, with dark blue eyes, and hands that offer cake and wine," are perpetually crowding round the traveller in this delicious district, and proffering to him their rustic presents. This was no doubt the case in former days, when the noble bard wrote his elegant poems—in the happy ancient days! when maidens were as yet generous, and men kindly! Now the degenerate peasantry of the district are much more inclined to ask than to give, and their blue eyes seem to have disappeared with their generosity.

But as it was a long time ago that the events of our story occurred, 'tis probable that the good Knight Ludwig of Hombourg was greeted upon his path by this fascinating peasantry; though we know not how he accepted their welcome. He continued his ride across the flat green country until he came to Rolandseck, whence he could command the Island of Nonnenwerth (that lies in the Rhine opposite that place), and all who went to it or passed from it.

Over the entrance of a little cavern in one of the rocks hanging above the Rhine-stream at Rolandseck, and covered with odoriferous cactuses and silvery magnolias, the traveller of the present day may perceive a rude broken image of a saint: that image represented the venerable Saint Buffo of Bonn, the patron of the Margrave; and Sir Ludwig, kneeling on the greensward, and reciting a censer, an ave, and a couple of acolytes before it, felt encouraged to think that the deed he meditated was about to be performed under the very eyes of his friend's sanctified patron. His devotion done (and the knight of those days was as pious as he was brave), Sir Ludwig, the gallant Hombourger, exclaimed with a loud voice:—

"Ho! hermit! holy hermit, art thou in thy cell?"

"Who calls the poor servant of heaven and Saint Buffo?" exclaimed a voice from the cavern; and presently, from beneath the wreaths of geranium and magnolia, appeared an intensely venerable, ancient, and majestic head—'twas that, we need not say, of Saint Buffo's solitary. A silver beard hanging to his knees gave his person an appearance of great respectability; his body was robed in simple brown serge, and girt with a knotted cord: his ancient feet were only defended from the prickles and stones by the rudest sandals, and his bald and polished head was bare.

"Holy hermit," said the knight, in a grave voice, "make ready thy ministry, for there is some one about to die."

"Where, son?"

"Here, father."

"Is he here, now?"

"Perhaps," said the stout warrior, crossing himself; "but not so if right prevail." At this moment he caught sight of a ferry-boat putting off from Nonnenwerth, with a knight on board. Ludwig knew at once, by the sinople reversed and the truncated gules on his surcoat, that it was Sir Gottfried of Godesberg.

"Be ready, father," said the good knight, pointing towards the advancing boat; and waving his hand by way of respect to the reverend hermit, without a further word, he vaulted into his saddle, and rode back for a few score of paces; when he wheeled round, and remained steady. His great lance and pennon rose in the air. His armor glistened in the sun; the chest and head of his battle-horse were similarly covered with steel. As Sir Gottfried, likewise armed and mounted (for his horse had been left at the ferry hard by), advanced up the road, he almost started at the figure before him—a glistening tower of steel.

"Are you the lord of this pass, Sir Knight?" said Sir Gottfried, haughtily, "or do you hold it against all comers, in honor of your lady-love?"

"I am not the lord of this pass. I do not hold it against all comers. I hold it but against one, and he is a liar and a traitor."

"As the matter concerns me not, I pray you let me pass," said Gottfried.

"The matter DOES concern thee, Gottfried of Godesberg. Liar and traitor! art thou coward, too?"

"Holy Saint Buffo! 'tis a fight!" exclaimed the old hermit (who, too, had been a gallant warrior in his day); and like the old war-horse that hears the trumpet's sound, and spite of his clerical profession, he prepared to look on at the combat with no ordinary eagerness, and sat down on the overhanging ledge of the rock, lighting his pipe, and affecting unconcern, but in reality most deeply interested in the event which was about to ensue.

As soon as the word "coward" had been pronounced by Sir Ludwig, his opponent, uttering a curse far too horrible to be inscribed here, had wheeled back his powerful piebald, and brought his lance to the rest.

"Ha! Beauseant!" cried he. "Allah humdillah!" 'Twas the battle-cry in Palestine of the irresistible Knights Hospitallers. "Look to thyself, Sir Knight, and for mercy from heaven! I will give thee none."

"A Bugo for Katzenellenbogen!" exclaimed Sir Ludwig, piously: that, too, was the well-known war-cry of his princely race.

"I will give the signal," said the old hermit, waving his pipe. "Knights, are you ready? One, two, three. LOS!" (let go.)

At the signal, the two steeds tore up the ground like whirlwinds; the two knights, two flashing perpendicular masses of steel, rapidly converged; the two lances met upon the two shields of either, and shivered, splintered, shattered into ten hundred thousand pieces, which whirled through the air here and there, among the rocks, or in the trees, or in the river. The two horses fell back trembling on their haunches, where they remained for half a minute or so.

"Holy Buffo! a brave stroke!" said the old hermit. "Marry, but a splinter wellnigh took off my nose!" The honest hermit waved his pipe in delight, not perceiving that one of the splinters had carried off the head of it, and rendered his favorite amusement impossible. "Ha! they are to it again! O my! how they go to with their great swords! Well stricken, gray! Well parried, piebald! Ha, that was a slicer! Go it, piebald! go it, gray!—go it, gray! go it, pie—Peccavi! peccavi!" said the old man, here suddenly closing his eyes, and falling down on his knees. "I forgot I was a man of peace." And the next moment, muttering a hasty matin, he sprung down the ledge of rock, and was by the side of the combatants.

The battle was over. Good knight as Sir Gottfried was, his strength and skill had not been able to overcome Sir Ludwig the Hombourger, with RIGHT on his side. He was bleeding at every point of his armor: he had been run through the body several times, and a cut in tierce, delivered with tremendous dexterity, had cloven the crown of his helmet of Damascus steel, and passing through the cerebellum and sensorium, had split his nose almost in twain.

His mouth foaming—his face almost green—his eyes full of blood—his brains spattered over his forehead, and several of his teeth knocked out,—the discomfited warrior presented a ghastly spectacle, as, reeling under the effects of the last tremendous blow which the Knight of Hombourg dealt, Sir Gottfried fell heavily from the saddle of his piebald charger; the frightened animal whisked his tail wildly with a shriek and a snort, plunged out his hind legs, trampling for one moment upon the feet of the prostrate Gottfried, thereby causing him to shriek with agony, and then galloped away riderless.

Away! ay, away!—away amid the green vineyards and golden cornfields; away up the steep mountains, where he frightened the eagles in their eyries; away down the clattering ravines, where the flashing cataracts tumble; away through the dark pine-forests, where the hungry wolves are howling away over the dreary wolds, where the wild wind walks alone; away through the plashing quagmires, where the will-o'-the-wisp slunk frightened among the reeds; away through light and darkness, storm and sunshine; away by tower and town, high-road and hamlet. Once a turnpike-man would have detained him; but, ha! ha! he charged the pike, and cleared it at a bound. Once the Cologne Diligence stopped the way: he charged the Diligence, he knocked off the cap of the conductor on the roof, and yet galloped wildly, madly, furiously, irresistibly on! Brave horse! gallant steed! snorting child of Araby! On went the horse, over mountains, rivers, turnpikes, apple-women; and never stopped until he reached a livery-stable in Cologne where his master was accustomed to put him up.

CHAPTER VI

THE CONFESSION

But we have forgotten, meanwhile, that prostrate individual. Having examined the wounds in his side, legs, head, and throat, the old hermit (a skilful leech) knelt down by the side of the vanquished one and said, "Sir Knight, it is my painful duty to state to you that you are in an exceedingly dangerous condition, and will not probably survive."

"Say you so, Sir Priest? then 'tis time I make my confession. Hearken you, Priest, and you, Sir Knight, whoever you be."

Sir Ludwig (who, much affected by the scene, had been tying his horse up to a tree), lifted his visor and said, "Gottfried of Godesberg! I am the friend of thy kinsman, Margrave Karl, whose happiness thou hast ruined; I am the friend of his chaste and virtuous lady, whose fair fame thou hast belied; I am the godfather of young Count Otto, whose heritage thou wouldst have appropriated. Therefore I met thee in deadly fight, and overcame thee, and have wellnigh finished thee. Speak on."

"I have done all this," said the dying man, "and here, in my last hour, repent me. The Lady Theodora is a spotless lady; the youthful Otto the true son of his father—Sir Hildebrandt is not his father, but his UNCLE."

"Gracious Buffo!" "Celestial Bugo!" here said the hermit and the Knight of Hombourg simultaneously, clasping their hands.

"Yes, his uncle; but with the BAR-SINISTER in his scutcheon. Hence he could never be acknowledged by the family; hence, too, the Lady Theodora's spotless purity (though the young people had been brought up together) could never be brought to own the relationship."

"May I repeat your confession?" asked the hermit.

"With the greatest pleasure in life: carry my confession to the Margrave, and pray him give me pardon. Were there—a notary-public present," slowly gasped the knight, the film of dissolution glazing over his eyes, "I would ask—you—two—gentlemen to witness it. I would gladly—sign the deposition—that is, if I could wr-wr-wr-wr-ite!" A faint shuddering smile—a quiver, a gasp, a gurgle—the blood gushed from his mouth in black volumes . . . .

"He will never sin more," said the hermit, solemnly.

"May heaven assoilzie him!" said Sir Ludwig. "Hermit, he was a gallant knight. He died with harness on his back and with truth on his lips: Ludwig of Hombourg would ask no other death. . . . ."

An hour afterwards the principal servants at the Castle of Godesberg were rather surprised to see the noble Lord Louis trot into the court-yard of the castle, with a companion on the crupper of his saddle. 'Twas the venerable hermit of Rolandseck, who, for the sake of greater celerity, had adopted this undignified conveyance, and whose appearance and little dumpy legs might well create hilarity among the "pampered menials" who are always found lounging about the houses of the great. He skipped off the saddle with considerable lightness however; and Sir Ludwig, taking the reverend man by the arm and frowning the jeering servitors into awe, bade one of them lead him to the presence of his Highness the Margrave.

"What has chanced?" said the inquisitive servitor. "The riderless horse of Sir Gottfried was seen to gallop by the outer wall anon. The Margrave's Grace has never quitted your lordship's chamber, and sits as one distraught."

"Hold thy prate, knave, and lead us on!" And so saying, the Knight and his Reverence moved into the well-known apartment, where, according to the servitor's description, the wretched Margrave sat like a stone.

Ludwig took one of the kind broken-hearted man's hands, the hermit seized the other, and began (but on account of his great age, with a prolixity which we shall not endeavor to imitate) to narrate the events which we have already described. Let the dear reader fancy, while his Reverence speaks, the glazed eyes of the Margrave gradually lighting up with attention; the flush of joy which mantles in his countenance—the start—the throb—the almost delirious outburst of hysteric exultation with which, when the whole truth was made known, he clasped the two messengers of glad tidings to his breast, with an energy that almost choked the aged recluse! "Ride, ride this instant to the Margravine—say I have wronged her, that it is all right, that she may come back—that I forgive her—that I apologize if you will"—and a secretary forthwith despatched a note to that effect, which was carried off by a fleet messenger.

"Now write to the Superior of the monastery at Cologne, and bid him send me back my boy, my darling, my Otto—my Otto of roses!" said the fond father, making the first play upon words he had ever attempted in his life. But what will not paternal love effect? The secretary (smiling at the joke) wrote another letter, and another fleet messenger was despatched on another horse.

"And now," said Sir Ludwig, playfully, "let us to lunch. Holy hermit, are you for a snack?"

The hermit could not say nay on an occasion so festive, and the three gentles seated themselves to a plenteous repast; for which the remains of the feast of yesterday offered, it need not be said, ample means.

"They will be home by dinner-time," said the exulting father. "Ludwig! reverend hermit! we will carry on till then." And the cup passed gayly round, and the laugh and jest circulated, while the three happy friends sat confidentially awaiting the return of the Margravine and her son.

But alas! said we not rightly at the commencement of a former chapter, that betwixt the lip and the raised wine-cup there is often many a spill? that our hopes are high, and often, too often, vain? About three hours after the departure of the first messenger, he returned, and with an exceedingly long face knelt down and presented to the Margrave a billet to the following effect:—

"CONVENT OF NONNENWERTH, Friday Afternoon.

"SIR—I have submitted too long to your ill-usage, and am disposed to bear it no more. I will no longer be made the butt of your ribald satire, and the object of your coarse abuse. Last week you threatened me with your cane! On Tuesday last you threw a wine-decanter at me, which hit the butler, it is true, but the intention was evident. This morning, in the presence of all the servants, you called me by the most vile, abominable name, which heaven forbid I should repeat! You dismissed me from your house under a false accusation. You sent me to this odious convent to be immured for life. Be it so! I will not come back, because, forsooth; you relent. Anything is better than a residence with a wicked, coarse, violent, intoxicated, brutal monster like yourself. I remain here for ever and blush to be obliged to sign myself

"THEODORA VON GODESBERG.

"P.S.—I hope you do not intend to keep all my best gowns, jewels, and wearing-apparel; and make no doubt you dismissed me from your house in order to make way for some vile hussy, whose eyes I would like to tear out. T. V. G."

## CHAPTER VII

THE SENTENCE

This singular document, illustrative of the passions of women at all times, and particularly of the manners of the early ages, struck dismay into the heart of the Margrave.

"Are her ladyship's insinuations correct?" asked the hermit, in a severe tone. "To correct a wife with a cane is a venial, I may say a justifiable practice; but to fling a bottle at her is ruin both to the liquor and to her."

"But she sent a carving-knife at me first," said the heartbroken husband. "O jealousy, cursed jealousy, why, why did I ever listen to thy green and yellow tongue?"

"They quarrelled; but they loved each other sincerely," whispered Sir Ludwig to the hermit: who began to deliver forthwith a lecture upon family discord and marital authority, which would have sent his two hearers to sleep, but for the arrival of the second messenger, whom the Margrave had despatched to Cologne for his son. This herald wore a still longer face than that of his comrade who preceded him.

"Where is my darling?" roared the agonized parent. "Have ye brought him with ye?"

"N—no," said the man, hesitating.

"I will flog the knave soundly when he comes," cried the father, vainly endeavoring, under an appearance of sternness, to hide his inward emotion and tenderness.

"Please, your Highness," said the messenger, making a desperate effort, "Count Otto is not at the convent."

"Know ye, knave, where he is?"

The swain solemnly said, "I do. He is THERE." He pointed as he spake to the broad Rhine, that was seen from the casement, lighted up by the magnificent hues of sunset.

"THERE! How mean ye THERE?" gasped the Margrave, wrought to a pitch of nervous fury.

"Alas! my good lord, when he was in the boat which was to conduct him to the convent, he—he jumped suddenly from it, and is dr—dr—owned."

"Carry that knave out and hang him!" said the Margrave, with a calmness more dreadful than any outburst of rage. "Let every man of the boat's crew be blown from the mouth of the cannon on the tower—except the coxswain, and let him be—"

What was to be done with the coxswain, no one knows; for at that moment, and overcome by his emotion, the Margrave sank down lifeless on the floor.

## CHAPTER VIII

THE CHILDE OF GODESBERG

It must be clear to the dullest intellect (if amongst our readers we dare venture to presume that a dull intellect should be found) that the cause of the Margrave's fainting-fit, described in the last chapter, was a groundless apprehension on the part of that too solicitous and credulous nobleman regarding the fate of his beloved child. No, young Otto was NOT drowned. Was ever hero of romantic story done to death so early in the tale? Young Otto was NOT drowned. Had such been the case, the Lord Margrave would infallibly have died at the close of the last chapter; and a few gloomy sentences at its close would have denoted how the lovely Lady Theodora became insane in the convent, and how Sir Ludwig determined, upon the demise of the old hermit (consequent upon the shock of hearing the news), to retire to the vacant hermitage, and assume the robe, the beard, the mortifications of the late venerable and solitary ecclesiastic. Otto was NOT drowned, and all those personages of our history are consequently alive and well.

The boat containing the amazed young Count—for he knew not the cause of his father's anger, and hence rebelled against the unjust sentence which the Margrave had uttered—had not rowed many miles, when the gallant boy rallied from his temporary surprise and despondency, and determined not to be a slave in any convent of any order: determined to make a desperate effort for escape. At a moment when the men were pulling hard against the tide, and Kuno, the coxswain, was looking carefully to steer the barge between some dangerous rocks and quicksands which are frequently met with in the majestic though dangerous river, Otto gave a sudden spring from the boat, and with one single flounce was in the boiling, frothing, swirling eddy of the stream.

Fancy the agony of the crew at the disappearance of their young lord! All loved him; all would have given their lives for him; but as they did not know how to swim, of course they declined to make any useless plunges in search of him, and stood on their oars in mute wonder and grief. ONCE, his fair head and golden ringlets were seen to arise from the water; TWICE, puffing and panting, it appeared for an instant again; THRICE, it rose but for one single moment: it was the last chance, and it sunk, sunk, sunk. Knowing the reception they would meet with from their liege lord, the men naturally did not go home to Godesberg, but putting in at the first creek on the opposite bank, fled into the Duke of Nassau's territory; where, as they have little to do with our tale, we will leave them.

But they little knew how expert a swimmer was young Otto. He had disappeared, it is true; but why? because he HAD DIVED. He calculated that his conductors would consider him drowned, and the desire of liberty lending him wings, (or we had rather say FINS, in this instance,) the gallant boy swam on beneath the water, never lifting his head for a single moment between Godesberg and Cologne—the distance being twenty-five or thirty miles.

Escaping from observation, he landed on the Deutz side of the river, repaired to a comfortable and quiet hostel there, saying he had had an accident from a boat, and thus accounting for the moisture of his habiliments, and while these were drying before a fire in his chamber, went snugly to bed, where he mused, not without amaze, on the strange events of the day. "This morning," thought he, "a noble, and heir to a princely estate—this evening an outcast, with but a few bank-notes which my mamma luckily gave me on my birthday. What a strange entry into life is this for a young man of my family! Well, I have courage and resolution: my first attempt in life has been a gallant and successful one; other dangers will be conquered by similar bravery." And recommending himself, his unhappy mother, and his mistaken father to the care of their patron saint, Saint Buffo, the gallant-hearted boy fell presently into such a sleep as only the young, the healthy, the innocent, and the extremely fatigued can enjoy.

The fatigues of the day (and very few men but would be fatigued after swimming wellnigh thirty miles under water) caused young Otto to sleep so profoundly, that he did not remark how, after Friday's sunset, as a natural consequence, Saturday's Phoebus illumined the world, ay, and sunk at his appointed hour. The serving-maidens of the hostel, peeping in, marked him sleeping, and blessing him for a pretty youth, tripped lightly from the chamber; the boots tried haply twice or thrice to call him (as boots will fain), but the lovely boy, giving another snore, turned on his side, and was quite unconscious of the interruption. In a word, the youth slept for six-and-thirty hours at an elongation; and the Sunday sun was shining and the bells of the hundred churches of Cologne were clinking and tolling in pious festivity, and the burghers and burgheresses of the town were trooping to vespers and morning service when Otto awoke.

As he donned his clothes of the richest Genoa velvet, the astonished boy could not at first account for his difficulty in putting them on. "Marry," said he, "these breeches that my blessed mother" (tears filled his fine eyes as he thought of her)—"that my blessed mother had made long on purpose, are now ten inches too short for me. Whir-r-r! my coat cracks i' the back, as in vain I try to buckle it round me; and the sleeves reach no farther than my elbows! What is this mystery? Am I grown fat and tall in a single night? Ah! ah! ah! ah! I have it."

The young and good-humored Childe laughed merrily. He bethought him of the reason of his mistake: his garments had shrunk from being five-and-twenty miles under water.

But one remedy presented itself to his mind; and that we need not say was to purchase new ones. Inquiring the way to the most genteel ready-made-clothes' establishment in the city of Cologne, and finding it was kept in the Minoriten Strasse, by an ancestor of the celebrated Moses of London, the noble Childe hied him towards the emporium; but you may be sure did not neglect to perform his religious duties by the way. Entering the cathedral, he made straight for the shrine of Saint Buffo, and hiding himself behind a pillar there (fearing he might be recognized by the archbishop, or any of his father's numerous friends in Cologne), he proceeded with his devotions, as was the practice of the young nobles of the age.

But though exceedingly intent upon the service, yet his eye could not refrain from wandering a LITTLE round about him, and he remarked with surprise that the whole church was filled with archers; and he remembered, too, that he had seen in the streets numerous other bands of men similarly attired in green. On asking at the cathedral porch the cause of this assemblage, one of the green ones said (in a jape), "Marry, youngster, YOU must be GREEN, not to know that we are all bound to the castle of his Grace Duke Adolf of Cleves, who gives an archery meeting once a year, and prizes for which we toxophilites muster strong."

Otto, whose course hitherto had been undetermined, now immediately settled what to do. He straightway repaired to the ready-made emporium of Herr Moses, and bidding that gentleman furnish him with an archer's complete dress, Moses speedily selected a suit from his vast stock, which fitted the youth to a T, and we need not say was sold at an exceedingly moderate price. So attired (and bidding Herr Moses a cordial farewell), young Otto was a gorgeous, a noble, a soul-inspiring boy to gaze on. A coat and breeches of the most brilliant pea-green, ornamented with a profusion of brass buttons, and fitting him with exquisite tightness, showed off a figure unrivalled for slim symmetry. His feet were covered with peaked buskins of buff leather, and a belt round his slender waist, of the same material, held his knife, his tobacco-pipe and pouch, and his long shining dirk; which, though the adventurous youth had as yet only employed it to fashion wicket-bails, or to cut bread-and-cheese, he was now quite ready to use against the enemy. His personal attractions were enhanced by a neat white hat, flung carelessly and fearlessly on one side of his open smiling countenance; and his lovely hair, curling in ten thousand yellow ringlets, fell over his shoulder like golden epaulettes, and down his back as far as the waist-buttons of his coat. I warrant me, many a lovely Colnerinn looked after the handsome Childe with anxiety, and dreamed that night of Cupid under the guise of "a bonny boy in green."

So accoutred, the youth's next thought was, that he must supply himself with a bow. This he speedily purchased at the most fashionable bowyer's, and of the best material and make. It was of ivory, trimmed with pink ribbon, and the cord of silk. An elegant quiver, beautifully painted and embroidered, was slung across his back, with a dozen of the finest arrows, tipped with steel of Damascus, formed of the branches of the famous Upas-tree of Java, and feathered with the wings of the ortolan. These purchases being completed (together with that of a knapsack, dressing-case, change, &c.), our young adventurer asked where was the hostel at which the archers were wont to assemble? and being informed that it was at the sign of the "Golden Stag," hied him to that house of entertainment, where, by calling for quantities of liquor and beer, he speedily made the acquaintance and acquired the good will of a company of his future comrades, who happened to be sitting in the coffee-room.

After they had eaten and drunken for all, Otto said, addressing them, "When go ye forth, gentles? I am a stranger here, bound as you to the archery meeting of Duke Adolf. An ye will admit a youth into your company 'twill gladden me upon my lonely way?"

The archers replied, "You seem so young and jolly, and you spend your gold so very like a gentleman, that we'll receive you in our band with pleasure. Be ready, for we start at half-past two!" At that hour accordingly the whole joyous company prepared to move, and Otto not a little increased his popularity among them by stepping out and having a conference with the landlord, which caused the latter to come into the room where the archers were assembled previous to departure, and to say, "Gentlemen, the bill is settled!"—words never ungrateful to an archer yet: no, marry, nor to a man of any other calling that I wot of.

They marched joyously for several leagues, singing and joking, and telling of a thousand feats of love and chase and war. While thus engaged, some one remarked to Otto, that he was not dressed in the regular uniform, having no feathers in his hat.

"I dare say I will find a feather," said the lad, smiling.

Then another gibed because his bow was new.

"See that you can use your old one as well, Master Wolfgang," said the undisturbed youth. His answers, his bearing, his generosity, his beauty, and his wit, inspired all his new toxophilite friends with interest and curiosity, and they longed to see whether his skill with the bow corresponded with their secret sympathies for him.

An occasion for manifesting this skill did not fail to present itself soon—as indeed it seldom does to such a hero of romance as young Otto was. Fate seems to watch over such: events occur to them just in the nick of time; they rescue virgins just as ogres are on the point of devouring them; they manage to be present at court and interesting ceremonies, and to see the most interesting people at the most interesting moment; directly an adventure is necessary for them, that adventure occurs: and I, for my part, have often wondered with delight (and never could penetrate the mystery of the subject) at the way in which that humblest of romance heroes, Signor Clown, when he wants anything in the Pantomime, straightway finds it to his hand. How is it that,—suppose he wishes to dress himself up like a woman for instance, that minute a coalheaver walks in with a shovel-hat that answers for a bonnet; at the very next instant a butcher's lad passing with a string of sausages and a bundle of bladders unconsciously helps Master Clown to a necklace and a tournure, and so on through the whole toilet? Depend upon it there is something we do not wot of in that mysterious overcoming of circumstances by great individuals: that apt and wondrous conjuncture of THE HOUR AND THE MAN; and so, for my part, when I heard the above remark of one of the archers, that Otto had never a feather in his bonnet, I felt sure that a heron would spring up in the next sentence to supply him with an aigrette.

And such indeed was the fact: rising out of a morass by which the archers were passing, a gallant heron, arching his neck, swelling his crest, placing his legs behind him, and his beak and red eyes against the wind, rose slowly, and offered the fairest mark in the world.

"Shoot, Otto," said one of the archers. "You would not shoot just now at a crow because it was a foul bird, nor at a hawk because it was a noble bird; bring us down yon heron: it flies slowly."

But Otto was busy that moment tying his shoestring, and Rudolf, the third best of the archers, shot at the bird and missed it.

"Shoot, Otto," said Wolfgang, a youth who had taken a liking to the young archer: "the bird is getting further and further."

But Otto was busy that moment whittling a willow-twig he had just cut. Max, the second best archer, shot and missed.

"Then," said Wolfgang, "I must try myself: a plague on you, young springald, you have lost a noble chance!"

Wolfgang prepared himself with all his care, and shot at the bird. "It is out of distance," said he, "and a murrain on the bird!"

Otto, who by this time had done whittling his willow-stick (having carved a capital caricature of Wolfgang upon it), flung the twig down and said carelessly, "Out of distance! Pshaw! We have two minutes yet," and fell to asking riddles and cutting jokes; to the which none of the archers listened, as they were all engaged, their noses in air, watching the retreating bird.

"Where shall I hit him?" said Otto.

"Go to," said Rudolf, "thou canst see no limb of him: he is no bigger than a flea."

"Here goes for his right eye!" said Otto; and stepping forward in the English manner (which his godfather having learnt in Palestine, had taught him), he brought his bowstring to his ear, took a good aim, allowing for the wind and calculating the parabola to a nicety. Whiz! his arrow went off.

He took up the willow-twig again and began carving a head of Rudolf at the other end, chatting and laughing, and singing a ballad the while.

The archers, after standing a long time looking skywards with their noses in the air, at last brought them down from the perpendicular to the horizontal position, and said, "Pooh, this lad is a humbug! The arrow's lost; let's go!"

"HEADS!" cried Otto, laughing. A speck was seen rapidly descending from the heavens; it grew to be as big as a crown-piece, then as a partridge, then as a tea-kettle, and flop! down fell a magnificent heron to the ground, flooring poor Max in its fall.

"Take the arrow out of his eye, Wolfgang," said Otto, without looking at the bird: "wipe it and put it back into my quiver."

The arrow indeed was there, having penetrated right through the pupil.

"Are you in league with Der Freischutz?" said Rudolf, quite amazed.

Otto laughingly whistled the "Huntsman's Chorus," and said, "No, my friend. It was a lucky shot: only a lucky shot. I was taught shooting, look you, in the fashion of merry England, where the archers are archers indeed."

And so he cut off the heron's wing for a plume for his hat; and the archers walked on, much amazed, and saying, "What a wonderful country that merry England must be!"

Far from feeling any envy at their comrade's success, the jolly archers recognized his superiority with pleasure; and Wolfgang and Rudolf especially held out their hands to the younker, and besought the honor of his friendship. They continued their walk all day, and when night fell made choice of a good hostel you may be sure, where over beer, punch, champagne, and every luxury, they drank to the health of the Duke of Cleves, and indeed each other's healths all round. Next day they resumed their march, and continued it without interruption, except to take in a supply of victuals here and there (and it was found on these occasions that Otto, young as he was, could eat four times as much as the oldest archer present, and drink to correspond); and these continued refreshments having given them more than ordinary strength, they determined on making rather a long march of it, and did not halt till after nightfall at the gates of the little town of Windeck.

What was to be done? the town-gates were shut. "Is there no hostel, no castle where we can sleep?" asked Otto of the sentinel at the gate. "I am so hungry that in lack of better food I think I could eat my grandmamma."

The sentinel laughed at this hyperbolical expression of hunger, and said, "You had best go sleep at the Castle of Windeck yonder;" adding with a peculiarly knowing look, "Nobody will disturb you there."

At that moment the moon broke out from a cloud, and showed on a hill hard by a castle indeed—but the skeleton of a castle. The roof was gone, the windows were dismantled, the towers were tumbling, and the cold moonlight pierced it through and through. One end of the building was, however, still covered in, and stood looking still more frowning, vast, and gloomy, even than the other part of the edifice.

"There is a lodging, certainly," said Otto to the sentinel, who pointed towards the castle with his bartizan; "but tell me, good fellow, what are we to do for a supper?"

"Oh, the castellan of Windeck will entertain you," said the man-at-arms with a grin, and marched up the embrasure; the while the archers, taking counsel among themselves, debated whether or not they should take up their quarters in the gloomy and deserted edifice.

"We shall get nothing but an owl for supper there," said young Otto. "Marry, lads, let us storm the town; we are thirty gallant fellows, and I have heard the garrison is not more than three hundred." But the rest of the party thought such a way of getting supper was not a very cheap one, and, grovelling knaves, preferred rather to sleep ignobly and without victuals, than dare the assault with Otto, and die, or conquer something comfortable.

One and all then made their way towards the castle. They entered its vast and silent halls, frightening the owls and bats that fled before them with hideous hootings and flappings of wings, and passing by a multiplicity of mouldy stairs, dank reeking roofs, and rickety corridors, at last came to an apartment which, dismal and dismantled as it was, appeared to be in rather better condition than the neighboring chambers, and they therefore selected it as their place of rest for the night. They then tossed up which should mount guard. The first two hours of watch fell to Otto, who was to be succeeded by his young though humble friend Wolfgang; and, accordingly, the Childe of Godesberg, drawing his dirk, began to pace upon his weary round; while his comrades, by various gradations of snoring, told how profoundly they slept, spite of their lack of supper.

'Tis needless to say what were the thoughts of the noble Childe as he performed his two hours' watch; what gushing memories poured into his full soul; what "sweet and bitter" recollections of home inspired his throbbing heart; and what manly aspirations after fame buoyed him up. "Youth is ever confident," says the bard. Happy, happy season! The moonlit hours passed by on silver wings, the twinkling stars looked friendly down upon him. Confiding in their youthful sentinel, sound slept the valorous toxophilites, as up and down, and there and back again, marched on the noble Childe. At length his repeater told him, much to his satisfaction, that it was half-past eleven, the hour when his watch was to cease; and so, giving a playful kick to the slumbering Wolfgang, that good-humored fellow sprung up from his lair, and, drawing his sword, proceeded to relieve Otto.

The latter laid him down for warmth's sake on the very spot which his comrade had left, and for some time could not sleep. Realities and visions then began to mingle in his mind, till he scarce knew which was which. He dozed for a minute; then he woke with a start; then he went off again; then woke up again. In one of these half-sleeping moments he thought he saw a figure, as of a woman in white, gliding into the room, and beckoning Wolfgang from it. He looked again. Wolfgang was gone. At that moment twelve o'clock clanged from the town, and Otto started up.

## CHAPTER IX

## THE LADY OF WINDECK

As the bell with iron tongue called midnight, Wolfgang the Archer, pacing on his watch, beheld before him a pale female figure. He did not know whence she came: but there suddenly she stood close to him. Her blue, clear, glassy eyes were fixed upon him. Her form was of faultless beauty; her face pale as the marble of the fairy statue, ere yet the sculptor's love had given it life. A smile played upon her features, but it was no warmer than the reflection of a moonbeam on a lake; and yet it was wondrous beautiful. A fascination stole over the senses of young Wolfgang. He stared at the lovely apparition with fixed eyes and distended jaws. She looked at him with ineffable archness. She lifted one beautifully rounded alabaster arm, and made a sign as if to beckon him towards her. Did Wolfgang—the young and lusty Wolfgang—follow? Ask the iron whether it follows the magnet?—ask the pointer whether it pursues the partridge through the stubble?—ask the youth whether the lollipop-shop does not attract him? Wolfgang DID follow. An antique door opened, as if by magic. There was no light, and yet they saw quite plain; they passed through the innumerable ancient chambers, and yet they did not wake any of the owls and bats roosting there. We know not through how many apartments the young couple passed; but at last they came to one where a feast was prepared: and on an antique table, covered with massive silver, covers were laid for two. The lady took her place at one end of the table, and with her sweetest nod beckoned Wolfgang to the other seat. He took it. The table was small, and their knees met. He felt as cold in his legs as if he were kneeling against an ice-well.

"Gallant archer," said she, "you must be hungry after your day's march. What supper will you have? Shall it be a delicate lobster-salad? or a dish of elegant tripe and onions? or a slice of boar's-head and truffles? or a Welsh rabbit a la cave au cidre? or a beefsteak and shallot? or a couple of rognons a la brochette? Speak, brave bowyer: you have but to order."

As there was nothing on the table but a covered silver dish, Wolfgang thought that the lady who proposed such a multiplicity of delicacies to him was only laughing at him; so he determined to try her with something extremely rare.

"Fair princess," he said, "I should like very much a pork-chop and some mashed potatoes."

She lifted the cover: there was such a pork-chop as Simpson never served, with a dish of mashed potatoes that would have formed at least six portions in our degenerate days in Rupert Street.

When he had helped himself to these delicacies, the lady put the cover on the dish again, and watched him eating with interest. He was for some time too much occupied with his own food to remark that his companion did not eat a morsel; but big as it was, his chop was soon gone; the shining silver of his plate was scraped quite clean with his knife, and, heaving a great sigh, he confessed a humble desire for something to drink.

"Call for what you like, sweet sir," said the lady, lifting up a silver filigree bottle, with an india-rubber cork, ornamented with gold.

"Then," said Master Wolfgang—for the fellow's tastes were, in sooth, very humble—"I call for half-and-half." According to his wish, a pint of that delicious beverage was poured from the bottle, foaming, into his beaker.

Having emptied this at a draught, and declared that on his conscience it was the best tap he ever knew in his life, the young man felt his appetite renewed; and it is impossible to say how many different dishes he called for. Only enchantment, he was afterwards heard to declare (though none of his friends believed him), could have given him the appetite he possessed on that extraordinary night. He called for another pork-chop and potatoes, then for pickled salmon; then he thought he would try a devilled turkey-wing. "I adore the devil," said he.

"So do I," said the pale lady, with unwonted animation; and the dish was served straightway. It was succeeded by black-puddings, tripe, toasted cheese, and—what was most remarkable—every one of the dishes which he desired came from under the same silver cover: which circumstance, when he had partaken of about fourteen different articles, he began to find rather mysterious.

"Oh," said the pale lady, with a smile, "the mystery is easily accounted for: the servants hear you, and the kitchen is BELOW." But this did not account for the manner in which more half-and-half, bitter ale, punch (both gin and rum), and even oil and vinegar, which he took with cucumber to his salmon, came out of the self-same bottle from which the lady had first poured out his pint of half-and-half.

"There are more things in heaven and earth, Voracio," said his arch entertainer, when he put this question to her, "than are dreamt of in your philosophy:" and, sooth to say, the archer was by this time in such a state, that he did not find anything wonderful more.

"Are you happy, dear youth?" said the lady, as, after his collation, he sank back in his chair.

"Oh, miss, ain't I?" was his interrogative and yet affirmative reply.

"Should you like such a supper every night, Wolfgang?" continued the pale one.

"Why, no," said he; "no, not exactly; not EVERY night: SOME nights I should like oysters."

"Dear youth," said she, "be but mine, and you may have them all the year round!" The unhappy boy was too far gone to suspect anything, otherwise this extraordinary speech would have told him that he was in suspicious company. A person who can offer oysters all the year round can live to no good purpose.

"Shall I sing you a song, dear archer?" said the lady.

"Sweet love!" said he, now much excited, "strike up, and I will join the chorus."

She took down her mandolin, and commenced a ditty. 'Twas a sweet and wild one. It told how a lady of high lineage cast her eyes on a peasant page; it told how nought could her love assuage, her suitor's wealth and her father's rage: it told how the youth did his foes engage; and at length they went off in the Gretna stage, the high-born dame and the peasant page. Wolfgang beat time, waggled his head, sung wofully out of tune as the song proceeded; and if he had not been too intoxicated with love and other excitement, he would have remarked how the pictures on the wall, as the lady sung, began to waggle their heads too, and nod and grin to the music. The song ended. "I am the lady of high lineage: Archer, will you be the peasant page?"

"I'll follow you to the devil!" said Wolfgang.

"Come," replied the lady, glaring wildly on him, "come to the chapel; we'll be married this minute!"

She held out her hand—Wolfgang took it. It was cold, damp,—deadly cold; and on they went to the chapel.

As they passed out, the two pictures over the wall, of a gentleman and lady, tripped lightly out of their frames, skipped noiselessly down to the ground, and making the retreating couple a profound curtsy and bow, took the places which they had left at the table.

Meanwhile the young couple passed on towards the chapel, threading innumerable passages, and passing through chambers of great extent. As they came along, all the portraits on the wall stepped out of their frames to follow them. One ancestor, of whom there was only a bust, frowned in the greatest rage, because, having no legs, his pedestal would not move; and several sticking-plaster profiles of the former Lords of Windeck looked quite black at being, for similar reasons, compelled to keep their places. However, there was a goodly procession formed behind Wolfgang and his bride; and by the time they reached the church, they had near a hundred followers.

The church was splendidly illuminated; the old banners of the old knights glittered as they do at Drury Lane. The organ set up of itself to play the "Bridesmaid's Chorus." The choir-chairs were filled with people in black.

"Come, love," said the pale lady.

"I don't see the parson," exclaimed Wolfgang, spite of himself rather alarmed.

"Oh, the parson! that's the easiest thing in the world! I say, bishop!" said the lady, stooping down.

Stooping down—and to what? Why, upon my word and honor, to a great brass plate on the floor, over which they were passing, and on which was engraven the figure of a bishop—and a very ugly bishop, too—with crosier and mitre, and lifted finger, on which sparkled the episcopal ring. "Do, my dear lord, come and marry us," said the lady, with a levity which shocked the feelings of her bridegroom.

The bishop got up; and directly he rose, a dean, who was sleeping under a large slate near him, came bowing and cringing up to him; while a canon of the cathedral (whose name was Schidnischmidt) began grinning and making fun at the pair. The ceremony was begun, and . . . .

As the clock struck twelve, young Otto bounded up, and remarked the absence of his companion Wolfgang. The idea he had had, that his friend disappeared in company with a white-robed female, struck him more and more. "I will follow them," said he; and, calling to the next on the watch (old Snozo, who was right unwilling to forego his sleep), he rushed away by the door through which he had seen Wolfgang and his temptress take their way.

That he did not find them was not his fault. The castle was vast, the chamber dark. There were a thousand doors, and what wonder that, after he had once lost sight of them, the intrepid Childe should not be able to follow in their steps? As might be expected, he took the wrong door, and wandered for at least three hours about the dark enormous solitary castle, calling out Wolfgang's name to the careless and indifferent echoes, knocking his young shins against the ruins scattered in the darkness, but still with a spirit entirely undaunted, and a firm resolution to aid his absent comrade. Brave Otto! thy exertions were rewarded at last!

For he lighted at length upon the very apartment where Wolfgang had partaken of supper, and where the old couple who had been in the picture-frames, and turned out to be the lady's father and mother, were now sitting at the table.

"Well, Bertha has got a husband at last," said the lady.

"After waiting four hundred and fifty-three years for one, it was quite time," said the gentleman. (He was dressed in powder and a pigtail, quite in the old fashion.)

"The husband is no great things," continued the lady, taking snuff. "A low fellow, my dear; a butcher's son, I believe. Did you see how the wretch ate at supper? To think my daughter should have to marry an archer!"

"There are archers and archers," said the old man. "Some archers are snobs, as your ladyship states; some, on the contrary, are gentlemen by birth, at least, though not by breeding. Witness young Otto, the Landgrave of Godesberg's son, who is listening at the door like a lackey, and whom I intend to run through the—"

"Law, Baron!" said the lady.

"I will, though," replied the Baron, drawing an immense sword, and glaring round at Otto: but though at the sight of that sword and that scowl a less valorous youth would have taken to his heels, the undaunted Childe advanced at once into the apartment. He wore round his neck a relic of St. Buffo (the tip of the saint's ear, which had been cut off at Constantinople). "Fiends! I command you to retreat!" said he, holding up this sacred charm, which his mamma had fastened on him; and at the sight of it, with an unearthly yell the ghosts of the Baron and the Baroness sprung back into their picture-frames, as clowns go through a clock in a pantomime.

He rushed through the open door by which the unlucky Wolfgang had passed with his demoniacal bride, and went on and on through the vast gloomy chambers lighted by the ghastly moonshine: the noise of the organ in the chapel, the lights in the kaleidoscopic windows, directed him towards that edifice. He rushed to the door: 'twas barred! He knocked: the beadles were deaf. He applied his inestimable relic to the lock, and—whiz! crash! clang! bang! whang!—the gate flew open! the organ went off in a fugue—the lights quivered over the tapers, and then went off towards the ceiling—the ghosts assembled rushed away with a skurry and a scream—the bride howled, and vanished—the fat bishop waddled back under his brass plate—the dean flounced down into his family vault—and the canon Schidnischmidt, who was making a joke, as usual, on the bishop, was obliged to stop at the very point of his epigram, and to disappear into the void whence he came.

Otto fell fainting at the porch, while Wolfgang tumbled lifeless down at the altar-steps; and in this situation the archers, when they arrived, found the two youths. They were resuscitated, as we scarce need say; but when, in incoherent accents, they came to tell their wondrous tale, some sceptics among the archers said—"Pooh! they were intoxicated!" while others, nodding their older heads, exclaimed—"THEY HAVE SEEN THE LADY OF WINDECK!" and recalled the stories of many other young men, who, inveigled by her devilish arts, had not been so lucky as Wolfgang, and had disappeared—for ever!

This adventure bound Wolfgang heart and soul to his gallant preserver; and the archers—it being now morning, and the cocks crowing lustily round about—pursued their way without further delay to the castle of the noble patron of toxophilites, the gallant Duke of Cleves.

CHAPTER X

THE BATTLE OF THE BOWMEN

Although there lay an immense number of castles and abbeys between Windeck and Cleves, for every one of which the guide-books have a legend and a ghost, who might, with the commonest stretch of ingenuity, be made to waylay our adventurers on the road; yet, as the journey would be thus almost interminable, let us cut it short by saying that the travellers reached Cleves without any further accident, and found the place thronged with visitors for the meeting next day.

And here it would be easy to describe the company which arrived, and make display of antiquarian lore. Now we would represent a cavalcade of knights arriving, with their pages carrying their shining helms of gold, and the stout esquires, bearers of lance and banner. Anon would arrive a fat abbot on his ambling pad, surrounded by the white-robed companions of his convent. Here should come the gleemen and jonglers, the minstrels, the mountebanks, the party-colored gipsies, the dark-eyed, nut-brown Zigeunerinnen; then a troop of peasants chanting Rhine-songs, and leading in their ox-drawn carts the peach-cheeked girls from the vine-lands. Next we would depict the litters blazoned with armorial bearings, from between the broidered curtains of which peeped out the swan-like necks and the haughty faces of the blond ladies of the castles. But for these descriptions we have not space; and the reader is referred to the account of the tournament in the ingenious novel of "Ivanhoe," where the above phenomena are described at length. Suffice it to say, that Otto and his companions arrived at the town of Cleves, and, hastening to a hostel, reposed themselves after the day's march, and prepared them for the encounter of the morrow.

That morrow came: and as the sports were to begin early, Otto and his comrades hastened to the field, armed with their best bows and arrows, you may be sure, and eager to distinguish themselves; as were the multitude of other archers assembled. They were from all neighboring countries—crowds of English, as you may fancy, armed with Murray's guide-books, troops of chattering Frenchmen, Frankfort Jews with roulette-tables, and Tyrolese, with gloves and trinkets—all hied towards the field where the butts were set up, and the archery practice was to be held. The Childe and his brother archers were, it need not be said, early on the ground.

But what words of mine can describe the young gentleman's emotion when, preceded by a band of trumpets, bagpipes, ophicleides, and other wind instruments, the Prince of Cleves appeared with the Princess Helen, his daughter? And ah! what expressions of my humble pen can do justice to the beauty of that young lady? Fancy every charm which decorates the person, every virtue which ornaments the mind, every accomplishment which renders charming mind and charming person doubly charming, and then you will have but a faint and feeble idea of the beauties of her Highness the Princess Helen. Fancy a complexion such as they say (I know not with what justice) Rowland's Kalydor imparts to the users of that cosmetic; fancy teeth to which orient pearls are like Wallsend coals; eyes, which were so blue, tender, and bright, that while they run you through with their lustre, they healed you with their kindness; a neck and waist, so ravishingly slender and graceful, that the least that is said about them the better; a foot which fell upon the flowers no heavier than a dew-drop—and this charming person set off by the most elegant toilet that ever milliner devised! The lovely Helen's hair (which was as black as the finest varnish for boots) was so long, that it was borne on a cushion several yards behind her by the maidens of her train; and a hat, set off with moss-roses, sunflowers, bugles, birds-of-paradise, gold lace, and pink ribbon, gave her a distingue air, which would have set the editor of the Morning Post mad with love.

It had exactly the same effect upon the noble Childe of Godesberg, as leaning on his ivory bow, with his legs crossed, he stood and gazed on her, as Cupid gazed on Psyche. Their eyes met: it was all over with both of them. A blush came at one and the same minute budding to the cheek of either. A simultaneous throb beat in those young hearts! They loved each other for ever from that instant. Otto still stood, cross-legged, enraptured, leaning on his ivory bow; but Helen, calling to a maiden for her pocket-handkerchief, blew her beautiful Grecian nose in order to hide her agitation. Bless ye, bless ye, pretty ones! I am old now; but not so old but that I kindle at the tale of love. Theresa MacWhirter too has lived and loved. Heigho!

Who is yon chief that stands behind the truck whereon are seated the Princess and the stout old lord, her father? Who is he whose hair is of the carroty hue? whose eyes, across a snubby bunch of a nose, are perpetually scowling at each other; who has a hump-back and a hideous mouth, surrounded with bristles, and crammed full of jutting yellow odious teeth. Although he wears a sky-blue doublet laced with silver, it only serves to render his vulgar punchy figure doubly ridiculous; although his nether garment is of salmon-colored velvet, it only draws the more attention to his legs, which are disgustingly crooked and bandy. A rose-colored hat, with towering pea-green ostrich-plumes, looks absurd on his bull-head; and though it is time of peace, the wretch is armed with a multiplicity of daggers, knives, yataghans, dirks, sabres, and scimitars, which testify his truculent and bloody disposition. 'Tis the terrible Rowski de Donnerblitz, Margrave of Eulenschreckenstein. Report says he is a suitor for the hand of the lovely Helen. He addresses various speeches of gallantry to her, and grins hideously as he thrusts his disgusting head over her lily shoulder. But she turns away from him! turns and shudders—ay, as she would at a black dose!

Otto stands gazing still, and leaning on his bow. "What is the prize?" asks one archer of another. There are two prizes—a velvet cap, embroidered by the hand of the Princess, and a chain of massive gold, of enormous value. Both lie on cushions before her.

"I know which I shall choose, when I win the first prize," says a swarthy, savage, and bandy-legged archer, who bears the owl gules on a black shield, the cognizance of the Lord Rowski de Donnerblitz.

"Which, fellow?" says Otto, turning fiercely upon him.

"The chain, to be sure!" says the leering archer. "You do not suppose I am such a flat as to choose that velvet gimcrack there?" Otto laughed in scorn, and began to prepare his bow. The trumpets sounding proclaimed that the sports were about to commence.

Is it necessary to describe them? No: that has already been done in the novel of "Ivanhoe" before mentioned. Fancy the archers clad in Lincoln green, all coming forward in turn, and firing at the targets.

Some hit, some missed; those that missed were fain to retire amidst the jeers of the multitudinous spectators. Those that hit began new trials of skill; but it was easy to see, from the first, that the battle lay between Squintoff (the Rowski archer) and the young hero with the golden hair and the ivory bow. Squintoff's fame as a marksman was known throughout Europe; but who was his young competitor? Ah? there was ONE heart in the assembly that beat most anxiously to know. 'Twas Helen's.

The crowning trial arrived. The bull's eye of the target, set up at three-quarters of a mile distance from the archers, was so small, that it required a very clever man indeed to see, much more to hit it; and as Squintoff was selecting his arrow for the final trial, the Rowski flung a purse of gold towards his archer, saying—"Squintoff, an ye win the prize, the purse is thine." "I may as well pocket it at once, your honor," said the bowman with a sneer at Otto. "This young chick, who has been lucky as yet, will hardly hit such a mark as that." And, taking his aim, Squintoff discharged his arrow right into the very middle of the bull's-eye.

"Can you mend that, young springald?" said he, as a shout rent the air at his success, as Helen turned pale to think that the champion of her secret heart was likely to be overcome, and as Squintoff, pocketing the Rowski's money, turned to the noble boy of Godesberg.

"Has anybody got a pea?" asked the lad. Everybody laughed at his droll request; and an old woman, who was selling porridge in the crowd, handed him the vegetable which he demanded. It was a dry and yellow pea. Otto, stepping up to the target, caused Squintoff to extract his arrow from the bull's-eye, and placed in the orifice made by the steel point of the shaft, the pea which he had received from the old woman. He then came back to his place. As he prepared to shoot, Helen was so overcome by emotion, that 'twas thought she would have fainted. Never, never had she seen a being so beautiful as the young hero now before her.

He looked almost divine. He flung back his long clusters of hair from his bright eyes and tall forehead; the blush of health mantled on his cheek, from which the barber's weapon had never shorn the down. He took his bow, and one of his most elegant arrows, and poising himself lightly on his right leg, he flung himself forward, raising his left leg on a level with his ear. He looked like Apollo, as he stood balancing himself there. He discharged his dart from the thrumming bowstring: it clove the blue air—whiz!

"HE HAS SPLIT THE PEA!" said the Princess, and fainted. The Rowski, with one eye, hurled an indignant look at the boy, while with the other he levelled (if aught so crooked can be said to level anything) a furious glance at his archer.

The archer swore a sulky oath. "He is the better man!" said he. "I suppose, young chap, you take the gold chain?"

"The gold chain?" said Otto. "Prefer a gold chain to a cap worked by that august hand? Never!" And advancing to the balcony where the Princess, who now came to herself, was sitting, he kneeled down before her, and received the velvet cap; which, blushing as scarlet as the cap itself, the Princess Helen placed on his golden ringlets. Once more their eyes met—their hearts thrilled. They had never spoken, but they knew they loved each other for ever.

"Wilt thou take service with the Rowski of Donnerblitz?" said that individual to the youth. "Thou shalt be captain of my archers in place of yon blundering nincompoop, whom thou hast overcome."

"Yon blundering nincompoop is a skilful and gallant archer," replied Otto, haughtily; "and I will NOT take service with the Rowski of Donnerblitz."

"Wilt thou enter the household of the Prince of Cleves?" said the father of Helen, laughing, and not a little amused at the haughtiness of the humble archer.

"I would die for the Duke of Cleves and HIS FAMILY," said Otto, bowing low. He laid a particular and a tender emphasis on the word family. Helen knew what he meant. SHE was the family. In fact her mother was no more, and her papa had no other offspring.

"What is thy name, good fellow," said the Prince, "that my steward may enroll thee?"

"Sir," said Otto, again blushing, "I am OTTO THE ARCHER."


CHAPTER XI

THE MARTYR OF LOVE

The archers who had travelled in company with young Otto gave a handsome dinner in compliment to the success of our hero; at which his friend distinguished himself as usual in the eating and drinking department. Squintoff, the Rowski bowman, declined to attend; so great was the envy of the brute at the youthful hero's superiority. As for Otto himself, he sat on the right hand of the chairman; but it was remarked that he could not eat. Gentle reader of my page! thou knowest why full well. He was too much in love to have any appetite; for though I myself when laboring under that passion, never found my consumption of victuals diminish, yet remember our Otto was a hero of romance, and they NEVER are hungry when they're in love.

The next day, the young gentleman proceeded to enroll himself in the corps of Archers of the Prince of Cleves, and with him came his attached squire, who vowed he never would leave him. As Otto threw aside his own elegant dress, and donned the livery of the House of Cleves, the noble Childe sighed not a little. 'Twas a splendid uniform 'tis true, but still it WAS a livery, and one of his proud spirit ill bears another's cognizances. "They are the colors of the Princess, however," said he, consoling himself; "and what suffering would I not undergo for HER?" As for Wolfgang, the squire, it may well be supposed that the good-natured, low-born fellow had no such scruples; but he was glad enough to exchange for the pink hose, the yellow jacket, the pea-green cloak, and orange-tawny hat, with which the Duke's steward supplied him, the homely patched doublet of green which he had worn for years past.

"Look at you two archers," said the Prince of Cleves to his guest, the Rowski of Donnerblitz, as they were strolling on the battlements after dinner, smoking their cigars as usual. His Highness pointed to our two young friends, who were mounting guard for the first time. "See yon two bowmen—mark their bearing! One is the youth who beat thy Squintoff, and t'other, an I mistake not, won the third prize at the butts. Both wear the same uniform—the colors of my house—yet wouldst not swear that the one was but a churl, and the other a noble gentleman?"

"Which looks like the nobleman?" said the Rowski, as black as thunder.

"WHICH? why, young Otto, to be sure," said the Princess Helen, eagerly. The young lady was following the pair; but under pretence of disliking the odor of the cigar, she had refused the Rowski's proffered arm, and was loitering behind with her parasol.

Her interposition in favor of her young protege only made the black and jealous Rowski more ill-humored. "How long is it, Sir Prince of Cleves," said he, "that the churls who wear your livery permit themselves to wear the ornaments of noble knights? Who but a noble dare wear ringlets such as yon springald's? Ho, archer!" roared he, "come, hither, fellow." And Otto stood before him. As he came, and presenting arms stood respectfully before the Prince and his savage guest, he looked for one moment at the lovely Helen—their eyes met, their hearts beat simultaneously: and, quick, two little blushes appeared in the cheek of either. I have seen one ship at sea answering another's signal so.

While they are so regarding each other, let us just remind our readers of the great estimation in which the hair was held in the North. Only nobles were permitted to wear it long. When a man disgraced himself, a shaving was sure to follow. Penalties were inflicted upon villains or vassals who sported ringlets. See the works of Aurelius Tonsor; Hirsutus de Nobilitate Capillari; Rolandus de Oleo Macassari; Schnurrbart; Fresirische Alterthumskunde, &c.

"We must have those ringlets of thine cut, good fellow," said the Duke of Cleves good-naturedly, but wishing to spare the feelings of his gallant recruit. "'Tis against the regulation cut of my archer guard."

"Cut off my hair!" cried Otto, agonized.

"Ay, and thine ears with it, yokel," roared Donnerblitz.

"Peace, noble Eulenschreckenstein," said the Duke with dignity: "let the Duke of Cleves deal as he will with his own men-at-arms. And you, young sir, unloose the grip of thy dagger."

Otto, indeed, had convulsively grasped his snickersnee, with intent to plunge it into the heart of the Rowski; but his politer feelings overcame him. "The count need not fear, my lord," said he: "a lady is present." And he took off his orange-tawny cap and bowed low. Ah! what a pang shot through the heart of Helen, as she thought that those lovely ringlets must be shorn from that beautiful head!

Otto's mind was, too, in commotion. His feelings as a gentleman—let us add, his pride as a man—for who is not, let us ask, proud of a good head of hair?—waged war within his soul. He expostulated with the Prince. "It was never in my contemplation," he said, "on taking service, to undergo the operation of hair-cutting."

"Thou art free to go or stay, Sir Archer," said the Prince pettishly. "I will have no churls imitating noblemen in my service: I will bandy no conditions with archers of my guard."

"My resolve is taken," said Otto, irritated too in his turn. "I will . . . . "

"What?" cried Helen, breathless with intense agitation.

"I will STAY," answered Otto. The poor girl almost fainted with joy. The Rowski frowned with demoniac fury, and grinding his teeth and cursing in the horrible German jargon, stalked away. "So be it," said the Prince of Cleves, taking his daughter's arm—"and here comes Snipwitz, my barber, who shall do the business for you." With this the Prince too moved on, feeling in his heart not a little compassion for the lad; for Adolf of Cleves had been handsome in his youth, and distinguished for the ornament of which he was now depriving his archer.

Snipwitz led the poor lad into a side-room, and there—in a word—operated upon him. The golden curls—fair curls that his mother had so often played with!—fell under the shears and round the lad's knees, until he looked as if he was sitting in a bath of sunbeams.

When the frightful act had been performed, Otto, who entered the little chamber in the tower ringleted like Apollo, issued from it as cropped as a charity-boy.

See how melancholy he looks, now that the operation is over!—And no wonder. He was thinking what would be Helen's opinion of him, now that one of his chief personal ornaments was gone. "Will she know me?" thought he; "will she love me after this hideous mutilation?"

Yielding to these gloomy thoughts, and, indeed, rather unwilling to be seen by his comrades, now that he was so disfigured, the young gentleman had hidden himself behind one of the buttresses of the wall, a prey to natural despondency; when he saw something which instantly restored him to good spirits. He saw the lovely Helen coming towards the chamber where the odious barber had performed upon him,—coming forward timidly, looking round her anxiously, blushing with delightful agitation,—and presently seeing, as she thought, the coast clear, she entered the apartment. She stooped down, and ah! what was Otto's joy when he saw her pick up a beautiful golden lock of his hair, press it to her lips, and then hide it in her bosom! No carnation ever blushed so redly as Helen did when she came out after performing this feat. Then she hurried straightway to her own apartments in the castle, and Otto, whose first impulse was to come out from his hiding-place, and, falling at her feet, call heaven and earth to witness to his passion, with difficulty restrained his feelings and let her pass: but the love-stricken young hero was so delighted with this evident proof of reciprocated attachment, that all regret at losing his ringlets at once left him, and he vowed he would sacrifice not only his hair, but his head, if need were, to do her service.

That very afternoon, no small bustle and conversation took place in the castle, on account of the sudden departure of the Rowski of Eulenschreckenstein, with all his train and equipage. He went away in the greatest wrath, it was said, after a long and loud conversation with the Prince. As that potentate conducted his guest to the gate, walking rather demurely and shamefacedly by his side, as he gathered his attendants in the court, and there mounted his charger, the Rowski ordered his trumpets to sound, and scornfully flung a largesse of gold among the servitors and men-at-arms of the House of Cleves, who were marshalled in the court. "Farewell, Sir Prince," said he to his host: "I quit you now suddenly; but remember, it is not my last visit to the Castle of Cleves." And ordering his band to play "See the Conquering Hero comes," he clattered away through the drawbridge. The Princess Helen was not present at his departure; and the venerable Prince of Cleves looked rather moody and chap-fallen when his guest left him. He visited all the castle defences pretty accurately that night, and inquired of his officers the state of the ammunition, provisions, &c. He said nothing; but the Princess Helen's maid did: and everybody knew that the Rowski had made his proposals, had been rejected, and, getting up in a violent fury, had called for his people, and sworn by his great gods that he would not enter the castle again until he rode over the breach, lance in hand, the conqueror of Cleves and all belonging to it.

No little consternation was spread through the garrison at the news: for everybody knew the Rowski to be one of the most intrepid and powerful soldiers in all Germany,—one of the most skilful generals.

Generous to extravagance to his own followers, he was ruthless to the enemy: a hundred stories were told of the dreadful barbarities exercised by him in several towns and castles which he had captured and sacked. And poor Helen had the pain of thinking, that in consequence of her refusal she was dooming all the men, women, and children of the principality to indiscriminate and horrible slaughter.

The dreadful surmises regarding a war received in a few days dreadful confirmation. It was noon, and the worthy Prince of Cleves was taking his dinner (though the honest warrior had had little appetite for that meal for some time past), when trumpets were heard at the gate; and presently the herald of the Rowski of Donnerblitz, clad in a tabard on which the arms of the Count were blazoned, entered the dining-hall. A page bore a steel gauntlet on a cushion; Bleu Sanglier had his hat on his head. The Prince of Cleves put on his own, as the herald came up to the chair of state where the sovereign sat.

"Silence for Bleu Sanglier," cried the Prince, gravely. "Say your say, Sir Herald."

"In the name of the high and mighty Rowski, Prince of Donnerblitz, Margrave of Eulenschreckenstein, Count of Krotenwald, Schnauzestadt, and Galgenhugel, Hereditary Grand Corkscrew of the Holy Roman Empire—to you, Adolf the Twenty-third, Prince of Cleves, I, Bleu Sanglier, bring war and defiance. Alone, and lance to lance, or twenty to twenty in field or in fort, on plain or on mountain, the noble Rowski defies you. Here, or wherever he shall meet you, he proclaims war to the death between you and him. In token whereof, here is his glove." And taking the steel glove from the page, Bleu Boar flung it clanging on the marble floor.

The Princess Helen turned deadly pale: but the Prince, with a good assurance, flung down his own glove, calling upon some one to raise the Rowski's; which Otto accordingly took up and presented to him, on his knee.

"Boteler, fill my goblet," said the Prince to that functionary, who, clothed in tight black hose, with a white kerchief, and a napkin on his dexter arm, stood obsequiously by his master's chair. The goblet was filled with Malvoisie: it held about three quarts; a precious golden hanap carved by the cunning artificer, Benvenuto the Florentine.

"Drink, Bleu Sanglier," said the Prince, "and put the goblet in thy bosom. Wear this chain, furthermore, for my sake." And so saying, Prince Adolf flung a precious chain of emeralds round the herald's neck. "An invitation to battle was ever a welcome call to Adolf of Cleves." So saying, and bidding his people take good care of Bleu Sanglier's retinue, the Prince left the hall with his daughter. All were marvelling at his dignity, courage, and generosity.

But, though affecting unconcern, the mind of Prince Adolf was far from tranquil. He was no longer the stalwart knight who, in the reign of Stanislaus Augustus, had, with his naked fist, beaten a lion to death in three minutes; and alone had kept the postern of Peterwaradin for two hours against seven hundred Turkish janissaries, who were assailing it. Those deeds which had made the heir of Cleves famous were done thirty years syne. A free liver since he had come into his principality, and of a lazy turn, he had neglected the athletic exercises which had made him in youth so famous a champion, and indolence had borne its usual fruits. He tried his old battle-sword—that famous blade with which, in Palestine, he had cut an elephant-driver in two pieces, and split asunder the skull of the elephant which he rode. Adolf of Cleves could scarcely now lift the weapon over his head. He tried his armor. It was too tight for him. And the old soldier burst into tears, when he found he could not buckle it. Such a man was not fit to encounter the terrible Rowski in single combat.

Nor could he hope to make head against him for any time in the field. The Prince's territories were small; his vassals proverbially lazy and peaceable; his treasury empty. The dismallest prospects were before him: and he passed a sleepless night writing to his friends for succor, and calculating with his secretary the small amount of the resources which he could bring to aid him against his advancing and powerful enemy.

Helen's pillow that evening was also unvisited by slumber. She lay awake thinking of Otto,—thinking of the danger and the ruin her refusal to marry had brought upon her dear papa. Otto, too, slept not: but HIS waking thoughts were brilliant and heroic: the noble Childe thought how he should defend the Princess, and win LOS and honor in the ensuing combat.

## CHAPTER XII

### THE CHAMPION

And now the noble Cleves began in good earnest to prepare his castle for the threatened siege. He gathered in all the available cattle round the property, and the pigs round many miles; and a dreadful slaughter of horned and snouted animals took place,—the whole castle resounding with the lowing of the oxen and the squeaks of the gruntlings, destined to provide food for the garrison. These, when slain, (her gentle spirit, of course, would not allow of her witnessing that disagreeable operation,) the lovely Helen, with the assistance of her maidens, carefully salted and pickled. Corn was brought in in great quantities, the Prince paying for the same when he had money, giving bills when he could get credit, or occasionally, marry, sending out a few stout men-at-arms to forage, who brought in wheat without money or credit either. The charming Princess, amidst the intervals of her labors, went about encouraging the garrison, who vowed to a man they would die for a single sweet smile of hers; and in order to make their inevitable sufferings as easy as possible to the gallant fellows, she and the apothecaries got ready a plenty of efficacious simples, and scraped a vast quantity of lint to bind their warriors' wounds withal. All the fortifications were strengthened; the fosses carefully filled with spikes and water; large stones placed over the gates, convenient to tumble on the heads of the assaulting parties; and caldrons prepared, with furnaces to melt up pitch, brimstone, boiling oil, &c., wherewith hospitably to receive them. Having the keenest eye in the whole garrison, young Otto was placed on the topmost tower, to watch for the expected coming of the beleaguering host.

They were seen only too soon. Long ranks of shining spears were seen glittering in the distance, and the army of the Rowski soon made its appearance in battle's magnificently stern array. The tents of the renowned chief and his numerous warriors were pitched out of arrow-shot of the castle, but in fearful proximity; and when his army had taken up its position, an officer with a flag of truce and a trumpet was seen advancing to the castle gate. It was the same herald who had previously borne his master's defiance to the Prince of Cleves. He came once more to the castle gate, and there proclaimed that the noble Count of Eulenschreckenstein was in arms without, ready to do battle with the Prince of Cleves, or his champion; that he would remain in arms for three days, ready for combat. If no man met him at the end of that period, he would deliver an assault, and would give quarter to no single soul in the garrison. So saying, the herald nailed his lord's gauntlet on the castle gate. As before, the Prince flung him over another glove from the wall; though how he was to defend himself from such a warrior, or get a champion, or resist the pitiless assault that must follow, the troubled old nobleman knew not in the least.

The Princess Helen passed the night in the chapel, vowing tons of wax-candles to all the patron saints of the House of Cleves, if they would raise her up a defender.

But how did the noble girl's heart sink—how were her notions of the purity of man shaken within her gentle bosom, by the dread intelligence which reached her the next morning, after the defiance of the Rowski! At roll-call it was discovered that he on whom she principally relied—he whom her fond heart had singled out as her champion, had proved faithless! Otto, the degenerate Otto, had fled! His comrade, Wolfgang, had gone with him. A rope was found dangling from the casement of their chamber, and they must have swum the moat and passed over to the enemy in the darkness of the previous night. "A pretty lad was this fair-spoken archer of thine!" said the Prince her father to her; "and a pretty kettle of fish hast thou cooked for the fondest of fathers." She retired weeping to her apartment. Never before had that young heart felt so wretched.

That morning, at nine o'clock, as they were going to breakfast, the Rowski's trumpets sounded. Clad in complete armor, and mounted on his enormous piebald charger, he came out of his pavilion, and rode slowly up and down in front of the castle. He was ready there to meet a champion.

Three times each day did the odious trumpet sound the same notes of defiance. Thrice daily did the steel-clad Rowski come forth challenging the combat. The first day passed, and there was no answer to his summons. The second day came and went, but no champion had risen to defend. The taunt of his shrill clarion remained without answer; and the sun went down upon the wretchedest father and daughter in all the land of Christendom.

The trumpets sounded an hour after sunrise, an hour after noon, and an hour before sunset. The third day came, but with it brought no hope. The first and second summons met no response. At five o'clock the old Prince called his daughter and blessed her. "I go to meet this Rowski," said he. "It may be we shall meet no more, my Helen—my child—the innocent cause of all this grief. If I shall fall to-night the Rowski's victim, 'twill be that life is nothing without honor." And so saying, he put into her hands a dagger, and bade her sheathe it in her own breast so soon as the terrible champion had carried the castle by storm.

This Helen most faithfully promised to do; and her aged father retired to his armory, and donned his ancient war-worn corselet. It had borne the shock of a thousand lances ere this, but it was now so tight as almost to choke the knightly wearer.

The last trumpet sounded—tantara! tantara!—its shrill call rang over the wide plains, and the wide plains gave back no answer. Again!—but when its notes died away, there was only a mournful, an awful silence. "Farewell, my child," said the Prince, bulkily lifting himself into his battle-saddle. "Remember the dagger. Hark! the trumpet sounds for the third time. Open, warders! Sound, trumpeters! and good St. Bendigo guard the right."

But Puffendorff, the trumpeter, had not leisure to lift the trumpet to his lips: when, hark! from without there came another note of another clarion!—a distant note at first, then swelling fuller. Presently, in brilliant variations, the full rich notes of the "Huntsman's Chorus" came clearly over the breeze; and a thousand voices of the crowd gazing over the gate exclaimed, "A champion! a champion!"

And, indeed, a champion HAD come. Issuing from the forest came a knight and squire: the knight gracefully cantering an elegant cream-colored Arabian of prodigious power—the squire mounted on an unpretending gray cob; which, nevertheless, was an animal of considerable strength and sinew. It was the squire who blew the trumpet, through the bars of his helmet; the knight's visor was completely down. A small prince's coronet of gold, from which rose three pink ostrich-feathers, marked the warrior's rank: his blank shield bore no cognizance. As gracefully poising his lance he rode into the green space where the Rowski's tents were pitched, the hearts of all present beat with anxiety, and the poor Prince of Cleves, especially, had considerable doubts about his new champion. "So slim a figure as that can never compete with Donnerblitz," said he, moodily, to his daughter; "but whoever he be, the fellow puts a good face on it, and rides like a man. See, he has touched the Rowski's shield with the point of his lance! By St. Bendigo, a perilous venture!"

The unknown knight had indeed defied the Rowski to the death, as the Prince of Cleves remarked from the battlement where he and his daughter stood to witness the combat; and so, having defied his enemy, the Incognito galloped round under the castle wall, bowing elegantly to the lovely Princess there, and then took his ground and waited for the foe. His armor blazed in the sunshine as he sat there, motionless, on his cream-colored steed. He looked like one of those fairy knights one has read of—one of those celestial champions who decided so many victories before the invention of gun powder.

The Rowski's horse was speedily brought to the door of his pavilion; and that redoubted warrior, blazing in a suit of magnificent brass armor, clattered into his saddle. Long waves of blood-red feathers bristled over his helmet, which was farther ornamented by two huge horns of the aurochs. His lance was painted white and red, and he whirled the prodigious beam in the air and caught it with savage glee. He laughed when he saw the slim form of his antagonist; and his soul rejoiced to meet the coming battle. He dug his spurs into the enormous horse he rode: the enormous horse snorted, and squealed, too, with fierce pleasure. He jerked and curveted him with a brutal playfulness, and after a few minutes' turning and wheeling, during which everybody had leisure to admire the perfection of his equitation, he cantered round to a point exactly opposite his enemy, and pulled up his impatient charger.

The old Prince on the battlement was so eager for the combat, that he seemed quite to forget the danger which menaced himself, should his slim champion be discomfited by the tremendous Knight of Donnerblitz. "Go it!" said he, flinging his truncheon into the ditch; and at the word, the two warriors rushed with whirling rapidity at each other.

And now ensued a combat so terrible, that a weak female hand, like that of her who pens this tale of chivalry, can never hope to do justice to the terrific theme. You have seen two engines on the Great Western line rush past each other with a pealing scream? So rapidly did the two warriors gallop towards one another; the feathers of either streamed yards behind their backs as they converged. Their shock as they met was as that of two cannon-balls; the mighty horses trembled and reeled with the concussion; the lance aimed at the Rowski's helmet bore off the coronet, the horns, the helmet itself, and hurled them to an incredible distance: a piece of the Rowski's left ear was carried off on the point of the nameless warrior's weapon. How had he fared? His adversary's weapon had glanced harmless along the blank surface of his polished buckler; and the victory so far was with him.

The expression of the Rowski's face, as, bareheaded, he glared on his enemy with fierce bloodshot eyeballs, was one worthy of a demon. The imprecatory expressions which he made use of can never be copied by a feminine pen.

His opponent magnanimously declined to take advantage of the opportunity thus offered him of finishing the combat by splitting his opponent's skull with his curtal-axe, and, riding back to his starting-place, bent his lance's point to the ground, in token that he would wait until the Count of Eulenschreckenstein was helmeted afresh.

"Blessed Bendigo!" cried the Prince, "thou art a gallant lance: but why didst not rap the Schelm's brain out?"

"Bring me a fresh helmet!" yelled the Rowski. Another casque was brought to him by his trembling squire.

As soon as he had braced it, he drew his great flashing sword from his side, and rushed at his enemy, roaring hoarsely his cry of battle. The unknown knight's sword was unsheathed in a moment, and at the next the two blades were clanking together the dreadful music of the combat!

The Donnerblitz wielded his with his usual savageness and activity. It whirled round his adversary's head with frightful rapidity. Now it carried away a feather of his plume; now it shore off a leaf of his coronet. The flail of the thrasher does not fall more swiftly upon the corn. For many minutes it was the Unknown's only task to defend himself from the tremendous activity of the enemy.

But even the Rowski's strength would slacken after exertion. The blows began to fall less thick anon, and the point of the unknown knight began to make dreadful play. It found and penetrated every joint of the Donnerblitz's armor. Now it nicked him in the shoulder where the vambrace was buckled to the corselet; now it bored a shrewd hole under the light brissart, and blood followed; now, with fatal dexterity, it darted through the visor, and came back to the recover deeply tinged with blood. A scream of rage followed the last thrust; and no wonder:—it had penetrated the Rowski's left eye.

His blood was trickling through a dozen orifices; he was almost choking in his helmet with loss of breath, and loss of blood, and rage. Gasping with fury, he drew back his horse, flung his great sword at his opponent's head, and once more plunged at him, wielding his curtal-axe.

Then you should have seen the unknown knight employing the same dreadful weapon! Hitherto he had been on his defence; now he began the attack; and the gleaming axe whirred in his hand like a reed, but descended like a thunderbolt! "Yield! yield! Sir Rowski," shouted he, in a calm, clear voice.

A blow dealt madly at his head was the reply. 'Twas the last blow that the Count of Eulenschreckenstein ever struck in battle! The curse was on his lips as the crushing steel descended into his brain, and split it in two. He rolled like a log from his horse: his enemy's knee was in a moment on his chest, and the dagger of mercy at his throat, as the knight once more called upon him to yield.

But there was no answer from within the helmet. When it was withdrawn, the teeth were crunched together; the mouth that should have spoken, grinned a ghastly silence: one eye still glared with hate and fury, but it was glazed with the film of death!

The red orb of the sun was just then dipping into the Rhine. The unknown knight, vaulting once more into his saddle, made a graceful obeisance to the Prince of Cleves and his daughter, without a word, and galloped back into the forest, whence he had issued an hour before sunset.

CHAPTER XIII

THE MARRIAGE

The consternation which ensued on the death of the Rowski, speedily sent all his camp-followers, army, &c. to the right-about. They struck their tents at the first news of his discomfiture; and each man laying hold of what he could, the whole of the gallant force which had marched under his banner in the morning had disappeared ere the sun rose.

On that night, as it may be imagined, the gates of the Castle of Cleves were not shut. Everybody was free to come in. Wine-butts were broached in all the courts; the pickled meat prepared in such lots for the siege was distributed among the people, who crowded to congratulate their beloved sovereign on his victory; and the Prince, as was customary with that good man, who never lost an opportunity of giving a dinner-party, had a splendid entertainment made ready for the upper classes, the whole concluding with a tasteful display of fireworks.

In the midst of these entertainments, our old friend the Count of Hombourg arrived at the castle. The stalwart old warrior swore by Saint Bugo that he was grieved the killing of the Rowski had been taken out of his hand. The laughing Cleves vowed by Saint Bendigo, Hombourg could never have finished off his enemy so satisfactorily as the unknown knight had just done.

But who was he? was the question which now agitated the bosom of these two old nobles. How to find him—how to reward the champion and restorer of the honor and happiness of Cleves? They agreed over supper that he should be sought for everywhere. Beadles were sent round the principal cities within fifty miles, and the description of the knight advertised, in the Journal de Francfort and the Allgemeine Zeitung. The hand of the Princess Helen was solemnly offered to him in these advertisements, with the reversion of the Prince of Cleves's splendid though somewhat dilapidated property.

"But we don't know him, my dear papa," faintly ejaculated that young lady. "Some impostor may come in a suit of plain armor, and pretend that he was the champion who overcame the Rowski (a prince who had his faults certainly, but whose attachment for me I can never forget); and how are you to say whether he is the real knight or not? There are so many deceivers in this world," added the Princess, in tears, "that one can't be too cautious now." The fact is, that she was thinking of the desertion of Otto in the morning; by which instance of faithlessness her heart was wellnigh broken.

As for that youth and his comrade Wolfgang, to the astonishment of everybody at their impudence, they came to the archers' mess that night, as if nothing had happened; got their supper, partaking both of meat and drink most plentifully; fell asleep when their comrades began to describe the events of the day, and the admirable achievements of the unknown warrior; and turning into their hammocks, did not appear on parade in the morning until twenty minutes after the names were called.

When the Prince of Cleves heard of the return of these deserters he was in a towering passion. "Where were you, fellows," shouted he, "during the time my castle was at its utmost need?"

Otto replied, "We were out on particular business."

"Does a soldier leave his post on the day of battle, sir?" exclaimed the Prince. "You know the reward of such—Death! and death you merit. But you are a soldier only of yesterday, and yesterday's victory has made me merciful. Hanged you shall not be, as you merit—only flogged, both of you. Parade the men, Colonel Ticklestern, after breakfast, and give these scoundrels five hundred apiece."

You should have seen how young Otto bounded, when this information was thus abruptly conveyed to him. "Flog ME!" cried he. "Flog Otto of—"

"Not so, my father," said the Princess Helen, who had been standing by during the conversation, and who had looked at Otto all the while with the most ineffable scorn. "Not so: although these PERSONS have forgotten their duty" (she laid a particularly sarcastic emphasis on the word persons), "we have had no need of their services, and have luckily found OTHERS more faithful. You promised your daughter a boon, papa; it is the pardon of these two PERSONS. Let them go, and quit a service they have disgraced; a mistress—that is, a master—they have deceived."

"Drum 'em out of the castle, Ticklestern; strip their uniforms from their backs, and never let me hear of the scoundrels again." So saying, the old Prince angrily turned on his heel to breakfast, leaving the two young men to the fun and derision of their surrounding comrades.

The noble Count of Hombourg, who was taking his usual airing on the ramparts before breakfast, came up at this juncture, and asked what was the row? Otto blushed when he saw him and turned away rapidly; but the Count, too, catching a glimpse of him, with a hundred exclamations of joyful surprise seized upon the lad, hugged him to his manly breast, kissed him most affectionately, and almost burst into tears as he embraced him. For, in sooth, the good Count had thought his godson long ere this at the bottom of the silver Rhine.

The Prince of Cleves, who had come to the breakfast-parlor window, (to invite his guest to enter, as the tea was made,) beheld this strange scene from the window, as did the lovely tea-maker likewise, with breathless and beautiful agitation. The old Count and the archer strolled up and down the battlements in deep conversation. By the gestures of surprise and delight exhibited by the former, 'twas easy to see the young archer was conveying some very strange and pleasing news to him; though the nature of the conversation was not allowed to transpire.

"A godson of mine," said the noble Count, when interrogated over his muffins. "I know his family; worthy people; sad scapegrace; ran away; parents longing for him; glad you did not flog him; devil to pay," and so forth. The Count was a man of few words, and told his tale in this brief, artless manner. But why, at its conclusion, did the gentle Helen leave the room, her eyes filled with tears? She left the room once more to kiss a certain lock of yellow hair she had pilfered. A dazzling, delicious thought, a strange wild hope, arose in her soul!

When she appeared again, she made some side-handed inquiries regarding Otto (with that gentle artifice oft employed by women); but he was gone. He and his companion were gone. The Count of Hombourg had likewise taken his departure, under pretext of particular business. How lonely the vast castle seemed to Helen, now that HE was no longer there. The transactions of the last few days; the beautiful archer-boy; the offer from the Rowski (always an event in a young lady's life); the siege of the castle; the death of her truculent admirer: all seemed like a fevered dream to her: all was passed away, and had left no trace behind. No trace?—yes! one: a little insignificant lock of golden hair, over which the young creature wept so much that she put it out of curl; passing hours and hours in the summer-house, where the operation had been performed.

On the second day (it is my belief she would have gone into a consumption and died of languor, if the event had been delayed a day longer,) a messenger, with a trumpet, brought a letter in haste to the Prince of Cleves, who was, as usual, taking refreshment. "To the High and Mighty Prince," &c. the letter ran. "The Champion who had the honor of engaging on Wednesday last with his late Excellency the Rowski of Donnerblitz, presents his compliments to H. S. H. the Prince of Cleves. Through the medium of the public prints the C. has been made acquainted with the flattering proposal of His Serene Highness relative to a union between himself (the Champion) and her Serene Highness the Princess Helen of Cleves. The Champion accepts with pleasure that polite invitation, and will have the honor of waiting upon the Prince and Princess of Cleves about half an hour after the receipt of this letter."

"Tol lol de rol, girl," shouted the Prince with heartfelt joy. (Have you not remarked, dear friend, how often in novel-books, and on the stage, joy is announced by the above burst of insensate monosyllables?) "Tol lol de rol. Don thy best kirtle, child; thy husband will be here anon." And Helen retired to arrange her toilet for this awful event in the life of a young woman. When she returned, attired to welcome her defender, her young cheek was as pale as the white satin slip and orange sprigs she wore.

She was scarce seated on the dais by her father's side, when a huge flourish of trumpets from without proclaimed the arrival of THE CHAMPION. Helen felt quite sick: a draught of ether was necessary to restore her tranquillity.

The great door was flung open. He entered,—the same tall warrior, slim, and beautiful, blazing in shining steel. He approached the Prince's throne, supported on each side by a friend likewise in armor. He knelt gracefully on one knee.

"I come," said he in a voice trembling with emotion, "to claim, as per advertisement, the hand of the lovely Lady Helen." And he held out a copy of the Allgemeine Zeitung as he spoke.

"Art thou noble, Sir Knight?" asked the Prince of Cleves.

"As noble as yourself," answered the kneeling steel.

"Who answers for thee?"

"I, Karl, Margrave of Godesberg, his father!" said the knight on the right hand, lifting up his visor.

"And I—Ludwig, Count of Hombourg, his godfather!" said the knight on the left, doing likewise.

The kneeling knight lifted up his visor now, and looked on Helen.

"I KNEW IT WAS," said she, and fainted as she saw Otto the Archer.

But she was soon brought to, gentles, as I have small need to tell ye. In a very few days after, a great marriage took place at Cleves under the patronage of Saint Bugo, Saint Buffo, and Saint Bendigo. After the marriage ceremony, the happiest and handsomest pair in the world drove off in a chaise-and-four, to pass the honeymoon at Kissingen. The Lady Theodora, whom we left locked up in her convent a long while since, was prevailed upon to come back to Godesberg, where she was reconciled to her husband. Jealous of her daughter-in-law, she idolized her son, and spoiled all her little grandchildren. And so all are happy, and my simple tale is done.

I read it in an old, old book, in a mouldy old circulating library. 'Twas written in the French tongue, by the noble Alexandre Dumas; but 'tis probable that he stole it from some other, and that the other had filched it from a former tale-teller. For nothing is new under the sun. Things die and are reproduced only. And so it is that the forgotten tale of the great Dumas reappears under the signature of

THERESA MACWHIRTER.

WHISTLEBINKIE, N.B., December 1.


REBECCA AND ROWENA

A ROMANCE UPON ROMANCE

BY MR. MICHAEL ANGELO TITMARSH

CHAPTER I

THE OVERTURE.—COMMENCEMENT OF THE BUSINESS

Well-beloved novel-readers and gentle patronesses of romance, assuredly it has often occurred to every one of you, that the books we delight in have very unsatisfactory conclusions, and end quite prematurely with page 320 of the third volume. At that epoch of the history it is well known that the hero is seldom more than thirty years old, and the heroine by consequence some seven or eight years younger; and I would ask any of you whether it is fair to suppose that people after the above age have nothing worthy of note in their lives, and cease to exist as they drive away from Saint George's, Hanover Square? You, dear young ladies, who get your knowledge of life from the circulating library, may be led to imagine that when the marriage business is done, and Emilia is whisked off in the new travelling-carriage, by the side of the enraptured Earl; or Belinda, breaking away from the tearful embraces of her excellent mother, dries her own lovely eyes upon the throbbing waistcoat of her bridegroom—you may be apt, I say, to suppose that all is over then; that Emilia and the Earl are going to be happy for the rest of their lives in his lordship's romantic castle in the North, and Belinda and her young clergyman to enjoy uninterrupted bliss in their rose-trellised parsonage in the West of England: but some there be among the novel-reading classes—old experienced folks—who know better than this. Some there be who have been married, and found that they have still something to see and to do, and to suffer mayhap; and that adventures, and pains, and pleasures, and taxes, and sunrises and settings, and the business and joys and griefs of life go on after, as before the nuptial ceremony.

Therefore I say, it is an unfair advantage which the novelist takes of hero and heroine, as of his inexperienced reader, to say good-by to the two former, as soon as ever they are made husband and wife; and I have often wished that additions should be made to all works of fiction which have been brought to abrupt terminations in the manner described; and that we should hear what occurs to the sober married man, as well as to the ardent bachelor; to the matron, as well as to the blushing spinster. And in this respect I admire (and would desire to imitate,) the noble and prolific French author, Alexandre Dumas, who carries his heroes from early youth down to the most venerable old age; and does not let them rest until they are so old, that it is full time the poor fellows should get a little peace and quiet. A hero is much too valuable a gentleman to be put upon the retired list, in the prime and vigor of his youth; and I wish to know what lady among us would like to be put on the shelf, and thought no longer interesting, because she has a family growing up, and is four or five and thirty years of age? I have known ladies at sixty, with hearts as tender and ideas as romantic as any young misses of sixteen. Let us have middle-aged novels then, as well as your extremely juvenile legends: let the young ones be warned that the old folks have a right to be interesting: and that a lady may continue to have a heart, although she is somewhat stouter than she was when a school-girl, and a man his feelings, although he gets his hair from Truefitt's.

Thus I would desire that the biographies of many of our most illustrious personages of romance should be continued by fitting hands, and that they should be heard of, until at least a decent age.—Look at Mr. James's heroes: they invariably marry young. Look at Mr. Dickens's: they disappear from the scene when they are mere chits. I trust these authors, who are still alive, will see the propriety of telling us something more about people in whom we took a considerable interest, and who must be at present strong and hearty, and in the full vigor of health and intellect. And in the tales of the great Sir Walter (may honor be to his name), I am sure there are a number of people who are untimely carried away from us, and of whom we ought to hear more.

My dear Rebecca, daughter of Isaac of York, has always, in my mind, been one of these; nor can I ever believe that such a woman, so admirable, so tender, so heroic, so beautiful, could disappear altogether before such another woman as Rowena, that vapid, flaxen-headed creature, who is, in my humble opinion, unworthy of Ivanhoe, and unworthy of her place as heroine. Had both of them got their rights, it ever seemed to me that Rebecca would have had the husband, and Rowena would have gone off to a convent and shut herself up, where I, for one, would never have taken the trouble of inquiring for her.

But after all she married Ivanhoe. What is to be done? There is no help for it. There it is in black and white at the end of the third volume of Sir Walter Scott's chronicle, that the couple were joined together in matrimony. And must the Disinherited Knight, whose blood has been fired by the suns of Palestine, and whose heart has been warmed in the company of the tender and beautiful Rebecca, sit down contented for life by the side of such a frigid piece of propriety as that icy, faultless, prim, niminy-piminy Rowena? Forbid it fate, forbid it poetical justice! There is a simple plan for setting matters right, and giving all parties their due, which is here submitted to the novel-reader. Ivanhoe's history MUST have had a continuation; and it is this which ensues. I may be wrong in some particulars of the narrative,—as what writer will not be?—but of the main incidents of the history, I have in my own mind no sort of doubt, and confidently submit them to that generous public which likes to see virtue righted, true love rewarded, and the brilliant Fairy descend out of the blazing chariot at the end of the pantomime, and make Harlequin and Columbine happy. What, if reality be not so, gentlemen and ladies; and if, after dancing a variety of jigs and antics, and jumping in and out of endless trap-doors and windows, through life's shifting scenes, no fairy comes down to make US comfortable at the close of the performance? Ah! let us give our honest novel-folks the benefit of their position, and not be envious of their good luck.

No person who has read the preceding volumes of this history, as the famous chronicler of Abbotsford has recorded them, can doubt for a moment what was the result of the marriage between Sir Wilfrid of

Ivanhoe and Lady Rowena. Those who have marked her conduct during her maidenhood, her distinguished politeness, her spotless modesty of demeanor, her unalterable coolness under all circumstances, and her lofty and gentlewomanlike bearing, must be sure that her married conduct would equal her spinster behavior, and that Rowena the wife would be a pattern of correctness for all the matrons of England.

Such was the fact. For miles around Rotherwood her character for piety was known. Her castle was a rendezvous for all the clergy and monks of the district, whom she fed with the richest viands, while she pinched herself upon pulse and water. There was not an invalid in the three Ridings, Saxon or Norman, but the palfrey of the Lady Rowena might be seen journeying to his door, in company with Father Glauber, her almoner, and Brother Thomas of Epsom, her leech. She lighted up all the churches in Yorkshire with wax-candles, the offerings of her piety. The bells of her chapel began to ring at two o'clock in the morning; and all the domestics of Rotherwood were called upon to attend at matins, at complins, at nones, at vespers, and at sermon. I need not say that fasting was observed with all the rigors of the Church; and that those of the servants of the Lady Rowena were looked upon with most favor whose hair-shirts were the roughest, and who flagellated themselves with the most becoming perseverance.

Whether it was that this discipline cleared poor Wamba's wits or cooled his humor, it is certain that he became the most melancholy fool in England, and if ever he ventured upon a pun to the shuddering poor servitors, who were mumbling their dry crusts below the salt, it was such a faint and stale joke that nobody dared to laugh at the innuendoes of the unfortunate wag, and a sickly smile was the best applause he could muster. Once, indeed, when Guffo, the goose-boy (a half-witted poor wretch), laughed outright at a lamentably stale pun which Wamba palmed upon him at supper-time, (it was dark, and the torches being brought in, Wamba said, "Guffo, they can't see their way in the argument, and are going TO THROW A LITTLE LIGHT UPON THE SUBJECT,") the Lady Rowena, being disturbed in a theological controversy with Father Willibald, (afterwards canonized as St. Willibald, of Bareacres, hermit and confessor,) called out to know what was the cause of the unseemly interruption, and Guffo and Wamba being pointed out as the culprits, ordered them straightway into the court-yard, and three dozen to be administered to each of them.

"I got you out of Front-de-Boeufs castle," said poor Wamba, piteously, appealing to Sir Wilfrid of Ivanhoe, "and canst thou not save me from the lash?"

"Yes, from Front-de-Boeuf's castle, WHERE YOU WERE LOCKED UP WITH THE JEWESS IN THE TOWER!" said Rowena, haughtily replying to the timid appeal of her husband. "Gurth, give him four dozen!"

And this was all poor Wamba got by applying for the mediation of his master.

In fact, Rowena knew her own dignity so well as a princess of the royal blood of England, that Sir Wilfrid of Ivanhoe, her consort, could scarcely call his life his own, and was made, in all things, to feel the inferiority of his station. And which of us is there acquainted with the sex that has not remarked this propensity in lovely woman, and how often the wisest in the council are made to be as fools at HER board, and the boldest in the battle-field are craven when facing her distaff?

"Where you were locked up with the Jewess in the tower," was a remark, too, of which Wilfrid keenly felt, and perhaps the reader will understand, the significancy. When the daughter of Isaac of York brought her diamonds and rubies—the poor gentle victim!—and, meekly laying them at the feet of the conquering Rowena, departed into foreign lands to tend the sick of her people, and to brood over the bootless passion which consumed her own pure heart, one would have thought that the heart of the royal lady would have melted before such beauty and humility, and that she would have been generous in the moment of her victory.

But did you ever know a right-minded woman pardon another for being handsome and more love-worthy than herself? The Lady Rowena did certainly say with mighty magnanimity to the Jewish maiden, "Come and live with me as a sister," as the former part of this history shows; but Rebecca knew in her heart that her ladyship's proposition was what is called BOSH (in that noble Eastern language with which Wilfrid the Crusader was familiar), or fudge, in plain Saxon; and retired with a broken, gentle spirit, neither able to bear the sight of her rival's happiness, nor willing to disturb it by the contrast of her own wretchedness. Rowena, like the most high-bred and virtuous of women, never forgave Isaac's daughter her beauty, nor her flirtation with Wilfrid (as the Saxon lady chose to term it); nor, above all, her admirable diamonds and jewels, although Rowena was actually in possession of them.

In a word, she was always flinging Rebecca into Ivanhoe's teeth. There was not a day in his life but that unhappy warrior was made to remember that a Hebrew damsel had been in love with him, and that a Christian lady of fashion could never forgive the insult. For instance, if Gurth, the swineherd, who was now promoted to be a gamekeeper and verderer, brought the account of a famous wild-boar in the wood, and proposed a hunt, Rowena would say, "Do, Sir Wilfrid, persecute these poor pigs: you know your friends the Jews can't abide them!" Or when, as it oft would happen, our lion-hearted monarch, Richard, in order to get a loan or a benevolence from the Jews, would roast a few of the Hebrew capitalists, or extract some of the principal rabbis' teeth, Rowena would exult and say, "Serve them right, the misbelieving wretches! England can never be a happy country until every one of these monsters is exterminated!" or else, adopting a strain of still more savage sarcasm, would exclaim, "Ivanhoe my dear, more persecution for the Jews! Hadn't you better interfere, my love? His Majesty will do anything for you; and, you know, the Jews were ALWAYS SUCH FAVORITES OF YOURS," or words to that effect. But, nevertheless, her ladyship never lost an opportunity of wearing Rebecca's jewels at court, whenever the Queen held a drawing-room; or at the York assizes and ball, when she appeared there: not of course because she took any interest in such things, but because she considered it her duty to attend, as one of the chief ladies of the county.

Thus Sir Wilfrid of Ivanhoe, having attained the height of his wishes, was, like many a man when he has reached that dangerous elevation, disappointed. Ah, dear friends, it is but too often so in life! Many a garden, seen from a distance, looks fresh and green, which, when beheld closely, is dismal and weedy; the shady walks melancholy and grass-grown; the bowers you would fain repose in, cushioned with stinging-nettles. I have ridden in a caique upon the waters of the Bosphorus, and looked upon the capital of the Soldan of Turkey. As seen from those blue waters, with palace and pinnacle, with gilded dome and towering cypress, it seemeth a very Paradise of Mahound: but, enter the city, and it is but a beggarly labyrinth of rickety huts and dirty alleys, where the ways are steep and the smells are foul, tenanted by mangy dogs and ragged beggars—a dismal illusion! Life is such, ah, well-a-day! It is only hope which is real, and reality is a bitterness and a deceit.

Perhaps a man with Ivanhoe's high principles would never bring himself to acknowledge this fact; but others did for him. He grew thin, and pined away as much as if he had been in a fever under the scorching sun of Ascalon. He had no appetite for his meals; he slept ill, though he was yawning all day. The jangling of the doctors and friars whom Rowena brought together did not in the least enliven him, and he would sometimes give proofs of somnolency during their disputes, greatly to the consternation of his lady. He hunted a good deal, and, I very much fear, as Rowena rightly remarked, that he might have an excuse for being absent from home. He began to like wine, too, who had been as sober as a hermit; and when he came back from Athelstane's (whither he would repair not unfrequently), the unsteadiness of his gait and the unnatural brilliancy of his eye were remarked by his lady: who, you may be sure, was sitting up for him. As for Athelstane, he swore by St. Wullstan that he was glad to have escaped a marriage with such a pattern of propriety; and honest Cedric the Saxon (who had been very speedily driven out of his daughter-in-law's castle) vowed by St. Waltheof that his son had bought a dear bargain.

So Sir Wilfrid of Ivanhoe became almost as tired of England as his royal master Richard was, (who always quitted the country when he had squeezed from his loyal nobles, commons, clergy, and Jews, all the money which he could get,) and when the lion-hearted Prince began to make war against the French King, in Normandy and Guienne, Sir Wilfrid pined like a true servant to be in company of the good champion, alongside of whom he had shivered so many lances, and dealt such woundy blows of sword and battle-axe on the plains of Jaffa or the breaches of Acre. Travellers were welcome at Rotherwood that brought news from the camp of the good King: and I warrant me that the knight listened with all his might when Father Drono, the chaplain, read in the St. James's Chronykyll (which was the paper of news he of Ivanhoe took in) of "another glorious triumph"—"Defeat of the French near Blois"—"Splendid victory at Epte, and narrow escape of the French King:" the which deeds of arms the learned scribes had to narrate.

However such tales might excite him during the reading, they left the Knight of Ivanhoe only the more melancholy after listening: and the more moody as he sat in his great hall silently draining his Gascony wine. Silently sat he and looked at his coats-of-mail hanging vacant on the wall, his banner covered with spider-webs, and his sword and axe rusting there. "Ah, dear axe," sighed he (into his drinking-horn)—"ah, gentle steel! that was a merry time when I sent thee crashing into the pate of the Emir Abdul Melik as he rode on the right of Saladin. Ah, my sword, my dainty headsman? my sweet split-rib? my razor of infidel beards! is the rust to eat thine edge off, and am I never more to wield thee in battle? What is the use of a shield on a wall, or a lance that has a cobweb for a pennon? O Richard, my good king, would I could hear once more thy voice in the front of the onset! Bones of Brian the Templar? would ye could rise from your grave at Templestowe, and that we might break another spear for honor and—and—" . . .

"And REBECCA," he would have said; but the knight paused here in rather a guilty panic: and her Royal Highness the Princess Rowena (as she chose to style herself at home) looked so hard at him out of her china-blue eyes, that Sir Wilfrid felt as if she was reading his thoughts, and was fain to drop his own eyes into his flagon.

In a word, his life was intolerable. The dinner hour of the twelfth century, it is known, was very early; in fact, people dined at ten o'clock in the morning: and after dinner Rowena sat mum under her canopy, embroidered with the arms of Edward the Confessor, working with her maidens at the most hideous pieces of tapestry, representing the tortures and martyrdoms of her favorite saints, and not allowing a soul to speak above his breath, except when she chose to cry out in her own shrill voice when a handmaid made a wrong stitch, or let fall a ball of worsted. It was a dreary life. Wamba, we have said, never ventured to crack a joke, save in a whisper, when he was ten miles from home; and then Sir Wilfrid Ivanhoe was too weary and blue-devilled to laugh; but hunted in silence, moodily bringing down deer and wild-boar with shaft and quarrel.

Then he besought Robin of Huntingdon, the jolly outlaw, nathless, to join him, and go to the help of their fair sire King Richard, with a score or two of lances. But the Earl of Huntingdon was a very different character from Robin Hood the forester. There was no more conscientious magistrate in all the county than his lordship: he was never known to miss church or quarter-sessions; he was the strictest game-proprietor in all the Riding, and sent scores of poachers to Botany Bay. "A man who has a stake in the country, my good Sir Wilfrid," Lord Huntingdon said, with rather a patronizing air (his lordship had grown immensely fat since the King had taken him into grace, and required a horse as strong as an elephant to mount him)—"a man with a stake in the country ought to stay IN the country. Property has its duties as well as its privileges, and a person of my rank is bound to live on the land from which he gets his living."

"'Amen!" sang out the Reverend —Tuck, his lordship's domestic chaplain, who had also grown as sleek as the Abbot of Jorvaulx, who was as prim as a lady in his dress, wore bergamot in his handkerchief, and had his poll shaved and his beard curled every day. And so sanctified was his Reverence grown, that he thought it was a shame to kill the pretty deer, (though he ate of them still hugely, both in pasties and with French beans and currant-jelly,) and being shown a quarter-staff upon a certain occasion, handled it curiously, and asked "what that ugly great stick was?"

Lady Huntingdon, late Maid Marian, had still some of her old fun and spirits, and poor Ivanhoe begged and prayed that she would come and stay at Rotherwood occasionally, and egayer the general dulness of that castle. But her ladyship said that Rowena gave herself such airs, and bored her so intolerably with stories of King Edward the Confessor, that she preferred any place rather than Rotherwood, which was as dull as if it had been at the top of Mount Athos.

The only person who visited it was Athelstane. "His Royal Highness the Prince" Rowena of course called him, whom the lady received with royal honors. She had the guns fired, and the footmen turned out with presented arms when he arrived; helped him to all Ivanhoe's favorite cuts of the mutton or the turkey, and forced her poor husband to light him to the state bedroom, walking backwards, holding a pair of wax-candles. At this hour of bedtime the Thane used to be in such a condition, that he saw two pair of candles and two Ivanhoes reeling before him. Let us hope it was not Ivanhoe that was reeling, but only his kinsman's brains muddled with the quantities of drink which it was his daily custom to consume. Rowena said it was the crack which the wicked Bois Guilbert, "the Jewess's OTHER lover, Wilfrid my dear," gave him on his royal skull, which caused the Prince to be disturbed so easily; but added, that drinking became a person of royal blood, and was but one of the duties of his station.

Sir Wilfrid of Ivanhoe saw it would be of no avail to ask this man to bear him company on his projected tour abroad; but still he himself was every day more and more bent upon going, and he long cast about for some means of breaking to his Rowena his firm resolution to join the King. He thought she would certainty fall ill if he communicated the news too abruptly to her: he would pretend a journey to York to attend a grand jury; then a call to London on law business or to buy stock; then he would slip over to Calais by the packet, by degrees as it were; and so be with the King before his wife knew that he was out of sight of Westminster Hall.

"Suppose your honor says you are going as your honor would say Bo! to a goose, plump, short, and to the point," said Wamba the Jester—who was Sir Wilfrid's chief counsellor and attendant—"depend on't her Highness would bear the news like a Christian woman."

"Tush, malapert! I will give thee the strap," said Sir Wilfrid, in a fine tone of high-tragedy indignation. "Thou knowest not the delicacy of the nerves of high-born ladies. An she faint not, write me down Hollander."

"I will wager my bauble against an Irish billet of exchange that she will let your honor go off readily: that is, if you press not the matter too strongly," Wamba answered, knowingly. And this Ivanhoe found to his discomfiture: for one morning at breakfast, adopting a degage air, as he sipped his tea, he said, "My love, I was thinking of going over to pay his Majesty a visit in Normandy." Upon which, laying down her muffin, (which, since the royal Alfred baked those cakes, had been the chosen breakfast cate of noble Anglo-Saxons, and which a kneeling page tendered to her on a salver, chased by the Florentine, Benvenuto Cellini,)—"When do you think of going, Wilfrid my dear?" the lady said; and the moment the tea-things were removed, and the tables and their trestles put away, she set about mending his linen, and getting ready his carpet-bag.

So Sir Wilfrid was as disgusted at her readiness to part with him as he had been weary of staying at home, which caused Wamba the Fool to say, "Marry, gossip, thou art like the man on ship-board, who, when the boatswain flogged him, did cry out 'Oh!' wherever the rope's-end fell on him: which caused Master Boatswain to say, 'Plague on thee, fellow, and a pize on thee, knave, wherever I hit thee there is no pleasing thee.'"

"And truly there are some backs which Fortune is always belaboring," thought Sir Wilfrid with a groan, "and mine is one that is ever sore."

So, with a moderate retinue, whereof the knave Wamba made one, and a large woollen comforter round his neck, which his wife's own white fingers had woven, Sir Wilfrid of Ivanhoe left home to join the King his master. Rowena, standing on the steps, poured out a series of prayers and blessings, most edifying to hear, as her lord mounted his charger, which his squires led to the door. "It was the duty of the British female of rank," she said, "to suffer all—ALL in the cause of her sovereign. SHE would not fear loneliness during the campaign: she would bear up against widowhood, desertion, and an unprotected situation."

"My cousin Athelstane will protect thee," said Ivanhoe, with profound emotion, as the tears trickled down his basenet; and bestowing a chaste salute upon the steel-clad warrior, Rowena modestly said "she hoped his Highness would be so kind."

Then Ivanhoe's trumpet blew: then Rowena waved her pocket-handkerchief: then the household gave a shout: then the pursuivant of the good Knight, Sir Wilfrid the Crusader, flung out his banner (which was argent, a gules cramoisy with three Moors impaled sable): then Wamba gave a lash on his mule's haunch, and Ivanhoe, heaving a great sigh, turned the tail of his war-horse upon the castle of his fathers.

As they rode along the forest, they met Athelstane the Thane powdering along the road in the direction of Rotherwood on his great dray-horse of a charger. "Good-by, good luck to you, old brick," cried the Prince, using the vernacular Saxon. "Pitch into those Frenchmen; give it 'em over the face and eyes; and I'll stop at home and take care of Mrs. I."

"Thank you, kinsman," said Ivanhoe—looking, however, not particularly well pleased; and the chiefs shaking hands, the train of each took its different way—Athelstane's to Rotherwood, Ivanhoe's towards his place of embarkation.

The poor knight had his wish, and yet his face was a yard long and as yellow as a lawyer's parchment; and having longed to quit home any time these three years past, he found himself envying Athelstane, because, forsooth, he was going to Rotherwood: which symptoms of discontent being observed by the witless Wamba, caused that absurd madman to bring his rebeck over his shoulder from his back, and to sing—

"ATRA CURA.

"Before I lost my five poor wits,
I mind me of a Romish clerk,
Who sang how Care, the phantom dark,
Beside the belted horseman sits.
Methought I saw the griesly sprite
Jump up but now behind my Knight."

"Perhaps thou didst, knave," said Ivanhoe, looking over his shoulder; and the knave went on with his jingle:

"And though he gallop as he may,
I mark that cursed monster black
Still sits behind his honor's back,
Tight squeezing of his heart alway.
Like two black Templars sit they there,
Beside one crupper, Knight and Care.

"No knight am I with pennoned spear,
To prance upon a bold destrere:
I will not have black Care prevail
Upon my long-eared charger's tail,
For lo, I am a witless fool,
And laugh at Grief and ride a mule."

And his bells rattled as he kicked his mule's sides.

"Silence, fool!" said Sir Wilfrid of Ivanhoe, in a voice both majestic and wrathful. "If thou knowest not care and grief, it is because thou knowest not love, whereof they are the companions. Who can love without an anxious heart? How shall there be joy at meeting, without tears at parting?" ("I did not see that his honor or my lady shed many anon," thought Wamba the Fool; but he was only a zany, and his mind was not right.) "I would not exchange my very sorrows for thine indifference," the knight continued. "Where there is a sun, there must be a shadow. If the shadow offend me, shall I put out my eyes and live in the dark? No! I am content with my fate, even such as it is. The Care of which thou speakest, hard though it may vex him, never yet rode down an honest man. I can bear him on my shoulders, and make my way through the world's press in spite of him; for my arm is strong, and my sword is keen, and my shield has no stain on it; and my heart, though it is sad, knows no guile." And here, taking a locket out of his waistcoat (which was made of chain-mail), the knight kissed the token, put it back under the waistcoat again, heaved a profound sigh, and stuck spurs into his horse.

As for Wamba, he was munching a black pudding whilst Sir Wilfrid was making the above speech, (which implied some secret grief on the knight's part, that must have been perfectly unintelligible to the fool,) and so did not listen to a single word of Ivanhoe's pompous remarks. They travelled on by slow stages through the whole kingdom, until they came to Dover, whence they took shipping for Calais. And in this little voyage, being exceedingly sea-sick, and besides elated at the thought of meeting his sovereign, the good knight cast away that profound melancholy which had accompanied him during the whole of his land journey.

CHAPTER II

THE LAST DAYS OF THE LION

From Calais Sir Wilfrid of Ivanhoe took the diligence across country to Limoges, sending on Gurth, his squire, with the horses and the rest of his attendants: with the exception of Wamba, who travelled not only as the knight's fool, but as his valet, and who, perched on the roof of the carriage, amused himself by blowing tunes upon the conducteur's French horn. The good King Richard was, as Ivanhoe learned, in the Limousin, encamped before a little place called Chalus; the lord whereof, though a vassal of the King's, was holding the castle against his sovereign with a resolution and valor which caused a great fury and annoyance on the part of the Monarch with the Lion Heart. For brave and magnanimous as he was, the Lion-hearted one did not love to be balked any more than another; and, like the royal animal whom he was said to resemble, he commonly tore his adversary to pieces, and then, perchance, had leisure to think how brave the latter had been. The Count of Chalus had found, it was said, a pot of money; the royal Richard wanted it. As the count denied that he had it, why did he not open the gates of his castle at once? It was a clear proof that he was guilty; and the King was determined to punish this rebel, and have his money and his life too.

He had naturally brought no breaching guns with him, because those instruments were not yet invented: and though he had assaulted the place a score of times with the utmost fury, his Majesty had been beaten back on every occasion, until he was so savage that it was dangerous to approach the British Lion. The Lion's wife, the lovely Berengaria, scarcely ventured to come near him. He flung the joint-stools in his tent at the heads of the officers of state, and kicked his aides-de-camp round his pavilion; and, in fact, a maid of honor, who brought a sack-posset in to his Majesty from the Queen after he came in from the assault, came spinning like a football out of the royal tent just as Ivanhoe entered it.

"Send me my drum-major to flog that woman!" roared out the infuriate King. "By the bones of St. Barnabas she has burned the sack! By St. Wittikind, I will have her flayed alive. Ha, St. George! ha, St. Richard! whom have we here?" And he lifted up his demi-culverin, or curtal-axe—a weapon weighing about thirteen hundredweight—and was about to fling it at the intruder's head, when the latter, kneeling gracefully on one knee, said calmly, "It is I, my good liege, Wilfrid of Ivanhoe."

"What, Wilfrid of Templestowe, Wilfrid the married man, Wilfrid the henpecked!" cried the King with a sudden burst of good-humor, flinging away the culverin from him, as though it had been a reed (it lighted three hundred yards off, on the foot of Hugo de Bunyon, who was smoking a cigar at the door of his tent, and caused that redoubted warrior to limp for some days after). "What, Wilfrid my gossip? Art come to see the lion's den? There are bones in it, man, bones and carcasses, and the lion is angry," said the King, with a terrific glare of his eyes. "But tush! we will talk of that anon. Ho! bring two gallons of hypocras for the King and the good Knight, Wilfrid of Ivanhoe. Thou art come in time, Wilfrid, for, by St. Richard and St. George, we will give a grand assault to-morrow. There will be bones broken, ha!"

"I care not, my liege," said Ivanhoe, pledging the sovereign respectfully, and tossing off the whole contents of the bowl of hypocras to his Highness's good health. And he at once appeared to be taken into high favor; not a little to the envy of many of the persons surrounding the King.

As his Majesty said, there was fighting and feasting in plenty before Chalus. Day after day, the besiegers made assaults upon the castle, but it was held so stoutly by the Count of Chalus and his gallant garrison, that each afternoon beheld the attacking-parties returning disconsolately to their tents, leaving behind them many of their own slain, and bringing back with them store of broken heads and maimed limbs, received in the unsuccessful onset. The valor displayed by Ivanhoe in all these contests was prodigious; and the way in which he escaped death from the discharges of mangonels, catapults, battering-rams, twenty-four pounders, boiling oil, and other artillery, with which the besieged received their enemies, was remarkable. After a day's fighting, Gurth and Wamba used to pick the arrows out of their intrepid master's coat-of-mail, as if they had been so many almonds in a pudding. 'Twas well for the good knight, that under his first coat-of-armor he wore a choice suit of Toledan steel, perfectly impervious to arrow-shots, and given to him by a certain Jew, named Isaac of York, to whom he had done some considerable services a few years back.

If King Richard had not been in such a rage at the repeated failures of his attacks upon the castle, that all sense of justice was blinded in the lion-hearted monarch, he would have been the first to acknowledge the valor of Sir Wilfrid of Ivanhoe, and would have given him a Peerage and the Grand Cross of the Bath at least a dozen times in the course of the siege: for Ivanhoe led more than a dozen storming parties, and with his own hand killed as many men (viz, two thousand three hundred and fifty-one) within six, as were slain by the lion-hearted monarch himself. But his Majesty was rather disgusted than pleased by his faithful servant's prowess; and all the courtiers, who hated Ivanhoe for his superior valor and dexterity (for he would kill you off a couple of hundreds of them of Chalus, whilst the strongest champions of the Kings host could not finish more than their two dozen of a day), poisoned the royal mind against Sir Wilfrid, and made the King look upon his feats of arms with an evil eye. Roger de Backbite sneeringly told the King that Sir Wilfrid had offered to bet an equal bet that he would kill more men than Richard himself in the next assault: Peter de Toadhole said that Ivanhoe stated everywhere that his Majesty was not the man he used to be; that pleasures and drink had enervated him; that he could neither ride, nor strike a blow with sword or axe, as he had been enabled to do in the old times in Palestine: and finally, in the twenty-fifth assault, in which they had very nearly carried the place, and in which onset Ivanhoe slew seven, and his Majesty six, of the sons of the Count de Chalus, its defender, Ivanhoe almost did for himself, by planting his banner before the King's upon the wall; and only rescued himself from utter disgrace by saving his Majesty's life several times in the course of this most desperate onslaught.

Then the luckless knight's very virtues (as, no doubt, my respected readers know,) made him enemies amongst the men—nor was Ivanhoe liked by the women frequenting the camp of the gay King Richard. His young Queen, and a brilliant court of ladies, attended the pleasure-loving monarch. His Majesty would transact business in the morning, then fight severely from after breakfast till about three o'clock in the afternoon; from which time, until after midnight, there was nothing but jigging and singing, feasting and revelry, in the royal tents. Ivanhoe, who was asked as a matter of ceremony, and forced to attend these entertainments, not caring about the blandishments of any of the ladies present, looked on at their ogling and dancing with a countenance as glum as an undertaker's, and was a perfect wet-blanket in the midst of the festivities. His favorite resort and conversation were with a remarkably austere hermit, who lived in the neighborhood of Chalus, and with whom Ivanhoe loved to talk about Palestine, and the Jews, and other grave matters of import, better than to mingle in the gayest amusements of the court of King Richard. Many a night, when the Queen and the ladies were dancing quadrilles and polkas (in which his Majesty, who was enormously stout as well as tall, insisted upon figuring, and in which he was about as graceful as an elephant dancing a hornpipe), Ivanhoe would steal away from the ball, and come and have a night's chat under the moon with his reverend friend. It pained him to see a man of the King's age and size dancing about with the young folks. They laughed at his Majesty whilst they flattered him: the pages and maids of honor mimicked the royal mountebank almost to his face; and, if Ivanhoe ever could have laughed, he certainly would one night when the King, in light-blue satin inexpressibles, with his hair in powder, chose to dance the minuet de la cour with the little Queen Berangeria.

Then, after dancing, his Majesty must needs order a guitar, and begin to sing. He was said to compose his own songs—words and music—but those who have read Lord Campobello's "Lives of the Lord Chancellors" are aware that there was a person by the name of Blondel, who, in fact, did all the musical part of the King's performances; and as for the words, when a king writes verses, we may be sure there will be plenty of people to admire his poetry. His Majesty would sing you a ballad, of which he had stolen every idea, to an air that was ringing on all the barrel-organs of Christendom, and, turning round to his courtiers, would say, "How do you like that? I dashed it off this morning." Or, "Blondel, what do you think of this movement in B flat?" or what not; and the courtiers and Blondel, you may be sure, would applaud with all their might, like hypocrites as they were.

One evening—it was the evening of the 27th March, 1199, indeed—his Majesty, who was in the musical mood, treated the court with a quantity of his so-called composition, until the people were fairly tired of clapping with their hands and laughing in their sleeves. First he sang an ORIGINAL air and poem, beginning

"Cherries nice, cherries nice, nice, come choose,
Fresh and fair ones, who'll refuse?" &c.

The which he was ready to take his affidavit he had composed the day before yesterday. Then he sang an equally ORIGINAL heroic melody, of which the chorus was

"Rule Britannia, Britannia rules the sea,
For Britons never, never, never slaves shall be," &c.

The courtiers applauded this song as they did the other, all except Ivanhoe, who sat without changing a muscle of his features, until the King questioned him, when the knight, with a bow said "he thought he had heard something very like the air and the words elsewhere." His Majesty scowled at him a savage glance from under his red bushy eyebrows; but Ivanhoe had saved the royal life that day, and the King, therefore, with difficulty controlled his indignation.

"Well," said he, "by St. Richard and St. George, but ye never heard THIS song, for I composed it this very afternoon as I took my bath after the melee. Did I not, Blondel?"

Blondel, of course, was ready to take an affidavit that his Majesty had done as he said, and the King, thrumming on his guitar with his great red fingers and thumbs, began to sing out of tune and as follows:—

"COMMANDERS OF THE FAITHFUL.

"The Pope he is a happy man,
His Palace is the Vatican,
And there he sits and drains his can:
The Pope he is a happy man.
I often say when I'm at home,
I'd like to be the Pope of Rome.

"And then there's Sultan Saladin,
That Turkish Soldan full of sin;
He has a hundred wives at least,
By which his pleasure is increased:
I've often wished, I hope no sin,
That I were Sultan Saladin.

"But no, the Pope no wife may choose,
And so I would not wear his shoes;
No wine may drink the proud Paynim,
And so I'd rather not be him:
My wife, my wine, I love I hope,
And would be neither Turk nor Pope."

"Encore! Encore! Bravo! Bis!" Everybody applauded the King's song with all his might: everybody except Ivanhoe, who preserved his abominable gravity: and when asked aloud by Roger de Backbite whether he had heard that too, said firmly, "Yes, Roger de Backbite; and so hast thou if thou darest but tell the truth."

"Now, by St. Cicely, may I never touch gittern again," bawled the King in a fury, "if every note, word, and thought be not mine; may I die in to-morrow's onslaught if the song be not my song. Sing thyself, Wilfrid of the Lanthorn Jaws; thou could'st sing a good song in old times." And with all his might, and with a forced laugh, the King, who loved brutal practical jests, flung his guitar at the head of Ivanhoe.

Sir Wilfrid caught it gracefully with one hand, and making an elegant bow to the sovereign, began to chant as follows:—

"KING CANUTE.

"King Canute was weary-hearted; he had reigned for years a score,
attling, struggling, pushing, fighting, killing much and robbing more;
And he thought upon his actions, walking by the wild sea-shore.

"'Twixt the Chancellor and Bishop walked the King with steps sedate,
Chamberlains and grooms came after, silversticks and goldsticks great,

Chaplains, aides-de-camp, and pages,—all the officers of state.

"Sliding after like his shadow, pausing when he chose to pause,
If a frown his face contracted, straight the courtiers dropped their jaws;
If to laugh the King was minded, out they burst in loud hee-haws.

"But that day a something vexed him, that was clear to old and young:
Thrice his Grace had yawned at table, when his favorite gleemen sung,
Once the Queen would have consoled him, but he bade her hold her tongue.

"'Something ails my gracious master,' cried the Keeper of the Seal.
'Sure, my lord, it is the lampreys served at dinner, or the veal?'
'Psha!' exclaimed the angry monarch. 'Keeper, 'tis not that I feel.

"''Tis the HEART, and not the dinner, fool, that doth my rest impair:
Can a King be great as I am, prithee, and yet know no care?
Oh, I'm sick, and tired, and weary.'—Some one cried, 'The King's arm-chair?'

"Then towards the lackeys turning, quick my Lord the Keeper nodded,
Straight the King's great chair was brought him, by two footmen able-bodied;
Languidly he sank into it: it was comfortably wadded.

"'Leading on my fierce companions,' cried be, 'over storm and brine,
I have fought and I have conquered! Where was glory like to mine?'
Loudly all the courtiers echoed: 'Where is glory like to thine?'

"'What avail me all my kingdoms? Weary am I now, and old;
Those fair sons I have begotten, long to see me dead and cold;
Would I were, and quiet buried, underneath the silent mould!

"'Oh, remorse, the writhing serpent! at my bosom tears and bites;
Horrid, horrid things I look on, though I put out all the lights;
Ghosts of ghastly recollections troop about my bed of nights.

"'Cities burning, convents blazing, red with sacrilegious fires;
Mothers weeping, virgins screaming, vainly for their slaughtered sires.'—
Such a tender conscience,' cries the Bishop, 'every one admires.

"'But for such unpleasant bygones, cease, my gracious lord, to search,
They're forgotten and forgiven by our Holy Mother Church;
Never, never does she leave her benefactors in the lurch.

"'Look! the land is crowned with minsters, which your Grace's bounty raised;
Abbeys filled with holy men, where you and Heaven are daily praised:
YOU, my lord, to think of dying? on my conscience I'm amazed!'

"'Nay, I feel,' replied King Canute, 'that my end is drawing near.'
'Don't say so,' exclaimed the courtiers (striving each to squeeze a tear).

'Sure your Grace is strong and lusty, and may live this fifty year.'

"'Live these fifty years!' the Bishop roared, with actions made to suit.
 'Are you mad, my good Lord Keeper, thus to speak of King Canute!
Men have lived a thousand years, and sure his Majesty will do't.

"'Adam, Enoch, Lamech, Cainan, Mahaleel, Methusela,
Lived nine hundred years apiece, and mayn't the King as well as they?'
'Fervently,' exclaimed the Keeper, 'fervently I trust he may.'

"'HE to die?' resumed the Bishop. 'He a mortal like to US?
Death was not for him intended, though communis omnibus:
Keeper, you are irreligious, for to talk and cavil thus.

"'With his wondrous skill in healing ne'er a doctor can compete,
Loathsome lepers, if he touch them, start up clean upon their feet;
Surely he could raise the dead up, did his Highness think it meet.

"'Did not once the Jewish captain stay the sun upon the hill,
And, the while he slew the foemen, bid the silver moon stand still?
So, no doubt, could gracious Canute, if it were his sacred will.'

"'Might I stay the sun above us, good Sir Bishop?' Canute cried;
'Could I bid the silver moon to pause upon her heavenly ride?
If the moon obeys my orders, sure I can command the tide.

"'Will the advancing waves obey me, Bishop, if I make the sign?'
Said the Bishop, bowing lowly, 'Land and sea, my lord, are thine.'
Canute turned towards the ocean—'Back!' he said, 'thou foaming brine

"'From the sacred shore I stand on, I command thee to retreat;
Venture not, thou stormy rebel, to approach thy master's seat:
Ocean, be thou still! I bid thee come not nearer to my feet!'

"But the sullen ocean answered with a louder, deeper roar,
And the rapid waves drew nearer, falling sounding on the shore;
Back the Keeper and the Bishop, back the King and courtiers bore.

"And he sternly bade them never more to kneel to human clay,
But alone to praise and worship That which earth and seas obey:
And his golden crown of empire never wore he from that day.
King Canute is dead and gone: Parasites exist alway."

At this ballad, which, to be sure, was awfully long, and as grave as a sermon, some of the courtiers tittered, some yawned, and some affected to be asleep and snore outright. But Roger de Backbite thinking to curry favor with the King by this piece of vulgarity, his Majesty fetched him a knock on the nose and a buffet on the ear, which, I warrant me, wakened Master Roger; to whom the King said, "Listen and be civil, slave; Wilfrid is singing about thee.—Wilfrid, thy ballad is long, but it is to the purpose, and I have grown cool during thy homily. Give me thy hand, honest friend. Ladies, good night. Gentlemen, we give the grand assault to-morrow; when I promise thee, Wilfrid, thy banner shall not be before mine."—And the King, giving his arm to her Majesty, retired into the private pavilion.

CHAPTER III

ST. GEORGE FOR ENGLAND

Whilst the royal Richard and his court were feasting in the camp outside the walls of Chalus, they of the castle were in the most miserable plight that may be conceived. Hunger, as well as the fierce assaults of the besiegers, had made dire ravages in the place. The garrison's provisions of corn and cattle, their very horses, dogs, and donkeys had been eaten up—so that it might well be said by Wamba "that famine, as well as slaughter, had THINNED the garrison." When the men of Chalus came on the walls to defend it against the scaling-parties of King Richard, they were like so many skeletons in armor; they could hardly pull their bowstrings at last, or pitch down stones on the heads of his Majesty's party, so weak had their arms become; and the gigantic Count of Chalus—a warrior as redoubtable for his size and strength as Richard Plantagenet himself—was scarcely able to lift up his battle-axe upon the day of that last assault, when Sir Wilfrid of Ivanhoe ran him through the—but we are advancing matters.

What should prevent me from describing the agonies of hunger which the Count (a man of large appetite) suffered in company with his heroic sons and garrison?—Nothing, but that Dante has already done the business in the notorious history of Count Ugolino; so that my efforts might be considered as mere imitations. Why should I not, if I were minded to revel in horrifying details, show you how the famished garrison drew lots, and ate themselves during the siege; and how the unlucky lot falling upon the Countess of Chalus, that heroic woman, taking an affectionate leave of her family, caused her large caldron in the castle kitchen to be set a-boiling, had onions, carrots and herbs, pepper and salt made ready, to make a savory soup, as the French like it; and when all things were quite completed, kissed her children, jumped into the caldron from off a kitchen stool, and so was stewed down in her flannel bed-gown? Dear friends, it is not from want of imagination, or from having no turn for the terrible or pathetic, that I spare you these details. I could give you some description that would spoil your dinner and night's rest, and make your hair stand on end. But why harrow your feelings? Fancy all the tortures and horrors that possibly can occur in a beleaguered and famished castle: fancy the feelings of men who know that no more quarter will be given them than they would get if they were peaceful Hungarian citizens kidnapped and brought to trial by his Majesty the Emperor of Austria; and then let us rush on to the breach and prepare once more to meet the assault of dreadful King Richard and his men.

On the 29th of March in the year 1199, the good King, having copiously partaken of breakfast, caused his trumpets to blow, and advanced with his host upon the breach of the castle of Chalus. Arthur de Pendennis bore his banner; Wilfrid of Ivanhoe fought on the King's right hand. Molyneux, Bishop of Bullocksmithy, doffed crosier and mitre for that day, and though fat and pursy, panted up the breach with the most resolute spirit, roaring out war-cries and curses, and wielding a prodigious mace of iron, with which he did good execution. Roger de Backbite was forced to come in attendance upon the sovereign, but took care to keep in the rear of his august master, and to shelter behind his huge triangular shield as much as possible. Many lords of note followed the King and bore the ladders; and as they were placed against the wall, the air was perfectly dark with the shower of arrows which the French archers poured out at the besiegers, and the cataract of stones, kettles, bootjacks, chests of drawers, crockery, umbrellas, congreve-rockets, bombshells, bolts and arrows and other missiles which the desperate garrison flung out on the storming-party. The King received a copper coal-scuttle right over his eyes, and a mahogany wardrobe was discharged at his morion, which would have felled an ox, and would have done for the King had not Ivanhoe warded it off skilfully. Still they advanced, the warriors falling around them like grass beneath the scythe of the mower.

The ladders were placed in spite of the hail of death raining round: the King and Ivanhoe were, of course, the first to mount them. Chalus stood in the breach, borrowing strength from despair; and roaring out, "Ha! Plantagenet, St. Barbacue for Chalus!" he dealt the King a crack across the helmet with his battle-axe, which shore off the gilt lion and crown that surmounted the steel cap. The King bent and reeled back; the besiegers were dismayed; the garrison and the Count of Chalus set up a shout of triumph: but it was premature.

As quick as thought Ivanhoe was into the Count with a thrust in tierce, which took him just at the joint of the armor, and ran him through as clean as a spit does a partridge. Uttering a horrid shriek, he fell back writhing; the King recovering staggered up the parapet; the rush of knights followed, and the union-jack was planted triumphantly on the walls, just as Ivanhoe,—but we must leave him for a moment.

"Ha, St. Richard!—ha, St. George!" the tremendous voice of the Lion-king was heard over the loudest roar of the onset. At every sweep of his blade a severed head flew over the parapet, a spouting trunk tumbled, bleeding, on the flags of the bartizan. The world hath never seen a warrior equal to that Lion-hearted Plantagenet, as he raged over the keep, his eyes flashing fire through the bars of his morion, snorting and chafing with the hot lust of battle. One by one les enfans de Chalus had fallen; there was only one left at last of all the brave race that had fought round the gallant Count:—only one, and but a boy, a fair-haired boy, a blue-eyed boy! he had been gathering pansies in the fields but yesterday—it was but a few years, and he was a baby in his mother's arms! What could his puny sword do against the most redoubted blade in Christendom?—and yet Bohemond faced the great champion of England, and met him foot to foot! Turn away, turn away, my dear young friends and kind-hearted ladies! Do not look at that ill-fated poor boy! his blade is crushed into splinters under the axe of the conqueror, and the poor child is beaten to his knee! . . .

"Now, by St. Barbacue of Limoges," said Bertrand de Gourdon, "the butcher will never strike down yonder lambling! Hold thy hand, Sir King, or, by St. Barbacue—"

Swift as thought the veteran archer raised his arblast to his shoulder, the whizzing bolt fled from the ringing string, and the next moment crashed quivering into the corselet of Plantagenet.

'Twas a luckless shot, Bertrand of Gourdon! Maddened by the pain of the wound, the brute nature of Richard was aroused: his fiendish appetite for blood rose to madness, and grinding his teeth, and with a curse too horrible to mention, the flashing axe of the royal butcher fell down on the blond ringlets of the child, and the children of Chalus were no more! . . .

I just throw this off by way of description, and to show what MIGHT be done if I chose to indulge in this style of composition; but as in the battles which are described by the kindly chronicler, of one of whose works this present masterpiece is professedly a continuation, everything passes off agreeably—the people are slain, but without any unpleasant sensation to the reader; nay, some of the most savage and blood-stained characters of history, such is the indomitable good-humor of the great novelist, become amiable, jovial companions, for whom one has a hearty sympathy—so, if you please, we will have this fighting business at Chalus, and the garrison and honest Bertrand of Gourdon, disposed of; the former, according to the usage of the good old times, having been hung up or murdered to a man, and the latter killed in the manner described by the late Dr. Goldsmith in his History.

As for the Lion-hearted, we all very well know that the shaft of Bertrand de Gourdon put an end to the royal hero—and that from that 29th of March he never robbed nor murdered any more. And we have legends in recondite books of the manner of the King's death.

"You must die, my son," said the venerable Walter of Rouen, as Berengaria was carried shrieking from the King's tent. "Repent, Sir King, and separate yourself from your children!"

"It is ill jesting with a dying man," replied the King. "Children have I none, my good lord bishop, to inherit after me."

"Richard of England," said the archbishop, turning up his fine eyes, "your vices are your children. Ambition is your eldest child, Cruelty is your second child, Luxury is your third child; and you have nourished them from your youth up. Separate yourself from these sinful ones, and prepare your soul, for the hour of departure draweth nigh."

Violent, wicked, sinful, as he might have been, Richard of England met his death like a Christian man. Peace be to the soul of the brave! When the news came to King Philip of France, he sternly forbade his courtiers to rejoice at the death of his enemy. "It is no matter of joy but of dolor," he said, "that the bulwark of Christendom and the bravest king of Europe is no more."

Meanwhile what has become of Sir Wilfrid of Ivanhoe, whom we left in the act of rescuing his sovereign by running the Count of Chalus through the body?

As the good knight stooped down to pick his sword out of the corpse of his fallen foe, some one coming behind him suddenly thrust a dagger into his back at a place where his shirt-of-mail was open (for Sir Wilfrid had armed that morning in a hurry, and it was his breast, not his back, that he was accustomed ordinarily to protect); and when poor Wamba came up on the rampart, which he did when the fighting was over,—being such a fool that he could not be got to thrust his head into danger for glory's sake—he found his dear knight with the dagger in his back lying without life upon the body of the Count de Chalus whom he had anon slain.

Ah, what a howl poor Wamba set up when he found his master killed! How he lamented over the corpse of that noble knight and friend! What mattered it to him that Richard the King was borne wounded to his tent, and that Bertrand de Gourdon was flayed alive? At another time the sight of this spectacle might have amused the simple knave; but now all his thoughts were of his lord: so good, so gentle, so kind, so loyal, so frank with the great, so tender to the poor, so truthful of speech, so modest regarding his own merit, so true a gentleman, in a word, that anybody might, with reason, deplore him.

As Wamba opened the dear knight's corselet, he found a locket round his neck, in which there was some hair; not flaxen like that of my Lady Rowena, who was almost as fair as an Albino, but as black, Wamba thought, as the locks of the Jewish maiden whom the knight had rescued in the lists of Templestowe. A bit of Rowena's hair was in Sir Wilfrid's possession, too; but that was in his purse along with his seal of arms, and a couple of groats: for the good knight never kept any money, so generous was he of his largesses when money came in.

Wamba took the purse, and seal, and groats, but he left the locket of hair round his master's neck, and when he returned to England never said a word about the circumstance. After all, how should he know whose hair it was? It might have been the knight's grandmother's hair for aught the fool knew; so he kept his counsel when he brought back the sad news and tokens to the disconsolate widow at Rotherwood.

The poor fellow would never have left the body at all, and indeed sat by it all night, and until the gray of the morning; when, seeing two suspicious-looking characters advancing towards him, he fled in dismay, supposing that they were marauders who were out searching for booty among the dead bodies; and having not the least courage, he fled from these, and tumbled down the breach, and never stopped running as fast as his legs would carry him, until he reached the tent of his late beloved master.

The news of the knight's demise, it appeared, had been known at his quarters long before; for his servants were gone, and had ridden off on his horses; his chests were plundered: there was not so much as a shirt-collar left in his drawers, and the very bed and blankets had been carried away by these FAITHFUL attendants. Who had slain Ivanhoe? That remains a mystery to the present day; but Roger de Backbite, whose nose he had pulled for defamation, and who was behind him in the assault at Chalus, was seen two years afterwards at the court of King John in an embroidered velvet waistcoat which Rowena could have sworn she had worked for Ivanhoe, and about which the widow would have made some little noise, but that—but that she was no longer a widow.

That she truly deplored the death of her lord cannot be questioned, for she ordered the deepest mourning which any milliner in York could supply, and erected a monument to his memory as big as a minster. But she was a lady of such fine principles, that she did not allow her grief to overmaster her; and an opportunity speedily arising for uniting the two best Saxon families in England, by an alliance between herself and the gentleman who offered himself to her, Rowena sacrificed her inclination to remain single, to her sense of duty; and contracted a second matrimonial engagement.

That Athelstane was the man, I suppose no reader familiar with life, and novels which are a rescript of life, and are all strictly natural and edifying, can for a moment doubt. Cardinal Pandulfo tied the knot for them: and lest there should be any doubt about Ivanhoe's death (for his body was never sent home after all, nor seen after Wamba ran away from it), his Eminence procured a Papal decree annulling the former marriage, so that Rowena became Mrs. Athelstane with a clear conscience. And who shall be surprised, if she was happier with the stupid and boozy Thane than with the gentle and melancholy Wilfrid? Did women never have a predilection for fools, I should like to know; or fall in love with donkeys, before the time of the amours of Bottom and Titania? Ah! Mary, had you not preferred an ass to a man, would you have married Jack Bray, when a Michael Angelo offered? Ah! Fanny, were you not a woman, would you persist in adoring Tom Hiccups, who beats you, and comes home tipsy from the Club? Yes, Rowena cared a hundred times more about tipsy Athelstane than ever she had done for gentle Ivanhoe, and so great was her infatuation about the former, that she would sit upon his knee in the presence of all her maidens, and let him smoke his cigars in the very drawing-room.

This is the epitaph she caused to be written by Father Drono (who piqued himself upon his Latinity) on the stone commemorating the death of her late lord:—

Hic est Guilfridus, belli dum vixit avidus:
Cum gladio et lancea, Normania et quoque Francia

Verbera dura dabat: per Turcos multum equitabat:
Guilbertum occidit: atque Hierosolyma vidit.
Heu! nunc sub fossa sunt tanti militis ossa,
Uxor Athelstani est conjux castissima Thani.

And this is the translation which the doggerel knave Wamba made of the Latin lines:

"REQUIESCAT.

"Under the stone you behold,
Buried, and coffined, and cold,
Lieth Sir Wilfrid the Bold.

"Always he marched in advance,
Warring in Flanders and France,
Doughty with sword and with lance.

"Famous in Saracen fight,
Rode in his youth the good knight,
Scattering Paynims in flight.

"Brian the Templar untrue,
Fairly in tourney he slew,
Saw Hierusalem too.

"Now he is buried and gone,
Lying beneath the gray stone:
Where shall you find such a one?

"Long time his widow deplored,
Weeping the fate of her lord,
Sadly cut off by the sword.

"When she was eased of her pain,
Came the good Lord Athelstane,
When her ladyship married again."

Athelstane burst into a loud laugh, when he heard it, at the last line, but Rowena would have had the fool whipped, had not the Thane interceded; and to him, she said, she could refuse nothing.

CHAPTER IV

IVANHOE REDIVIVUS

I trust nobody will suppose, from the events described in the last chapter, that our friend Ivanhoe is really dead. Because we have given him an epitaph or two and a monument, are these any reasons that he should be really gone out of the world? No: as in the pantomime, when we see Clown and Pantaloon lay out Harlequin and cry over him, we are always sure that Master Harlequin will be up at the next minute alert and shining in his glistening coat; and, after giving a box on the ears to the pair of them, will be taking a dance with Columbine, or leaping gayly through the clock-face, or into the three-pair-of-stairs' window:—so Sir Wilfrid, the Harlequin of our Christmas piece, may be run through a little, or may make believe to be dead, but will assuredly rise up again when he is wanted, and show himself at the right moment.

The suspicious-looking characters from whom Wamba ran away were no cut-throats and plunderers, as the poor knave imagined, but no other than Ivanhoe's friend, the hermit, and a reverend brother of his, who visited the scene of the late battle in order to see if any Christians still survived there, whom they might shrive and get ready for heaven, or to whom they might possibly offer the benefit of their skill as leeches. Both were prodigiously learned in the healing art; and had about them those precious elixirs which so often occur in romances, and with which patients are so miraculously restored. Abruptly dropping his master's head from his lap as he fled, poor Wamba caused the knight's pate to fall with rather a heavy thump to the ground, and if the knave had but stayed a minute longer, he would have heard Sir Wilfrid utter a deep groan. But though the fool heard him not, the holy hermits did; and to recognize the gallant Wilfrid, to withdraw the enormous dagger still sticking out of his back, to wash the wound with a portion of the precious elixir, and to pour a little of it down his throat, was with the excellent hermits the work of an instant: which remedies being applied, one of the good men took the knight by the heels and the other by the head, and bore him daintily from the castle to their hermitage in a neighboring rock. As for the Count of Chalus, and the remainder of the slain, the hermits were too much occupied with Ivanhoe's case to mind them, and did not, it appears, give them any elixir: so that, if they are really dead, they must stay on the rampart stark and cold; or if otherwise, when the scene closes upon them as it does now, they may get up, shake themselves, go to the slips and drink a pot of porter, or change their stage-clothes and go home to supper. My dear readers, you may settle the matter among yourselves as you like. If you wish to kill the characters really off, let them be dead, and have done with them: but, entre nous, I don't believe they are any more dead than you or I are, and sometimes doubt whether there is a single syllable of truth in this whole story.

Well, Ivanhoe was taken to the hermits' cell, and there doctored by the holy fathers for his hurts; which were of such a severe and dangerous order, that he was under medical treatment for a very considerable time. When he woke up from his delirium, and asked how long he had been ill, fancy his astonishment when he heard that he had been in the fever for six years! He thought the reverend fathers were joking at first, but their profession forbade them from that sort of levity; and besides, he could not possibly have got well any sooner, because the story would have been sadly put out had he appeared earlier. And it proves how good the fathers were to him, and how very nearly that scoundrel of a Roger de Backbite's dagger had finished him, that he did not get well under this great length of time; during the whole of which the fathers tended him without ever thinking of a fee. I know of a kind physician in this town who does as much sometimes; but I won't do him the ill service of mentioning his name here.

Ivanhoe, being now quickly pronounced well, trimmed his beard, which by this time hung down considerably below his knees, and calling for his suit of chain-armor, which before had fitted his elegant person as tight as wax, now put it on, and it bagged and hung so loosely about him, that even the good friars laughed at his absurd appearance. It was impossible that he should go about the country in such a garb as that: the very boys would laugh at him: so the friars gave him one of their old gowns, in which he disguised himself, and after taking an affectionate farewell of his friends, set forth on his return to his native country. As he went along, he learned that Richard was dead, that John reigned, that Prince Arthur had been poisoned, and was of course made acquainted with various other facts of public importance recorded in Pinnock's Catechism and the Historic Page.

But these subjects did not interest him near so much as his own private affairs; and I can fancy that his legs trembled under him, and his pilgrim's staff shook with emotion, as at length, after many perils, he came in sight of his paternal mansion of Rotherwood, and saw once more the chimneys smoking, the shadows of the oaks over the grass in the sunset, and the rooks winging over the trees. He heard the supper gong sounding: he knew his way to the door well enough; he entered the familiar hall with a benedicite, and without any more words took his place.

You might have thought for a moment that the gray friar trembled and his shrunken cheek looked deadly pale; but he recovered himself presently: nor could you see his pallor for the cowl which covered his face.

A little boy was playing on Athelstane's knee; Rowena smiling and patting the Saxon Thane fondly on his broad bullhead, filled him a huge cup of spiced wine from a golden jug. He drained a quart of the liquor, and, turning round, addressed the friar:—

"And so, gray frere, thou sawest good King Richard fall at Chalus by the bolt of that felon bowman?"

"We did, an it please you. The brothers of our house attended the good King in his last moments: in truth, he made a Christian ending!"

"And didst thou see the archer flayed alive? It must have been rare sport," roared Athelstane, laughing hugely at the joke. "How the fellow must have howled!"

"My love!" said Rowena, interposing tenderly, and putting a pretty white finger on his lip.

"I would have liked to see it too," cried the boy.

"That's my own little Cedric, and so thou shalt. And, friar, didst see my poor kinsman Sir Wilfrid of Ivanhoe? They say he fought well at Chalus!"

"My sweet lord," again interposed Rowena, "mention him not."

"Why? Because thou and he were so tender in days of yore—when you could not bear my plain face, being all in love with his pale one?"

"Those times are past now, dear Athelstane," said his affectionate wife, looking up to the ceiling.

"Marry, thou never couldst forgive him the Jewess, Rowena."

"The odious hussy! don't mention the name of the unbelieving creature," exclaimed the lady.

"Well, well, poor Wil was a good lad—a thought melancholy and milksop though. Why, a pint of sack fuddled his poor brains."

"Sir Wilfrid of Ivanhoe was a good lance," said the friar. "I have heard there was none better in Christendom. He lay in our convent after his wounds, and it was there we tended him till he died. He was buried in our north cloister."

"And there's an end of him," said Athelstane. "But come, this is dismal talk. Where's Wamba the Jester? Let us have a song. Stir up, Wamba, and don't lie like a dog in the fire! Sing us a song, thou crack-brained jester, and leave off whimpering for bygones. Tush, man! There be many good fellows left in this world."

"There be buzzards in eagles' nests," Wamba said, who was lying stretched before the fire, sharing the hearth with the Thane's dogs. "There be dead men alive, and live men dead. There be merry songs and dismal songs. Marry, and the merriest are the saddest sometimes. I will leave off motley and wear black, gossip Athelstane. I will turn howler at funerals, and then, perhaps, I shall be merry. Motley is fit for mutes, and black for fools. Give me some drink, gossip, for my voice is as cracked as my brain."

"Drink and sing, thou beast, and cease prating," the Thane said.

And Wamba, touching his rebeck wildly, sat up in the chimney-side and curled his lean shanks together and began:—

"LOVE AT TWO SCORE.

"Ho! pretty page, with dimpled chin,
That never has known the barber's shear,
All your aim is woman to win—
This is the way that boys begin—
Wait till you've come to forty year!

"Curly gold locks cover foolish brains,
Billing and cooing is all your cheer,
Sighing and singing of midnight strains
Under Bonnybells' window-panes.
Wait till you've come to forty year!

"Forty times over let Michaelmas pass,
Grizzling hair the brain doth clear;
Then you know a boy is an ass,
Then you know the worth of a lass,
Once you have come to forty year.

"Pledge me round, I bid ye declare,
All good fellows whose beards are gray:
Did not the fairest of the fair
Common grow, and wearisome, ere
Ever a month was passed away?

"The reddest lips that ever have kissed,
The brightest eyes that ever have shone,
May pray and whisper and we not list,

Or look away and never be missed,
Ere yet ever a month was gone.

"Gillian's dead, Heaven rest her bier,
How I loved her twenty years syne!
Marian's married, but I sit here,
Alive and merry at forty year,
Dipping my nose in the Gascon wine."

"Who taught thee that merry lay, Wamba, thou son of Witless?" roared Athelstane, clattering his cup on the table and shouting the chorus.

"It was a good and holy hermit, sir, the pious clerk of Copmanhurst, that you wot of, who played many a prank with us in the days that we knew King Richard. Ah, noble sir, that was a jovial time and a good priest."

"They say the holy priest is sure of the next bishopric, my love," said Rowena. "His Majesty hath taken him into much favor. My Lord of Huntingdon looked very well at the last ball; but I never could see any beauty in the Countess—a freckled, blowsy thing, whom they used to call Maid Marian: though, for the matter of that, what between her flirtations with Major Littlejohn and Captain Scarlett, really—"

"Jealous again—haw! haw!" laughed Athelstane.

"I am above jealousy, and scorn it," Rowena answered, drawing herself up very majestically.

"Well, well, Wamba's was a good song," Athelstane said.

"Nay, a wicked song," said Rowena, turning up her eyes as usual. "What! rail at woman's love? Prefer a filthy wine cup to a true wife? Woman's love is eternal, my Athelstane. He who questions it would be a blasphemer were he not a fool. The well-born and well-nurtured gentlewoman loves once and once only."

"I pray you, madam, pardon me, I—I am not well," said the gray friar, rising abruptly from his settle, and tottering down the steps of the dais. Wamba sprung after him, his bells jingling as he rose, and casting his arms around the apparently fainting man, he led him away into the court. "There be dead men alive and live men dead," whispered he. "There be coffins to laugh at and marriages to cry over. Said I not sooth, holy friar?" And when they had got out into the solitary court, which was deserted by all the followers of the Thane, who were mingling in the drunken revelry in the hall, Wamba, seeing that none were by, knelt down, and kissing the friar's garment, said, "I knew thee, I knew thee, my lord and my liege!"

"Get up," said Wilfrid of Ivanhoe, scarcely able to articulate: "only fools are faithful."

And he passed on, and into the little chapel where his father lay buried. All night long the friar spent there: and Wamba the Jester lay outside watching as mute as the saint over the porch.

When the morning came, Wumba was gone; and the knave being in the habit of wandering hither and thither as he chose, little notice was taken of his absence by a master and mistress who had not much sense of humor. As for Sir Wilfrid, a gentleman of his delicacy of feelings could not be expected to remain in a house where things so naturally disagreeable to him were occurring, and he quitted Rotherwood incontinently, after paying a dutiful visit to the tomb where his old father, Cedric, was buried; and hastened on to York, at which city he made himself known to the family attorney, a most respectable man, in whose hands his ready money was deposited, and took up a sum sufficient to fit himself out with credit, and a handsome retinue, as became a knight of consideration. But he changed his name, wore a wig and spectacles, and disguised himself entirely, so that it was impossible his friends or the public should know him, and thus metamorphosed, went about whithersoever his fancy led him. He was present at a public ball at York, which the lord mayor gave, danced Sir Roger de Coverley in the very same set with Rowena—(who was disgusted that Maid Marian took precedence of her)—he saw little Athelstane overeat himself at the supper and pledge his big father in a cup of sack; he met the Reverend Mr. Tuck at a missionary meeting, where he seconded a resolution proposed by that eminent divine;—in fine, he saw a score of his old acquaintances, none of whom recognized in him the warrior of Palestine and Templestowe. Having a large fortune and nothing to do, he went about this country performing charities, slaying robbers, rescuing the distressed, and achieving noble feats of arms. Dragons and giants existed in his day no more, or be sure he would have had a fling at them: for the truth is, Sir Wilfrid of Ivanhoe was somewhat sick of the life which the hermits of Chalus had restored to him, and felt himself so friendless and solitary that he would not have been sorry to come to an end of it. Ah, my dear friends and intelligent British public, are there not others who are melancholy under a mask of gayety, and who, in the midst of crowds, are lonely? Liston was a most melancholy man; Grimaldi had feelings; and there are others I wot of:—but psha!—let us have the next chapter.

CHAPTER V

IVANHOE TO THE RESCUE

The rascally manner in which the chicken-livered successor of Richard of the Lion-heart conducted himself to all parties, to his relatives, his nobles, and his people, is a matter notorious, and set forth clearly in the Historic Page: hence, although nothing, except perhaps success, can, in my opinion, excuse disaffection to the sovereign, or appearance in armed rebellion against him, the loyal reader will make allowance for two of the principal personages of this narrative, who will have to appear in the present chapter in the odious character of rebels to their lord and king. It must be remembered, in partial exculpation of the fault of Athelstane and Rowena, (a fault for which they were bitterly punished, as you shall presently hear,) that the monarch exasperated his subjects in a variety of ways,—that before he murdered his royal nephew, Prince Arthur, there was a great question whether he was the rightful king of England at all,—that his behavior as an uncle, and a family man, was likely to wound the feelings of any lady and mother,—finally, that there were palliations for the conduct of Rowena and Ivanhoe, which it now becomes our duty to relate.

When his Majesty destroyed Prince Arthur, the Lady Rowena, who was one of the ladies of honor to the Queen, gave up her place at court at once, and retired to her castle of Rotherwood. Expressions made use of by her, and derogatory to the character of the sovereign, were carried to the monarch's ears, by some of those parasites, doubtless, by whom it is the curse of kings to be attended; and John swore, by St. Peter's teeth, that he would be revenged upon the haughty Saxon lady,—a kind of oath which, though he did not trouble himself about all other oaths, he was never known to break. It was not for some years after he had registered this vow, that he was enabled to keep it.

Had Ivanhoe been present at Ronen, when the King meditated his horrid designs against his nephew, there is little doubt that Sir Wilfrid would have prevented them, and rescued the boy: for Ivanhoe was, as we need scarcely say, a hero of romance; and it is the custom and duty of all gentlemen of that profession to be present on all occasions of historic interest, to be engaged in all conspiracies, royal interviews, and remarkable occurrences: and hence Sir Wilfrid would certainly have rescued the young Prince, had he been anywhere in the neighborhood of Rouen, where the foul tragedy occurred. But he was a couple of hundred leagues off, at Chalus, when the circumstance happened; tied down in his bed as crazy as a Bedlamite, and raving ceaselessly in the Hebrew tongue (which he had caught up during a previous illness in which he was tended by a maiden of that nation) about a certain Rebecca Ben Isaacs, of whom, being a married man, he never would have thought, had he been in his sound senses. During this delirium, what were politics to him, or he to politics? King John or King Arthur was entirely indifferent to a man who announced to his nurse-tenders, the good hermits of Chalus before mentioned, that he was the Marquis of Jericho, and about to marry Rebecca the Queen of Sheba. In a word, he only heard of what had occurred when he reached England, and his senses were restored to him. Whether was he happier, sound of brain and entirely miserable, (as any man would be who found so admirable a wife as Rowena married again,) or perfectly crazy, the husband of the beautiful Rebecca? I don't know which he liked best.

Howbeit the conduct of King John inspired Sir Wilfrid with so thorough a detestation of that sovereign, that he never could be brought to take service under him; to get himself presented at St. James's, or in any way to acknowledge, but by stern acquiescence, the authority of the sanguinary successor of his beloved King Richard. It was Sir Wilfrid of Ivanhoe, I need scarcely say, who got the Barons of England to league together and extort from the king that famous instrument and palladium of our liberties at present in the British Museum, Great Russell Street, Bloomsbury—the Magna Charta. His name does not naturally appear in the list of Barons, because he was only a knight, and a knight in disguise too: nor does Athelstane's signature figure on that document. Athelstane, in the first place, could not write; nor did he care a pennypiece about politics, so long as he could drink his wine at home undisturbed, and have his hunting and shooting in quiet.

It was not until the King wanted to interfere with the sport of every gentleman in England (as we know by reference to the Historic Page that this odious monarch did), that Athelstane broke out into open rebellion, along with several Yorkshire squires and noblemen. It is recorded of the King, that he forbade every man to hunt his own deer; and, in order to secure an obedience to his orders, this Herod of a monarch wanted to secure the eldest sons of all the nobility and gentry, as hostages for the good behavior of their parents.

Athelstane was anxious about his game—Rowena was anxious about her son. The former swore that he would hunt his deer in spite of all Norman tyrants—the latter asked, should she give up her boy to the ruffian who had murdered his own nephew?* The speeches of both were brought to the King at York; and, furious, he ordered an instant attack upon Rotherwood, and that the lord and lady of that castle should be brought before him dead or alive.

*See Hume, Giraldus Cambrensis, The Monk of Croyland, and Pinnock's Catechism.

Ah, where was Wilfrid of Ivanhoe, the unconquerable champion, to defend the castle against the royal party? A few thrusts from his lance would have spitted the leading warriors of the King's host: a few cuts from his sword would have put John's forces to rout. But the lance and sword of Ivanhoe were idle on this occasion. "No, be hanged to me!" said the knight, bitterly, "THIS is a quarrel in which I can't interfere. Common politeness forbids. Let yonder ale-swilling Athelstane defend his—ha, ha—WIFE; and my Lady Rowena guard her—ha, ha, ha—SON." And he laughed wildly and madly; and the sarcastic, way in which he choked and gurgled out the words "wife" and "son" would have made you shudder to hear.

When he heard, however, that, on the fourth day of the siege, Athelstane had been slain by a cannon-ball, (and this time for good, and not to come to life again as he had done before,) and that the widow (if so the innocent bigamist may be called) was conducting the defence of Rotherwood herself with the greatest intrepidity, showing herself upon the walls with her little son, (who bellowed like a bull, and did not like the fighting at all,) pointing the guns and encouraging the garrison in every way—better feelings returned to the bosom of the Knight of Ivanhoe, and summoning his men, he armed himself quickly and determined to go forth to the rescue.

He rode without stopping for two days and two nights in the direction of Rotherwood, with such swiftness and disregard for refreshment, indeed, that his men dropped one by one upon the road, and he arrived alone at the lodge-gate of the park. The windows were smashed; the door stove in; the lodge, a neat little Swiss cottage, with a garden where the pinafores of Mrs. Gurth's children might have been seen hanging on the gooseberry-bushes in more peaceful times, was now a ghastly heap of smoking ruins: cottage, bushes, pinafores, children lay mangled together, destroyed by the licentious soldiery of an infuriate monarch! Far be it from me to excuse the disobedience of Athelstane and Rowena to their sovereign; but surely, surely this cruelty might have been spared.

Gurth, who was lodge-keeper, was lying dreadfully wounded and expiring at the flaming and violated threshold of his lately picturesque home. A catapult and a couple of mangonels had done his business. The faithful fellow, recognizing his master, who had put up his visor and forgotten his wig and spectacles in the agitation of the moment, exclaimed, "Sir Wilfrid! my dear master—praised be St. Waltheof—there may be yet time—my beloved mistr—master Athelst . . ." He sank back, and never spoke again.

Ivanhoe spurred on his horse Bavieca madly up the chestnut avenue. The castle was before him; the western tower was in flames; the besiegers were pressing at the southern gate; Athelstane's banner, the bull rampant, was still on the northern bartizan. "An Ivanhoe, an Ivanhoe!" he bellowed out, with a shout that overcame all the din of battle: "Nostre Dame a la rescousse!" And to hurl his lance through the midriff of Reginald de Bracy, who was commanding the assault—who fell howling with anguish—to wave his battle-axe over his own head, and cut off those of thirteen men-at-arms, was the work of an instant. "An Ivanhoe, an Ivanhoe!" he still shouted, and down went a man as sure as he said "hoe!"

"Ivanhoe! Ivanhoe!" a shrill voice cried from the top of the northern bartizan. Ivanhoe knew it.

"Rowena my love, I come!" he roared on his part. "Villains! touch but a hair of her head, and I . . ."

Here, with a sudden plunge and a squeal of agony, Bavieca sprang forward wildly, and fell as wildly on her back, rolling over and over upon the knight. All was dark before him; his brain reeled; it whizzed; something came crashing down on his forehead. St. Waltheof and all the saints of the Saxon calendar protect the knight! . . .

When he came to himself, Wamba and the lieutenant of his lances were leaning over him with a bottle of the hermit's elixir. "We arrived here the day after the battle," said the fool; "marry, I have a knack of that."

"Your worship rode so deucedly quick, there was no keeping up with your worship," said the lieutenant.

"The day—after—the bat—" groaned Ivanhoe. "Where is the Lady Rowena?"

"The castle has been taken and sacked," the lieutenant said, and pointed to what once WAS Rotherwood, but was now only a heap of smoking ruins. Not a tower was left, not a roof, not a floor, not a single human being! Everything was flame and ruin, smash and murther!

Of course Ivanhoe fell back fainting again among the ninety-seven men-at-arms whom he had slain; and it was not until Wamba had applied a second, and uncommonly strong dose of the elixir that he came to life again. The good knight was, however, from long practice, so accustomed to the severest wounds, that he bore them far more easily than common folk, and thus was enabled to reach York upon a litter, which his men constructed for him, with tolerable ease.

Rumor had as usual advanced before him; and he heard at the hotel where he stopped, what had been the issue of the affair at Rotherwood. A minute or two after his horse was stabbed, and Ivanhoe knocked down, the western bartizan was taken by the storming-party which invested it, and every soul slain, except Rowena and her boy; who were tied upon horses and carried away, under a secure guard, to one of the King's castles—nobody knew whither: and Ivanhoe was recommended by the hotel-keeper (whose house he had used in former times) to reassume his wig and spectacles, and not call himself by his own name any more, lest some of the King's people should lay hands on him. However, as he had killed everybody round about him, there was but little danger of his discovery; and the Knight of the Spectacles, as he was called, went about York quite unmolested, and at liberty to attend to his own affairs.

We wish to be brief in narrating this part of the gallant hero's existence; for his life was one of feeling rather than affection, and the description of mere sentiment is considered by many well-informed persons to be tedious. What WERE his sentiments now, it may be asked, under the peculiar position in which he found himself? He had done his duty by Rowena, certainly: no man could say otherwise. But as for being in love with her any more, after what had occurred, that was a different question. Well, come what would, he was determined still to continue doing his duty by her;—but as she was whisked away the deuce knew whither, how could he do anything? So he resigned himself to the fact that she was thus whisked away.

He, of course, sent emissaries about the country to endeavor to find out where Rowena was: but these came back without any sort of intelligence; and it was remarked, that he still remained in a perfect state of resignation. He remained in this condition for a year, or more; and it was said that he was becoming more cheerful, and he certainly was growing rather fat. The Knight of the Spectacles was voted an agreeable man in a grave way; and gave some very elegant, though quiet, parties, and was received in the best society of York.

It was just at assize-time, the lawyers and barristers had arrived, and the town was unusually gay; when, one morning, the attorney, whom we have mentioned as Sir Wilfrid's man of business, and a most respectable man, called upon his gallant client at his lodgings, and said he had a communication of importance to make. Having to communicate with a client of rank, who was condemned to be hanged for forgery, Sir Roger de Backbite, the attorney said, he had been to visit that party in the condemned cell; and on the way through the yard, and through the bars of another cell, had seen and recognized an old acquaintance of Sir Wilfrid of Ivanhoe—and the lawyer held him out, with a particular look, a note, written on a piece of whity-brown paper.

What were Ivanhoe's sensations when he recognized the handwriting of Rowena!—he tremblingly dashed open the billet, and read as follows:—

"MY DEAREST IVANHOE,—For I am thine now as erst, and my first love was ever—ever dear to me. Have I been near thee dying for a whole year, and didst thou make no effort to rescue thy Rowena? Have ye given to others—I mention not their name nor their odious creed—the heart that ought to be mine? I send thee my forgiveness from my dying pallet of straw.—I forgive thee the insults I have received, the cold and hunger I have endured, the failing health of my boy, the bitterness of my prison, thy infatuation about that Jewess, which made our married life miserable, and which caused thee, I am sure, to go abroad to look after her. I forgive thee all my wrongs, and fain would bid thee farewell. Mr. Smith hath gained over my gaoler—he will tell thee how I may see thee. Come and console my last hour by promising that thou wilt care for my boy—HIS boy who fell like a hero (when thou wert absent) combating by the side of ROWENA."

The reader may consult his own feelings, and say whether Ivanhoe was likely to be pleased or not by this letter: however, he inquired of Mr. Smith, the solicitor, what was the plan which that gentleman had devised for the introduction to Lady Rowena, and was informed that he was to get a barrister's gown and wig, when the gaoler would introduce him into the interior of the prison. These decorations, knowing several gentlemen of the Northern Circuit, Sir Wilfrid of Ivanhoe easily procured, and with feelings of no small trepidation, reached the cell, where, for the space of a year, poor Rowena had been immured.

If any person have a doubt of the correctness, of the historical exactness of this narrative, I refer him to the "Biographie Universelle" (article Jean sans Terre), which says, "La femme d'un baron auquel on vint demander son fils, repondit, 'Le roi pense-t-il que je confierai mon fils a un homme qui a egorge son neveu de sa propre main?' Jean fit enlever la mere et l'enfant, et la laissa MOURIR DE FAIM dans les cachots."

I picture to myself, with a painful sympathy, Rowena undergoing this disagreeable sentence. All her virtues, her resolution, her chaste energy and perseverance, shine with redoubled lustre, and, for the first time since the commencement of the history, I feel that I am partially reconciled to her. The weary year passes—she grows weaker and more languid, thinner and thinner! At length Ivanhoe, in the disguise of a barrister of the Northern Circuit, is introduced to her cell, and finds his lady in the last stage of exhaustion, on the straw of her dungeon, with her little boy in her arms. She has preserved his life at the expense of her own, giving him the whole of the pittance which her gaolers allowed her, and perishing herself of inanition.

There is a scene! I feel as if I had made it up, as it were, with this lady, and that we part in peace, in consequence of my providing her with so sublime a death-bed. Fancy Ivanhoe's entrance—their recognition—the faint blush upon her worn features—the pathetic way in which she gives little Cedric in charge to him, and his promises of protection.

"Wilfrid, my early loved," slowly gasped she, removing her gray hair from her furrowed temples, and gazing on her boy fondly, as he nestled on Ivanhoe's knee—"promise me, by St. Waltheof of Templestowe—promise me one boon!"

"I do," said Ivanhoe, clasping the boy, and thinking it was to that little innocent the promise was intended to apply.

"By St. Waltheof?"

"By St. Waltheof!"

"Promise me, then," gasped Rowena, staring wildly at him, "that you never will marry a Jewess?"

"By St. Waltheof," cried Ivanhoe, "this is too much, Rowena!"—But he felt his hand grasped for a moment, the nerves then relaxed, the pale lips ceased to quiver—she was no more!


CHAPTER VI

IVANHOE THE WIDOWER

Having placed young Cedric at school at the hall of Dotheboyes, in Yorkshire, and arranged his family affairs, Sir Wilfrid of Ivanhoe quitted a country which had no longer any charms for him, and in which his stay was rendered the less agreeable by the notion that King John would hang him, if ever he could lay hands on the faithful follower of King Richard and Prince Arthur.

But there was always in those days a home and occupation for a brave and pious knight. A saddle on a gallant war-horse, a pitched field against the Moors, a lance wherewith to spit a turbaned infidel, or a road to Paradise carved out by his scimitar,—these were the height of the ambition of good and religious warriors; and so renowned a champion as Sir Wilfrid of Ivanhoe was sure to be well received wherever blows were stricken for the cause of Christendom. Even among the dark Templars, he who had twice overcome the most famous lance of their Order was a respected though not a welcome guest: but among the opposition company of the Knights of St. John, he was admired and courted beyond measure; and always affectioning that Order, which offered him, indeed, its first rank and commanderies, he did much good service; fighting in their ranks for the glory of heaven and St. Waltheof, and slaying many thousands of the heathen in Prussia, Poland, and those savage Northern countries. The only fault that the great and gallant, though severe and ascetic Folko of Heydenbraten, the chief of the Order of St. John, found with the melancholy warrior, whose lance did such good service to the cause, was, that he did not persecute the Jews as so religious a knight should. He let off sundry captives of that persuasion whom he had taken with his sword and his spear, saved others from torture, and actually ransomed the two last grinders of a venerable rabbi (that Roger de Cartright, an English knight of the Order, was about to extort from the elderly Israelite,) with a hundred crowns and a gimmal ring, which were all the property he possessed. Whenever he so ransomed or benefited one of this religion, he would moreover give them a little token or a message (were the good knight out of money), saying, "Take this token, and remember this deed was done by Wilfrid the Disinherited, for the services whilome rendered to him by Rebecca, the daughter of Isaac of York!" So among themselves, and in their meetings and synagogues, and in their restless travels from land to land, when they of Jewry cursed and reviled all Christians, as such abominable heathens will, they nevertheless excepted the name of the Desdichado, or the doubly-disinherited as he now was, the Desdichado-Doblado.

The account of all the battles, storms, and scaladoes in which Sir Wilfrid took part, would only weary the reader; for the chopping off one heathen's head with an axe must be very like the decapitation of any other unbeliever. Suffice it to say, that wherever this kind of work was to be done, and Sir Wilfrid was in the way, he was the man to perform it. It would astonish you were you to see the account that Wamba kept of his master's achievements, and of the Bulgarians, Bohemians, Croatians, slain or maimed by his hand. And as, in those days, a reputation for valor had an immense effect upon the soft hearts of women, and even the ugliest man, were he a stout warrior, was looked upon with favor by Beauty: so Ivanhoe, who was by no means ill-favored, though now becoming rather elderly, made conquests over female breasts as well as over Saracens, and had more than one direct offer of marriage made to him by princesses, countesses, and noble ladies possessing both charms and money, which they were anxious to place at the disposal of a champion so renowned. It is related that the Duchess Regent of Kartoffelberg offered him her hand, and the ducal crown of Kartoffelberg, which he had rescued from the unbelieving Prussians; but Ivanhoe evaded the Duchess's offer, by riding away from her capital secretly at midnight and hiding himself in a convent of Knights Hospitallers on the borders of Poland. And it is a fact that the Princess Rosalia Seraphina of Pumpernickel, the most lovely woman of her time, became so frantically attached to him, that she followed him on a campaign, and was discovered with his baggage disguised as a horse-boy. But no princess, no beauty, no female blandishments had any charms for Ivanhoe: no hermit practised a more austere celibacy. The severity of his morals contrasted so remarkably with the lax and dissolute manner of the young lords and nobles in the courts which he frequented, that these young springalds would sometimes sneer and call him Monk and Milksop; but his courage in the day of battle was so terrible and admirable, that I promise you the youthful libertines did not sneer THEN; and the most reckless of them often turned pale when they couched their lances to follow Ivanhoe. Holy Waltheof! it was an awful sight to see him with his pale calm face, his shield upon his breast, his heavy lance before him, charging a squadron of heathen Bohemians, or a regiment of Cossacks! Wherever he saw the enemy, Ivanhoe assaulted him: and when people remonstrated with him, and said if he attacked such and such a post, breach, castle, or army, he would be slain, "And suppose I be?" he answered, giving them to understand that he would as lief the Battle of Life were over altogether.

While he was thus making war against the Northern infidels news was carried all over Christendom of a catastrophe which had befallen the good cause in the South of Europe, where the Spanish Christians had met with such a defeat and massacre at the hands of the Moors as had never been known in the proudest day of Saladin.

Thursday, the 9th of Shaban, in the 605th year of the Hejira, is known all over the West as the amun-al-ark, the year of the battle of Alarcos, gained over the Christians by the Moslems of Andaluz, on which fatal day Christendom suffered a defeat so signal, that it was feared the Spanish peninsula would be entirely wrested away from the dominion of the Cross. On that day the Franks lost 150,000 men and 30,000 prisoners. A man-slave sold among the unbelievers for a dirhem; a donkey for the same; a sword, half a dirhem; a horse, five dirhems. Hundreds of thousands of these various sorts of booty were in the possession of the triumphant followers of Yakoobal-Mansoor. Curses on his head! But he was a brave warrior, and the Christians before him seemed to forget that they were the descendants of the brave Cid, the Kanbitoor, as the Moorish hounds (in their jargon) denominated the famous Campeador.

A general move for the rescue of the faithful in Spain—a crusade against the infidels triumphing there, was preached throughout Europe by all the most eloquent clergy; and thousands and thousands of valorous knights and nobles, accompanied by well-meaning varlets and vassals of the lower sort, trooped from all sides to the rescue. The Straits of Gibel-al-Tariff, at which spot the Moor, passing from

Barbary, first planted his accursed foot on the Christian soil, were crowded with the galleys of the Templars and the Knights of St. John, who flung succors into the menaced kingdoms of the peninsula; the inland sea swarmed with their ships hasting from their forts and islands, from Rhodes and Byzantium, from Jaffa and Ascalon. The Pyrenean peaks beheld the pennons and glittered with the armor of the knights marching out of France into Spain; and, finally, in a ship that set sail direct from Bohemia, where Sir Wilfrid happened to be quartered at the time when the news of the defeat of Alarcos came and alarmed all good Christians, Ivanhoe landed at Barcelona, and proceeded to slaughter the Moors forthwith.

He brought letters of introduction from his friend Folko of Heydenbraten, the Grand Master of the Knights of Saint John, to the venerable Baldomero de Garbanzos, Grand Master of the renowned order of Saint Jago. The chief of Saint Jago's knights paid the greatest respect to a warrior whose fame was already so widely known in Christendom; and Ivanhoe had the pleasure of being appointed to all the posts of danger and forlorn hopes that could be devised in his honor. He would be called up twice or thrice in a night to fight the Moors: he led ambushes, scaled breaches, was blown up by mines; was wounded many hundred times (recovering, thanks to the elixir, of which Wamba always carried a supply); he was the terror of the Saracens, and the admiration and wonder of the Christians.

To describe his deeds, would, I say, be tedious; one day's battle was like that of another. I am not writing in ten volumes like Monsieur Alexandre Dumas, or even in three like other great authors. We have no room for the recounting of Sir Wilfrid's deeds of valor. Whenever he took a Moorish town, it was remarked, that he went anxiously into the Jewish quarter, and inquired amongst the Hebrews, who were in great numbers in Spain, for Rebecca, the daughter of Isaac. Many Jews, according to his wont, he ransomed, and created so much scandal by this proceeding, and by the manifest favor which he showed to the people of that nation, that the Master of Saint Jago remonstrated with him, and it is probable he would have been cast into the Inquisition and roasted, but that his prodigious valor and success against the Moors counterbalanced his heretical partiality for the children of Jacob.

It chanced that the good knight was present at the siege of Xixona in Andalusia, entering the breach first, according to his wont, and slaying, with his own hand, the Moorish lieutenant of the town, and several hundred more of its unbelieving defenders. He had very nearly done for the Alfaqui, or governor—a veteran warrior with a crooked scimitar and a beard as white as snow—but a couple of hundred of the Alfaqui's bodyguard flung themselves between Ivanhoe and their chief, and the old fellow escaped with his life, leaving a handful of his beard in the grasp of the English knight. The strictly military business being done, and such of the garrison as did not escape put, as by right, to the sword, the good knight, Sir Wilfrid of Ivanhoe, took no further part in the proceedings of the conquerors of that ill-fated place. A scene of horrible massacre and frightful reprisals ensued, and the Christian warriors, hot with victory and flushed with slaughter, were, it is to be feared, as savage in their hour of triumph as ever their heathen enemies had been.

Among the most violent and least scrupulous was the ferocious Knight of Saint Jago, Don Beltran de Cuchilla y Trabuco y Espada y Espelon. Raging through the vanquished city like a demon, he slaughtered indiscriminately all those infidels of both sexes whose wealth did not tempt him to a ransom, or whose beauty did not reserve them for more frightful calamities than death. The slaughter over, Don Beltran took up his quarters in the Albaycen, where the Alfaqui had lived who had so narrowly escaped the sword of Ivanhoe; but the wealth, the treasure, the slaves, and the family of the fugitive chieftain, were left in possession of the conqueror of Xixona. Among the treasures, Don Beltran recognized with a savage joy the coat-armors and ornaments of many brave and unfortunate companions-in-arms who had fallen in the fatal battle of Alarcos. The sight of those bloody relics added fury to his cruel disposition, and served to steel a heart already but little disposed to sentiments of mercy.

Three days after the sack and plunder of the place, Don Beltran was seated in the hall-court lately occupied by the proud Alfaqui, lying in his divan, dressed in his rich robes, the fountains playing in the centre, the slaves of the Moor ministering to his scarred and rugged Christian conqueror. Some fanned him with peacocks' pinions, some danced before him, some sang Moor's melodies to the plaintive notes of a guzla, one—it was the only daughter of the Moor's old age, the young Zutulbe, a rosebud of beauty—sat weeping in a corner of the gilded hall: weeping for her slain brethren, the pride of Moslem chivalry, whose heads were blackening in the blazing sunshine on the portals without, and for her father, whose home had been thus made desolate.

He and his guest, the English knight Sir Wilfrid, were playing at chess, a favorite amusement with the chivalry of the period, when a messenger was announced from Valencia, to treat, if possible, for the ransom of the remaining part of the Alfaqui's family. A grim smile lighted up Don Beltran's features as he bade the black slave admit the messenger. He entered. By his costume it was at once seen that the bearer of the flag of truce was a Jew—the people were employed continually then as ambassadors between the two races at war in Spain.

"I come," said the old Jew (in a voice which made Sir Wilfrid start), "from my lord the Alfaqui to my noble senor, the invincible Don Beltran de Cuchilla, to treat for the ransom of the Moor's only daughter, the child of his old age and the pearl of his affection."

"A pearl is a valuable jewel, Hebrew. What does the Moorish dog bid for her?" asked Don Beltran, still smiling grimly.

"The Alfaqui offers 100,000 dinars, twenty-four horses with their caparisons, twenty-four suits of plate-armor, and diamonds and rubies to the amount of 1,000,000 dinars."

"Ho, slaves!" roared Don Beltran, "show the Jew my treasury of gold. How many hundred thousand pieces are there?" And ten enormous chests were produced in which the accountant counted 1,000 bags of 1,000 dirhems each, and displayed several caskets of jewels containing such a treasure of rubies, smaragds, diamonds, and jacinths, as made the eyes of the aged ambassador twinkle with avarice.

"How many horses are there in my stable?" continued Don Beltran; and Muley, the master of the horse, numbered three hundred fully caparisoned; and there was, likewise, armor of the richest sort for as many cavaliers, who followed the banner of this doughty captain.

"I want neither money nor armor," said the ferocious knight; "tell this to the Alfaqui, Jew. And I will keep the child, his daughter, to serve the messes for my dogs, and clean the platters for my scullions."

"Deprive not the old man of his child," here interposed the Knight of Ivanhoe; "bethink thee, brave Don Beltran, she is but an infant in years."

"She is my captive, Sir Knight," replied the surly Don Beltran; "I will do with my own as becomes me."

"Take 200,000 dirhems," cried the Jew; "more!—anything! The Alfaqui will give his life for his child!"

"Come hither, Zutulbe!—come hither, thou Moorish pearl!" yelled the ferocious warrior; "come closer, my pretty black-eyed houri of heathenesse! Hast heard the name of Beltran de Espada y Trabuco?"

"There were three brothers of that name at Alarcos, and my brothers slew the Christian dogs!" said the proud young girl, looking boldly at Don Beltran, who foamed with rage.

"The Moors butchered my mother and her little ones, at midnight, in our castle of Murcia," Beltran said.

"Thy father fled like a craven, as thou didst, Don Beltran!" cried the high-spirited girl.

"By Saint Jago, this is too much!" screamed the infuriated nobleman; and the next moment there was a shriek, and the maiden fell to the ground with Don Beltran's dagger in her side.

"Death is better than dishonor!" cried the child, rolling on the blood-stained marble pavement. "I—I spit upon thee, dog of a Christian!" and with this, and with a savage laugh, she fell back and died.

"Bear back this news, Jew, to the Alfaqui," howled the Don, spurning the beauteous corpse with his foot. "I would not have ransomed her for all the gold in Barbary!" And shuddering, the old Jew left the apartment, which Ivanhoe quitted likewise.

When they were in the outer court, the knight said to the Jew, "Isaac of York, dost thou not know me?" and threw back his hood, and looked at the old man.

The old Jew stared wildly, rushed forward as if to seize his hand, then started back, trembling convulsively, and clutching his withered hands over his face, said, with a burst of grief, "Sir Wilfrid of Ivanhoe!—no, no!—I do not know thee!"

"Holy mother! what has chanced?" said Ivanhoe, in his turn becoming ghastly pale; "where is thy daughter—where is Rebecca?"

"Away from me!" said the old Jew, tottering. "Away Rebecca is—dead!"

When the Disinherited Knight heard that fatal announcement, he fell to the ground senseless, and was for some days as one perfectly distraught with grief. He took no nourishment and uttered no word. For weeks he did not relapse out of his moody silence, and when he came partially to himself again, it was to bid his people to horse, in a hollow voice, and to make a foray against the Moors. Day after day he issued out against these infidels, and did nought but slay and slay. He took no plunder as other knights did, but left that to his followers; he uttered no war-cry, as was the manner of chivalry, and he gave no quarter, insomuch that the "silent knight" became the dread of all the Paynims of Granada and Andalusia, and more fell by his lance than by that of any the most clamorous captains of the troops in arms against them. Thus the tide of battle turned, and the Arab historian, El Makary, recounts how, at the great battle of Al Akab, called by the Spaniards Las Navas, the Christians retrieved their defeat at Alarcos, and absolutely killed half a milllion of Mahometans. Fifty thousand of these, of course, Don Wilfrid took to his own lance; and it was remarked that the melancholy warrior seemed somewhat more easy in spirits after that famous feat of arms.

## CHAPTER VII

THE END OF THE PERFORMANCE

In a short time the terrible Sir Wilfrid of Ivanhoe had killed off so many of the Moors, that though those unbelieving miscreants poured continual reinforcements into Spain from Barbary, they could make no head against the Christian forces, and in fact came into battle quite discouraged at the notion of meeting the dreadful silent knight. It was commonly believed amongst them, that the famous Malek Ric, Richard of England, the conqueror of Saladin, had come to life again, and was battling in the Spanish hosts—that this, his second life, was a charmed one, and his body inaccessible to blow of scimitar or thrust of spear—that after battle he ate the hearts and drank the blood of many young Moors for his supper: a thousand wild legends were told of Ivanhoe, indeed, so that the Morisco warriors came half vanquished into the field, and fell an easy prey to the Spaniards, who cut away among them without mercy. And although none of the Spanish historians whom I have consulted make mention of Sir Wilfrid as the real author of the numerous triumphs which now graced the arms of the good cause, this is not in the least to be wondered at, in a nation that has always been notorious for bragging, and for the non-payment of their debts of gratitude as of their other obligations, and that writes histories of the Peninsular war with the Emperor Napoleon, without making the slightest mention of his Grace the Duke of Wellington, or of the part taken by BRITISH VALOR in that transaction. Well, it must be confessed, on the other hand, that we brag enough of our fathers' feats in those campaigns: but this is not the subject at present under consideration.

To be brief, Ivanhoe made such short work with the unbelievers, that the monarch of Aragon, King Don Jayme, saw himself speedily enabled to besiege the city of Valencia, the last stronghold which the Moors had in his dominions, and garrisoned by many thousands of those infidels under the command of their King Aboo Abdallah Mahommed, son of Yakoobal-Mansoor. The Arabian historian El Makary gives a full account of the military precautions taken by Aboo Abdallah to defend his city; but as I do not wish to make a parade of my learning, or to write a costume novel, I shall pretermit any description of the city under its Moorish governors.

Besides the Turks who inhabited it, there dwelt within its walls great store of those of the Hebrew nation, who were always protected by the Moors during their unbelieving reign in Spain; and who were, as we very well know, the chief physicians, the chief bankers, the chief statesmen, the chief artists and musicians, the chief everything, under the Moorish kings. Thus it is not surprising that the Hebrews, having their money, their liberty, their teeth, their lives, secure under the Mahometan domination, should infinitely prefer it to the Christian sway; beneath which they were liable to be deprived of every one of these benefits.

Among these Hebrews of Valencia, lived a very ancient Israelite—no other than Isaac of York before mentioned, who came into Spain with his daughter, soon after Ivanhoe's marriage, in the third volume of the first part of this history. Isaac was respected by his people for the money which he possessed, and his daughter for her admirable good qualities, her beauty, her charities, and her remarkable medical skill.

The young Emir Aboo Abdallah was so struck by her charms, that though she was considerably older than his Highness, he offered to marry her, and install her as Number 1 of his wives; and Isaac of York would not have objected to the union, (for such mixed marriages were not uncommon between the

Hebrews and Moors in those days,) but Rebecca firmly yet respectfully declined the proposals of the prince, saying that it was impossible she should unite herself with a man of a creed different to her own.

Although Isaac was, probably, not over-well pleased at losing this chance of being father-in-law to a royal highness, yet as he passed among his people for a very strict character, and there were in his family several rabbis of great reputation and severity of conduct, the old gentleman was silenced by this objection of Rebecca's, and the young lady herself applauded by her relatives for her resolute behavior. She took their congratulations in a very frigid manner, and said that it was her wish not to marry at all, but to devote herself to the practice of medicine altogether, and to helping the sick and needy of her people. Indeed, although she did not go to any public meetings, she was as benevolent a creature as the world ever saw: the poor blessed her wherever they knew her, and many benefited by her who guessed not whence her gentle bounty came.

But there are men in Jewry who admire beauty, and, as I have even heard, appreciate money too, and Rebecca had such a quantity of both, that all the most desirable bachelors of the people were ready to bid for her. Ambassadors came from all quarters to propose for her. Her own uncle, the venerable Ben Solomons, with a beard as long as a cashmere goat's, and a reputation for learning and piety which still lives in his nation, quarrelled with his son Moses, the red-haired diamond-merchant of Trebizond, and his son Simeon, the bald bill-broker of Bagdad, each putting in a claim for their cousin. Ben Minories came from London and knelt at her feet; Ben Jochanan arrived from Paris, and thought to dazzle her with the latest waistcoats from the Palais Royal; and Ben Jonah brought her a present of Dutch herrings, and besought her to come back and be Mrs. Ben Jonah at the Hague.

Rebecca temporized as best she might. She thought her uncle was too old. She besought dear Moses and dear Simeon not to quarrel with each other, and offend their father by pressing their suit. Ben Minories from London, she said, was too young, and Jochanan from Paris, she pointed out to Isaac of York, must be a spendthrift, or he would not wear those absurd waistcoats. As for Ben Jonah, she said, she could not bear the notion of tobacco and Dutch herrings: she wished to stay with her papa, her dear papa. In fine, she invented a thousand excuses for delay, and it was plain that marriage was odious to her. The only man whom she received with anything like favor, was young Bevis Marks of London, with whom she was very familiar. But Bevis had come to her with a certain token that had been given to him by an English knight, who saved him from a fagot to which the ferocious Hospitaller Folko of Heydenbraten was about to condemn him. It was but a ring, with an emerald in it, that Bevis knew to be sham, and not worth a groat. Rebecca knew about the value of jewels too; but ah! she valued this one more than all the diamonds in Prester John's turban. She kissed it; she cried over it; she wore it in her bosom always and when she knelt down at night and morning, she held it between her folded hands on her neck. . . . Young Bevis Marks went away finally no better off than the others; the rascal sold to the King of France a handsome ruby, the very size of the bit of glass in Rebecca's ring; but he always said he would rather have had her than ten thousand pounds: and very likely he would, for it was known she would at once have a plum to her fortune.

These delays, however, could not continue for ever; and at a great family meeting held at Passover-time, Rebecca was solemnly ordered to choose a husband out of the gentlemen there present; her aunts pointing out the great kindness which had been shown to her by her father, in permitting her to choose for herself. One aunt was of the Solomon faction, another aunt took Simeon's side, a third most venerable old lady—the head of the family, and a hundred and forty-four years of age—was ready to pronounce a curse upon her, and cast her out, unless she married before the month was over. All the jewelled heads of all the old ladies in council, all the beards of all the family, wagged against her: it must have been an awful sight to witness.

At last, then, Rebecca was forced to speak. "Kinsmen!" she said, turning pale, "when the Prince Abou Abdil asked me in marriage, I told you I would not wed but with one of my own faith."

"She has turned Turk," screamed out the ladies. "She wants to be a princess, and has turned Turk," roared the rabbis.

"Well, well," said Isaac, in rather an appeased tone, "let us hear what the poor girl has got to say. Do you want to marry his royal highness, Rebecca? Say the word, yes or no."

Another groan burst from the rabbis—they cried, shrieked, chattered, gesticulated, furious to lose such a prize; as were the women, that she should reign over them a second Esther.

"Silence," cried out Isaac; "let the girl speak. Speak boldly, Rebecca dear, there's a good girl."

Rebecca was as pale as a stone. She folded her arms on her breast, and felt the ring there. She looked round all the assembly, and then at Isaac. "Father," she said, in a thrilling low steady voice, "I am not of your religion—I am not of the Prince Boabdil's religion—I—I am of HIS religion."

"His! whose, in the name of Moses, girl?" cried Isaac.

Rebecca clasped her hands on her beating chest and looked round with dauntless eyes. "Of his," she said, "who saved my life and your honor: of my dear, dear champion's. I never can be his, but I will be no other's. Give my money to my kinsmen; it is that they long for. Take the dross, Simeon and Solomon, Jonah and Jochanan, and divide it among you, and leave me. I will never be yours, I tell you, never. Do you think, after knowing him and hearing him speak,—after watching him wounded on his pillow, and glorious in battle" (her eyes melted and kindled again as she spoke these words), "I can mate with such as you? Go. Leave me to myself. I am none of yours. I love him—I love him. Fate divides us—long, long miles separate us; and I know we may never meet again. But I love and bless him always. Yes, always. My prayers are his; my faith is his. Yes, my faith is your faith, Wilfrid—Wilfrid! I have no kindred more, —I am a Christian!"

At this last word there was such a row in the assembly, as my feeble pen would in vain endeavor to depict. Old Isaac staggered back in a fit, and nobody took the least notice of him. Groans, curses, yells of men, shrieks of women, filled the room with such a furious jabbering, as might have appalled any heart less stout than Rebecca's; but that brave woman was prepared for all; expecting, and perhaps hoping, that death would be her instant lot. There was but one creature who pitied her, and that was her cousin and father's clerk, little Ben Davids, who was but thirteen, and had only just begun to carry a bag, and whose crying and boo-hooing, as she finished speaking, was drowned in the screams and maledictions of the elder Israelites. Ben Davids was madly in love with his cousin (as boys often are with ladies of twice their age), and he had presence of mind suddenly to knock over the large brazen lamp on the table, which illuminated the angry conclave; then, whispering to Rebecca to go up to her own room and lock herself in, or they would kill her else, he took her hand and led her out.

From that day she disappeared from among her people. The poor and the wretched missed her, and asked for her in vain. Had any violence been done to her, the poorer Jews would have risen and put all

Isaac's family to death; and besides, her old flame, Prince Boabdil, would have also been exceedingly wrathful. She was not killed then, but, so to speak, buried alive, and locked up in Isaac's back-kitchen: an apartment into which scarcely any light entered, and where she was fed upon scanty portions of the most mouldy bread and water. Little Ben Davids was the only person who visited her, and her sole consolation was to talk to him about Ivanhoe, and how good and how gentle he was; how brave and how true; and how he slew the tremendous knight of the Templars, and how he married a lady whom Rebecca scarcely thought worthy of him, but with whom she prayed he might be happy; and of what color his eyes were, and what were the arms on his shield—viz, a tree with the word "Desdichado" written underneath, &c. &c. &c.: all which talk would not have interested little Davids, had it come from anybody else's mouth, but to which he never tired of listening as it fell from her sweet lips.

So, in fact, when old Isaac of York came to negotiate with Don Beltran de Cuchilla for the ransom of the Alfaqui's daughter of Xixona, our dearest Rebecca was no more dead than you and I; and it was in his rage and fury against Ivanhoe that Isaac told that cavalier the falsehood which caused the knight so much pain and such a prodigious deal of bloodshed to the Moors: and who knows, trivial as it may seem, whether it was not that very circumstance which caused the destruction in Spain of the Moorish power?

Although Isaac, we may be sure, never told his daughter that Ivanhoe had cast up again, yet Master Ben Davids did, who heard it from his employer; and he saved Rebecca's life by communicating the intelligence, for the poor thing would have infallibly perished but for this good news. She had now been in prison four years three months and twenty-four days, during which time she had partaken of nothing but bread and water (except such occasional tit-bits as Davids could bring her—and these were few indeed; for old Isaac was always a curmudgeon, and seldom had more than a pair of eggs for his own and Davids' dinner); and she was languishing away, when the news came suddenly to revive her. Then, though in the darkness you could not see her cheeks, they began to bloom again: then her heart began to beat and her blood to flow, and she kissed the ring on her neck a thousand times a day at least; and her constant question was, "Ben Davids! Ben Davids! when is he coming to besiege Valencia?" She knew he would come: and, indeed, the Christians were encamped before the town ere a month was over.

And now, my dear boys and girls, I think I perceive behind that dark scene of the back-kitchen (which is just a simple flat, painted stone-color, that shifts in a minute,) bright streaks of light flashing out, as though they were preparing a most brilliant, gorgeous, and altogether dazzling illumination, with effects never before attempted on any stage. Yes, the fairy in the pretty pink tights and spangled muslin is getting into the brilliant revolving chariot of the realms of bliss.—Yes, most of the fiddlers and trumpeters have gone round from the orchestra to join in the grand triumphal procession, where the whole strength of the company is already assembled, arrayed in costumes of Moorish and Christian chivalry, to celebrate the "Terrible Escalade," the "Rescue of Virtuous Innocence"—the "Grand Entry of the Christians into Valencia"—"Appearance of the Fairy Day-Star," and "Unexampled displays of pyrotechnic festivity." Do you not, I say, perceive that we are come to the end of our history; and, after a quantity of rapid and terrific fighting, brilliant change of scenery, and songs, appropriate or otherwise, are bringing our hero and heroine together? Who wants a long scene at the last? Mammas are putting the girls' cloaks and boas on; papas have gone out to look for the carriage, and left the box-door swinging open, and letting in the cold air: if there WERE any stage-conversation, you could not hear it, for the scuffling of the people who are leaving the pit. See, the orange-women are preparing to retire. To-morrow their play-bills will be as so much waste-paper—so will some of our masterpieces, woe is me: but lo! here we come to Scene the last, and Valencia is besieged and captured by the Christians.

Who is the first on the wall, and who hurls down the green standard of the Prophet? Who chops off the head of the Emir Aboo What-d'ye-call'im, just as the latter has cut over the cruel Don Beltran de Cuchillay &c.? Who, attracted to the Jewish quarter by the shrieks of the inhabitants who are being slain by the Moorish soldiery, and by a little boy by the name of Ben Davids, who recognizes the knight by his shield, finds Isaac of York egorge on a threshold, and clasping a large back-kitchen key? Who but Ivanhoe—who but Wilfrid? "An Ivanhoe to the rescue," he bellows out; he has heard that news from little Ben Davids which makes him sing. And who is it that comes out of the house—trembling—panting —with her arms out—in a white dress—with her hair down—who is it but dear Rebecca? Look, they rush together, and Master Wamba is waving an immense banner over them, and knocks down a circumambient Jew with a ham, which he happens to have in his pocket. . . . As for Rebecca, now her head is laid upon Ivanhoe's heart, I shall not ask to hear what she is whispering, or describe further that scene of meeting; though I declare I am quite affected when I think of it. Indeed I have thought of it any time these five-and-twenty years—ever since, as a boy at school, I commenced the noble study of novels—ever since the day when, lying on sunny slopes of half-holidays, the fair chivalrous figures and beautiful shapes of knights and ladies were visible to me—ever since I grew to love Rebecca, that sweetest creature of the poet's fancy, and longed to see her righted.

That she and Ivanhoe were married, follows of course; for Rowena's promise extorted from him was, that he would never wed a Jewess, and a better Christian than Rebecca now was never said her catechism. Married I am sure they were, and adopted little Cedric; but I don't think they had any other children, or were subsequently very boisterously happy. Of some sort of happiness melancholy is a characteristic, and I think these were a solemn pair, and died rather early.

THE HISTORY OF THE NEXT FRENCH REVOLUTION

[FROM A FORTHCOMING HISTORY OF EUROPE]

CHAPTER I

It is seldom that the historian has to record events more singular than those which occurred during this year, when the Crown of France was battled for by no less than four pretenders, with equal claims, merits, bravery, and popularity. First in the list we place—His Royal Highness Louis Anthony Frederick Samuel Anna Maria, Duke of Brittany, and son of Louis XVI. The unhappy Prince, when a prisoner with his unfortunate parents in the Temple, was enabled to escape from that place of confinement, hidden (for the treatment of the ruffians who guarded him had caused the young Prince to dwindle down astonishingly) in the cocked-hat of the Representative, Roederer. It is well known that, in the troublous revolutionary times, cocked-hats were worn of a considerable size.

He passed a considerable part of his life in Germany; was confined there for thirty years in the dungeons of Spielberg; and, escaping thence to England, was, under pretence of debt, but in reality from political hatred, imprisoned there also in the Tower of London. He must not be confounded with any other of the persons who laid claim to be children of the unfortunate victim of the first Revolution.

The next claimant, Henri of Bordeaux, is better known. In the year 1843 he held his little fugitive court in furnished lodgings, in a forgotten district of London, called Belgrave Square. Many of the nobles of France flocked thither to him, despising the persecutions of the occupant of the throne; and some of the chiefs of the British nobility—among whom may be reckoned the celebrated and chivalrous Duke of Jenkins—aided the adventurous young Prince with their counsels, their wealth, and their valor.

The third candidate was his Imperial Highness Prince John Thomas Napoleon—a fourteenth cousin of the late Emperor; and said by some to be a Prince of the House of Gomersal. He argued justly that, as the immediate relatives of the celebrated Corsican had declined to compete for the crown which was their right, he, Prince John Thomas, being next in succession, was, undoubtedly, heir to the vacant imperial throne. And in support of his claim, he appealed to the fidelity of Frenchmen and the strength of his good sword.

His Majesty Louis Philippe was, it need not be said, the illustrious wielder of the sceptre which the three above-named princes desired to wrest from him. It does not appear that the sagacious monarch was esteemed by his subjects, as such a prince should have been esteemed. The light-minded people, on the contrary, were rather weary than otherwise of his sway. They were not in the least attached to his amiable family, for whom his Majesty with characteristic thrift had endeavored to procure satisfactory allowances. And the leading statesmen of the country, whom his Majesty had disgusted, were suspected of entertaining any but feelings of loyalty towards his house and person.

It was against the above-named pretenders that Louis Philippe (now nearly a hundred years old), a prince amongst sovereigns, was called upon to defend his crown.

The city of Paris was guarded, as we all know, by a hundred and twenty-four forts, of a thousand guns each—provisioned for a considerable time, and all so constructed as to fire, if need were, upon the palace of the Tuileries. Thus, should the mob attack it, as in August 1792, and July 1830, the building could be razed to the ground in an hour; thus, too, the capital was quite secure from foreign invasion. Another defence against the foreigners was the state of the roads. Since the English companies had retired, half a mile only of railroad had been completed in France, and thus any army accustomed, as those of Europe now are, to move at sixty miles an hour, would have been ennuye'd to death before they could have marched from the Rhenish, the Maritime, the Alpine, or the Pyrenean frontier upon the capital of France. The French people, however, were indignant at this defect of communication in their territory, and said, without the least show of reason, that they would have preferred that the five hundred and seventy-five thousand billions of francs which had been expended upon the fortifications should have been laid out in a more peaceful manner. However, behind his forts, the King lay secure.

As it is our aim to depict in as vivid a manner as possible the strange events of the period, the actions, the passions of individuals and parties engaged, we cannot better describe them than by referring to contemporary documents, of which there is no lack. It is amusing at the present day to read in the pages of the Moniteur and the Journal des Debats the accounts of the strange scenes which took place.

The year 1884 had opened very tranquilly. The Court of the Tuileries had been extremely gay. The three-and-twenty youngest Princes of England, sons of her Majesty Victoria, had enlivened the balls by their presence; the Emperor of Russia and family had paid their accustomed visit; and the King of the Belgians had, as usual, made his visit to his royal father-in-law, under pretence of duty and pleasure, but really to demand payment of the Queen of the Belgians' dowry, which Louis Philippe of Orleans still resolutely declined to pay. Who would have thought that in the midst of such festivity danger was lurking rife, in the midst of such quiet, rebellion?

Charenton was the great lunatic asylum of Paris, and it was to this repository that the scornful journalist consigned the pretender to the throne of Louis XVI.

But on the next day, viz. Saturday, the 29th February, the same journal contained a paragraph of a much more startling and serious import; in which, although under a mask of carelessness, it was easy to see the Government alarm.

On Friday, the 28th February, the Journal des Debats contained a paragraph, which did not occasion much sensation at the Bourse, so absurd did its contents seem. It ran as follows:—

"ENCORE UN LOUIS XVII.! A letter from Calais tells us that a strange personage lately landed from England (from Bedlam we believe) has been giving himself out to be the son of the unfortunate Louis XVI. This is the twenty-fourth pretender of the species who has asserted that his father was the august victim of the Temple. Beyond his pretensions, the poor creature is said to be pretty harmless; he is accompanied by one or two old women, who declare they recognize in him the Dauphin; he does not make any attempt to seize upon his throne by force of arms, but waits until heaven shall conduct him to it.

"If his Majesty comes to Paris, we presume he will TAKE UP his quarters in the palace of Charenton.

"We have not before alluded to certain rumors which have been afloat (among the lowest canaille and the vilest estaminets of the metropolis), that a notorious personage—why should we hesitate to mention the name of the Prince John Thomas Napoleon?—has entered France with culpable intentions, and revolutionary views. The Moniteur of this morning, however, confirms the disgraceful fact. A pretender is on our shores; an armed assassin is threatening our peaceful liberties; a wandering, homeless cut-throat is robbing on our highways; and the punishment of his crime awaits him. Let no considerations of the past defer that just punishment; it is the duty of the legislator to provide for THE FUTURE. Let the full powers of the law be brought against him, aided by the stern justice of the public force. Let him be tracked, like a wild beast, to his lair, and meet the fate of one. But the sentence has, ere this, been certainly executed. The brigand, we hear, has been distributing (without any effect) pamphlets among the low ale-houses and peasantry of the department of the Upper Rhine (in which he lurks); and the Police have an easy means of tracking his footsteps.

"Corporal Crane, of the Gendarmerie, is on the track of the unfortunate young man. His attempt will only serve to show the folly of the pretenders, and the love, respect, regard, fidelity, admiration, reverence, and passionate personal attachment in which we hold our beloved sovereign."

"SECOND EDITION!

"CAPTURE OF THE PRINCE.

"A courier has just arrived at the Tuileries with a report that after a scuffle between Corporal Crane and the 'Imperial Army,' in a water-barrel, whither the latter had retreated, victory has remained with the former. A desperate combat ensued in the first place, in a hay-loft, whence the pretender was ejected with immense loss. He is now a prisoner—and we dread to think what his fate may be! It will warn future aspirants, and give Europe a lesson which it is not likely to forget. Above all, it will set beyond a doubt the regard, respect, admiration, reverence, and adoration which we all feel for our sovereign."

"THIRD EDITION.

"A second courier has arrived. The infatuated Crane has made common cause with the Prince, and forever forfeited the respect of Frenchmen. A detachment of the 520th Leger has marched in pursuit of the pretender and his dupes. Go, Frenchmen, go and conquer! Remember that it is our rights you guard, our homes which you march to defend; our laws which are confided to the points of your unsullied bayonets;—above all, our dear, dear sovereign, around whose throne you rally!

"Our feelings overpower us. Men of the 520th, remember your watchword is Gemappes,—your countersign, Valmy."

"The Emperor of Russia and his distinguished family quitted the Tuileries this day. His Imperial Majesty embraced his Majesty the King of the French with tears in his eyes, and conferred upon their RR. HH. the Princes of Nemours and Joinville, the Grand Cross of the Order of the Blue Eagle."

"His Majesty passed a review of the Police force. The venerable monarch was received with deafening cheers by this admirable and disinterested body of men. Those cheers were echoed in all French hearts. Long, long may our beloved Prince be among us to receive them!"


CHAPTER II

HENRY V. AND NAPOLEON III

Sunday, February 30th.

We resume our quotations from the Debats, which thus introduces a third pretender to the throne:—

"Is this distracted country never to have peace? While on Friday we recorded the pretensions of a maniac to the great throne of France; while on Saturday we were compelled to register the culpable attempts of one whom we regard as a ruffian, murderer, swindler, forger, burglar, and common pickpocket, to gain over the allegiance of Frenchmen—it is to-day our painful duty to announce a THIRD invasion—yes, a third invasion. The wretched, superstitious, fanatic Duke of Bordeaux has landed at Nantz, and has summoned the Vendeans and the Bretons to mount the white cockade.

"Grand Dieu! are we not happy under the tricolor? Do we not repose under the majestic shadow of the best of kings? Is there any name prouder than that of Frenchman; any subject more happy than that of our sovereign? Does not the whole French family adore their father? Yes. Our lives, our hearts, our blood, our fortune, are at his disposal: it was not in vain that we raised, it is not the first time we have rallied round, the august throne of July. The unhappy Duke is most likely a prisoner by this time; and the martial court which shall be called upon to judge one infamous traitor and pretender, may at the same moment judge another. Away with both! let the ditch of Vincennes (which has been already fatal to his race) receive his body, too, and with it the corpse of the other pretender. Thus will a great crime be wiped out of history, and the manes of a slaughtered martyr avenged!

"One word more. We hear that the Duke of Jenkins accompanies the descendant of Caroline of Naples. An ENGLISH DUKE, entendez-vous! An English Duke, great heaven! and the Princes of England still dancing in our royal halls! Where, where will the perfidy of Albion end?"

"The King reviewed the third and fourth battalions of Police. The usual heart-rending cheers accompanied the monarch, who looked younger than ever we saw him—ay, as young as when he faced the Austrian cannon at Valmy and scattered their squadrons at Gemappes.

"Rations of liquor, and crosses of the Legion of Honor, were distributed to all the men.

"The English Princes quitted the Tuileries in twenty-three coaches-and-four. They were not rewarded with crosses of the Legion of Honor. This is significant."

"The Dukes of Joinville and Nemours left the palace for the departments of the Loire and Upper Rhine, where they will take the command of the troops. The Joinville regiment—Cavalerie de la Marine—is one of the finest in the service."

"Orders have been given to arrest the fanatic who calls himself Duke of Brittany, and who has been making some disturbances in the Pas de Calais."

"ANECDOTE OF HIS MAJESTY.—At the review of troops (Police) yesterday, his Majesty, going up to one old grognard and pulling him by the ear, said, 'Wilt thou have a cross or another ration of wine?' The old hero, smiling archly, answered, 'Sire, a brave man can gain a cross any day of battle, but it is hard for him sometimes to get a drink of wine.' We need not say that he had his drink, and the generous sovereign sent him the cross and ribbon too."

On the next day, the Government journals began to write in rather a despondent tone regarding the progress of the pretenders to the throne. In spite of their big talking, anxiety is clearly manifested, as appears from the following remarks of the Debats:—

"The courier from the Rhine department," says the Debats, "brings us the following astounding Proclamation:—

"'Strasburg, xxii. Nivose: Decadi. 92nd year of the Republic, one and indivisible. We, John Thomas Napoleon, by the constitutions of the Empire, Emperor of the French Republic, to our marshals, generals, officers, and soldiers, greeting:

"'Soldiers!

"'From the summit of the Pyramids forty centuries look down upon you. The sun of Austerlitz has risen once more. The Guard dies, but never surrenders. My eagles, flying from steeple to steeple, never shall droop till they perch on the towers of Notre Dame.

"'Soldiers! the child of YOUR FATHER has remained long in exile. I have seen the fields of Europe where your laurels are now withering, and I have communed with the dead who repose beneath them. They ask where are our children? Where is France? Europe no longer glitters with the shine of its triumphant bayonets—echoes no more with the shouts of its victorious cannon. Who could reply to such a question save with a blush?—And does a blush become the cheeks of Frenchmen?

"'No. Let us wipe from our faces that degrading mark of shame. Come, as of old, and rally round my eagles! You have been subject to fiddling prudence long enough. Come, worship now at the shrine of Glory! You have been promised liberty, but you have had none. I will endow you with the true, the real freedom. When your ancestors burst over the Alps, were they not free? Yes; free to conquer. Let us imitate the example of those indomitable myriads; and, flinging a defiance to Europe, once more trample over her; march in triumph into her prostrate capitals, and bring her kings with her treasures at our feet. This is the liberty worthy of Frenchmen.

"'Frenchmen! I promise you that the Rhine shall be restored to you; and that England shall rank no more among the nations. I will have a marine that shall drive her ships from the seas; a few of my brave regiments will do the rest. Henceforth, the traveller in that desert island shall ask, "Was it this wretched corner of the world that for a thousand years defied Frenchmen?"

"'Frenchmen, up and rally!—I have flung my banner to the breezes; 'tis surrounded by the faithful and the brave. Up, and let our motto be, LIBERTY, EQUALITY, WAR ALL OVER THE WORLD!

"'NAPOLEON III.

"'The Marshal of the Empire, HARICOT.'

"Such is the Proclamation! such the hopes that a brutal-minded and bloody adventurer holds out to our country. 'War all over the world,' is the cry of the savage demon; and the fiends who have rallied round him echo it in concert. We were not, it appears, correct in stating that a corporal's guard had been sufficient to seize upon the marauder, when the first fire would have served to conclude his miserable life. But, like a hideous disease, the contagion has spread; the remedy must be dreadful. Woe to those on whom it will fall!

"His Royal Highness the Prince of Joinville, Admiral of France, has hastened, as we before stated, to the disturbed districts, and takes with him his Cavalerie de la Marine. It is hard to think that the blades of those chivalrous heroes must be buried in the bosoms of Frenchmen: but so be it: it is those monsters who have asked for blood, not we. It is those ruffians who have begun the quarrel, not we. WE remain calm and hopeful, reposing under the protection of the dearest and best of sovereigns.

"The wretched pretender, who called himself Duke of Brittany, has been seized, according to our prophecy: he was brought before the Prefect of Police yesterday, and his insanity being proved beyond a doubt, he has been consigned to a strait-waistcoat at Charenton. So may all incendiary enemies of our Government be overcome!

"His Royal Highness the Duke of Nemours is gone into the department of the Loire, where he will speedily put an end to the troubles in the disturbed districts of the Bocage and La Vendee. The foolish young Prince, who has there raised his standard, is followed, we hear, by a small number of wretched persons, of whose massacre we expect every moment to receive the news. He too has issued his Proclamation, and our readers will smile at its contents:

"'WE HENRY, Fifth of the Name, King of France and Navarre, to all whom it may concern, greeting:

"'After years of exile we have once more unfurled in France the banner of the lilies. Once more the white plume of Henri IV. floats in the crest of his little son (petit fils)! Gallant nobles! worthy burgesses! honest commons of my realm, I call upon you to rally round the oriflamme of France, and summon the ban arriereban of my kingdoms. To my faithful Bretons I need not appeal. The country of Duguesclin has loyalty for an heirloom! To the rest of my subjects, my atheist misguided subjects, their father makes one last appeal. Come to me, my children! your errors shall be forgiven. Our Holy Father, the Pope, shall intercede for you. He promised it when, before my departure on this expedition, I kissed his inviolable toe!

"'Our afflicted country cries aloud for reforms. The infamous universities shall be abolished. Education shall no longer be permitted. A sacred and wholesome inquisition shall be established. My faithful nobles shall pay no more taxes. All the venerable institutions of our country shall be restored as they existed before 1788. Convents and monasteries again shall ornament our country, the calm nurseries of saints and holy women! Heresy shall be extirpated with paternal severity, and our country shall be free once more.

"'His Majesty the King of Ireland, my august ally, has sent, under the command of His Royal Highness Prince Daniel, his Majesty's youngest son, an irresistible IRISH BRIGADE, to co-operate in the good work. His Grace the Lion of Judah, the canonized patriarch of Tuam, blessed their green banner before they set forth. Henceforth may the lilies and the harp be ever twined together. Together we will make a crusade against the infidels of Albion, and raze their heretic domes to the ground. Let our cry be, Vive la France! down with England! Montjoie St. Denis!

"'BY THE KING.

"'The Secretary of State and Grand Inquisitor. . . LA ROUE. The Marshal of France. . . POMADOUR DE L'AILE DE PIGEON. The General Commander-in-Chief of the Irish Brigade in the service of his Most Christian Majesty. . . DANIEL, PRINCE OF BALLYBUNION.

'HENRI.'"

"His Majesty reviewed the admirable Police force, and held a council of Ministers in the afternoon. Measures were concerted for the instant putting down of the disturbances in the departments of the Rhine and Loire, and it is arranged that on the capture of the pretenders, they shall be lodged in separate cells in the prison of the Luxembourg: the apartments are already prepared, and the officers at their posts.

"The grand banquet that was to be given at the palace to-day to the diplomatic body, has been put off; all the ambassadors being attacked with illness, which compels them to stay at home."

"The ambassadors despatched couriers to their various Governments."

"His Majesty the King of the Belgians left the palace of the Tuileries."

CHAPTER III

We will now resume the narrative, and endeavor to compress, in a few comprehensive pages, the facts which are more diffusely described in the print from which we have quoted.

It was manifest, then, that the troubles in the departments were of a serious nature, and that the forces gathered round the two pretenders to the crown were considerable. They had their supporters too in Paris—as what party indeed has not? and the venerable occupant of the throne was in a state of considerable anxiety, and found his declining years by no means so comfortable as his virtues and great age might have warranted.

His paternal heart was the more grieved when he thought of the fate reserved to his children, grandchildren, and great-grandchildren, now sprung up around him in vast numbers. The King's grandson, the Prince Royal, married to a Princess of the house of Schlippen-Schloppen, was the father of fourteen children, all handsomely endowed with pensions by the State. His brother, the Count D'Eu, was similarly blessed with a multitudinous offspring. The Duke of Nemours had no children; but the Princes of Joinville, Aumale, and Montpensier (married to the Princesses Januaria and Februaria, of Brazil, and the Princess of the United States of America, erected into a monarchy, 4th July, 1856, under the Emperor Duff Green I.) were the happy fathers of immense families—all liberally apportioned by the Chambers, which had long been entirely subservient to his Majesty Louis Philippe.

The Duke of Aumale was King of Algeria, having married (in the first instance) the Princess Badroulboudour, a daughter of his Highness Abd-El-Kader. The Prince of Joinville was adored by the nation, on account of his famous victory over the English fleet under the command of Admiral the Prince of Wales, whose ship, the "Richard Cobden," of 120 guns, was taken by the "Belle-Poule" frigate of 36; on which occasion forty-five other ships of war and 79 steam-frigates struck their colors to about one-fourth the number of the heroic French navy. The victory was mainly owing to the gallantry of the celebrated French horse-marines, who executed several brilliant charges under the orders of the intrepid Joinville; and though the Irish Brigade, with their ordinary modesty, claimed the honors of the day, yet, as only three of that nation were present in the action, impartial history must award the palm to the intrepid sons of Gaul.

With so numerous a family quartered on the nation, the solicitude of the admirable King may be conceived, lest a revolution should ensue, and fling them on the world once more. How could he support so numerous a family? Considerable as his wealth was (for he was known to have amassed about a hundred and thirteen billions, which were lying in the caves of the Tuileries), yet such a sum was quite insignificant, when divided among his progeny; and, besides, he naturally preferred getting from the nation as much as his faithful people could possibly afford.

Seeing the imminency of the danger, and that money, well applied, is often more efficacious than the conqueror's sword, the King's Ministers were anxious that he should devote a part of his savings to the carrying on of the war. But, with the cautiousness of age, the monarch declined this offer; he preferred, he said, throwing himself upon his faithful people, who, he was sure, would meet, as became them, the coming exigency. The Chambers met his appeal with their usual devotion. At a solemn convocation of those legislative bodies, the King, surrounded by his family, explained the circumstances and the danger. His Majesty, his family, his Ministers, and the two Chambers, then burst into tears, according to immemorial usage, and raising their hands to the ceiling, swore eternal fidelity to the dynasty and to France, and embraced each other affectingly all round.

It need not be said that in the course of that evening two hundred Deputies of the Left left Paris, and joined the Prince John Thomas Napoleon, who was now advanced as far as Dijon: two hundred and fifty-three (of the Right, the Centre, and Round the Corner,) similarly quitted the capital to pay their homage to the Duke of Bordeaux. They were followed, according to their several political predilections, by the various Ministers and dignitaries of the State. The only Minister who remained in Paris was Marshal Thiers, Prince of Waterloo (he had defeated the English in the very field where they had obtained formerly a success, though the victory was as usual claimed by the Irish Brigade); but age had ruined the health and diminished the immense strength of that gigantic leader, and it is said his only reason for remaining in Paris was because a fit of the gout kept him in bed.

The capital was entirely tranquil. The theatres and cafes were open as usual, and the masked balls attended with great enthusiasm: confiding in their hundred and twenty-four forts, the light-minded people had nothing to fear.

Except in the way of money, the King left nothing undone to conciliate his people. He even went among them with his umbrella; but they were little touched with that mark of confidence. He shook hands with everybody; he distributed crosses of the Legion of Honor in such multitudes, that red ribbon rose two hundred per cent in the market (by which his Majesty, who speculated in the article, cleared a tolerable sum of money). But these blandishments and honors had little effect upon an apathetic people; and the enemy of the Orleans dynasty, the fashionable young nobles of the Henriquinquiste party, wore gloves perpetually, for fear (they said) that they should be obliged to shake hands with the best of kings; while the republicans adopted coats without button-holes, lest they should be forced to hang red ribbons in them. The funds did not fluctuate in the least.

The proclamations of the several pretenders had had their effect. The young men of the schools and the estaminets (celebrated places of public education) allured by the noble words of Prince Napoleon, "Liberty, equality, war all over the world!" flocked to his standard in considerable numbers: while the noblesse naturally hastened to offer their allegiance to the legitimate descendant of Saint Louis.

And truly, never was there seen a more brilliant chivalry than that collected round the gallant Prince Henry! There was not a man in his army but had lacquered boots and fresh white kid-gloves at morning and evening parade. The fantastic and effeminate but brave and faithful troops were numbered off into different legions: there was the Fleur-d'Orange regiment; the Eau-de-Rose battalion; the Violet-Pomatum volunteers; the Eau-de-Cologne cavalry—according to the different scents which they affected. Most of the warriors wore lace ruffles; all powder and pigtails, as in the real days of chivalry. A band of heavy dragoons under the command of Count Alfred de Horsay made themselves conspicuous for their discipline, cruelty, and the admirable cut of their coats; and with these celebrated horsemen came from England the illustrious Duke of Jenkins with his superb footmen. They were all six feet high. They all wore bouquets of the richest flowers: they wore bags, their hair slightly powdered, brilliant shoulder-knots, and cocked-hats laced with gold. They wore the tight knee-pantaloon of velveteen peculiar to this portion of the British infantry: and their legs were so superb, that the Duke of Bordeaux, embracing with tears their admirable leader on parade, said, "Jenkins, France never saw such calves until now." The weapon of this tremendous militia was an immense club or cane, reaching from the sole of the foot to the nose, and heavily mounted with gold. Nothing could stand before this terrific weapon, and the breast-plates and plumed morions of the French cuirassiers would have been undoubtedly crushed beneath them, had they ever met in mortal combat. Between this part of the Prince's forces and the Irish auxiliaries there was a deadly animosity. Alas, there always is such in camps! The sons of Albion had not forgotten the day when the children of Erin had been subject to their devastating sway.

The uniform of the latter was various—the rich stuff called corps-du-roy (worn by Coeur de Lion at Agincourt) formed their lower habiliments for the most part: the national frieze* yielded them tail-coats. The latter was generally torn in a fantastic manner at the elbows, skirts, and collars, and fastened with every variety of button, tape, and string. Their weapons were the caubeen, the alpeen, and the doodeen of the country—the latter a short but dreadful weapon of offence. At the demise of the venerable Theobald Mathew, the nation had laid aside its habit of temperance, and universal intoxication betokened their grief; it became afterwards their constant habit. Thus do men ever return to the haunts of their childhood: such a power has fond memory over us! The leaders of this host seem to have been, however, an effeminate race; they are represented by contemporary historians as being passionately fond of FLYING KITES. Others say they went into battle armed with "bills," no doubt rude weapons; for it is stated that foreigners could never be got to accept them in lieu of their own arms. The Princes of Mayo, Donegal, and Connemara, marched by the side of their young and royal chieftain, the Prince of Ballybunion, fourth son of Daniel the First, King of the Emerald Isle.

* Were these in any way related to the chevaux-de-frise on which the French cavalry were mounted?

Two hosts then, one under the Eagles, and surrounded by the republican imperialists, the other under the antique French Lilies, were marching on the French capital. The Duke of Brittany, too, confined in the lunatic asylum of Charenton, found means to issue a protest against his captivity, which caused only derision in the capital. Such was the state of the empire, and such the clouds that were gathering round the Sun of Orleans!

CHAPTER IV

THE BATTLE OF RHEIMS

It was not the first time that the King had had to undergo misfortunes; and now, as then, he met them like a man. The Prince of Joinville was not successful in his campaign against the Imperial Pretender: and that bravery which had put the British fleet to flight, was found, as might be expected, insufficient against the irresistible courage of native Frenchmen. The Horse Marines, not being on their own element, could not act with their usual effect. Accustomed to the tumult of the swelling seas, they were easily unsaddled on terra firma and in the Champagne country.

It was literally in the Champagne country that the meeting between the troops under Joinville and Prince Napoleon took place! for both armies had reached Rheims, and a terrific battle was fought underneath the walls. For some time nothing could dislodge the army of Joinville, entrenched in the champagne cellars of Messrs. Ruinart, Moet, and others; but making too free with the fascinating liquor, the army at length became entirely drunk: on which the Imperialists, rushing into the cellars, had an easy victory over them; and, this done, proceeded to intoxicate themselves likewise.

The Prince of Joinville, seeing the deroute of his troops, was compelled with a few faithful followers to fly towards Paris, and Prince Napoleon remained master of the field of battle. It is needless to recapitulate the bulletin which he published the day after the occasion, so soon as he and his secretaries were in a condition to write: eagles, pyramids, rainbows, the sun of Austerlitz, &c., figured in the proclamation, in close imitation of his illustrious uncle. But the great benefit of the action was this: on arousing from their intoxication, the late soldiers of Joinville kissed and embraced their comrades of the Imperial army, and made common cause with them.

"Soldiers!" said the Prince, on reviewing them the second day after the action, "the Cock is a gallant bird; but he makes way for the Eagle! Your colors are not changed. Ours floated on the walls of Moscow—yours on the ramparts of Constantine; both are glorious. Soldiers of Joinville! we give you welcome, as we would welcome your illustrious leader, who destroyed the fleets of Albion. Let him join us! We will march together against that perfidious enemy.

"But, Soldiers! intoxication dimmed the laurels of yesterday's glorious day! Let us drink no more of the fascinating liquors of our native Champagne. Let us remember Hannibal and Capua; and, before we plunge into dissipation, that we have Rome still to conquer!

"Soldiers! Seltzer-water is good after too much drink. Wait awhile, and your Emperor will lead you into a Seltzer-water country. Frenchmen! it lies BEYOND THE RHINE!"

Deafening shouts of "Vive l'Empereur!" saluted this allusion of the Prince, and the army knew that their natural boundary should be restored to them. The compliments to the gallantry of the Prince of Joinville likewise won all hearts, and immensely advanced the Prince's cause. The Journal des Debats did not know which way to turn. In one paragraph it called the Emperor "a sanguinary tyrant, murderer, and pickpocket;" in a second it owned he was "a magnanimous rebel, and worthy of forgiveness;" and, after proclaiming "the brilliant victory of the Prince of Joinville," presently denominated it a "funeste journee."

The next day the Emperor, as we may now call him, was about to march on Paris, when Messrs. Ruinart and Moet were presented, and requested to be paid for 300,000 bottles of wine. "Send three hundred thousand more to the Tuileries," said the Prince, sternly: "our soldiers will be thirsty when they reach Paris." And taking Moet with him as a hostage, and promising Ruinart that he would have him shot unless he obeyed, with trumpets playing and eagles glancing in the sun, the gallant Imperial army marched on their triumphant way.


CHAPTER V

THE BATTLE OF TOURS

We have now to record the expedition of the Prince of Nemours against his advancing cousin, Henry V. His Royal Highness could not march against the enemy with such a force as he would have desired to bring against them; for his royal father, wisely remembering the vast amount of property he had stowed away under the Tuileries, refused to allow a single soldier to quit the forts round the capital, which thus was defended by one hundred and forty-four thousand guns (eighty-four-pounders), and four hundred and thirty-two thousand men:—little enough, when one considers that there were but three men to a gun. To provision this immense army, and a population of double the amount within the walls, his Majesty caused the country to be scoured for fifty miles round, and left neither ox, nor ass, nor blade of grass. When appealed to by the inhabitants of the plundered district, the royal Philip replied, with tears in his eyes, that his heart bled for them—that they were his children—that every cow taken from the meanest peasant was like a limb torn from his own body; but that duty must be done, that the interests of the country demanded the sacrifice, and that in fact, they might go to the deuce. This the unfortunate creatures certainly did.

The theatres went on as usual within the walls. The Journal des Debats stated every day that the pretenders were taken; the Chambers sat—such as remained—and talked immensely about honor, dignity, and the glorious revolution of July; and the King, as his power was now pretty nigh absolute over them, thought this a good opportunity to bring in a bill for doubling his children's allowances all round.

Meanwhile the Duke of Nemours proceeded on his march; and as there was nothing left within fifty miles of Paris wherewith to support his famished troops, it may be imagined that he was forced to ransack the next fifty miles in order to maintain them. He did so. But the troops were not such as they should have been, considering the enemy with whom they had to engage.

The fact is, that most of the Duke's army consisted of the National Guard; who, in a fit of enthusiasm, and at the cry of "LA PATRIE EN DANGER" having been induced to volunteer, had been eagerly accepted by his Majesty, anxious to lessen as much as possible the number of food-consumers in his beleaguered capital. It is said even that he selected the most gormandizing battalions of the civic force to send forth against the enemy: viz, the grocers, the rich bankers, the lawyers, &c. Their parting with their families was very affecting. They would have been very willing to recall their offer of marching, but companies of stern veterans closing round them, marched them to the city gates, which were closed upon them; and thus perforce they were compelled to move on. As long as he had a bottle of brandy and a couple of sausages in his holsters, the General of the National Guard, Odillon Barrot, talked with tremendous courage. Such was the power of his eloquence over the troops, that, could he have come up with the enemy while his victuals lasted, the issue of the combat might have been very different. But in the course of the first day's march he finished both the sausages and the brandy, and became quite uneasy, silent, and crest-fallen.

It was on the fair plains of Touraine, by the banks of silver Loire, that the armies sat down before each other, and the battle was to take place which had such an effect upon the fortunes of France. 'Twas a brisk day of March: the practised valor of Nemours showed him at once what use to make of the army under his orders, and having enfiladed his National Guard battalions, and placed his artillery in echelons, he formed his cavalry into hollow squares on the right and left of his line, flinging out a cloud of howitzers to fall back upon the main column. His veteran infantry he formed behind his National Guard—politely hinting to Odillon Barrot, who wished to retire under pretence of being exceedingly unwell, that the regular troops would bayonet the National Guard if they gave way an inch: on which their General, turning very pale, demurely went back to his post. His men were dreadfully discouraged; they had slept on the ground all night; they regretted their homes and their comfortable nightcaps in the Rue St. Honore: they had luckily fallen in with a flock of sheep and a drove of oxen at Tours the day before; but what were these, compared to the delicacies of Chevet's or three courses at Vefour's? They mournfully cooked their steaks and cutlets on their ramrods, and passed a most wretched night.

The army of Henry was encamped opposite to them for the most part in better order. The noble cavalry regiments found a village in which they made themselves pretty comfortable, Jenkins's Foot taking possession of the kitchens and garrets of the buildings. The Irish Brigade, accustomed to lie abroad, were quartered in some potato fields, where they sang Moore's melodies all night. There were, besides the troops regular and irregular, about three thousand priests and abbes with the army, armed with scourging-whips, and chanting the most lugubrious canticles: these reverend men were found to be a hindrance rather than otherwise to the operations of the regular forces.

It was a touching sight, on the morning before the battle, to see the alacrity with which Jenkins's regiment sprung up at the FIRST reveille of the bell, and engaged (the honest fellows!) in offices almost menial for the benefit of their French allies. The Duke himself set the example, and blacked to a nicety the boots of Henri. At half-past ten, after coffee, the brilliant warriors of the cavalry were ready; their clarions rung to horse, their banners were given to the wind, their shirt-collars were exquisitely starched, and the whole air was scented with the odors of their pomatums and pocket-handkerchiefs.

Jenkins had the honor of holding the stirrup for Henri. "My faithful Duke!" said the Prince, pulling him by the shoulder-knot, "thou art always at THY POST." "Here, as in Wellington Street, sire," said the hero, blushing. And the Prince made an appropriate speech to his chivalry, in which allusions to the lilies, Saint Louis, Bayard and Henri Quatre, were, as may be imagined, not spared. "Ho! standard-bearer!" the Prince concluded, "fling out my oriflamme. Noble gents of France, your King is among you to-day!"

Then turning to the Prince of Ballybunion, who had been drinking whiskey-punch all night with the Princes of Donegal and Connemara, "Prince," he said, "the Irish Brigade has won every battle in the French history—we will not deprive you of the honor of winning this. You will please to commence the attack with your brigade." Bending his head until the green plumes of his beaver mingled with the mane of the Shetland pony which he rode, the Prince of Ireland trotted off with his aides-de-camp; who rode the same horses, powerful grays, with which a dealer at Nantz had supplied them on their and the Prince's joint bill at three months.

The gallant sons of Erin had wisely slept until the last minute in their potato-trenches, but rose at once at the summons of their beloved Prince. Their toilet was the work of a moment—a single shake and it was done. Rapidly forming into a line, they advanced headed by their Generals,—who, turning their steeds into a grass-field, wisely determined to fight on foot. Behind them came the line of British foot under the illustrious Jenkins, who marched in advance perfectly collected, and smoking a Manilla cigar. The cavalry were on the right and left of the infantry, prepared to act in pontoon, in echelon, or in ricochet, as occasion might demand. The Prince rode behind, supported by his Staff, who were almost all of them bishops, archdeacons, or abbes; and the body of ecclesiastics followed, singing to the sound, or rather howl, of serpents and trombones, the Latin canticles of the Reverend Franciscus O'Mahony, lately canonized under the name of Saint Francis of Cork.

The advanced lines of the two contending armies were now in presence—the National Guard of Orleans and the Irish Brigade. The white belts and fat paunches of the Guard presented a terrific appearance; but it might have been remarked by the close observer, that their faces were as white as their belts, and the long line of their bayonets might be seen to quiver. General Odillon Barrot, with a cockade as large as a pancake, endeavored to make a speech: the words honneur, patrie, Francais, champ de bataille might be distinguished; but the General was dreadfully flustered, and was evidently more at home in the Chamber of Deputies than in the field of war.

The Prince of Ballybunion, for a wonder, did not make a speech. "Boys," said he, "we've enough talking at the Corn Exchange; bating's the word now." The Green-Islanders replied with a tremendous hurroo, which sent terror into the fat bosoms of the French.

"Gentlemen of the National Guard," said the Prince, taking off his hat and bowing to Odillon Barrot, "will ye be so igsthramely obleeging as to fire first." This he said because it had been said at Fontenoy, but chiefly because his own men were only armed with shillelaghs, and therefore could not fire.

But this proposal was very unpalatable to the National Guardsmen: for though they understood the musket-exercise pretty well, firing was the thing of all others they detested—the noise, and the kick of the gun, and the smell of the powder being very unpleasant to them. "We won't fire," said Odillon Barrot, turning round to Colonel Saugrenue and his regiment of the line—which, it may be remembered, was formed behind the National Guard.

"Then give them the bayonet," said the Colonel, with a terrific oath. "Charge, corbleu!"

At this moment, and with the most dreadful howl that ever was heard, the National Guard was seen to rush forwards wildly, and with immense velocity, towards the foe. The fact is, that the line regiment behind them, each selecting his man, gave a poke with his bayonet between the coat-tails of the Nationals, and those troops bounded forward with an irresistible swiftness.

Nothing could withstand the tremendous impetus of that manoeuvre. The Irish Brigade was scattered before it, as chaff before the wind. The Prince of Ballybunion had barely time to run Odillon Barrot through the body, when he too was borne away in the swift rout. They scattered tumultuously, and fled for twenty miles without stopping. The Princes of Donegal and Connemara were taken prisoners; but though they offered to give bills at three months, and for a hundred thousand pounds, for their ransom, the offer was refused, and they were sent to the rear; when the Duke of Nemours, hearing they were Irish Generals, and that they had been robbed of their ready money by his troops, who had taken them prisoners, caused a comfortable breakfast to be supplied to them, and lent them each a sum of money. How generous are men in success!—the Prince of Orleans was charmed with the conduct of his National Guards, and thought his victory secure. He despatched a courier to Paris with the brief words, "We met the enemy before Tours. The National Guard has done its duty. The troops of the pretender are routed. Vive le Roi!" The note, you may be sure, appeared in the Journal des Debats, and the editor, who only that morning had called Henri V. "a great prince, an august exile," denominated him instantly a murderer, slave, thief, cut-throat, pickpocket, and burglar.

CHAPTER VI

THE ENGLISH UNDER JENKINS

But the Prince had not calculated that there was a line of British infantry behind the routed Irish Brigade. Borne on with the hurry of the melee, flushed with triumph, puffing and blowing with running, and forgetting, in the intoxication of victory, the trifling bayonet-pricks which had impelled them to the charge, the conquering National Guardsmen found themselves suddenly in presence of Jenkins's Foot.

They halted all in a huddle, like a flock of sheep.

"UP, FOOT, AND AT THEM!" were the memorable words of the Duke Jenkins, as, waving his baton, he pointed towards the enemy, and with a tremendous shout the stalwart sons of England rushed on!—Down went plume and cocked-hat, down went corporal and captain, down went grocer and tailor, under the long staves of the indomitable English Footmen. "A Jenkins! a Jenkins!" roared the Duke, planting a blow which broke the aquiline nose of Major Arago, the celebrated astronomer. "St. George for Mayfair!" shouted his followers, strewing the plain with carcasses. Not a man of the Guard escaped; they fell like grass before the mower.

"They are gallant troops, those yellow-plushed Anglais," said the Duke of Nemours, surveying them with his opera-glass. "'Tis a pity they will all be cut up in half an hour. Concombre! take your dragoons, and do it!" "Remember Waterloo, boys!" said Colonel Concombre, twirling his moustache, and a thousand sabres flashed in the sun, and the gallant hussars prepared to attack the Englishmen.

Jenkins, his gigantic form leaning on his staff, and surveying the havoc of the field, was instantly aware of the enemy's manoeuvre. His people were employed rifling the pockets of the National Guard, and had made a tolerable booty, when the great Duke, taking a bell out of his pocket, (it was used for signals in his battalion in place of fife or bugle,) speedily called his scattered warriors together. "Take the muskets of the Nationals," said he. They did so. "Form in square, and prepare to receive cavalry!" By the time Concombre's regiment arrived, he found a square of bristling bayonets with Britons behind them!

The Colonel did not care to attempt to break that tremendous body. "Halt!" said he to his men.

"Fire!" screamed Jenkins, with eagle swiftness; but the guns of the National Guard not being loaded, did not in consequence go off. The hussars gave a jeer of derision, but nevertheless did not return to the attack, and seeing some of the Legitimist cavalry at hand, prepared to charge upon them.

The fate of those carpet warriors was soon decided. The Millefleur regiment broke before Concombre's hussars instantaneously; the Eau-de-Rose dragoons stuck spurs into their blood horses, and galloped far out of reach of the opposing cavalry; the Eau-de-Cologne lancers fainted to a man, and the regiment of Concombre, pursuing its course, had actually reached the Prince and his aides-de-camp, when the clergymen coming up formed gallantly round the oriflamme, and the bassoons and serpents braying again, set up such a shout of canticles, and anathemas, and excommunications, that the horses of Concombre's dragoons in turn took fright, and those warriors in their turn broke and fled. As soon as they turned, the Vendean riflemen fired amongst them and finished them: the gallant Concombre fell; the intrepid though diminutive Cornichon, his major, was cut down; Cardon was wounded a la moelle, and the wife of the fiery Navet was that day a widow. Peace to the souls of the brave! In defeat or in victory, where can the soldier find a more fitting resting-place than the glorious field of carnage? Only a few disorderly and dispirited riders of Concombre's regiment reached Tours at night. They had left it but the day before, a thousand disciplined and high-spirited men!

Knowing how irresistible a weapon is the bayonet in British hands, the intrepid Jenkins determined to carry on his advantage, and charged the Saugrenue light infantry (now before him) with COLD STEEL. The Frenchmen delivered a volley, of which a shot took effect in Jenkins's cockade, but did not abide the crossing of the weapons. "A Frenchman dies, but never surrenders," said Saugrenue, yielding up his sword, and his whole regiment were stabbed, trampled down, or made prisoners. The blood of the Englishmen rose in the hot encounter. Their curses were horrible; their courage tremendous. "On! on!" hoarsely screamed they; and a second regiment met them and was crushed, pounded in the hurtling, grinding encounter. "A Jenkins, a Jenkins!" still roared the heroic Duke: "St. George for Mayfair!" The Footmen of England still yelled their terrific battle-cry, "Hurra, hurra!" On they went; regiment after regiment was annihilated, until, scared at the very trample of the advancing warriors, the dismayed troops of France screaming fled. Gathering his last warriors round about him, Nemours determined to make a last desperate effort. 'Twas vain: the ranks met; the next moment the truncheon of the Prince of Orleans was dashed from his hand by the irresistible mace of the Duke Jenkins; his horse's shins were broken by the same weapon. Screaming with agony the animal fell. Jenkins's hand was at the Duke's collar in a moment, and had he not gasped out, "Je me rends!" he would have been throttled in that dreadful grasp!

Three hundred and forty-two standards, seventy-nine regiments, their baggage, ammunition, and treasure-chests, fell into the hands of the victorious Duke. He had avenged the honor of Old England; and himself presenting the sword of the conquered Nemours to Prince Henri, who now came up, the Prince bursting into tears, fell on his neck and said, "Duke, I owe my crown to my patron saint and you." It was indeed a glorious victory: but what will not British valor attain?

The Duke of Nemours, having despatched a brief note to Paris, saying, "Sire, all is lost except honor!" was sent off in confinement; and in spite of the entreaties of his captor, was hardly treated with decent politeness. The priests and the noble regiments who rode back when the affair was over, were for having the Prince shot at once, and murmured loudly against "cet Anglais brutal" who interposed in behalf of the prisoner. Henri V. granted the Prince his life; but, no doubt misguided by the advice of his noble and ecclesiastical counsellors, treated the illustrious English Duke with marked coldness, and did not even ask him to supper that night.

"Well!" said Jenkins, "I and my merry men can sup alone." And, indeed, having had the pick of the plunder of about 28,000 men, they had wherewithal to make themselves pretty comfortable. The prisoners (25,403) were all without difficulty induced to assume the white cockade. Most of them had those marks of loyalty ready sewn in their flannel-waistcoats, where they swore they had worn them ever since 1830. This we may believe, and we will; but the Prince Henri was too politic or too good-humored in the moment of victory, to doubt the sincerity of his new subjects' protestations, and received the Colonels and Generals affably at his table.

The next morning a proclamation was issued to the united armies. "Faithful soldiers of France and Navarre," said the Prince, "the saints have won for us a great victory—the enemies of our religion have been overcome—the lilies are restored to their native soil. Yesterday morning at eleven o'clock the army under my command engaged that which was led by his SERENE Highness the Duke de Nemours. Our forces were but a third in number when compared with those of the enemy. My faithful chivalry and nobles made the strength, however, equal.

"The regiments of Fleur-d'Orange, Millefleur, and Eau-de-Cologne covered themselves with glory: they sabred many thousands of the enemy's troops. Their valor was ably seconded by the gallantry of my ecclesiastical friends: at a moment of danger they rallied round my banner, and forsaking the crosier for the sword, showed that they were of the church militant indeed.

"My faithful Irish auxiliaries conducted themselves with becoming heroism—but why particularize when all did their duty? How remember individual acts when all were heroes?" The Marshal of France, Sucre d'Orgeville, Commander of the Army of H.M. Christian Majesty, recommended about three thousand persons for promotion; and the indignation of Jenkins and his brave companions may be imagined when it is stated that they were not even mentioned in the despatch!

As for the Princes of Ballybunion, Donegal, and Connemara, they wrote off despatches to their Government, saying, "The Duke of Nemours is beaten, and a prisoner! The Irish Brigade has done it all!"

On which his Majesty the King of the Irish, convoking his Parliament at the Corn Exchange Palace, Dublin, made a speech, in which he called Louis Philippe an "old miscreant," and paid the highest compliments to his son and his troops. The King on this occasion knighted Sir Henry Sheehan, Sir Gavan Duffy (whose journals had published the news), and was so delighted with the valor of his son, that he despatched him his order of the Pig and Whistle (1st class), and a munificent present of five hundred thousand pounds—in a bill at three months. All Dublin was illuminated; and at a ball at the Castle the Lord Chancellor Smith (Earl of Smithereens) getting extremely intoxicated, called out the Lord Bishop of Galway (the Dove), and they fought in the Phoenix Park. Having shot the Right Reverend Bishop through the body, Smithereens apologized. He was the same practitioner who had rendered himself so celebrated in the memorable trial of the King—before the Act of Independence.

Meanwhile, the army of Prince Henri advanced with rapid strides towards Paris, whither the History likewise must hasten; for extraordinary were the events preparing in that capital.

CHAPTER VII

THE LEAGUER OF PARIS

By a singular coincidence, on the very same day when the armies of Henri V. appeared before Paris from the Western Road, those of the Emperor John Thomas Napoleon arrived from the North. Skirmishes took place between the advanced-guards of the two parties, and much slaughter ensued.

"Bon!" thought King Louis Philippe, who examined them from his tower; "they will kill each other. This is by far the most economical way of getting rid of them." The astute monarch's calculations were admirably exposed by a clever remark of the Prince of Ballybunion. "Faix, Harry," says he (with a familiarity which the punctilious son of Saint Louis resented), "you and him yandther—the Emperor, I mane—are like the Kilkenny cats, dear."

"Et que font-ils ces chats de Kilkigny, Monsieur le Prince de Ballybunion?" asked the Most Christian King haughtily.

Prince Daniel replied by narrating the well-known apologue of the animals "ating each other all up but their TEELS; and that's what you and Imparial Pop yondther will do, blazing away as ye are," added the jocose and royal boy.

"Je prie votre Altesse Royale de vaguer a ses propres affaires," answered Prince Henri sternly: for he was an enemy to anything like a joke; but there is always wisdom in real wit, and it would have been well for his Most Christian Majesty had he followed the facetious counsels of his Irish ally.

The fact is, the King, Henri, had an understanding with the garrisons of some of the forts, and expected all would declare for him. However, of the twenty-four forts which we have described, eight only—and by the means of Marshal Soult, who had grown extremely devout of late years—declared for Henri, and raised the white flag: while eight others, seeing Prince John Thomas Napoleon before them in the costume of his revered predecessor, at once flung open their gates to him, and mounted the tricolor with the eagle. The remaining eight, into which the Princes of the blood of Orleans had thrown themselves, remained constant to Louis Philippe. Nothing could induce that Prince to quit the Tuileries.

His money was there, and he swore he would remain by it. In vain his sons offered to bring him into one of the forts—he would not stir without his treasure. They said they would transport it thither; but no, no: the patriarchal monarch, putting his finger to his aged nose, and winking archly, said "he knew a trick worth two of that," and resolved to abide by his bags.

The theatres and cafes remained open as usual: the funds rose three centimes. The Journal des Debats published three editions of different tones of politics: one, the Journal de l'Empire, for the Napoleonites; the Journal de la Legitimite another, very complimentary to the Legitimate monarch; and finally, the original edition, bound heart and soul to the dynasty of July. The poor editor, who had to write all three, complained not a little that his salary was not raised: but the truth is, that, by altering the names, one article did indifferently for either paper. The Duke of Brittany, under the title of Louis XVII., was always issuing manifestoes from Charenton, but of these the Parisians took little heed: the Charivari proclaimed itself his Gazette, and was allowed to be very witty at the expense of the three pretenders.

As the country had been ravaged for a hundred miles round, the respective Princes of course were for throwing themselves into the forts, where there was plenty of provision; and, when once there, they speedily began to turn out such of the garrison as were disagreeable to them, or had an inconvenient appetite, or were of a doubtful fidelity. These poor fellows turned into the road, had no choice but starvation; as to getting into Paris, that was impossible: a mouse could not have got into the place, so admirably were the forts guarded, without having his head taken off by a cannon-ball. Thus the three conflicting parties stood, close to each other, hating each other, "willing to wound and yet afraid to strike"—the victuals in the forts, from the prodigious increase of the garrisons, getting smaller every day. As for Louis Philippe in his palace, in the centre of the twenty-four forts, knowing that a spark from one might set them all blazing away, and that he and his money-bags might be blown into eternity in ten minutes, you may fancy his situation was not very comfortable.

But his safety lay in his treasure. Neither the Imperialists nor the Bourbonites were willing to relinquish the two hundred and fifty billions in gold; nor would the Princes of Orleans dare to fire upon that considerable sum of money, and its possessor, their revered father. How was this state of things to end? The Emperor sent a note to his Most Christian Majesty (for they always styled each other in this manner in their communications), proposing that they should turn out and decide the quarrel sword in hand; to which proposition Henri would have acceded, but that the priests, his ghostly counsellors, threatened to excommunicate him should he do so. Hence this simple way of settling the dispute was impossible.

The presence of the holy fathers caused considerable annoyance in the forts. Especially the poor English, as Protestants, were subject to much petty persecution, to the no small anger of Jenkins, their commander. And it must be confessed that these intrepid Footmen were not so amenable to discipline as they might have been. Remembering the usages of merry England, they clubbed together, and swore they would have four meals of meat a day, wax-candles in the casemates, and their porter. These demands were laughed at: the priests even called upon them to fast on Fridays; on which a general mutiny broke out in the regiment; and they would have had a FOURTH standard raised before Paris—viz., that of England—but the garrison proving too strong for them, they were compelled to lay down their sticks; and, in consideration of past services, were permitted to leave the forts. 'Twas well for them! as you shall hear.

The Prince of Ballybunion and the Irish force were quartered in the fort which, in compliment to them, was called Fort Potato, and where they made themselves as comfortable as circumstances would admit. The Princes had as much brandy as they liked, and passed their time on the ramparts playing at dice, or pitch-and-toss (with the halfpenny that one of them somehow had) for vast sums of money, for which they gave their notes-of-hand. The warriors of their legion would stand round delighted; and it was, "Musha, Master Dan, but that's a good throw!" "Good luck to you, Misther Pat, and throw thirteen this time!" and so forth. But this sort of inaction could not last long. They had heard of the treasures amassed in the palace of the Tuileries: they sighed when they thought of the lack of bullion in their green and beautiful country. They panted for war! They formed their plan.

## CHAPTER VIII

THE BATTLE OF THE FORTS

On the morning of the 26th October, 1884, as his Majesty Louis Philippe was at breakfast reading the Debats newspaper, and wishing that what the journal said about "Cholera Morbus in the Camp of the Pretender Henri,"—"Chicken-pox raging in the Forts of the Traitor Bonaparte,"—might be true, what was his surprise to hear the report of a gun; and at the same instant—whiz! came an eighty-four-pound ball through the window and took off the head of the faithful Monsieur de Montalivet, who was coming in with a plate of muffins.

"Three francs for the window," said the monarch; "and the muffins of course spoiled!" and he sat down to breakfast very peevishly. Ah, King Louis Philippe, that shot cost thee more than a window-pane—more than a plate of muffins—it cost thee a fair kingdom and fifty millions of tax-payers.

The shot had been fired from Fort Potato. "Gracious heavens!" said the commander of the place to the Irish Prince, in a fury, "What has your Highness done?" "Faix," replied the other, "Donegal and I saw a sparrow on the Tuileries, and we thought we'd have a shot at it, that's all." "Hurroo! look out for squalls," here cried the intrepid Hibernian; for at this moment one of Paixhans' shells fell into the counterscarp of the demilune on which they were standing, and sent a ravelin and a couple of embrasures flying about their ears.

Fort Twenty-three, which held out for Louis Philippe, seeing Fort Twenty-four, or Potato, open a fire on the Tuileries, instantly replied by its guns, with which it blazed away at the Bourbonite fort. On seeing this, Fort Twenty-two, occupied by the Imperialists, began pummelling Twenty-three; Twenty-one began at Twenty-two; and in a quarter of an hour the whole of this vast line of fortification was in a blaze of flame, flashing, roaring, cannonading, rocketing, bombing, in the most tremendous manner. The world has never perhaps, before or since, heard such an uproar. Fancy twenty-four thousand guns thundering at each other. Fancy the sky red with the fires of hundreds of thousands of blazing, brazen meteors; the air thick with impenetrable smoke—the universe almost in a flame! for the noise of the cannonading was heard on the peaks of the Andes, and broke three windows in the English factory at Canton. Boom, boom, boom! for three days incessantly the gigantic—I may say, Cyclopean battle went on: boom, boom, boom, bong! The air was thick with cannon-balls: they hurtled, they jostled each other in the heavens, and fell whizzing, whirling, crashing, back into the very forts from which they came. Boom, boom, boom, bong—brrwrrwrrr!

On the second day a band might have been seen (had the smoke permitted it) assembling at the sally-port of Fort Potato, and have been heard (if the tremendous clang of the cannonading had allowed it) giving mysterious signs and countersigns. "Tom," was the word whispered, "Steele" was the sibilated response. (It is astonishing how, in the roar of elements, THE HUMAN WHISPER hisses above all!) It was the Irish Brigade assembling. "Now or never, boys!" said their leaders; and sticking their doodeens into their mouths, they dropped stealthily into the trenches, heedless of the broken glass and sword-blades; rose from those trenches; formed in silent order; and marched to Paris. They knew they could arrive there unobserved—nobody, indeed, remarked their absence.

The frivolous Parisians were, in the meanwhile, amusing themselves at their theatres and cafes as usual; and a new piece, in which Arnal performed, was the universal talk of the foyers: while a new feuilleton by Monsieur Eugene Sue, kept the attention of the reader so fascinated to the journal, that they did not care in the least for the vacarme without the walls.


CHAPTER IX

LOUIS XVII

The tremendous cannonading, however, had a singular effect upon the inhabitants of the great public hospital of Charenton, in which it may be remembered Louis XVII. had been, as in mockery, confined. His majesty of demeanor, his calm deportment, the reasonableness of his pretensions, had not failed to strike with awe and respect his four thousand comrades of captivity. The Emperor of China, the Princess of the Moon, Julius Caesar, Saint Genevieve, the patron saint of Paris, the Pope of Rome, the Cacique of Mexico, and several singular and illustrious personages who happened to be confined there, all held a council with Louis XVII.; and all agreed that now or never was the time to support his legitimate pretensions to the Crown of France. As the cannons roared around them, they howled with furious delight in response. They took counsel together: Dr. Pinel and the infamous jailers, who, under the name of keepers, held them in horrible captivity, were pounced upon and overcome in a twinkling. The strait-waistcoats were taken off from the wretched captives languishing in the dungeons; the guardians were invested in these shameful garments, and with triumphant laughter plunged under the Douches. The gates of the prison were flung open, and they marched forth in the blackness of the storm!

On the third day, the cannonading was observed to decrease; only a gun went off fitfully now and then.

On the fourth day, the Parisians said to one another, "Tiens! ils sont fatigues, les cannoniers des forts!"—and why? Because there was no more powder?—Ay, truly, there WAS no more powder.

There was no more powder, no more guns, no more gunners, no more forts, no more nothing. THE FORTS HAD BLOWN EACH OTHER UP. The battle-roar ceased. The battle-clouds rolled off. The silver moon, the twinkling stars, looked blandly down from the serene azure,—and all was peace—stillness—the stillness of death. Holy, holy silence!

Yes: the battle of Paris was over. And where were the combatants? All gone—not one left!—And where was Louis Philippe? The venerable Prince was a captive in the Tuileries; the Irish Brigade was encamped around it: they had reached the palace a little too late; it was already occupied by the partisans of his Majesty Louis XVII.

That respectable monarch and his followers better knew the way to the Tuileries than the ignorant sons of Erin. They burst through the feeble barriers of the guards; they rushed triumphant into the kingly halls of the palace; they seated the seventeenth Louis on the throne of his ancestors; and the Parisians read in the Journal des Debats, of the fifth of November; an important article, which proclaimed that the civil war was concluded:—

"The troubles which distracted the greatest empire in the world are at an end. Europe, which marked with sorrow the disturbances which agitated the bosom of the Queen of Nations, the great leader of Civilization, may now rest in peace. That monarch whom we have long been sighing for; whose image has lain hidden, and yet oh! how passionately worshipped, in every French heart, is with us once more. Blessings be on him; blessings—a thousand blessings upon the happy country which is at length restored to his beneficent, his legitimate, his reasonable sway!

"His Most Christian Majesty Louis XVII. yesterday arrived at his palace of the Tulleries, accompanied by his august allies. His Royal Highness the Duke of Orleans has resigned his post as Lieutenant-General of the kingdom, and will return speedily to take up his abode at the Palais Royal. It is a great mercy that the children of his Royal Highness, who happened to be in the late forts round Paris, (before the bombardment which has so happily ended in their destruction,) had returned to their father before the commencement of the cannonading. They will continue, as heretofore, to be the most loyal supporters of order and the throne.

"None can read without tears in their eyes our august monarch's proclamation.

"'Louis, by &c.—

"'My children! After nine hundred and ninety-nine years of captivity, I am restored to you. The cycle of events predicted by the ancient Magi, and the planetary convolutions mentioned in the lost Sibylline books, have fulfilled their respective idiosyncrasies, and ended (as always in the depths of my dungeons I confidently expected) in the triumph of the good Angel, and the utter discomfiture of the abominable Blue Dragon.

"'When the bombarding began, and the powers of darkness commenced their hellish gunpowder evolutions, I was close by—in my palace of Charenton, three hundred and thirty-three thousand miles off, in the ring of Saturn—I witnessed your misery. My heart was affected by it, and I said, "Is the multiplication-table a fiction? are the signs of the Zodiac mere astronomers' prattle?"

"'I clapped chains, shrieking and darkness, on my physician, Dr. Pinel. The keepers I shall cause to be roasted alive. I summoned my allies round about me. The high contracting Powers came to my bidding: monarchs from all parts of the earth; sovereigns from the Moon and other illumined orbits; the white necromancers, and the pale imprisoned genii. I whispered the mystic sign, and the doors flew open. We entered Paris in triumph, by the Charenton bridge. Our luggage was not examined at the Octroi. The bottle-green ones were scared at our shouts, and retreated, howling: they knew us, and trembled.

"'My faithful Peers and Deputies will rally around me. I have a friend in Turkey—the Grand Vizier of the Mussulmans: he was a Protestant once—Lord Brougham by name. I have sent to him to legislate for us: he is wise in the law, and astrology, and all sciences; he shall aid my Ministers in their councils. I have written to him by the post. There shall be no more infamous mad-houses in France, where poor souls shiver in strait-waistcoats.

"'I recognized Louis Philippe, my good cousin. He was in his counting-house, counting out his money, as the old prophecy warned me. He gave me up the keys of his gold; I shall know well how to use it. Taught by adversity, I am not a spendthrift, neither am I a miser. I will endow the land with noble institutions instead of diabolical forts. I will have no more cannon founded. They are a curse and shall be melted—the iron ones into railroads; the bronze ones into statues of beautiful saints, angels, and wise men; the copper ones into money, to be distributed among my poor. I was poor once, and I love them.

"'There shall be no more poverty; no more wars; no more avarice; no more passports; no more custom-houses; no more lying: no more physic.

"'My Chambers will put the seal to these reforms. I will it. I am the king.

(Signed) 'Louis.'"

"Some alarm was created yesterday by the arrival of a body of the English Foot-Guard under the Duke of Jenkins; they were at first about to sack the city, but on hearing that the banner of the lilies was once more raised in France, the Duke hastened to the Tuileries, and offered his allegiance to his Majesty. It was accepted: and the Plush Guard has been established in place of the Swiss, who waited on former sovereigns."

"The Irish Brigade quartered in the Tuileries are to enter our service. Their commander states that they took every one of the forts round Paris, and having blown them up, were proceeding to release Louis XVII., when they found that august monarch, happily, free. News of their glorious victory has been conveyed to Dublin, to his Majesty the King of the Irish. It will be a new laurel to add to his green crown!"

And thus have we brought to a conclusion our history of the great French Revolution of 1884. It records the actions of great and various characters; the deeds of various valor; it narrates wonderful reverses of fortune; it affords the moralist scope for his philosophy; perhaps it gives amusement to the merely idle reader. Nor must the latter imagine, because there is not a precise moral affixed to the story, that its tendency is otherwise than good. He is a poor reader, for whom his author is obliged to supply a moral application. It is well in spelling-books and for children; it is needless for the reflecting spirit. The drama of Punch himself is not moral: but that drama has had audiences all over the world. Happy he, who in our dark times can cause a smile! Let us laugh then, and gladden in the sunshine, though it be but as the ray upon the pool, that flickers only over the cold black depths below!

COX'S DIARY

THE ANNOUNCEMENT

On the 1st of January, 1838, I was the master of a lovely shop in the neighborhood of Oxford Market; of a wife, Mrs. Cox; of a business, both in the shaving and cutting line, established three-and-thirty years; of a girl and boy respectively of the ages of eighteen and thirteen; of a three-windowed front, both to my first and second pair; of a young foreman, my present partner, Mr. Orlando Crump; and of that celebrated mixture for the human hair, invented by my late uncle, and called Cox's Bohemian Balsam of Tokay, sold in pots at two-and-three and three-and-nine. The balsam, the lodgings, and the old-established cutting and shaving business brought me in a pretty genteel income. I had my girl, Jemimarann, at Hackney, to school; my dear boy, Tuggeridge, plaited her hair beautifully; my wife at the counter (behind the tray of patent soaps, &c.) cut as handsome a figure as possible; and it was my hope that Orlando and my girl, who were mighty soft upon one another, would one day be joined together in Hyming, and, conjointly with my son Tug, carry on the business of hairdressers when their father was either dead or a gentleman: for a gentleman me and Mrs. C. determined I should be.

Jemima was, you see, a lady herself, and of very high connections: though her own family had met with crosses, and was rather low. Mr. Tuggeridge, her father, kept the famous tripe-shop near the "Pigtail and Sparrow," in the Whitechapel Road; from which place I married her; being myself very fond of the article, and especially when she served it to me—the dear thing!

Jemima's father was not successful in business: and I married her, I am proud to confess it, without a shilling. I had my hands, my house, and my Bohemian balsam to support her!—and we had hopes from her uncle, a mighty rich East India merchant, who, having left this country sixty years ago as a cabin-boy, had arrived to be the head of a great house in India, and was worth millions, we were told.

Three years after Jemimarann's birth (and two after the death of my lamented father-in-law), Tuggeridge (head of the great house of Budgurow and Co.) retired from the management of it; handed over his shares to his son, Mr. John Tuggeridge, and came to live in England, at Portland Place, and Tuggeridgeville, Surrey, and enjoy himself. Soon after, my wife took her daughter in her hand and went, as in duty bound, to visit her uncle: but whether it was that he was proud and surly, or she somewhat sharp in her way, (the dear girl fears nobody, let me have you to know,) a desperate quarrel took place between them; and from that day to the day of his death, he never set eyes on her. All that he would condescend to do, was to take a few dozen of lavender-water from us in the course of the year, and to send his servants to be cut and shaved by us. All the neighbors laughed at this poor ending of our expectations, for Jemmy had bragged not a little; however, we did not care, for the connection was always a good one, and we served Mr. Hock, the valet; Mr. Bar, the coachman; and Mrs. Breadbasket, the housekeeper, willingly enough. I used to powder the footman, too, on great days, but never in my life saw old Tuggeridge, except once: when he said "Oh, the barber!" tossed up his nose, and passed on.

One day—one famous day last January—all our Market was thrown into a high state of excitement by the appearance of no less than three vehicles at our establishment. As me, Jemmy, my daughter, Tug, and Orlando, were sitting in the back-parlor over our dinner (it being Christmas-time, Mr. Crump had treated the ladies to a bottle of port, and was longing that there should be a mistletoe-bough: at which proposal my little Jemimarann looked as red as a glass of negus):—we had just, I say, finished the port, when, all of a sudden, Tug bellows out, "La, Pa, here's uncle Tuggeridge's housekeeper in a cab!"

And Mrs. Breadbasket it was, sure enough—Mrs. Breadbasket in deep mourning, who made her way, bowing and looking very sad, into the back shop. My wife, who respected Mrs. B. more than anything else in the world, set her a chair, offered her a glass of wine, and vowed it was very kind of her to come. "La, mem," says Mrs. B., "I'm sure I'd do anything to serve your family, for the sake of that poor dear Tuck-Tuck-tug-guggeridge, that's gone."

"That's what?" cries my wife.

"What, gone?" cried Jemimarann, bursting out crying (as little girls will about anything or nothing); and Orlando looking very rueful, and ready to cry too.

"Yes, gaw—" Just as she was at this very "gaw" Tug roars out, "La, Pa! here's Mr. Bar, uncle Tug's coachman!"

It was Mr. Bar. When she saw him, Mrs. Breadbasket stepped suddenly back into the parlor with my ladies. "What is it, Mr. Bar?" says I; and as quick as thought, I had the towel under his chin, Mr. Bar in the chair, and the whole of his face in a beautiful foam of lather. Mr. Bar made some resistance.—"Don't think of it, Mr. Cox," says he; "don't trouble yourself, sir." But I lathered away and never minded. "And what's this melancholy event, sir," says I, "that has spread desolation in your family's bosoms? I can feel for your loss, sir—I can feel for your loss."

I said so out of politeness, because I served the family, not because Tuggeridge was my uncle—no, as such I disown him.

Mr. Bar was just about to speak. "Yes, sir," says he, "my master's gaw—" when at the "gaw" in walks Mr. Hock, the own man!—the finest gentleman I ever saw.

"What, YOU here, Mr. Bar!" says he.

"Yes, I am, sir; and haven't I a right, sir?"

"A mighty wet day, sir," says I to Mr. Hock—stepping up and making my bow. "A sad circumstance too, sir! And is it a turn of the tongs that you want to-day, sir? Ho, there, Mr. Crump!"

"Turn, Mr. Crump, if you please, sir," said Mr. Hock, making a bow: "but from you, sir, never—no, never, split me!—and I wonder how some fellows can have the INSOLENCE to allow their MASTERS to shave them!" With this, Mr. Hock flung himself down to be curled: Mr. Bar suddenly opened his mouth in order to reply; but seeing there was a tiff between the gentlemen, and wanting to prevent a quarrel, I rammed the Advertiser into Mr. Hock's hands, and just popped my shaving-brush into Mr. Bar's mouth—a capital way to stop angry answers.

Mr. Bar had hardly been in the chair one second, when whir comes a hackney-coach to the door, from which springs a gentleman in a black coat with a bag.

"What, you here!" says the gentleman. I could not help smiling, for it seemed that everybody was to begin by saying, "What, YOU here!" "Your name is Cox, sir?" says he; smiling too, as the very pattern of mine. "My name, sir, is Sharpus,—Blunt, Hone and Sharpus, Middle Temple Lane,—and I am proud to salute you, sir; happy,—that is to say, sorry to say that Mr. Tuggeridge, of Portland Place, is dead, and your lady is heiress, in consequence, to one of the handsomest properties in the kingdom."

At this I started, and might have sunk to the ground, but for my hold of Mr. Bar's nose; Orlando seemed putrified to stone, with his irons fixed to Mr. Hock's head; our respective patients gave a wince out:—Mrs. C., Jemimarann, and Tug, rushed from the back shop, and we formed a splendid tableau such as the great Cruikshank might have depicted.

"And Mr. John Tuggeridge, sir?" says I.

"Why—hee, hee, hee!" says Mr. Sharpus. "Surely you know that he was only the—hee, hee, hee!—the natural son!"

You now can understand why the servants from Portland Place had been so eager to come to us. One of the house-maids heard Mr. Sharpus say there was no will, and that my wife was heir to the property, and not Mr. John Tuggeridge: this she told in the housekeeper's room; and off, as soon as they heard it, the whole party set, in order to be the first to bear the news.

We kept them, every one in their old places; for, though my wife would have sent them about their business, my dear Jemimarann just hinted, "Mamma, you know THEY have been used to great houses, and we have not; had we not better keep them for a little?"—Keep them, then, we did, to show us how to be gentlefolks.

I handed over the business to Mr. Crump without a single farthing of premium, though Jemmy would have made me take four hundred pounds for it; but this I was above: Crump had served me faithfully, and have the shop he should.

## FIRST ROUT

We were speedily installed in our fine house: but what's a house without friends? Jemmy made me CUT all my old acquaintances in the Market, and I was a solitary being; when, luckily, an old acquaintance of ours, Captain Tagrag, was so kind as to promise to introduce us into distinguished society. Tagrag was the son of a baronet, and had done us the honor of lodging with us for two years; when we lost sight of him, and of his little account, too, by the way. A fortnight after, hearing of our good fortune, he was among us again, however; and Jemmy was not a little glad to see him, knowing him to be a baronet's son, and very fond of our Jemimarann. Indeed, Orlando (who is as brave as a lion) had on one occasion absolutely beaten Mr. Tagrag for being rude to the poor girl: a clear proof, as Tagrag said afterwards, that he was always fond of her.

Mr. Crump, poor fellow, was not very much pleased by our good fortune, though he did all he could to try at first; and I told him to come and take his dinner regular, as if nothing had happened. But to this Jemima very soon put a stop, for she came very justly to know her stature, and to look down on Crump, which she bid her daughter to do; and, after a great scene, in which Orlando showed himself very rude and angry, he was forbidden the house—for ever!

So much for poor Crump. The Captain was now all in all with us. "You see, sir," our Jemmy would say, "we shall have our town and country mansion, and a hundred and thirty thousand pounds in the funds, to leave between our two children; and, with such prospects, they ought surely to have the first society of England." To this Tagrag agreed, and promised to bring us acquainted with the very pink of the fashion; ay, and what's more, did.

First, he made my wife get an opera-box, and give suppers on Tuesdays and Saturdays. As for me, he made me ride in the Park: me and Jemimarann, with two grooms behind us, who used to laugh all the way, and whose very beards I had shaved. As for little Tug, he was sent straight off to the most fashionable school in the kingdom, the Reverend Doctor Pigney's, at Richmond.

Well, the horses, the suppers, the opera-box, the paragraphs in the papers about Mr. Coxe Coxe (that's the way: double your name and stick an "e" to the end of it, and you are a gentleman at once), had an effect in a wonderfully short space of time, and we began to get a very pretty society about us. Some of old Tug's friends swore they would do anything for the family, and brought their wives and daughters to see dear Mrs. Coxe and her charming girl; and when, about the first week in February, we announced a grand dinner and ball for the evening of the twenty-eighth, I assure you there was no want of company: no, nor of titles neither; and it always does my heart good even to hear one mentioned.

Let me see. There was, first, my Lord Dunboozle, an Irish peer, and his seven sons, the Honorable Messieurs Trumper (two only to dinner): there was Count Mace, the celebrated French nobleman, and his Excellency Baron von Punter from Baden; there was Lady Blanche Bluenose, the eminent literati, author of "The Distrusted" "The Distorted," "The Disgusted," "The Disreputable One," and other poems; there was the Dowager Lady Max and her daughter, the Honorable Miss Adelaide Blueruin; Sir Charles Codshead, from the City; and Field-Marshal Sir Gorman O'Gallagher, K.A., K.B., K.C., K.W., K.X., in the service of the Republic of Guatemala: my friend Tagrag and his fashionable acquaintance, little Tom Tufthunt, made up the party. And when the doors were flung open, and Mr. Hock, in black, with a white napkin, three footmen, coachman, and a lad whom Mrs. C. had dressed in sugar-loaf buttons and called a page, were seen round the dinner-table, all in white gloves, I promise you I felt a thrill of elation, and thought to myself—Sam Cox, Sam Cox, who ever would have expected to see you here?

After dinner, there was to be, as I said, an evening-party; and to this Messieurs Tagrag and Tufthunt had invited many of the principal nobility that our metropolis had produced. When I mention, among the company to tea, her Grace the Duchess of Zero, her son the Marquis of Fitzurse, and the Ladies North Pole her daughters; when I say that there were yet OTHERS, whose names may be found in the Blue Book, but shan't, out of modesty, be mentioned here, I think I've said enough to show that, in our time, No. 96, Portland Place, was the resort of the best of company.

It was our first dinner, and dressed by our new cook, Munseer Cordongblew. I bore it very well; eating, for my share, a filly dysol allamater dotell, a cutlet soubeast, a pully bashymall, and other French dishes: and, for the frisky sweet wine, with tin tops to the bottles, called Champang, I must say that me and Mrs. Coxe-Tuggeridge Coxe drank a very good share of it (but the Claret and Jonnysberger, being sour, we did not much relish). However, the feed, as I say, went off very well: Lady Blanche Bluenose sitting next to me, and being so good as to put me down for six copies of all her poems; the Count and Baron von Punter engaging Jemimarann for several waltzes, and the Field-Marshal plying my dear Jemmy with Champagne, until, bless her! her dear nose became as red as her new crimson satin gown, which, with a blue turban and bird-of-paradise feathers, made her look like an empress, I warrant.

Well, dinner past, Mrs. C. and the ladies went off:—thunder-under-under came the knocks at the door; squeedle-eedle-eedle, Mr. Wippert's fiddlers began to strike up; and, about half-past eleven, me and the gents thought it high time to make our appearance. I felt a LITTLE squeamish at the thought of meeting a couple of hundred great people; but Count Mace and Sir Gorman O'Gallagher taking each an arm, we reached, at last, the drawing-room.

The young ones in company were dancing, and the Duchess and the great ladies were all seated, talking to themselves very stately, and working away at the ices and macaroons. I looked out for my pretty Jemimarann amongst the dancers, and saw her tearing round the room along with Baron Punter, in what they call a gallypard; then I peeped into the circle of the Duchesses, where, in course, I expected to find Mrs. C.; but she wasn't there! She was seated at the further end of the room, looking very sulky;

and I went up and took her arm, and brought her down to the place where the Duchesses were. "Oh, not there!" said Jemmy, trying to break away. "Nonsense, my dear," says I: "you are missis, and this is your place." Then going up to her ladyship the Duchess, says I, "Me and my missis are most proud of the honor of seeing of you."

The Duchess (a tall red-haired grenadier of a woman) did not speak.

I went on: "The young ones are all at it, ma'am, you see; and so we thought we would come and sit down among the old ones. You and I, ma'am, I think, are too stiff to dance."

"Sir!" says her Grace.

"Ma'am," says I, "don't you know me? My name's Cox. Nobody's introduced me; but, dash it, it's my own house, and I may present myself—so give us your hand, ma'am."

And I shook hers in the kindest way in the world; but—would you believe it?—the old cat screamed as if my hand had been a hot 'tater. "Fitzurse! Fitzurse!" shouted she, "help! help!" Up scuffled all the other Dowagers—in rushed the dancers. "Mamma! mamma!" squeaked Lady Julia North Pole. "Lead me to my mother," howled Lady Aurorer: and both came up and flung themselves into her arms. "Wawt's the raw?" said Lord Fitzurse, sauntering up quite stately.

"Protect me from the insults of this man," says her Grace. "Where's Tufthunt? he promised that not a soul in this house should speak to me."

"My dear Duchess," said Tufthunt, very meek.

"Don't Duchess ME, sir. Did you not promise they should not speak; and hasn't that horrid tipsy wretch offered to embrace me? Didn't his monstrous wife sicken me with her odious familiarities? Call my people, Tufthunt! Follow me, my children!"

"And my carriage," "And mine," "And mine!" shouted twenty more voices. And down they all trooped to the hall: Lady Blanche Bluenose and Lady Max among the very first; leaving only the Field-Marshal and one or two men, who roared with laughter ready to split.

"Oh, Sam," said my wife, sobbing, "why would you take me back to them? they had sent me away before! I only asked the Duchess whether she didn't like rum-shrub better than all your Maxarinos and Curasosos: and—would you believe it?—all the company burst out laughing; and the Duchess told me just to keep off, and not to speak till I was spoken to. Imperence! I'd like to tear her eyes out."

And so I do believe my dearest Jemmy would!


A DAY WITH THE SURREY HOUNDS

Our ball had failed so completely that Jemmy, who was bent still upon fashion, caught eagerly at Tagrag's suggestion, and went down to Tuggeridgeville. If we had a difficulty to find friends in town, here there was none: for the whole county came about us, ate our dinners and suppers, danced at our balls—ay, and spoke to us too. We were great people in fact: I a regular country gentleman; and as such,

Jemmy insisted that I should be a sportsman, and join the county hunt. "But," says I, "my love, I can't ride." "Pooh! Mr. C." said she, "you're always making difficulties: you thought you couldn't dance a quadrille; you thought you couldn't dine at seven o'clock; you thought you couldn't lie in bed after six; and haven't you done every one of these things? You must and you shall ride!" And when my Jemmy said "must and shall," I knew very well there was nothing for it: so I sent down fifty guineas to the hunt, and, out of compliment to me, the very next week, I received notice that the meet of the hounds would take place at Squashtail Common, just outside my lodge-gates.

I didn't know what a meet was; and me and Mrs. C. agreed that it was most probable the dogs were to be fed there. However, Tagrag explained this matter to us, and very kindly promised to sell me a horse, a delightful animal of his own; which, being desperately pressed for money, he would let me have for a hundred guineas, he himself having given a hundred and fifty for it.

Well, the Thursday came: the hounds met on Squashtail Common; Mrs. C. turned out in her barouche to see us throw off; and, being helped up on my chestnut horse, Trumpeter, by Tagrag and my head groom, I came presently round to join them.

Tag mounted his own horse; and, as we walked down the avenue, "I thought," he said, "you told me you knew how to ride; and that you had ridden once fifty miles on a stretch!"

"And so I did," says I, "to Cambridge, and on the box too."

"ON THE BOX!" says he; "but did you ever mount a horse before?"

"Never," says I, "but I find it mighty easy."

"Well," says he, "you're mighty bold for a barber; and I like you, Coxe, for your spirit." And so we came out of the gate.

As for describing the hunt, I own, fairly, I can't. I've been at a hunt, but what a hunt is—why the horses WILL go among the dogs and ride them down—why the men cry out "yooooic"—why the dogs go snuffing about in threes and fours, and the huntsman says, "Good Towler—good Betsy," and we all of us after him say, "Good Towler—good Betsy" in course: then, after hearing a yelp here and a howl there, tow, row, yow, yow, yow! burst out, all of a sudden, from three or four of them, and the chap in a velvet cap screeches out (with a number of oaths I shan't repeat here), "Hark, to Ringwood!" and then, "There he goes!" says some one; and all of a sudden, helter skelter, skurry hurry, slap bang, whooping, screeching and hurraing, blue-coats and red-coats, bays and grays, horses, dogs, donkeys, butchers, baro-knights, dustmen, and blackguard boys, go tearing all together over the common after two or three of the pack that yowl loudest. Why all this is, I can't say; but it all took place the second Thursday of last March, in my presence.

Up to this, I'd kept my seat as well as the best, for we'd only been trotting gently about the field until the dogs found; and I managed to stick on very well; but directly the tow-rowing began, off went Trumpeter like a thunderbolt, and I found myself playing among the dogs like the donkey among the chickens. "Back, Mr. Coxe," holloas the huntsman; and so I pulled very hard, and cried out, "Wo!" but he wouldn't; and on I went galloping for the dear life. How I kept on is a wonder; but I squeezed my knees in very tight, and shoved my feet very hard into the stirrups, and kept stiff hold of the scruff of

Trumpeter's neck, and looked betwixt his ears as well as ever I could, and trusted to luck: for I was in a mortal fright, sure enough, as many a better man would be in such a case, let alone a poor hairdresser.

As for the hounds, after my first riding in among them, I tell you honestly, I never saw so much as the tip of one of their tails; nothing in this world did I see except Trumpeter's dun-colored mane, and that I gripped firm: riding, by the blessing of luck, safe through the walking, the trotting, the galloping, and never so much as getting a tumble.

There was a chap at Croydon very well known as the "Spicy Dustman," who, when he could get no horse to ride to the hounds, turned regularly out on his donkey; and on this occasion made one of us. He generally managed to keep up with the dogs by trotting quietly through the cross-roads, and knowing the country well. Well, having a good guess where the hounds would find, and the line that sly Reynolds (as they call the fox) would take, the Spicy Dustman turned his animal down the lane from Squashtail to Cutshins Common; across which, sure enough, came the whole hunt. There's a small hedge and a remarkably fine ditch here: some of the leading chaps took both, in gallant style; others went round by a gate, and so would I, only I couldn't; for Trumpeter would have the hedge, and be hanged to him, and went right for it.

Hoop! if ever you DID try a leap! Out go your legs, out fling your arms, off goes your hat; and the next thing you feel—that is, I did—is a most tremendous thwack across the chest, and my feet jerked out of the stirrups: me left in the branches of a tree; Trumpeter gone clean from under me, and walloping and floundering in the ditch underneath. One of the stirrup-leathers had caught in a stake, and the horse couldn't get away: and neither of us, I thought, ever WOULD have got away: but all of a sudden, who should come up the lane but the Spicy Dustman!

"Holloa!" says I, "you gent, just let us down from this here tree!"

"Lor'!" says he, "I'm blest if I didn't take you for a robin."

"Let's down," says I; but he was all the time employed in disengaging Trumpeter, whom he got out of the ditch, trembling and as quiet as possible. "Let's down," says I. "Presently," says he; and taking off his coat, he begins whistling and swishing down Trumpeter's sides and saddle; and when he had finished, what do you think the rascal did?—he just quietly mounted on Trumpeter's back, and shouts out, "Git down yourself, old Bearsgrease; you've only to drop! I'LL give your 'oss a hairing arter them 'ounds; and you—vy, you may ride back my pony to Tuggeridgeweal!" And with this, I'm blest if he didn't ride away, leaving me holding, as for the dear life, and expecting every minute the branch would break.

It DID break too, and down I came into the slush; and when I got out of it, I can tell you I didn't look much like the Venuses or the Apollor Belvidearis what I used to dress and titivate up for my shop window when I was in the hairdressing line, or smell quite so elegant as our rose-oil. Faugh! what a figure I was!

I had nothing for it but to mount the dustman's donkey (which was very quietly cropping grass in the hedge), and to make my way home; and after a weary, weary journey, I arrived at my own gate.

A whole party was assembled there. Tagrag, who had come back; their Excellencies Mace and Punter, who were on a visit; and a number of horses walking up and down before the whole of the gentlemen of the hunt, who had come in after losing their fox! "Here's Squire Coxe!" shouted the grooms. Out rushed the servants, out poured the gents of the hunt, and on trotted poor me, digging into the donkey, and everybody dying with laughter at me.

Just as I got up to the door, a horse came galloping up, and passed me; a man jumped down, and taking off a fantail hat, came up, very gravely, to help me down.

"Squire," says he, "how came you by that there hanimal? Jist git down, will you, and give it to its howner?"

"Rascal!" says I, "didn't you ride off on my horse?"

"Was there ever sich ingratitude?" says the Spicy. "I found this year 'oss in a pond, I saves him from drowning, I brings him back to his master, and he calls me a rascal!"

The grooms, the gents, the ladies in the balcony, my own servants, all set up a roar at this; and so would I, only I was so deucedly ashamed, as not to be able to laugh just then.

And so my first day's hunting ended. Tagrag and the rest declared I showed great pluck, and wanted me to try again; but "No," says I, "I HAVE been."

## THE FINISHING TOUCH

I was always fond of billiards: and, in former days, at Grogram's in Greek Street, where a few jolly lads of my acquaintance used to meet twice a week for a game, and a snug pipe and beer, I was generally voted the first man of the club; and could take five from John the marker himself. I had a genius, in fact, for the game; and now that I was placed in that station of life where I could cultivate my talents, I gave them full play, and improved amazingly. I do say that I think myself as good a hand as any chap in England.

The Count and his Excellency Baron von Punter were, I can tell you, astonished by the smartness of my play: the first two or three rubbers Punter beat me, but when I came to know his game, I used to knock him all to sticks; or, at least, win six games to his four: and such was the betting upon me; his Excellency losing large sums to the Count, who knew what play was, and used to back me. I did not play except for shillings, so my skill was of no great service to me.

One day I entered the billiard-room where these three gentlemen were high in words. "The thing shall not be done," I heard Captain Tagrag say: "I won't stand it."

"Vat, begause you would have de bird all to yourzelf, hey?" said the Baron.

"You sall not have a single fezare of him, begar," said the Count: "ve vill blow you, M. de Taguerague; parole d'honneur, ve vill."

"What's all this, gents," says I, stepping in, "about birds and feathers?"

"Oh," says Tagrag, "we were talking about—about—pigeon-shooting; the Count here says he will blow a bird all to pieces at twenty yards, and I said I wouldn't stand it, because it was regular murder."

"Oh, yase, it was bidgeon-shooting," cries the Baron: "and I know no better sbort. Have you been bidgeon-shooting, my dear Squire? De fon is gabidal."

"No doubt," says I, "for the shooters, but mighty bad sport for the PIGEON." And this joke set them all a-laughing ready to die. I didn't know then what a good joke it WAS, neither; but I gave Master Baron, that day, a precious good beating, and walked off with no less than fifteen shillings of his money.

As a sporting man, and a man of fashion, I need not say that I took in the Flare-up regularly; ay, and wrote one or two trifles in that celebrated publication (one of my papers, which Tagrag subscribed for me, Philo-pestitiaeamicus, on the proper sauce for teal and widgeon—and the other, signed Scru-tatos, on the best means of cultivating the kidney species of that vegetable—made no small noise at the time, and got me in the paper a compliment from the editor). I was a constant reader of the Notices to Correspondents, and, my early education having been rayther neglected (for I was taken from my studies and set, as is the custom in our trade, to practise on a sheep's head at the tender age of nine years, before I was allowed to venture on the humane countenance,)—I say, being thus curtailed and cut off in my classical learning, I must confess I managed to pick up a pretty smattering of genteel information from that treasury of all sorts of knowledge; at least sufficient to make me a match in learning for all the noblemen and gentlemen who came to our house. Well, on looking over the Flare-up notices to correspondents, I read, one day last April, among the notices, as follows:—

"'Automodon.' We do not know the precise age of Mr. Baker of Covent Garden Theatre; nor are we aware if that celebrated son of Thespis is a married man.

"'Ducks and Green-peas' is informed, that when A plays his rook to B's second Knight's square, and B, moving two squares with his Queen's pawn, gives check to his adversary's Queen, there is no reason why B's Queen should not take A's pawn, if B be so inclined.

"'F. L. S.' We have repeatedly answered the question about Madame Vestris: her maiden name was Bartolozzi, and she married the son of Charles Mathews, the celebrated comedian.

"'Fair Play.' The best amateur billiard and ecarte player in England, is Coxe Tuggeridge Coxe, Esq., of Portland Place, and Tuggeridgeville: Jonathan, who knows his play, can only give him two in a game of a hundred; and, at the cards, NO man is his superior. Verbum sap.

"'Scipio Americanus' is a blockhead."

I read this out to the Count and Tagrag, and both of them wondered how the Editor of that tremendous Flare-up should get such information; and both agreed that the Baron, who still piqued himself absurdly on his play, would be vastly annoyed by seeing me preferred thus to himself. We read him the paragraph, and preciously angry he was. "Id is," he cried, "the tables" (or "de DABELS," as he called them),—"de horrid dabels; gom viz me to London, and dry a slate-table, and I vill beat you." We all roared at this; and the end of the dispute was, that, just to satisfy the fellow, I agreed to play his Excellency at slate-tables, or any tables he chose.

"Gut," says he, "gut; I lif, you know, at Abednego's, in de Quadrant; his dabels is goot; ve vill blay dere, if you vill." And I said I would: and it was agreed that, one Saturday night, when Jemmy was at the Opera, we should go to the Baron's rooms, and give him a chance.

We went, and the little Baron had as fine a supper as ever I saw: lots of Champang (and I didn't mind drinking it), and plenty of laughing and fun. Afterwards, down we went to billiards. "Is dish Misther Coxsh, de shelebrated player?" says Mr. Abednego, who was in the room, with one or two gentlemen of his own persuasion, and several foreign noblemen, dirty, snuffy, and hairy, as them foreigners are. "Is dish Misther Coxsh? blesh my hart, it is a honor to see you; I have heard so much of your play."

"Come, come," says I, "sir"—for I'm pretty wide awake—"none of your gammon; you're not going to book ME."

"No, begar, dis fish you not catch," says Count Mace.

"Dat is gut!—haw! haw!" snorted the Baron. "Hook him! Lieber Himmel, you might dry and hook me as well. Haw! haw!"

Well, we went to play. "Five to four on Coxe," screams out the Count.—"Done and done," says another nobleman. "Ponays," says the Count.—"Done," says the nobleman. "I vill take your six crowns to four," says the Baron.—"Done," says I. And, in the twinkling of an eye, I beat him once making thirteen off the balls without stopping.

We had some more wine after this; and if you could have seen the long faces of the other noblemen, as they pulled out their pencils and wrote I.O.U.'s for the Count! "Va toujours, mon cher," says he to me, "you have von for me three hundred pounds."

"I'll blay you guineas dis time," says the Baron. "Zeven to four you must give me though." And so I did: and in ten minutes THAT game was won, and the Baron handed over his pounds. "Two hundred and sixty more, my dear, dear Coxe," says the Count: "you are mon ange gardien!" "Wot a flat Misther Coxsh is, not to back his luck," I hoard Abednego whisper to one of the foreign noblemen.

"I'll take your seven to four, in tens," said I to the Baron. "Give me three," says he, "and done." I gave him three, and lost the game by one. "Dobbel, or quits," says he. "Go it," says I, up to my mettle: "Sam Coxe never says no;" and to it we went. I went in, and scored eighteen to his five. "Holy Moshesh!" says Abednego, "dat little Coxsh is a vonder! who'll take odds?"

"I'll give twenty to one," says I, "in guineas."

"Ponays; yase, done," screams out the Count.

"BONIES, done," roars out the Baron: and, before I could speak, went in, and—would you believe it?—in two minutes he somehow made the game!

Oh, what a figure I cut when my dear Jemmy heard of this afterwards! In vain I swore it was guineas: the Count and the Baron swore to ponies; and when I refused, they both said their honor was concerned, and they must have my life, or their money. So when the Count showed me actually that, in spite of this bet (which had been too good to resist) won from me, he had been a very heavy loser by the night; and brought me the word of honor of Abednego, his Jewish friend, and the foreign noblemen, that ponies had been betted;—why, I paid them one thousand pounds sterling of good and lawful money.—But I've not played for money since: no, no; catch me at THAT again if you can.

## A NEW DROP-SCENE AT THE OPERA

No lady is a lady without having a box at the Opera: so my Jemmy, who knew as much about music,—bless her!—as I do about Sanscrit, algebra, or any other foreign language, took a prime box on the second tier. It was what they called a double box; it really COULD hold two, that is, very comfortably; and we got it a great bargain—for five hundred a year! Here, Tuesdays and Saturdays, we used regularly to take our places, Jemmy and Jemimarann sitting in front; me, behind: but as my dear wife used to wear a large fantail gauze hat with ostrich feathers, birds-of-paradise, artificial flowers, and tags of muslin or satin, scattered all over it, I'm blest if she didn't fill the whole of the front of the box; and it was only by jumping and dodging, three or four times in the course of the night, that I could manage to get a sight of the actors. By kneeling down, and looking steady under my darling Jemmy's sleeve, I DID contrive, every now and then, to have a peep of Senior Lablash's boots, in the "Puritanny," and once actually saw Madame Greasi's crown and head-dress in "Annybalony."

What a place that Opera is, to be sure! and what enjoyments us aristocracy used to have! Just as you have swallowed down your three courses (three curses I used to call them;—for so, indeed, they are, causing a deal of heartburns, headaches, doctor's bills, pills, want of sleep, and such like)—just, I say, as you get down your three courses, which I defy any man to enjoy properly unless he has two hours of drink and quiet afterwards, up comes the carriage, in bursts my Jemmy, as fine as a duchess, and scented like our shop. "Come, my dear," says she, "it's 'Normy' to—night" (or "Annybalony," or the "Nosey di Figaro," or the "Gazzylarder," as the case may be). "Mr. Foster strikes off punctually at eight, and you know it's the fashion to be always present at the very first bar of the aperture." And so off we are obliged to budge, to be miserable for five hours, and to have a headache for the next twelve, and all because it's the fashion!

After the aperture, as they call it, comes the opera, which, as I am given to understand, is the Italian for singing. Why they should sing in Italian, I can't conceive; or why they should do nothing BUT sing. Bless us! how I used to long for the wooden magpie in the "Gazzylarder" to fly up to the top of the church-steeple, with the silver spoons, and see the chaps with the pitchforks come in and carry off that wicked Don June. Not that I don't admire Lablash, and Rubini, and his brother, Tomrubini: him who has that fine bass voice, I mean, and acts the Corporal in the first piece, and Don June in the second; but three hours is a LITTLE too much, for you can't sleep on those little rickety seats in the boxes.

The opera is bad enough; but what is that to the bally? You SHOULD have seen my Jemmy the first night when she stopped to see it; and when Madamsalls Fanny and Theresa Hustler came forward, along with a gentleman, to dance, you should have seen how Jemmy stared, and our girl blushed, when Madamsall Fanny, coming forward, stood on the tips of only five of her toes, and raising up the other five, and the foot belonging to them, almost to her shoulder, twirled round, and round, and round, like a teetotum, for a couple of minutes or more; and as she settled down, at last, on both feet, in a natural decent posture, you should have heard how the house roared with applause, the boxes clapping with all their might, and waving their handkerchiefs; the pit shouting, "Bravo!" Some people, who, I suppose, were rather angry at such an exhibition, threw bunches of flowers at her; and what do you think she did? Why, hang me, if she did not come forward, as though nothing had happened, gather up the things they had thrown at her, smile, press them to her heart, and begin whirling round again faster than ever. Talk about coolness, I never saw such in all MY born days.

"Nasty thing!" says Jemmy, starting up in a fury; "if women WILL act so, it serves them right to be treated so."

"Oh, yes! she acts beautifully," says our friend his Excellency, who along with Baron von Punter and Tagrag, used very seldom to miss coming to our box.

"She may act very beautifully, Munseer, but she don't dress so; and I am very glad they threw that orange-peel and all those things at her, and that the people waved to her to get off."

Here his Excellency, and the Baron and Tag, set up a roar of laughter.

"My dear Mrs. Coxe," says Tag, "those are the most famous dancers in the world; and we throw myrtle, geraniums, and lilies and roses at them, in token of our immense admiration!"

"Well, I never!" said my wife; and poor Jemimarann slunk behind the curtain, and looked as red as it almost. After the one had done the next begun; but when, all of a sudden, a somebody came skipping and bounding in, like an Indian-rubber ball, flinging itself up, at least six feet from the stage, and there shaking about its legs like mad, we were more astonished than ever!

"That's Anatole," says one of the gentlemen.

"Anna who?" says my wife; and she might well be mistaken: for this person had a hat and feathers, a bare neck and arms, great black ringlets, and a little calico frock, which came down to the knees.

"Anatole. You would not think he was sixty-three years old, he's as active as a man of twenty."

"HE!" shrieked out my wife; "what, is that there a man? For shame! Munseer. Jemimarann, dear, get your cloak, and come along; and I'll thank you, my dear, to call our people, and let us go home."

You wouldn't think, after this, that my Jemmy, who had shown such a horror at the bally, as they call it, should ever grow accustomed to it; but she liked to hear her name shouted out in the crush-room, and so would stop till the end of everything; and, law bless you! in three weeks from that time, she could look at the ballet as she would at a dancing-dog in the streets, and would bring her double-barrelled opera-glass up to her eyes as coolly as if she had been a born duchess. As for me, I did at Rome as Rome does; and precious fun it used to be, sometimes.

My friend the Baron insisted one night on my going behind the scenes; where, being a subscriber, he said I had what they call my ONTRAY. Behind, then, I went; and such a place you never saw nor heard of! Fancy lots of young and old gents of the fashion crowding round and staring at the actresses practising their steps. Fancy yellow snuffy foreigners, chattering always, and smelling fearfully of tobacco. Fancy scores of Jews, with hooked-noses and black muzzles, covered with rings, chains, sham diamonds, and gold waistcoats. Fancy old men dressed in old nightgowns, with knock-knees, and dirty flesh-colored cotton stockings, and dabs of brick-dust on their wrinkled old chops, and tow-wigs (such wigs!) for the bald ones, and great tin spears in their hands mayhap, or else shepherds' crooks, and fusty garlands of flowers made of red and green baize. Fancy troops of girls giggling, chattering, pushing to and fro, amidst old black canvas, Gothic halls, thrones, pasteboard Cupids, dragons, and such like. Such dirt, darkness, crowd, confusion and gabble of all conceivable languages was never known!

If you COULD but have seen Munseer Anatole! Instead of looking twenty, he looked a thousand. The old man's wig was off, and a barber was giving it a touch with the tongs; Munseer was taking snuff himself, and a boy was standing by with a pint of beer from the public-house at the corner of Charles Street.

I met with a little accident during the three-quarters of an hour which they allow for the entertainment of us men of fashion on the stage, before the curtain draws up for the bally, while the ladies in the boxes are gaping, and the people in the pit are drumming with their feet and canes in the rudest manner possible, as though they couldn't wait.

Just at the moment before the little bell rings and the curtain flies up, and we scuffle off to the sides (for we always stay till the very last moment), I was in the middle of the stage, making myself very affable to the fair figgerantys which was spinning and twirling about me, and asking them if they wasn't cold, and such like politeness, in the most condescending way possible, when a bolt was suddenly withdrawn, and down I popped, through a trap in the stage, into the place below. Luckily I was stopped by a piece of machinery, consisting of a heap of green blankets and a young lady coming up as Venus rising from the sea. If I had not fallen so soft, I don't know what might have been the consequence of the collusion. I never told Mrs. Coxe, for she can't bear to hear of my paying the least attention to the fair sex.

STRIKING A BALANCE

Next door to us, in Portland Place, lived the Right Honorable the Earl of Kilblazes, of Kilmacrasy Castle, County Kildare, and his mother the Dowager Countess. Lady Kilblazes had a daughter, Lady Juliana Matilda MacTurk, of the exact age of our dear Jemimarann; and a son, the Honorable Arthur Wellington Anglesea Blucher Bulow MacTurk, only ten months older than our boy Tug.

My darling Jemmy is a woman of spirit, and, as become her station, made every possible attempt to become acquainted with the Dowager Countess of Kilblazes, which her ladyship (because, forsooth, she was the daughter of the Minister, and Prince of Wales's great friend, the Earl of Portansherry) thought fit to reject. I don't wonder at my Jemmy growing so angry with her, and determining, in every way, to put her ladyship down. The Kilblazes' estate is not so large as the Tuggeridge property by two thousand a year at least; and so my wife, when our neighbors kept only two footmen, was quite authorized in having three; and she made it a point, as soon as ever the Kilblazes' carriage-and-pair came round, to have out her own carriage-and-four.

Well, our box was next to theirs at the Opera; only twice as big. Whatever masters went to Lady Juliana, came to my Jemimarann; and what do you think Jemmy did? she got her celebrated governess, Madame de Flicflac, away from the Countess, by offering a double salary. It was quite a treasure, they said, to have Madame Flicflac: she had been (to support her father, the Count, when he emigrated) a FRENCH dancer at the ITALIAN Opera. French dancing, and Italian, therefore, we had at once, and in the best style: it is astonishing how quick and well she used to speak—the French especially.

Master Arthur MacTurk was at the famous school of the Reverend Clement Coddler, along with a hundred and ten other young fashionables, from the age of three to fifteen; and to this establishment Jemmy sent our Tug, adding forty guineas to the hundred and twenty paid every year for the boarders. I think I found out the dear soul's reason; for, one day, speaking about the school to a mutual acquaintance of ours and the Kilblazes, she whispered to him that "she never would have thought of sending her darling boy at the rate which her next-door neighbors paid; THEIR lad, she was sure, must be starved: however, poor people, they did the best they could on their income!"

Coddler's, in fact, was the tip-top school near London: he had been tutor to the Duke of Buckminster, who had set him up in the school, and, as I tell you, all the peerage and respectable commoners came to it. You read in the bill, (the snopsis, I think, Coddler called it,) after the account of the charges for board, masters, extras, &c.—"Every young nobleman (or gentleman) is expected to bring a knife, fork, spoon, and goblet of silver (to prevent breakage), which will not be returned; a dressing-gown and slippers; toilet-box, pomatum, curling-irons, &c. &c. The pupil must on NO ACCOUNT be allowed to have more than ten guineas of pocket-money, unless his parents particularly desire it, or he be above fifteen years of age. WINE will be an extra charge; as are warm, vapor, and douche baths. CARRIAGE EXERCISE will be provided at the rate of fifteen guineas per quarter. It is EARNESTLY REQUESTED that no young nobleman (or gentleman) be allowed to smoke. In a place devoted to THE CULTIVATION OF POLITE LITERATURE, such an ignoble enjoyment were profane.

"CLEMENT CODDLER, M. A.,

"Chaplain and late tutor to his Grace the Duke of Buckminster.

"MOUNT PARNASSUS, RICHMOND, SURREY."

To this establishment our Tug was sent. "Recollect, my dear," said his mamma, "that you are a Tuggeridge by birth, and that I expect you to beat all the boys in the school; especially that Wellington MacTurk, who, though he is a lord's son, is nothing to you, who are the heir of Tuggeridgeville."

Tug was a smart young fellow enough, and could cut and curl as well as any young chap of his age: he was not a bad hand at a wig either, and could shave, too, very prettily; but that was in the old time, when we were not great people: when he came to be a gentleman, he had to learn Latin and Greek, and had a deal of lost time to make up for, on going to school.

However, we had no fear; for the Reverend Mr. Coddler used to send monthly accounts of his pupil's progress, and if Tug was not a wonder of the world, I don't know who was. It was

General behavior......excellent.
English...............very good.
French................tres bien.
Latin.................optime.

And so on:—he possessed all the virtues, and wrote to us every month for money. My dear Jemmy and I determined to go and see him, after he had been at school a quarter; we went, and were shown by Mr. Coddler, one of the meekest, smilingest little men I ever saw, into the bedrooms and eating-rooms (the dromitaries and refractories he called them), which were all as comfortable as comfortable might be. "It is a holiday, today," said Mr. Coddler; and a holiday it seemed to be. In the dining-room were half a dozen young gentlemen playing at cards ("All tip-top nobility," observed Mr. Coddler);—in the bedrooms there was only one gent: he was lying on his bed, reading novels and smoking cigars. "Extraordinary genius!" whispered Coddler. "Honorable Tom Fitz-Warter, cousin of Lord Byron's; smokes all day; and has written the SWEETEST poems you can imagine. Genius, my dear madam, you know—genius must have its way." "Well, UPON my word," says Jemmy, "if that's genius, I had rather that Master Tuggeridge Coxe Tuggeridge remained a dull fellow."

"Impossible, my dear madam," said Coddler. "Mr. Tuggeridge Coxe COULDN'T be stupid if he TRIED."

Just then up comes Lord Claude Lollypop, third son of the Marquis of Allycompane. We were introduced instantly: "Lord Claude Lollypop, Mr. and Mrs. Coxe." The little lord wagged his head, my wife bowed very low, and so did Mr. Coddler; who, as he saw my lord making for the playground, begged him to show us the way.—"Come along," says my lord; and as he walked before us, whistling, we had leisure to remark the beautiful holes in his jacket, and elsewhere.

About twenty young noblemen (and gentlemen) were gathered round a pastry-cook's shop at the end of the green. "That's the grub-shop," said my lord, "where we young gentlemen wot has money buys our wittles, and them young gentlemen wot has none, goes tick."

Then we passed a poor red-haired usher sitting on a bench alone. "That's Mr. Hicks, the Husher, ma'am," says my lord. "We keep him, for he's very useful to throw stones at, and he keeps the chaps' coats when there's a fight, or a game at cricket.—Well, Hicks, how's your mother? what's the row now?" "I believe, my lord," said the usher, very meekly, "there is a pugilistic encounter somewhere on the premises—the Honorable Mr. Mac—"

"Oh! COME along," said Lord Lollypop, "come along: this way, ma'am! Go it, ye cripples!" And my lord pulled my dear Jemmy's gown in the kindest and most familiar way, she trotting on after him, mightily pleased to be so taken notice of, and I after her. A little boy went running across the green. "Who is it, Petitoes?" screams my lord. "Turk and the barber," pipes Petitoes, and runs to the pastry-cook's like mad. "Turk and the ba—," laughs out my lord, looking at us. "HURRA! THIS way, ma'am!" And turning round a corner, he opened a door into a court-yard, where a number of boys were collected, and a great noise of shrill voices might be heard. "Go it, Turk!" says one. "Go it, barber!" says another. "PUNCH HITH LIFE OUT!" roars another, whose voice was just cracked, and his clothes half a yard too short for him!

Fancy our horror when, on the crowd making way, we saw Tug pummelling away at the Honorable Master MacTurk! My dear Jemmy, who don't understand such things, pounced upon the two at once, and, with one hand tearing away Tug, sent him spinning back into the arms of his seconds, while, with the other, she clawed hold of Master MacTurk's red hair, and, as soon as she got her second hand free, banged it about his face and ears like a good one.

"You nasty—wicked—quarrelsome—aristocratic" (each word was a bang)—"aristocratic—oh! oh! oh!"—Here the words stopped; for what with the agitation, maternal solicitude, and a dreadful kick on the shins which, I am ashamed to say, Master MacTurk administered, my dear Jemmy could bear it no longer, and sunk fainting away in my arms.

## DOWN AT BEULAH

Although there was a regular cut between the next-door people and us, yet Tug and the Honorable Master MacTurk kept up their acquaintance over the back-garden wall, and in the stables, where they were fighting, making friends, and playing tricks from morning to night, during the holidays. Indeed, it was from young Mac that we first heard of Madame de Flicflac, of whom my Jemmy robbed Lady

Kilblazes, as I before have related. When our friend the Baron first saw Madame, a very tender greeting passed between them; for they had, as it appeared, been old friends abroad. "Sapristie," said the Baron, in his lingo, "que fais-tu ici, Amenaide?" "Et toi, mon pauvre Chicot," says she, "est-ce qu'on t'a mis a la retraite? Il parait que tu n'es plus General chez Franco—" "CHUT!" says the Baron, putting his finger to his lips.

"What are they saying, my dear?" says my wife to Jemimarann, who had a pretty knowledge of the language by this time.

"I don't know what 'Sapristie' means, mamma; but the Baron asked Madame what she was doing here? and Madame said, 'And you, Chicot, you are no more a General at Franco.'—Have I not translated rightly, Madame?"

"Oui, mon chou, mon ange. Yase, my angel, my cabbage, quite right. Figure yourself, I have known my dear Chicot dis twenty years."

"Chicot is my name of baptism," says the Baron; "Baron Chicot de Punter is my name."

"And being a General at Franco," says Jemmy, "means, I suppose, being a French General?"

"Yes, I vas," said he, "General Baron de Punter—n'est 'a pas, Amenaide?"

"Oh, yes!" said Madame Flicflac, and laughed; and I and Jemmy laughed out of politeness: and a pretty laughing matter it was, as you shall hear.

About this time my Jemmy became one of the Lady-Patronesses of that admirable institution, "The Washerwoman's-Orphans' Home;" Lady de Sudley was the great projector of it; and the manager and chaplain, the excellent and Reverend Sidney Slopper. His salary, as chaplain, and that of Doctor Leitch, the physician (both cousins of her ladyship's), drew away five hundred pounds from the six subscribed to the Charity: and Lady de Sudley thought a fete at Beulah Spa, with the aid of some of the foreign princes who were in town last year, might bring a little more money into its treasury. A tender appeal was accordingly drawn up, and published in all the papers:—

"APPEAL.

"BRITISH WASHERWOMAN'S-ORPHANS' HOME.

"The 'Washerwoman's-Orphans' Home' has now been established seven years: and the good which it has effected is, it may be confidently stated, INCALCULABLE. Ninety-eight orphan children of Washerwomen have been lodged within its walls. One hundred and two British Washerwomen have been relieved when in the last state of decay. ONE HUNDRED AND NINETY-EIGHT THOUSAND articles of male and female dress have been washed, mended, buttoned, ironed, and mangled in the Establishment. And, by an arrangement with the governors of the Foundling, it is hoped that THE BABY-LINEN OF THAT HOSPITAL will be confided to the British Washerwoman's Home!

"With such prospects before it, is it not sad, is it not lamentable to think, that the Patronesses of the Society have been compelled to reject the applications of no less than THREE THOUSAND EIGHT HUNDRED AND ONE BRITISH WASHERWOMEN, from lack of means for their support? Ladies of England!

Mothers of England! to you we appeal. Is there one of you that will not respond to the cry in behalf of these deserving members of our sex?

"It has been determined by the Ladies-Patronesses to give a fete at Beulah Spa, on Thursday, July 25; which will be graced with the first foreign and native TALENT; by the first foreign and native RANK; and where they beg for the attendance of every WASHERWOMAN'S FRIEND."

Her Highness the Princess of Schloppenzollernschwigmaringen, the Duke of Sacks-Tubbingen, His Excellency Baron Strumpff, His Excellency Lootf-Allee-Koolee-Bismillah-Mohamed-Rusheed-Allah, the Persian Ambassador, Prince Futtee-Jaw, Envoy from the King of Oude, His Excellency Don Alonzo di Cachachero-y-Fandango-y-Castanete, the Spanish Ambassador, Count Ravioli, from Milan, the Envoy of the Republic of Topinambo, and a host of other fashionables, promised to honor the festival: and their names made a famous show in the bills. Besides these, we had the celebrated band of Moscow-musiks, the seventy-seven Transylvanian trumpeters, and the famous Bohemian Minnesingers; with all the leading artists of London, Paris, the Continent, and the rest of Europe.

I leave you to fancy what a splendid triumph for the British Washerwoman's Home was to come off on that day. A beautiful tent was erected, in which the Ladies-Patronesses were to meet: it was hung round with specimens of the skill of the washerwomen's orphans; ninety-six of whom were to be feasted in the gardens, and waited on by the Ladies-Patronesses.

Well, Jemmy and my daughter, Madame de Flicflac, myself, the Count, Baron Punter, Tug, and Tagrag, all went down in the chariot and barouche-and-four, quite eclipsing poor Lady Kilblazes and her carriage-and-two.

There was a fine cold collation, to which the friends of the Ladies-Patronesses were admitted; after which, my ladies and their beaux went strolling through the walks; Tagrag and the Count having each an arm of Jemmy; the Baron giving an arm apiece to Madame and Jemimarann. Whilst they were walking, whom should they light upon but poor Orlando Crump, my successor in the perfumery and hair-cutting.

"Orlando!" says Jemimarann, blushing as red as a label, and holding out her hand.

"Jemimar!" says he, holding out his, and turning as white as pomatum.

"SIR!" says Jemmy, as stately as a duchess.

"What! madam," says poor Crump, "don't you remember your shopboy?"

"Dearest mamma, don't you recollect Orlando?" whimpers Jemimarann, whose hand he had got hold of.

"Miss Tuggeridge Coxe," says Jemmy, "I'm surprised of you. Remember, sir, that our position is altered, and oblige me by no more familiarity."

"Insolent fellow!" says the Baron, "vat is dis canaille?"

"Canal yourself, Mounseer," says Orlando, now grown quite furious: he broke away, quite indignant, and was soon lost in the crowd. Jemimarann, as soon as he was gone, began to look very pale and ill; and her mamma, therefore, took her to a tent, where she left her along with Madame Flicflac and the Baron; going off herself with the other gentlemen, in order to join us.

It appears they had not been seated very long, when Madame Flicflac suddenly sprung up, with an exclamation of joy, and rushed forward to a friend whom she saw pass.

The Baron was left alone with Jemimarann; and, whether it was the champagne, or that my dear girl looked more than commonly pretty, I don't know; but Madame Flicflac had not been gone a minute, when the Baron dropped on his knees, and made her a regular declaration.

Poor Orlando Crump had found me out by this time, and was standing by my side, listening, as melancholy as possible, to the famous Bohemian Minnesingers, who were singing the celebrated words of the poet Gothy:—

"Ich bin ya hupp lily lee, du bist ya hupp lily lee.
Wir sind doch hupp lily lee, hupp la lily lee."
"Chorus—Yodle-odle-odle-odle-odle-odle hupp! yodle-odle-aw-o-o-o!"

They were standing with their hands in their waistcoats, as usual, and had just come to the "o-o-o," at the end of the chorus of the forty-seventh stanza, when Orlando started: "That's a scream!" says he. "Indeed it is," says I; "and, but for the fashion of the thing, a very ugly scream too:" when I heard another shrill "Oh!" as I thought; and Orlando bolted off, crying, "By heavens, it's HER voice!" "Whose voice?" says I. "Come and see the row," says Tag. And off we went, with a considerable number of people, who saw this strange move on his part.

We came to the tent, and there we found my poor Jemimarann fainting; her mamma holding a smelling-bottle; the Baron, on the ground, holding a handkerchief to his bleeding nose; and Orlando squaring at him, and calling on him to fight if he dared.

My Jemmy looked at Crump very fierce. "Take that feller away," says she; "he has insulted a French nobleman, and deserves transportation, at the least."

Poor Orlando was carried off. "I've no patience with the little minx," says Jemmy, giving Jemimarann a pinch. "She might be a Baron's lady; and she screams out because his Excellency did but squeeze her hand."

"Oh, mamma! mamma!" sobs poor Jemimarann, "but he was t-t-tipsy."

"T-t-tipsy! and the more shame for you, you hussy, to be offended with a nobleman who does not know what he is doing."

A TOURNAMENT

"I say, Tug," said MacTurk, one day soon after our flareup at Beulah, "Kilblazes comes of age in October, and then we'll cut you out, as I told you: the old barberess will die of spite when she hears what we are going to do. What do you think? we're going to have a tournament!" "What's a tournament?" says Tug, and so said his mamma when she heard the news; and when she knew what a tournament was, I think, really, she WAS as angry as MacTurk said she would be, and gave us no peace for days together. "What!" says she, "dress up in armor, like play-actors, and run at each other with spears? The Kilblazes must be mad!" And so I thought, but I didn't think the Tuggeridges would be mad too, as they were: for, when Jemmy heard that the Kilblazes' festival was to be, as yet, a profound secret, what does she do, but send down to the Morning Post a flaming account of

"THE PASSAGE OF ARMS AT TUGGERIDGEVIILLE!

"The days of chivalry are NOT past. The fair Castellane of T-gg-r-dgeville, whose splendid entertainments have so often been alluded to in this paper, has determined to give one, which shall exceed in splendor even the magnificence of the Middle Ages. We are not at liberty to say more; but a tournament, at which His Ex-l-ncy B-r-n de P-nt-r and Thomas T-gr-g, Esq., eldest son of Sir Th—s T-gr-g, are to be the knights-defendants against all comers; a QUEEN OF BEAUTY, of whose loveliness every frequenter of fashion has felt the power; a banquet, unexampled in the annals of Gunter; and a ball, in which the recollections of ancient chivalry will blend sweetly with the soft tones of Weippert and Collinet, are among the entertainments which the Ladye of T-gg-ridgeville has prepared for her distinguished guests."

The Baron was the life of the scheme; he longed to be on horseback, and in the field at Tuggeridgeville, where he, Tagrag, and a number of our friends practised: he was the very best tilter present; he vaulted over his horse, and played such wonderful antics, as never were done except at Ducrow's.

And now—oh that I had twenty pages, instead of this short chapter, to describe the wonders of the day!—Twenty-four knights came from Ashley's at two guineas a head. We were in hopes to have had Miss Woolford in the character of Joan of Arc, but that lady did not appear. We had a tent for the challengers, at each side of which hung what they called ESCOACHINGS, (like hatchments, which they put up when people die,) and underneath sat their pages, holding their helmets for the tournament. Tagrag was in brass armor (my City connections got him that famous suit); his Excellency in polished steel. My wife wore a coronet, modelled exactly after that of Queen Catharine, in "Henry V.;" a tight gilt jacket, which set off dear Jemmy's figure wonderfully, and a train of at least forty feet. Dear Jemimarann was in white, her hair braided with pearls. Madame de Flicflac appeared as Queen Elizabeth; and Lady Blanche Bluenose as a Turkish princess. An alderman of London and his lady; two magistrates of the county, and the very pink of Croydon; several Polish noblemen; two Italian counts (besides our Count); one hundred and ten young officers, from Addiscombe College, in full uniform, commanded by Major-General Sir Miles Mulligatawney, K.C.B., and his lady; the Misses Pimminy's Finishing Establishment, and fourteen young ladies, all in white: the Reverend Doctor Wapshot, and forty-nine young gentlemen, of the first families, under his charge—were SOME only of the company. I leave you to fancy that, if my Jemmy did seek for fashion, she had enough of it on this occasion. They wanted me to have mounted again, but my hunting-day had been sufficient; besides, I ain't big enough for a real knight: so, as Mrs. Coxe insisted on my opening the Tournament—and I knew it was in vain to resist—the Baron and Tagrag had undertaken to arrange so that I might come off with safety, if I came off at all. They had procured from the Strand Theatre a famous stud of hobby-horses, which they told me had been trained for the use of the great Lord Bateman. I did not know exactly what they were till they arrived; but as they had belonged to a lord, I thought it was all right, and consented; and I found it the best sort of riding, after all, to appear to be on horseback and walk safely a-foot at the same time; and it was impossible to come down as long as I kept on my own legs: besides, I could cuff and pull my steed about as much as I liked, without fear of his biting or kicking in return. As Lord of the Tournament, they placed in my hands a lance, ornamented spirally, in blue and gold: I thought of the pole over my old shop door, and almost wished myself there again, as I capered up to the battle in my helmet and breastplate, with all the trumpets blowing and drums beating at the time. Captain Tagrag was my opponent, and preciously we poked each other, till, prancing about, I put my foot on my horse's petticoat behind, and down I came, getting a thrust from the Captain, at the same time, that almost broke my shoulder-bone. "This was sufficient," they said, "for the laws of chivalry;" and I was glad to get off so.

After that the gentlemen riders, of whom there were no less than seven, in complete armor, and the professionals, now ran at the ring; and the Baron was far, far the most skilful.

"How sweetly the dear Baron rides," said my wife, who was always ogling at him, smirking, smiling, and waving her handkerchief to him. "I say, Sam," says a professional to one of his friends, as, after their course, they came cantering up, and ranged under Jemmy's bower, as she called it:—"I say, Sam, I'm blowed if that chap in harmer mustn't have been one of hus." And this only made Jemmy the more pleased; for the fact is, the Baron had chosen the best way of winning Jemimarann by courting her mother.

The Baron was declared conqueror at the ring; and Jemmy awarded him the prize, a wreath of white roses, which she placed on his lance; he receiving it gracefully, and bowing, until the plumes of his helmet mingled with the mane of his charger, which backed to the other end of the lists; then galloping back to the place where Jemimarann was seated, he begged her to place it on his helmet. The poor girl blushed very much, and did so. As all the people were applauding, Tagrag rushed up, and, laying his hand on the Baron's shoulder, whispered something in his ear, which made the other very angry, I suppose, for he shook him off violently. "Chacun pour soi," says he, "Monsieur de Taguerague,"—which means, I am told, "Every man for himself." And then he rode away, throwing his lance in the air, catching it, and making his horse caper and prance, to the admiration of all beholders.

After this came the "Passage of Arms." Tagrag and the Baron ran courses against the other champions; ay, and unhorsed two apiece; whereupon the other three refused to turn out; and preciously we laughed at them, to be sure!

"Now, it's OUR turn, Mr. CHICOT," says Tagrag, shaking his fist at the Baron: "look to yourself, you infernal mountebank, for, by Jupiter, I'll do my best!" And before Jemmy and the rest of us, who were quite bewildered, could say a word, these two friends were charging away, spears in hand, ready to kill each other. In vain Jemmy screamed; in vain I threw down my truncheon: they had broken two poles before I could say "Jack Robinson," and were driving at each other with the two new ones. The Baron had the worst of the first course, for he had almost been carried out of his saddle. "Hark you, Chicot!" screamed out Tagrag, "next time look to your head!" And next time, sure enough, each aimed at the head of the other.

Tagrag's spear hit the right place; for it carried off the Baron's helmet, plume, rose-wreath and all; but his Excellency hit truer still—his lance took Tagrag on the neck, and sent him to the ground like a stone.

"He's won! he's won!" says Jemmy, waving her handkerchief; Jemimarann fainted, Lady Blanche screamed, and I felt so sick that I thought I should drop. All the company were in an uproar: only the Baron looked calm, and bowed very gracefully, and kissed his hand to Jemmy; when, all of a sudden, a Jewish-looking man springing over the barrier, and followed by three more, rushed towards the Baron. "Keep the gate, Bob!" he hollas out. "Baron, I arrest you, at the suit of Samuel Levison, for—"

But he never said for what; shouting out, "Aha!" and "Sapprrrristie!" and I don't know what, his Excellency drew his sword, dug his spurs into his horse, and was over the poor bailiff, and off before another word. He had threatened to run through one of the bailiff's followers, Mr. Stubbs, only that gentleman made way for him; and when we took up the bailiff, and brought him round by the aid of a little brandy-and-water, he told us all. "I had a writ againsht him, Mishter Coxsh, but I didn't vant to shpoil shport; and, beshidesh, I didn't know him until dey knocked off his shteel cap!"

Here was a pretty business!

## OVER-BOARDED AND UNDER-LODGED

We had no great reason to brag of our tournament at Tuggeridgeville: but, after all, it was better than the turn-out at Kilblazes, where poor Lord Heydownderry went about in a black velvet dressing-gown, and the Emperor Napoleon Bonypart appeared in a suit of armor and silk stockings, like Mr. Pell's friend in Pickwick; we, having employed the gentlemen from Astley's Antitheatre, had some decent sport for our money.

We never heard a word from the Baron, who had so distinguished himself by his horsemanship, and had knocked down (and very justly) Mr. Nabb, the bailiff, and Mr. Stubbs, his man, who came to lay hands upon him. My sweet Jemmy seemed to be very low in spirits after his departure, and a sad thing it is to see her in low spirits: on days of illness she no more minds giving Jemimarann a box on the ear, or sending a plate of muffins across a table at poor me, than she does taking her tea.

Jemmy, I say, was very low in spirits; but, one day (I remember it was the day after Captain Higgins called, and said he had seen the Baron at Boulogne), she vowed that nothing but change of air would do her good, and declared that she should die unless she went to the seaside in France. I knew what this meant, and that I might as well attempt to resist her as to resist her Gracious Majesty in Parliament assembled; so I told the people to pack up the things, and took four places on board the "Grand Turk" steamer for Boulogne.

The travelling-carriage, which, with Jemmy's thirty-seven boxes and my carpet-bag, was pretty well loaded, was sent on board the night before; and we, after breakfasting in Portland Place (little did I think it was the—but, poh! never mind), went down to the Custom House in the other carriage, followed by a hackney-coach and a cab, with the servants, and fourteen bandboxes and trunks more, which were to be wanted by my dear girl in the journey.

The road down Cheapside and Thames Street need not be described: we saw the Monument, a memento of the wicked Popish massacre of St. Bartholomew;—why erected here I can't think, as St. Bartholomew is in Smithfield;—we had a glimpse of Billingsgate, and of the Mansion House, where we saw the two-and-twenty-shilling-coal smoke coming out of the chimneys, and were landed at the Custom House in safety. I felt melancholy, for we were going among a people of swindlers, as all Frenchmen are thought to be; and, besides not being able to speak the language, leaving our own dear country and honest countrymen.

Fourteen porters came out, and each took a package with the greatest civility; calling Jemmy her ladyship, and me your honor; ay, and your honoring and my ladyshipping even my man and the maid in the cab. I somehow felt all over quite melancholy at going away. "Here, my fine fellow," says I to the coachman, who was standing very respectful, holding his hat in one hand and Jemmy's jewel-case in the other—"Here, my fine chap," says I, "here's six shillings for you;" for I did not care for the money.

"Six what?" says he.

"Six shillings, fellow," shrieks Jemmy, "and twice as much as your fare."

"Feller, marm!" says this insolent coachman. "Feller yourself, marm: do you think I'm a-going to kill my horses, and break my precious back, and bust my carriage, and carry you, and your kids, and your traps for six hog?" And with this the monster dropped his hat, with my money in it, and doubling his fist put it so very near my nose that I really thought he would have made it bleed. "My fare's heighteen shillings," says he, "hain't it?—hask hany of these gentlemen."

"Why, it ain't more than seventeen-and-six," says one of the fourteen porters; "but if the gen'l'man IS a gen'l'man, he can't give no less than a suffering anyhow."

I wanted to resist, and Jemmy screamed like a Turk; but, "Holloa!" says one. "What's the row?" says another. "Come, dub up!" roars a third. And I don't mind telling you, in confidence, that I was so frightened that I took out the sovereign and gave it. My man and Jemmy's maid had disappeared by this time: they always do when there's a robbery or a row going on.

I was going after them. "Stop, Mr. Ferguson," pipes a young gentleman of about thirteen, with a red livery waistcoat that reached to his ankles, and every variety of button, pin, string, to keep it together. "Stop, Mr. Heff," says he, taking a small pipe out of his mouth, "and don't forgit the cabman."

"What's your fare, my lad?" says I.

"Why, let's see—yes—ho!—my fare's seven-and-thirty and eightpence eggs—acly."

The fourteen gentlemen holding the luggage, here burst out and laughed very rudely indeed; and the only person who seemed disappointed was, I thought, the hackney-coachman. "Why, YOU rascal!" says Jemmy, laying hold of the boy, "do you want more than the coachman?"

"Don't rascal ME, marm!" shrieks the little chap in return. "What's the coach to me? Vy, you may go in an omlibus for sixpence if you like; vy don't you go and buss it, marm? Vy did you call my cab, marm? Vy am I to come forty mile, from Scarlot Street, Po'tl'nd Street, Po'tl'nd Place, and not git my fare, marm? Come, give me a suffering and a half, and don't keep my hoss avaiting all day." This speech, which takes some time to write down, was made in about the fifth part of a second; and, at the end of it, the young gentleman hurled down his pipe, and, advancing towards Jemmy, doubled his fist, and seemed to challenge her to fight.

My dearest girl now turned from red to be as pale as white Windsor, and fell into my arms. What was I to do? I called "Policeman!" but a policeman won't interfere in Thames Street; robbery is licensed there. What was I to do? Oh! my heart beats with paternal gratitude when I think of what my Tug did!

As soon as this young cab-chap put himself into a fighting attitude, Master Tuggeridge Coxe—who had been standing by laughing very rudely, I thought—Master Tuggeridge Coxe, I say, flung his jacket suddenly into his mamma's face (the brass buttons made her start and recovered her a little), and, before we could say a word was in the ring in which we stood (formed by the porters, nine orangemen and women, I don't know how many newspaper-boys, hotel-cads, and old-clothesmen), and, whirling about two little white fists in the face of the gentleman in the red waistcoat, who brought up a great pair of black ones to bear on the enemy, was engaged in an instant.

But la bless you! Tug hadn't been at Richmond School for nothing; and MILLED away one, two, right and left—like a little hero as he is, with all his dear mother's spirit in him. First came a crack which sent a long dusky white hat—that looked damp and deep like a well, and had a long black crape-rag twisted round it—first came a crack which sent this white hat spinning over the gentleman's cab and scattered among the crowd a vast number of things which the cabman kept in it,—such as a ball of string, a piece of candle, a comb, a whip-lash, a little warbler, a slice of bacon, &c. &c.

The cabman seemed sadly ashamed of this display, but Tug gave him no time: another blow was planted on his cheekbone; and a third, which hit him straight on the nose, sent this rude cabman straight down to the ground.

"Brayvo, my lord!" shouted all the people around.

"I won't have no more, thank yer," said the little cabman, gathering himself up. "Give us over my fare, vil yer, and let me git away?"

"What's your fare, NOW, you cowardly little thief?" says Tug.

"Vy, then, two-and-eightpence," says he. "Go along,—you KNOW it is!" and two-and-eightpence he had; and everybody applauded Tug, and hissed the cab-boy, and asked Tug for something to drink. We heard the packet-bell ringing, and all run down the stairs to be in time.

I now thought our troubles would soon be over; mine were, very nearly so, in one sense at least: for after Mrs. Coxe and Jemimarann, and Tug, and the maid, and valet, and valuables had been handed across, it came to my turn. I had often heard of people being taken up by a PLANK, but seldom of their being set down by one. Just as I was going over, the vessel rode off a little, the board slipped, and down I soused into the water. You might have heard Mrs. Coxe's shriek as far as Gravesend; it rung in my ears as I went down, all grieved at the thought of leaving her a disconsolate widder. Well, up I came again, and caught the brim of my beaver-hat—though I have heard that drowning men catch at straws:—I floated, and hoped to escape by hook or by crook; and, luckily, just then, I felt myself suddenly jerked by the waistband of my whites, and found myself hauled up in the air at the end of a boat-hook, to the sound of "Yeho! yeho! yehoi! yehoi!" and so I was dragged aboard. I was put to bed, and had swallowed so much water that it took a very considerable quantity of brandy to bring it to a proper mixture in my inside. In fact, for some hours I was in a very deplorable state.

NOTICE TO QUIT

Well, we arrived at Boulogne; and Jemmy, after making inquiries, right and left, about the Baron, found that no such person was known there; and being bent, I suppose, at all events, on marrying her daughter to a lord, she determined to set off for Paris, where, as he had often said, he possessed a magnificent —hotel he called it;—and I remember Jemmy being mightily indignant at the idea; but hotel, we found afterwards, means only a house in French, and this reconciled her. Need I describe the road from Boulogne to Paris? or need I describe that Capitol itself? Suffice it to say, that we made our appearance there, at "Murisse's Hotel," as became the family of Coxe Tuggeridge; and saw everything worth seeing in the metropolis in a week. It nearly killed me, to be sure; but, when you're on a pleasure-party in a foreign country, you must not mind a little inconvenience of this sort.

Well, there is, near the city of Paris, a splendid road and row of trees, which—I don't know why—is called the Shandeleezy, or Elysian Fields, in French: others, I have heard, call it the Shandeleery; but mine I know to be the correct pronunciation. In the middle of this Shandeleezy is an open space of ground, and a tent where, during the summer, Mr. Franconi, the French Ashley, performs with his horses and things. As everybody went there, and we were told it was quite the thing, Jemmy agreed that we should go too; and go we did.

It's just like Ashley's: there's a man just like Mr. Piddicombe, who goes round the ring in a huzzah-dress, cracking a whip; there are a dozen Miss Woolfords, who appear like Polish princesses, Dihannas, Sultannas, Cachuchas, and heaven knows what! There's the fat man, who comes in with the twenty-three dresses on, and turns out to be the living skeleton! There's the clowns, the sawdust, the white horse that dances a hornpipe, the candles stuck in hoops, just as in our own dear country.

My dear wife, in her very finest clothes, with all the world looking at her, was really enjoying this spectacle (which doesn't require any knowledge of the language, seeing that the dumb animals don't talk it), when there came in, presently, "the great Polish act of the Sarmatian horse-tamer, on eight steeds," which we were all of us longing to see. The horse-tamer, to music twenty miles an hour, rushed in on four of his horses, leading the other four, and skurried round the ring. You couldn't see him for the sawdust, but everybody was delighted, and applauded like mad. Presently, you saw there were only three horses in front: he had slipped one more between his legs, another followed, and it was clear that the consequences would be fatal, if he admitted any more. The people applauded more than ever; and when, at last, seven and eight were made to go in, not wholly, but sliding dexterously in and out, with the others, so that you did not know which was which, the house, I thought, would come down with applause; and the Sarmatian horse-tamer bowed his great feathers to the ground. At last the music grew slower, and he cantered leisurely round the ring; bending, smirking, seesawing, waving his whip, and laying his hand on his heart, just as we have seen the Ashley's people do. But fancy our astonishment when, suddenly, this Sarmatian horse-tamer, coming round with his four pair at a canter, and being opposite our box, gave a start, and a—hupp! which made all his horses stop stock-still at an instant.

"Albert!" screamed my dear Jemmy: "Albert! Bahbahbah—baron!" The Sarmatian looked at her for a minute; and turning head over heels, three times, bolted suddenly off his horses, and away out of our sight.

It was HIS EXCELLENCY THE BARON DE PUNTER!

Jemmy went off in a fit as usual, and we never saw the Baron again; but we heard, afterwards, that Punter was an apprentice of Franconi's, and had run away to England, thinking to better himself, and had joined Mr. Richardson's army; but Mr. Richardson, and then London, did not agree with him; and we saw the last of him as he sprung over the barriers at the Tuggeridgeville tournament.

"Well, Jemimarann," says Jemmy, in a fury, "you shall marry Tagrag; and if I can't have a baroness for a daughter, at least you shall be a baronet's lady." Poor Jemimarann only sighed: she knew it was of no use to remonstrate.

Paris grew dull to us after this, and we were more eager than ever to go back to London: for what should we hear, but that that monster, Tuggeridge, of the City—old Tug's black son, forsooth!—was going to contest Jemmy's claim to the property, and had filed I don't know how many bills against us in Chancery! Hearing this, we set off immediately, and we arrived at Boulogne, and set off in that very same "Grand Turk" which had brought us to France.

If you look in the bills, you will see that the steamers leave London on Saturday morning, and Boulogne on Saturday night; so that there is often not an hour between the time of arrival and departure. Bless us! bless us! I pity the poor Captain that, for twenty-four hours at a time, is on a paddle-box, roaring out, "Ease her! Stop her!" and the poor servants, who are laying out breakfast, lunch, dinner, tea, supper;—breakfast, lunch, dinner, tea, supper again;—for layers upon layers of travellers, as it were; and most of all, I pity that unhappy steward, with those unfortunate tin-basins that he must always keep an eye over. Little did we know what a storm was brooding in our absence; and little were we prepared for the awful, awful fate that hung over our Tuggeridgeville property.

Biggs, of the great house of Higgs, Biggs, and Blatherwick, was our man of business: when I arrived in London I heard that he had just set off to Paris after me. So we started down to Tuggeridgeville instead of going to Portland Place. As we came through the lodge-gates, we found a crowd assembled within them; and there was that horrid Tuggeridige on horseback, with a shabby-looking man, called Mr. Scapgoat, and his man of business, and many more. "Mr. Scapgoat," says Tuggeridge, grinning, and handing him over a sealed paper, "here's the lease; I leave you in possession, and wish you good morning."

"In possession of what?" says the rightful lady of Tuggeridgeville, leaning out of the carriage-window. She hated black Tuggeridge, as she called him, like poison: the very first week of our coming to Portland Place, when he called to ask restitution of some plate which he said was his private property, she called him a base-born blackamoor, and told him to quit the house. Since then there had been law squabbles between us without end, and all sorts of writings, meetings, and arbitrations.

"Possession of my estate of Tuggeridgeville, madam," roars he, "left me by my father's will, which you have had notice of these three weeks, and know as well as I do."

"Old Tug left no will," shrieked Jemmy; "he didn't die to leave his estates to blackamoors—to negroes—to base-born mulatto story-tellers; if he did may I be —"

"Oh, hush! dearest mamma," says Jemimarann. "Go it again, mother!" says Tug, who is always sniggering.

"What is this business, Mr. Tuggeridge?" cried Tagrag (who was the only one of our party that had his senses). "What is this will?"

"Oh, it's merely a matter of form," said the lawyer, riding up. "For heaven's sake, madam, be peaceable; let my friends, Higgs, Biggs, and Blatherwick, arrange with me. I am surprised that none of their people are here. All that you have to do is to eject us; and the rest will follow, of course."

"Who has taken possession of this here property?" roars Jemmy, again.

"My friend Mr. Scapgoat," said the lawyer.—Mr. Scapgoat grinned.

"Mr. Scapgoat," said my wife, shaking her fist at him (for she is a woman of no small spirit), "if you don't leave this ground I'll have you pushed out with pitchforks, I will—you and your beggarly blackamoor yonder." And, suiting the action to the word, she clapped a stable fork into the hands of one of the gardeners, and called another, armed with a rake, to his help, while young Tug set the dog at their heels, and I hurrahed for joy to see such villany so properly treated.

"That's sufficient, ain't it?" said Mr. Scapgoat, with the calmest air in the world. "Oh, completely," said the lawyer. "Mr. Tuggeridge, we've ten miles to dinner. Madam, your very humble servant." And the whole posse of them rode away.

## LAW LIFE ASSURANCE

We knew not what this meant, until we received a strange document from Higgs, in London—which begun, "Middlesex to wit. Samuel Cox, late of Portland Place, in the city of Westminster, in the said county, was attached to answer Samuel Scapgoat, of a plea, wherefore, with force and arms, he entered into one messuage, with the appurtenances, which John Tuggeridge, Esq., demised to the said Samuel Scapgoat, for a term which is not yet expired, and ejected him." And it went on to say that "we, with force of arms, viz, with swords, knives, and staves, had ejected him." Was there ever such a monstrous falsehood? when we did but stand in defence of our own; and isn't it a sin that we should have been turned out of our rightful possessions upon such a rascally plea?

Higgs, Biggs, and Blatherwick had evidently been bribed; for would you believe it?—they told us to give up possession at once, as a will was found, and we could not defend the action. My Jemmy refused their proposal with scorn, and laughed at the notion of the will: she pronounced it to be a forgery, a vile blackamoor forgery; and believes, to this day, that the story of its having been made thirty years ago, in Calcutta, and left there with old Tug's papers, and found there, and brought to England, after a search made by order of Tuggeridge junior, is a scandalous falsehood.

Well, the cause was tried. Why need I say anything concerning it? What shall I say of the Lord Chief Justice, but that he ought to be ashamed of the wig he sits in? What of Mr. — and Mr. —, who exerted their eloquence against justice and the poor? On our side, too, was no less a man than Mr. Serjeant Binks, who, ashamed I am, for the honor of the British bar, to say it, seemed to have been bribed too: for he actually threw up his case! Had he behaved like Mr. Mulligan, his junior—and to whom, in this humble way, I offer my thanks—all might have been well. I never knew such an effect produced, as when Mr. Mulligan, appearing for the first time in that court, said, "Standing here upon the pidestal of secred Thamis; seeing around me the arnymints of a profission I rispict; having before me a vinnerable judge, and an enlightened jury—the counthry's glory, the netion's cheap defender, the poor man's priceless palladium: how must I thrimble, my lard, how must the blush bejew my cheek—" (somebody cried out, "O CHEEKS!" In the court there was a dreadful roar of laughing; and when order was established, Mr. Mulligan continued:)—"My lard, I heed them not; I come from a counthry accustomed to opprission, and as that counthry—yes, my lard, THAT IRELAND—(do not laugh, I am proud of it)—is ever, in spite of her tyrants, green, and lovely, and beautiful: my client's cause, likewise, will rise shuperior to the malignant imbecility—I repeat, the MALIGNANT IMBECILITY—of those who would thrample it down; and in whose teeth, in my client's name, in my counthry's—ay, and MY OWN—I, with folded arrums, hurl a scarnful and eternal defiance!"

"For heaven's sake, Mr. Milligan"—("MULLIGAN, ME LARD," cried my defender)—"Well, Mulligan, then, be calm, and keep to your brief."

Mr. Mulligan did; and for three hours and a quarter, in a speech crammed with Latin quotations, and unsurpassed for eloquence, he explained the situation of me and my family; the romantic manner in which Tuggeridge the elder gained his fortune, and by which it afterwards came to my wife; the state of Ireland; the original and virtuous poverty of the Coxes—from which he glanced passionately, for a few minutes (until the judge stopped him), to the poverty of his own country; my excellence as a husband, father, landlord; my wife's, as a wife, mother, landlady. All was in vain—the trial went against us. I was soon taken in execution for the damages; five hundred pounds of law expenses of my own, and as much more of Tuggeridge's. He would not pay a farthing, he said, to get me out of a much worse place than the Fleet. I need not tell you that along with the land went the house in town, and the money in the funds. Tuggeridge, he who had thousands before, had it all. And when I was in prison, who do you think would come and see me? None of the Barons, nor Counts, nor Foreign Ambassadors, nor Excellencies, who used to fill our house, and eat and drink at our expense,—not even the ungrateful Tagrag!

I could not help now saying to my dear wife, "See, my love, we have been gentlefolks for exactly a year, and a pretty life we have had of it. In the first place, my darling, we gave grand dinners, and everybody laughed at us."

"Yes, and recollect how ill they made you," cries my daughter.

"We asked great company, and they insulted us."

"And spoilt mamma's temper," said Jemimarann.

"Hush! Miss," said her mother; "we don't want YOUR advice."

"Then you must make a country gentleman of me."

"And send Pa into dunghills," roared Tug.

"Then you must go to operas, and pick up foreign Barons and Counts."

"Oh, thank heaven, dearest papa, that we are rid of them," cries my little Jemimarann, looking almost happy, and kissing her old pappy.

"And you must make a fine gentleman of Tug there, and send him to a fine school."

"And I give you my word," says Tug, "I'm as ignorant a chap as ever lived."

"You're an insolent saucebox," says Jemmy; "you've learned that at your fine school."

"I've learned something else, too, ma'am; ask the boys if I haven't," grumbles Tug.

"You hawk your daughter about, and just escape marrying her to a swindler."

"And drive off poor Orlando," whimpered my girl.

"Silence! Miss," says Jemmy, fiercely.

"You insult the man whose father's property you inherited, and bring me into this prison, without hope of leaving it: for he never can help us after all your bad language." I said all this very smartly; for the fact is, my blood was up at the time, and I determined to rate my dear girl soundly.

"Oh! Sammy," said she, sobbing (for the poor thing's spirit was quite broken), "it's all true; I've been very, very foolish and vain, and I've punished my dear husband and children by my follies, and I do so, so repent them!" Here Jemimarann at once burst out crying, and flung herself into her mamma's arms, and the pair roared and sobbed for ten minutes together. Even Tug looked queer: and as for me, it's a most extraordinary thing, but I'm blest if seeing them so miserable didn't make me quite happy.—I don't think, for the whole twelve months of our good fortune, I had ever felt so gay as in that dismal room in the Fleet, where I was locked up.

Poor Orlando Crump came to see us every day; and we, who had never taken the slightest notice of him in Portland Place, and treated him so cruelly that day at Beulah Spa, were only too glad of his company now. He used to bring books for my girl, and a bottle of sherry for me; and he used to take home Jemmy's fronts and dress them for her; and when locking-up time came, he used to see the ladies home to their little three-pair bedroom in Holborn, where they slept now, Tug and all. "Can the bird forget its nest?" Orlando used to say (he was a romantic young fellow, that's the truth, and blew the flute and read Lord Byron incessantly, since he was separated from Jemimarann). "Can the bird, let loose in eastern climes, forget its home? Can the rose cease to remember its beloved bulbul?—Ah, no! Mr. Cox, you made me what I am, and what I hope to die—a hairdresser. I never see a curling-irons before I entered your shop, or knew Naples from brown Windsor. Did you not make over your house, your furniture, your emporium of perfumery, and nine-and-twenty shaving customers, to me? Are these trifles? Is Jemimarann a trifle? if she would allow me to call her so. Oh, Jemimarann, your Pa found me in the workhouse, and made me what I am. Conduct me to my grave, and I never, never shall be different!" When he had said this, Orlando was so much affected, that he rushed suddenly on his hat and quitted the room.

Then Jemimarann began to cry too. "Oh, Pa!" said she, "isn't he—isn't he a nice young man?"

"I'm HANGED if he ain't," says Tug. "What do you think of his giving me eighteenpence yesterday, and a bottle of lavender-water for Mimarann?"

"He might as well offer to give you back the shop at any rate," says Jemmy.

"What! to pay Tuggeridge's damages? My dear, I'd sooner die than give Tuggeridge the chance."

Tuggeridge vowed that I should finish my days there, when he put me in prison. It appears that we both had reason to be ashamed of ourselves; and were, thank God! I learned to be sorry for my bad feelings toward him, and he actually wrote to me to say—

"SIR,—I think you have suffered enough for faults which, I believe, do not lie with you, so much as your wife; and I have withdrawn my claims which I had against you while you were in wrongful possession of my father's estates. You must remember that when, on examination of my father's papers, no will was found, I yielded up his property, with perfect willingness, to those who I fancied were his legitimate heirs. For this I received all sorts of insults from your wife and yourself (who acquiesced in them); and when the discovery of a will, in India, proved MY just claims, you must remember how they were met, and the vexatious proceedings with which you sought to oppose them.

"I have discharged your lawyer's bill; and, as I believe you are more fitted for the trade you formerly exercised than for any other, I will give five hundred pounds for the purchase of a stock and shop, when you shall find one to suit you.

"I enclose a draft for twenty pounds to meet your present expenses. You have, I am told, a son, a boy of some spirit: if he likes to try his fortune abroad, and go on board an Indiaman, I can get him an appointment; and am, Sir, your obedient servant,

"JOHN TUGGERIDGE"

It was Mrs. Breadbasket, the housekeeper, who brought this letter, and looked mighty contemptuous as she gave it.

"I hope, Breadbasket, that your master will send me my things at any rate," cries Jemmy. "There's seventeen silk and satin dresses, and a whole heap of trinkets, that can be of no earthly use to him."

"Don't Breadbasket me, mem, if you please, mem. My master says that them things is quite obnoxious to your sphere of life. Breadbasket, indeed!" And so she sailed out.

Jemmy hadn't a word; she had grown mighty quiet since we have been in misfortune: but my daughter looked as happy as a queen; and Tug, when he heard of the ship, gave a jump that nearly knocked down poor Orlando. "Ah, I suppose you'll forget me now?" says he with a sigh; and seemed the only unhappy person in company.

"Why, you conceive, Mr. Crump," says my wife, with a great deal of dignity, "that, connected as we are, a young man born in a work—"

"Woman!" cried I (for once in my life determined to have my own way), "hold your foolish tongue. Your absurd pride has been the ruin of us hitherto; and, from this day, I'll have no more of it. Hark ye, Orlando, if you will take Jemimarann, you may have her; and if you'll take five hundred pounds for a half-share of the shop, they're yours; and THAT'S for you, Mrs. Cox."

And here we are, back again. And I write this from the old back shop, where we are all waiting to see the new year in. Orlando sits yonder, plaiting a wig for my Lord Chief Justice, as happy as may be; and Jemimarann and her mother have been as busy as you can imagine all day long, and are just now giving the finishing touches to the bridal-dresses: for the wedding is to take place the day after to-morrow. I've cut seventeen heads off (as I say) this very day; and as for Jemmy, I no more mind her than I do the Emperor of China and all his Tambarins. Last night we had a merry meeting of our friends and neighbors, to celebrate our reappearance among them; and very merry we all were. We had a capital fiddler, and we kept it up till a pretty tidy hour this morning. We begun with quadrills, but I never could do 'em well; and after that, to please Mr. Crump and his intended, we tried a gallopard, which I found anything but easy: for since I am come back to a life of peace and comfort, it's astonishing how stout I'm getting. So we turned at once to what Jemmy and me excels in—a country dance; which is rather surprising, as we was both brought up to a town life. As for young Tug, he showed off in a sailor's hornpipe: which Mrs. Cox says is very proper for him to learn, now he is intended for the sea. But stop! here comes in the punchbowls; and if we are not happy, who is? I say I am like the Swish people, for I can't flourish out of my native HAIR.

## William Makepeace Thackeray – A Short Biography

William Makepeace Thackeray, was born on July 18th, 1811 in Calcutta, then British India, where his father, Richmond Thackeray was the secretary to the Board of Revenue in the British East India Company. His mother, Anne Becher also worked for the British East India Company.

His father died in 1815, and his mother sent Thackeray to England the following year while she remained in India and would, sometime later, marry her childhood sweetheart. En-route to England the ship stopped for provisions on St. Helena. The Imprisoned Napoleon was pointed out to him by a servant with the words that he "eats three sheep every day, and all the little children he can lay hands on!"

Finally, back in England the young Thackeray was sent to school, initially in Southampton and Chiswick, before being moved to Charterhouse School. Charterhouse and Thackeray did not take to each other but the time became a valuable source for his later work "Slaughterhouse". Despite his less than respectful recalling of his time with them Charterhouse placed a monument in the chapel after his death.

In his final year at Charterhouse a troubling illness delayed his departure to attend Cambridge University. Over the course of his life Thackeray would suffer from ill health, much of it brought about for his fondness for "gluttling and gorging". Excess was something he could enjoy and for a man who stood some 6' 3" it would appear to the eye that, initially at least, his large frame could absorb much of that excess.

However, Thackeray's lazy attitude to completely mastering anything he set his mind too, especially where ambition for academia was involved, meant he departed Cambridge little more than a year after joining. He had however published two short works in University periodicals. As an author, he would have quite some impact on English literature in the years to come, so it seems difficult to reconcile that he felt no urgency to pursue writing at that time.

He now spent some time travelling across Europe stopping at both Paris, to study art, and to winter in Weimar. Back in London a final attempt was made on a professional career. This time studying law at Middle Temple. It lasted no more than a few months.

Now, having reached 21, he received his father's inheritance. It was a very substantial estate of 17,000 pounds, an enormous sum of money at the time. However, although Thackeray had youth he lacked a little in energy and certainly much financial experience. He funded not one but two newspapers, and neither was to prove successful. Gambling seemed enjoyable and certainly he had money to lose, which he did on a regular basis. Further investments in two soon-to-fail Indian banks quickly ensured little of his good fortune remained.

He now had to consider taking up yet another profession. Thackeray turned to art hoping that his studies in Paris would prove of benefit. Unfortunately, they did not. His ambivalent attitude continued until on August 20th, 1836 he married the 20-year-old, Isabella Gethin Shawe. It seemed to prove a turning point in many ways.

The marriage would produce three daughters; Anne Isabella in 1837, Jane, in 1838, who tragically died in infancy and Harriet Marian in 1840.

Now, as a husband and father, Thackeray seemed at last to understand his responsibilities to nurture and provide.

His early efforts at "writing for his life" were to establish his career as a foremost author. His main employment was with Fraser's Magazine, a sharp-witted and sharp-tongued conservative publication for which he produced art criticism, short fictional sketches, and who would also serialise two of his novels. He also found time, between 1837 and 1840 to review books for The Times and to make regular contributions to The Morning Chronicle and The Foreign Quarterly Review.

In his earliest works, which he wrote under various pseudonyms including; Charles James Yellowplush, Michael Angelo Titmarsh and George Savage Fitz-Boodle, he tended towards savagery in his attacks on high society, military prowess, the institution of marriage and hypocrisy.

Between May 1839 and February 1840 Fraser's published Catherine. Originally intended as a satire of the Newgate school of crime fiction, it ended up being more of a picaresque tale. Thackeray also began work on what would eventually become A Shabby Genteel Story.

However, Thackeray, having successfully found a career that he cared about and had the talent for, found that his personal life was about to descend into chaos. After the birth of her third child in 1840, Isabella, sank into depression. At first Thackeray, didn't think too much of it. He needed to work to earn an income to support his family and finding that Isabella was distracting both herself and him he realised he could get no work done at home and so spent more and more time away until finally, in September 1840, it dawned upon him how serious his wife's condition had become. Struck by guilt, he set out with his wife to Ireland. During the boat crossing she threw herself into the sea, but was thankfully pulled from the waters. Her mother who had little understanding of her daughter's illness was of little help and perhaps a hinderance. After four-weeks they returned to England. From November 1840 to February 1842 Isabella was in and out of professional care, as her condition waxed and waned.

Isabella eventually deteriorated into a permanent state of detachment. Thackeray desperately sought cures for her, but nothing worked, and she ended up in two different asylums in or near Paris until 1845, after which Thackeray took her back to England, where he installed her with a Mrs Bakewell at Camberwell. Despite her condition Isabella would outlive her husband by 3 decades.

After his wife's illness Thackeray became a de facto widower, never able to establish another permanent relationship.

In 1843, through his connection to the illustrator John Leech, whom he had met at Charterhouse, he began writing for the newly created magazine Punch, in which he published The Snob Papers, later collected as The Book of Snobs. Thackeray was a regular contributor to Punch until 1854.

Thackeray had earlier received some success with two travel books, The Paris Sketch Book and The Irish Sketch Book, the latter marked by hostility to Irish Catholics. The book appealed to British prejudices, and on that basis Thackeray now became Punch's Irish expert, often under the pseudonym Hibernis Hibernior. It was Thackeray's writings that were the basis for Punch's notoriously harsh, hostile and condescending depictions of the Irish during the devastating Irish Famine (1845–51).

As well as his regular columns and contributions Thackeray worked on his novels. In The Luck of Barry Lyndon, which was serialised in Fraser's in 1844, he explored the situation of an outsider trying to achieve status in high society, a theme he developed more successfully a few years later with Vanity Fair.

Thackeray achieved more recognition with his Snob Papers (serialised 1846/7, and published as a book in 1848), but the work that really established his fame was the novel Vanity Fair, which first appeared in serialised instalments beginning in January 1847.

Published as a book the novel had a slow start but eventually sales rose to 7,000 copies a month. Just as importantly, it was the book that everybody was talking about. Thackeray finally had a name that gained notice and was reviewed in journals such as the famed, and much sought after, Edinburgh Review.

The accolades and success also gave him a respite from writing everything in a manner that would help ensure income rather than literary respect. Even before Vanity Fair completed its serial run Thackeray had become a celebrity, sought after by the very lords and ladies whom he satirised. with the character of Becky Sharp, the artist's daughter who rises high by manipulating all around her.

Pendennis followed in 1849-50, but it was interrupted halfway through writing for 3 months by a severe illness. Some accounts say it was cholera. Pendennis is a semi-autobiographical bildungsroman that draws on, among other things, Thackeray's disappointments in college, his ambivalent relationship with his mother, and his insider's knowledge of the London publishing world.

This novel ran at the same time as Charles Dicken's David Copperfield, and their dual appearance brought about the first of many comparisons with Dickens. Thackeray, for his part, felt that he and Dickens were battling for supremacy, though he would never equal Dickens's popularity, except with the critics.

Interestingly the two were involved in a spat which became known as the "Garrick Club affair". Thackeray and Dickens had skirmished over the "Dignity of Literature" and had other slight disagreements but this literary quarrel caused a rift in their friendship that lasted almost until the end of Thackeray's life. The relationship was healed only in Thackeray's last months, through a surprise meeting and handshake on the steps of a London club. Thackeray had taken offense at some personal remarks in a column by Edmund Yates and demanded an apology, eventually taking the affair to the Garrick Club committee. Already upset with Thackeray for an indiscreet remark about his affair with Ellen Ternan, Dickens championed Yates, helping him to write letters both to Thackeray and, in his defense, to the club's committee. Despite the intervention of Dickens, Yates eventually lost the vote of the Club's members, but the quarrel was laid out for the public in journal articles and pamphlets. "What pains me most," Thackeray said at the time, "is that Dickens should have been his adviser, and next that I should have had to lay a heavy hand on a young man who, I take it, has been cruelly punished by the issue of the affair, and I believe is hardly aware of the nature of his own offence, and doesn't even now understand that a gentleman should resent the monstrous insult which he volunteered".

Aside from these quarrelsome, distracting literary disagreements and Isabella's on-going illness life was good for Thackeray. He was to remain as he put it "at the top of the tree," for the rest of his life. The works for which he is so well remembered; Vanity Fair and Barry Lyndon had established that but he continued to write and produce novels, stories, sketches and works profusely.

To remain at such a high level in both quality and quantity is somewhat surprising given the continuation and escalation of various illnesses which continued to haunt him.

With Isabella still unwell Thackeray did seek out other women, in particular Mrs Jane Brookfield. Despite his hopes, it always felt that he was pursuing her as she battled the problems of her own marriage and turned to Thackeray for comfort and support. A source for these relationships often came on the lecture tours of Great Britain and the United States which he now entertained. These tours gave the public a chance to see and hear their hero's and provided another valuable source of income for those invited to tour. Whilst in in New York he met the Baxter family. Sally, the eldest daughter, enchanted the novelist—as a number of vibrant, intelligent, beautiful young women had done before her—and she became the model for Ethel Newcome. He visited her on his second tour of the States when she was married to a South Carolina gentleman. His choosing of married women in the shape of both Jane and Sally was ill-advised and both relationships led nowhere but did take quite some time to disassemble and for reason to set in.

In 1852, The History of Henry Esmond was published as a 3-volume novel without first being serialised and in a special type meant to imitate the appearance of an eighteenth-century book. This was the most carefully planned of Thackeray's novels. The book was celebrated for its brilliance, and Thackeray recognized it as "the very best I can do". At the time, it caused a sensation thanks to its controversial ending, wherein the hero marries a woman who early in the novel seemed more like a "mother" to him.

The eighteenth-century held a great attraction for Thackeray and he had previously set both Barry Lyndon and Catherine there as well as the sequel to Esmond, The Virginians, which takes place in North America and includes George Washington as a character.

Thackeray had twice visited the United States on lecture tours during this period as well as given lectures in London on the English humorists of the eighteenth century, and on the first four Hanoverian monarchs. The latter were published in a book as The Four Georges.

Interestingly Thackeray also decided that Politics was something he could more than dabble in. In Oxford he stood as an independent for Parliament. He was narrowly beaten by Cardwell, a politician who was substituted for the man Thackeray thought he was going to run against, although Thackeray's advocacy of entertainment on the Sabbath would have done little to help his campaign. Even so the margin of his defeat was only 1,070 votes, to Thackeray's 1,005.

In 1860 Thackeray became editor of the newly established Cornhill Magazine, a role he never felt truly comfortable in, preferring to contribute as a columnist on the Roundabout Papers. However, the financial compensation was by all accounts quite extraordinary. The Cornhill began its history with a record circulation and a number of distinguished contributors swayed onboard by Thackeray's reputation. It was in the Cornhill that he serialised his last complete novel, The Adventures of Philip in 1861-62. (After his death, the incomplete Denis Duval would also appear there in 1864).

After two years as editor he stepped down, primarily to concentrate on writing novels again. A piece he wrote for the Cornhill at this time "Thorns in the Cushion," one of The Roundabout Papers, fondly assembles the pains he felt in rejecting manuscripts on the one hand and receiving criticism of the magazine on the other. It seemed a good time to move on.

Thackeray's health had worsened during the 1850s and he was plagued by a recurring stricture of the urethra that laid him up for days at a time. He also felt that he had lost much of his creative impetus. He worsened matters by excessively eating and drinking, and avoiding exercise, though he enjoyed horseback-riding. He has been described as "the greatest literary glutton who ever lived". Indeed, his main activity apart from writing was eating and drinking and many of his stories include elaborate scenes and themes on his fondness for them.

On December 23$^{rd}$, 1863, William Makepeace Thackeray, after returning from dining out and before dressing for bed, suffered a massive stroke. He was found dead on his bed the following morning. He was only fifty-two.

His death was entirely unexpected, and shocked family, friends and indeed the entire Nation.

It is said that at his funeral service thousands of mourners turned out to witness his passing. He was buried on December 29$^{th}$ at Kensal Green Cemetery, London.


William Makepeace Thackeray – A Concise Bibliography

The Yellowplush Papers (1837)
Catherine (1839–40)
A Shabby Genteel Story (1840)
Second Funeral of Napoleon (1841)
The Irish Sketchbook (1843)
The Luck of Barry Lyndon (1844)
Notes of a Journey from Cornhill to Grand Cairo (1846)
Mrs. Perkins's Ball (1846), under the name M. A. Titmarsh
Stray Papers: Being Stories, Reviews, Verses, and Sketches (1821-1847)
The Book of Snobs (1848)
Vanity Fair (1848)
Pendennis (1848–1850)
Rebecca and Rowena (1850)
The Paris Sketchbook (1840)
Men's Wives (1852)
The History of Henry Esmond (1852)
The English Humorists of the Eighteenth Century (1853)
The Newcomes (1855)

The Rose and the Ring (1855)
The Virginians (1857–1859)
Lovel the Widower (1860)
Four Georges (1860-1861)
The Adventures of Philip (1862)
Roundabout Papers (1863)
Denis Duval (1864)
The English Humorists of the eighteenth century: A Series of Six Lectures (1867)
Ballads (1869)
Burlesques (1869)
The Orphan of Pimlico (1876)

Thackeray wrote a numerous number of articles for magazines and the like as well as contributing many picture sketches to articles and his own books. Many were then collected and published together. We have listed his major works only for this bibliography.

www.ingramcontent.com/pod-product-compliance
Lightning Source LLC
Chambersburg PA
CBHW060535260626
47161CB00003B/916